THE ADOPTED ONE

The Adopted One is a fictionalised autobiography. All characters in this publication are fictitious and any resemblance to real persons, living or dead is purely coincidental.

 New Generation Publishing

THE ADOPTED ONE

By

Heather Rogers

ACKNOWLEDGEMENTS

I would like to thank Maria Czanerle for her time and support.

I DEDICATE THIS BOOK TO ADOPTED PEOPLE EVERYWHERE.

THE PARTING

She stood with breath abated and knew what she must do
How could she ever forgive herself but she had thought it through
No more the struggling days ahead for her two children dear
She had found them another home instead and one day would make it clear
That if their father had not gone away to fight the war
She would not have met another man whom she had fallen for
He promised her another life in a land of milk and honey
But said he could not take her children as he did not have the money
By now she'd fallen pregnant and could see no other way
Her husband did not want her so with her new love she had to stay
The orphanage door opened and amongst the noise and din
A woman dressed all in white said 'Won't you please step in?'
She had to sign some papers and left the children's things
Her mind was wracked with torment as she thought of what love brings
She flung her arms around them and whispered 'I won't be long.'
They started crying for her but she knew she must be strong
She headed for the doorway and took a backward look
And saw them huddled on a bench, faces streaming like a brook

She thought 'You'll thank me one day for doing you this turn'
And did not think their hearts would break and all life long they'd yearn
To see the mother they had lost and hold her in their arms
She only thought of the man she loved as she was besotted by his charms.

Heather Rogers

CHAPTER 1

'We know something about you that you don't know,' Naomi's school chum, Rhys, taunted as they walked home from High School.

'What is it?' Naomi asked, wondering what Rhys was going to come out with. Although he teased her on a regular basis, she thought this time she detected more malice in his voice.

His friend Dai lurched forward. 'I'd kill myself if I was you, but I'm not saying.'

'You don't know anything,' Naomi sneered. 'Anyway you always had too much to say for yourself, Dai.' With that, she turned and walked down the street tossing back her long auburn curls, leaving Dai to stew in his own embarrassment.

She made her way along the path that had been furrowed by the feet of countless miners as they made their way to and from the pit that acted as the backdrop to the village.

Rhys caught up with her and snarled, 'You're a spoilt only child, Naomi Williams, and you think you're *it* dressed up in your fine frocks, don't you?' He blocked her way and stood there menacingly, staring at her. 'But *I'd* rather be me than *you* any day.'

'I don't know what you're talking about, so leave me alone,' she shouted. As her anger started to rise, it flushed her cheeks pinker than the warm summer sun had already managed. 'I never *did* really like you,' she continued.

'Oh, didn't you?' Rhys's eyes flashed in contempt. 'Well, at least I'm not adopted, like *you*.'

Naomi froze. These stupid hateful boys were making things up. It could never be true, she thought to herself biting into her lower lip. 'You're both liars and I hate you,' she shouted, angrily. She was hurting inside.

'Ask your parents then,' Rhys smirked, triumphantly. 'I dare you.'

Doubt hit her. After all, her parents were much older than the other children's and she'd often thought they looked more like her grandparents. Was this why? She felt sick with fear. Her thoughts raced wildly.

'That'll teach you to be nasty to me,' mocked Rhys, a grin of self-satisfaction spreading across his face.

'I'm not adopted, so there,' Naomi shouted as her heart thudded against her ribs.

'My Nana Bell told me you were,' Rhys gloated.

Appalled, Naomi stared at him. This couldn't be true. It had to be a nightmare. But suddenly a memory surfaced. *'She's highly strung. I expect it's in the blood. But we'll never know,'* she once overheard her mother remark to her sister, Maud.

As tears welled up she pushed the boys aside and ran home as fast as her legs would carry her, her mind whirling with what she had been told.

Once inside the house she was too frightened to confront her parents, knowing full well she would get a hiding for making such a dreadful thing up if it wasn't true. Fearfully, she pushed away the idea. Of course it wasn't true. She was fourteen not four and Mam would have told her. At least, that's what she hoped. The thought of being adopted was getting more frightening by the minute.

Finding it hard to keep up the pretence that nothing was wrong she went to bed early in order to give herself time in the quiet of her room to think up a plan of action.

There was an hour to go before her parents would leave the house on their way to the Rugby grounds to watch their home team play Ebbw Vale. Each minute dragged. The strain of waiting was driving her mad and so was the increasing gnawing in her stomach.

Clenching her teeth she bided her time and, after waving off her parents as they disappeared round the corner of the street, she took a deep breath before making her way up the stairs. She was fully aware that delving into her mother's private things would certainly be a punishable offence. However, the fear of a hiding was pushed aside by the urgent need to find out the truth and this spurred her on as she went into her parents' bedroom.

She stared round the room and knew the most likely place to find any evidence would be in her mother's wardrobe. She'd often seen her put receipts and papers in an old biscuit tin which she kept in there.

Opening the wardrobe door she began to rummage inside, trying hard not to misplace anything. Eventually she found the tin hidden under some woollen blankets that had been put away for the summer.

Slowly prising the lid open, she ran her fingers through the mass of receipts and insurance papers. This yielded nothing. Then she saw a large, faded brown envelope which was at the very bottom. Instinctively she knew that this was what she was looking for.

As she sat down on the bed to steady herself she carefully opened the unsealed envelope. She unfolded its contents and stared at the print, catching her breath when her eyes fell upon the words written in bold letters across the top of the page. ADOPTION ORDER.

The words chilled her. Rhys was right after all, she thought to herself as she sat nervously fingering the paper and staring into space. As the realization set in she turned her attention to an enclosed letter and read on.

According to the solicitor's fees she'd been handed over for the sum of ten shillings when she was only two years old. Tears started to form in her eyes.

Still unable to grasp that this was anything to do with her she looked back at the adoption order. Her birth parents' names glared out at her. She gulped hard not wanting to believe it.

Their address was in London. The nail was finally hammered home when she saw that the date of birth on the document corresponded with her own. It was as if an electric shock had pulsed through her. How could anyone part with a child of that age?

Sickening bile rose in her throat. She knew now she was different. From that day on she realized things would never be the same for her. Why would her real parents do this? Who was she? Her eyes blurred with tears and, as she wiped them away, she caught sight of herself in the dressing-table mirror. Pointing to her reflection she cried, 'This is me! This is me!'

The discovery cut into her like a knife. Wounded, she began to rock back and forth, sobbing uncontrollably. Her world, as she knew it, had come to an end. Nothing seemed real anymore. Why hadn't she been told before? Her mind began to work ten to the dozen. Was this the reason she never looked remotely like anyone else in the family? She'd thought about it fleetingly in the past, but had never made any connection with the possibility of being adopted. There was also the fact that no-one had ever blurted out the truth. In the small coal-mining village where she lived, gossip was rife and any such news would have been common knowledge.

Maybe it wasn't true. Maybe this was all just a misunderstanding. As she looked back down at the papers it gave her no comfort. It was there for all to see.

For what seemed like ages she sat sobbing, clutching the adoption order in her hand, and it wasn't until she glanced at the bedside-table clock that she realized that May and Jack Williams, her adopted parents, would soon return. Never again would she be able to look at them in the same light.

How would she be able to hold herself together? She didn't know, but at that moment she felt like pummelling their chests and shouting and screaming in anger at them. Her life had been one big lie.

Hastily, she replaced the documents exactly as she had found them, then looked in the mirror and rubbed her eyes dry in order to take away the signs that she had been crying. As her mind was in a state of confusion she decided to wait until the time was right to have it out with her *parents*. Her heart ached and she knew she would never be able to rest until she came face to face with the woman who had given birth to her.

As the days passed the pain remained with her and her adoption was always on her mind. She found it difficult to keep her composure around her adoptive parents but she managed, knowing she would have to choose her time carefully if she didn't want to end up with a good slapping.

Her plan, however, was ruined when one evening she arrived home late from the Chapel youth club, having dawdled along. As soon as she stepped through the door, her mother flew at her.

'Where have you been?' she shouted angrily. 'You're late.'

'I wish you wouldn't keep on about the time. All the other girls stay out later than nine o'clock,' Naomi retorted.

'Yes, maybe, but the other girls are asking to have their fingers burnt by hanging around street corners,' her mother snapped.

'And what's that supposed to mean?' asked Naomi, naïvely.

'Never you mind, girl. I don't know what's wrong

with you of late but you've grown extremely moody.'

'Is that so?' Naomi, challenged. 'Perhaps I've had cause to.'

'And what do you mean by that?' said her mother, in a warning voice.

'Wouldn't you like to know?' Naomi shouted, standing defiantly, whilst inside she was seething with anger.

'You're asking for a slap, my girl.' Her mother stepped forward. 'We've done a lot for you that you don't know about.'

Her father jumped out of his armchair. 'Curb your mouth now, woman. We'll have none of that talk.' He glared at her.

'Well, it's time she knew about things, especially now she's getting above herself.'

'Keep your mouth shut about that affair, woman. I'm tired enough after a long shift down the pit as it is,' said Jack sternly, as he tried to push his way between them.

'What's in the tree comes out in the branches, you know,' muttered May, flashing her eyes at him.

'What on earth are you talking about, *Mother?*' asked Naomi in a sarcastic sounding voice. 'Anything I should know about?'

May slammed her fist on the table, eyes ablaze, as if she was at breaking point. 'You've got a lot to be thankful for, my girl, and you should be grateful you were never left in the children's home.'

There was a sudden appalled silence.

'No! May, don't say any more,' shouted Jack, his face white with shock. 'Your mother's not well. Don't take any notice,' he said to Naomi, giving her a travesty of a smile.

May's mouth tightened. 'She must be told before anything happens to me, Jack.'

'But not like this. You promised we'd sit her down,' said Jack, wringing his hands.

'I know all about my adoption if that's what it's all about. My life's been full of secrets and lies, which I don't thank you for,' Naomi blurted out. She clenched her teeth. It angered her even more to think that her Dad was avoiding the issue by bringing up the fact that her mother wasn't well. Her mother had suffered with poor health as long as she could remember.

The silence was deadly. Naomi felt physically sick.

Her parents looked at each other in horror until Jack broke the silence.

'But there *is* something you don't know,' he said trying to compose himself. 'The doctor wants your mother admitted into the Miners' Hospital for tests soon.' He stopped momentarily, as if trying to find the right words, and Naomi suddenly noticed how much he seemed to age in those few, fleeting, seconds. 'He's worried it may be cancer.'

The fight immediately left her and she looked at her Dad questioningly.

'Cancer? Why on earth didn't you tell me?' she cried. Finding out she was adopted was horrific, but now this?

'Mother didn't want to worry you, so we decided to wait until she had her admission date,' said Jack, turning to his wife with a pitiful look.

Naomi shook her head. 'I don't believe this is happening. Mam, I should have been first to know you were going into hospital. I'm awfully sorry for upsetting you, and you know I will be eternally grateful for all you've done, but never telling me the fact that I was adopted is a grievance I find hard to bear.'

'I suggest you put your adoption behind you,' said May, abruptly, 'and with regards to me being admitted into hospital I was going to explain things tonight. That was the reason I was tetchy when you arrived home late. Anyway, let's hear no more on either subject. I'm going up to my bed, and suggest you do the same. I'm so tired I can hardly think straight.'

Naomi fought hard to control her emotions. There were hundreds of questions she needed to ask. She was no longer a child and hated being treated like one, but it was typical of her mother not wanting to go into things.

'Yes, Mam,' she said quietly, biting into her lip. She had no intention of causing any further distress so ran up the stairs calling 'Nos da,' over the banister as she went. Tears filled her eyes when she entered her bedroom, and she threw herself face first, onto her bed.

Her mind was in a turmoil. She somehow knew that the cancer had already struck and had begun to gain its stranglehold. It didn't bear thinking about. The only reason she hadn't picked up on what was happening with her mother was because she'd been so absorbed with herself and her adoption issues.

As her conscience began to prick her, she buried her head in the pillow and sobbed, dreading the thought of what tomorrow might bring.

CHAPTER 2

The following week Naomi won the school Eisteddfod with her poetry and song. She had the honour to sit in the Bardic chair in front of all the other pupils and couldn't wait to run home to tell her parents about her achievement, hoping she would be able to cheer up her mother.

'I sat in the Bardic chair with a crown of laurel leaves on my head in front of the whole school, Mam,' she said excitedly, hoping for some praise. 'My poem was chosen over everyone else's *and* I came first with my singing. The headmaster told me I have a fine soprano voice and should have singing lessons,' she swanked, dancing around the room. 'What do you think about that then, Mam?'

Her mother towered above her glowering. 'Singing lessons indeed? You can put that idea right out of your mind, my girl. You're too full of yourself lately and I certainly don't want someone singing like Madam Patti in my home,' she snapped sternly, tapping her fingers on the sideboard.

Naomi stared at her mother, stunned, thinking she would have been proud of what she'd accomplished. After all Madam Patti was a famous opera singer who had toured the world so why didn't she want her daughter to better herself. After mulling things round in her head she thought it best not to get into an argument because she could tell by her mother's voice that her nerves were fraught and didn't fancy one of her swipes.

Her shoulders sagged. She knew full well that she would never live up to her mother's expectations, whatever she did. Still, she'd be finishing school that summer, which would mean she'd be more independent when she earned a wage.

As soon as school broke up, Naomi found herself employment at the local foundry as a trainee copy typist/telephonist and after she'd worked her week in hand she hurried home excitedly with her wages.

'Your first wage packet,' said her mother, opening it up.

Naomi felt proud to be able to contribute to the household, but looked at her mother in amazement when she put several half crowns on the table.

'Here's fifteen shillings for bus fares, stockings, and the like,' she said, looking at her daughter approvingly.

Naomi was stunned. 'But Mam, I'm fifteen nearly sixteen and none of the other girls hand all their money over. They pay something for their keep and have the rest to spend on themselves.' She groaned as she stared down at the paltry sum of money she'd been given.

'I don't care what the other girls do. You live by my rules, and if you think I'm letting you go around looking like some common trollop, buying any old thing to wear, you're mistaken.'

Naomi was enraged. Her mother did not have a clue as to the latest fashion. It grieved her to think that she was still in control as to what she could dress in. She had hoped to catch one of the ladies'dress shops open in the High Street, where a flowered flared skirt costing twelve shillings and sixpence had caught her eye. Now her hopes were dashed and she felt her anger rise.

'I'll move out then,' said Naomi cockily, thinking her harsh words might make her mother change her mind.

'Over my dead body,' shouted her mother, grimacing.

Before Naomi could retaliate, she saw the colour suddenly drain from her mother's face and she began to tremble. 'I feel dreadful. Quick, go and fetch your father,' she cried, trying to grasp hold of the table to steady herself.

Naomi rushed to her side, lifting her thin frame onto the settee. 'I'm calling the doctor first,' she insisted, on seeing the state she was in.

Her mother's eyes filled up with tears as she looked up at her.

'I'm sorry for rowing with you Mam.'

A trickle of tears fell down her mother's face. 'You keep the money, girl. I won't need it where I'm going.' She sank back on the settee, looking as if all the fight had gone out of her.

Naomi looked at her aghast, and knew she meant every word. 'I'll run down to the pit and fetch Da,' she said, panicking. She knew her father would want to be on the scene when the doctor arrived, so scurried out of the house as fast as her legs would carry her.

Within the hour Jack was back at the house, and the doctor had contacted the ambulance service. Looking bewildered and drawn May, with Jack by her side, was taken into the Miners' Hospital.

Things were happening too fast for Naomi who was trying her hardest to keep a stiff upper lip. Despite the tempestuous relationship she'd had with her mother she greatly admired her for the woman she was. Being from two different moulds hadn't helped things between them, but knowing that her mother had gone without over the years to clothe and feed her had spoken volumes.

Autumn had set in before May Williams was allowed to be discharged from hospital. Naomi knew deep down that her mother was being sent home to die so did all she could to help her father turn the front room into a bedroom as her mother had become too weak to be able to climb the stairs.

Jack had always been a strong, capable man despite working many years down the pit, but it was plain to see by the ashen colour of his sunken features that he was far from well, himself.

Naomi was worried to death about both her parents and, despite working full-time, she kept the home running like clockwork as her mother would have wanted and pushed all thoughts of her adoption into the back of her mind.

In order to settle her mother in when she arrived home Naomi asked for time off but was only granted a few hours leave. She felt angry about this but the foundry manager was notorious for wanting his pound of flesh from his workforce.

As soon as she heard the ambulance arrive outside Naomi ran to the door to welcome her mother home. 'We've put your bed in the front room, Mam, and I've dusted and polished all round,' she said, wanting so much to please.

Her mother's eyes were riveted on the hallstand as soon as she stepped inside. 'That's as maybe, but I see you've neglected to clean the old oak hall-stand.'

Naomi sighed. Nothing had changed. She looked into the face of her Mam, whose faded blue eyes darted around the place. Swallowing hard, Naomi gave the hallstand a quick flick of the duster, determined to do her best. She presumed it was her mother's way of stating that her authority still counted in the household, which she fully understood.

A few minutes later May's sister, Maud, appeared at the door, followed by Mrs Evans, one of the neighbours. Both women offered to take turns in helping out whilst Naomi returned to work.

It was only then it became clear to her that her mother was now a complete invalid and round-the-clock care was needed.

Sunday was Naomi's busiest day. After cleaning out the grate and lighting the fires, she put a small joint of beef in the oven for Sunday lunch, and carried on baking some cakes for tea. There was always plenty of work to do around the house, so Naomi got on with it as well as she could. She was fully aware that her mother's health was failing rapidly and dreaded the outcome of it all.

Later on that morning the Queen's nurses called to attend to May. Naomi was glad of their help because it took a little of the work load off her shoulders.

Several minutes after they'd gone, she hurried into the parlour with a cup of tea and was surprised to find her mother sitting up in bed, staring round the room as if in a trance.

'What is it, Mam?'

'My father's just left. He called in to see me with his dogs.'

Naomi felt her stomach turn over. She barely remembered her grandparents, as both of them died when she was young.

'I'm just going to dish up dinner now, Mam,' she said, handing her the tea. 'I won't be long.' Before turning to go back into the scullery Naomi stared at her mother for a few brief seconds and had a strong feeling that her time had come.

Knowing that her mother was a deeply religious woman, she doubted whether she feared death, and marvelled at her courage as she watched her endure the pain of her cancer without complaint.

On leaving the room she found it hard to fight back the tears, and gritted her teeth.

Back in the scullery she dished up the Sunday roast. She knew her father would be home from work very soon which would make her feel a lot easier in herself. She was frightened that her mother might die when she was home alone and knew she would be at a loss as to what to do.

After placing her mother's Sunday lunch on a tray she made her way back into the front room.

On opening the door she looked at her mother aghast, as she saw her stretching her arms out towards the window.

'What on earth's the matter, Mam? What's out there?'

'Can't you see the lovely cross filled with red roses outside?'

Naomi stared through the window pane and all she could see were a few neighbours making their way home from morning service at the local chapel. At that moment she felt a cold chill creep down her spine and was lost for words.

'I'm coming…I'm coming,' her mother cried, with a radiant look on her face.

Naomi stared at her, speechless. All this talk had frightened her, and by now she was convinced that her mother was losing her mind.

'I've always kept a tight rein on you for your own good,' announced her mother, turning to her. 'So don't ever think of raking up your past because it will do you no good whatsoever.'

The words seemed final to Naomi who was trying her hardest to control her emotions.

Suddenly, her mother fell back onto her pillows and began to shiver. 'Quick, bank up the fire, there's a good girl. I've suddenly gone cold from the waist down.'

Naomi felt flummoxed. She put down the dinner tray and attended to the fire, then hastily covered up her mother's legs with a blanket.

Her mother's words whirled round in her head, but she knew only too well that she would never be able to comply with her wishes.

Shortly after tea, Naomi made her way to the little

Welsh Chapel on the hillside. It was her treat of the week where she could sing her favourite Welsh hymns to her heart's content with the friends she had known since Sunday school. She was head over heels in love with Vincent, one of the lads who attended the Chapel, but she knew nothing could ever come of it because he had been granted a place at University and would shortly be leaving the town.

After the evening service was over she stayed chatting with everyone for several minutes before taking the short cut home over the fields. The cold November wind was biting, making her feel chilled to the bone.

Once inside the house she walked quietly into the front room and felt unnerved when she heard her mother making strange noises as she slept. She tried to wake her with no response, and panicked. 'Dada, come quickly, there's something wrong with Mam's breathing, and she won't wake up.'

Her father hurried straight in and stopped in his tracks. 'Oh, my God! It's the death rattles,' he said, putting his hands up to his face. 'You stay here while I telephone Mr Taylor, your Aunt Mauds' neighbour. And I'll give Mrs Evans a knock on the way.'

He left a bewildered looking Naomi staring at her mother, fearful of what could happen whilst she was there on her own.

Shortly afterwards, her father reappeared with Mrs Evans and before very long her aunt Maud arrived, looking very flustered. Both women sat by the side of the bed looking anxiously at May whilst Naomi made herself comfortable at the bottom of the bed. Nothing seemed real to her any more.

May Williams drew her last breath shortly after midnight. Naomi sat looking on in disbelief. She lived in the hope that her mother had gone to heaven. Their life together had been fraught with difficulties. How she wished she could make up for all those times, but it was too late now.

She watched in silence as her beloved Dad closed her mother's eyes and then placed two pennies on them. She'd never seen a corpse before and found it all overwhelming.

Within minutes of her mother dying her Aunt Maud and Mrs Evans began busying themselves laying her mother out in readiness for the undertaker.

'Going to make us all a nice cup of tea, is it?' suggested her Dad, as he wiped the tears from his eyes.

Naomi knew her father's cure for all ills was a nice cup of tea so she disappeared without a quibble, relieved to have something to do.

After hurriedly putting the kettle on to boil she looked through the scullery window to the starlit sky and wondered if her mother was looking down at her. In a state of shock and bewilderment she broke down crying.

Everything seemed like a blur to Naomi on the day of the funeral. The rain was coming down in sheets but that didn't deter the large number of people who attended.

Jack Williams and his daughter quietly acknowledged each person as they stepped into the funeral parlour. Naomi secretly hoped that her birth mother might suddenly emerge and was sad not to have seen a stranger in sight, calling herself stupid for even thinking such things at such a time.

On entering the house after the service, her aunt Maud turned up her nose when she saw the spread Naomi had prepared for the funeral tea. 'You could have cut several more plates of sandwiches, my girl. What were you thinking of? Duw! We must put on a good show you know.'

Gritting her teeth, Naomi flung her coat onto the hallstand, and began buttering some more bread. She wasn't used to her aunt giving her orders and resented it.

After the funeral tea, everyone went their separate ways. Once all the crockery and cutlery was neatly placed on the pantry shelves, Naomi sat down in an armchair by the fire feeling relieved it was all over. Just as she kicked off her best shoes, which had been pinching her toes all day, her father came into the room looking extremely pale. Naomi's heart went out to him.

'What is it Dad? Anything else I can get you, like another cuppa?'

Her father ran his hand through his wispy grey hair, and shook his head. 'I just wanted you to know that now your mother's gone, her strict rule keeping will be a thing of the past.'

Naomi heaved a huge sigh. 'Thank you Da, that's wonderful,' she said, flinging her arms round him. She felt as if a great burden had suddenly been removed from her shoulders and was fully aware that her mother would turn in her grave if she had heard the conversation.

As far as she was concerned, the world was now her oyster, and there would be no stopping her finding her roots.

CHAPTER 3

Six months had passed since her mother's death and Naomi had thought long and hard about searching for her birth mother. In the end she finally decided it would be best to leave things well alone whilst her father was still in mourning.

She missed her adoptive mother and was grateful for all she had done but, as the deep yearning to find her natural mother grew more intense by the day, she knew she would never be able to rest until she had broached the subject.

One Saturday afternoon Naomi was surprised to see her father out of mourning as he came in through the door wearing a smart brown corduroy jacket and trousers.

'Where's tea, girl? I'm starving,' he said, taking off his jacket. 'Like the new rig-out?'

'It's smashing, Dad. You *do* look smart.' The thought flashed through her mind that he may have taken up with another woman, knowing what a good looking man he was, but she cringed at the idea. 'Are you off anywhere special then?'

Her father's eyes glinted. 'Yes, you could say that.'

'Welsh Rarebit coming up, with lashings of brown sauce,' said Naomi, wondering what her father had been up to. 'You really look pleased with yourself, Da. Had a win on the horses, is it?' Naomi laid the food down before him, itching to know what was going on.

He shook his head, and began to tuck into his food.

'Come on Da let me into your secret, *please*,' said Naomi, eaten up with curiosity.

'Well I was thinking it was high time we had a break so I decided to book us a coach holiday touring the continent.'

'You're kidding me,' said Naomi looking at him in

astonishment. She could hardly believe her ears. Her ambition had always been to travel abroad. 'Are you pulling my leg again, Da? Or have you robbed the bank?' she giggled.

'If you must know there was money left over after paying your Mother's funeral expenses So I decided to put it to good use and when the passports are sorted, we shall be off to enjoy the delights of Europe.'

A gleeful Naomi shrieked in delight. 'You're not joking then! Just wait until I tell the girls in the office. They'll be green with envy.'

She had no intentions of upsetting her father with adoption issues now he'd broken this good news to her. They could be put on the back boiler for when the time was right.

The holiday soon came around and with much eagerness Naomi and her father boarded the coach which was to take them across the Channel to a hotel in Ostend.

It was during the first day of the holiday when Naomi and her father struck up a conversation with a young man who was sat drinking coffee at the same table in the hotel lounge. They soon found out that he was holidaying on his own and quickly asked him if he would like to join them on the excursions.

'My name's Peter, and I would be glad to accompany you. My friend let me down at the last minute you see.'

Naomi took an instant liking to Peter, with his handsome looks and tousled blonde hair. She thought he had a funny accent but he was smartly turned out, which she knew would go down well with her Dad.

'Where are you from then?' she asked, intent on finding out as much as she could about the stranger.

'I'm from north London,' he answered, giving her a

huge smile.

'We were just about to look at the trips offered on this brochure so feel free to take a seat,' grinned Naomi, moving up for him to sit down beside her.

From that day on the three of them spent the rest of the holiday together as they toured through northern Europe. Naomi was elated to think they had all forged such a good friendship in such a short time and there wasn't a day that went by when she didn't hear her father chuckling at Peter's jokes. She was pleased that life had taken on a new meaning for him, and overjoyed that her beloved Da had regained his sense of humour.

When the holiday finally came to a close Naomi was reluctant to return home. She'd tasted another side to life and yearned for more.

During their last morning together Peter suggested they walk down to the beach whilst her father was attending to his packing. Naomi jumped at the idea and, as they walked hand in hand watching the sun's rays dappling on the sea shore, Naomi knew this moment would be forever etched in her mind. They walked without speaking as if the slightest whisper would spoil the tranquillity and togetherness they were sharing.

On the way back to the hotel Peter proposed they stopped for a coffee before she boarded the coach for her homeward journey. Naomi eagerly accepted his offer and soon made herself comfortable outside a nearby café, which looked out onto the sea.

'I wish this holiday could last forever,' she sighed, leaning back into her chair.

Peter took her hand in his. 'Just because the holiday's ending doesn't mean that we won't see each other again. I've a feeling we were meant for each other and wondered if you'd consider being my girl friend?'

Naomi's eyes lit up. She could hardly contain her

excitement. 'But I live nowhere near London.'

'Distance is no problem. I've a car,' he announced, smiling.

Her heart leapt. 'Well, you must be rich. Only the doctor and well off business people own cars where I live.'

'Well, I don't know about that,' he laughed. 'As soon as I was of age my father bought me one as a 21st birthday present.'

Naomi looked at him in awe, astounded at his father's generosity and more than a little curious as to how Peter's father could afford it. Before she could find out more Peter dug deep into his trouser pocket and produced a maroon coloured jewellery box. 'I've bought this for you to remember me by,' he said, placing it on the table.

Naomi opened the box and gasped when she found a beautiful gold crucifix and chain inside, something she'd always wanted.

'I can't possibly take this from you. It's far too expensive,' she said, feeling overwhelmed by his kindness.

He closed her hand over the box. 'You must accept it as a token of my love, and there'll be more where that comes from, *my girl.*'

'Thank you ever so much,' said Naomi unable to believe her luck. *My girl,* she thought to herself. No-one had ever called her that apart from her parents or aunt, but now…well, it meant that she was now properly courting with someone who could possibly help her to better herself.

'You must know,' said Peter, looking into her eyes, 'that I've fallen headlong in love with you, and if your father agrees, would you consider us getting engaged at Christmas?'

Naomi nearly choked on her coffee. Christmas was

only four months away. She was enjoying the attention, but fully intended taking her time over such things now that she was as free as a bird. She smiled at him, avoiding the issue. Somehow the thought of being tied down in her teenage years did not appeal. There was plenty of time for that.

'Well, I'll have to think about it,' she said coyly, trying her best not to upset him.

Peter squeezed her hand. 'Promise you'll write to me then,' he urged, gazing into her eyes.

She could tell he was well smitten with her. 'Of course I will,' she declared, whilst fastening the cross and chain round her neck.

After leaving the café they strolled arm in arm back to the hotel, where she found her father impatiently waiting outside with the suitcases.

'I wondered where you'd got to, cariad. Hurry up, the coach will be leaving soon,' he said, glancing down at his newly bought wrist watch.

'I like your watch, Da,' exclaimed Naomi, 'but take a look at the cross and chain Peter's bought for me,' she said, sticking her chest out.

Her father raised his eyebrows. 'You've got a good one there, my girl, so you'd better look after him.' He turned to shake hands with Peter as they prepared to board the coach. 'I've enjoyed your company Peter. You're welcome to visit us any time. I've written our address down on a slip of paper for you.'

Peter took it, looking pleased with himself and, after kissing Naomi goodbye, he gave them a final wave as the coach pulled away.

For the rest of the journey Naomi slumped down in her seat then stuck her head in a book so that no-one would see her tears.

A few days later Naomi was thrilled when she received

a letter from Peter inviting her up to London to meet his parents the following Sunday. She was over the moon at the thought of visiting his family and, as the excitement built up in her, she began to romanticise about finding her birth mother.

When her father arrived home from work, she didn't give him chance to take off his coat before rushing up to him. 'What do you think Dad? I've been invited up to London to meet Peter's parents,' she cried, waving the letter in her hand.

Her father's face beamed. 'He's just the sort of lad I'd like to see you settle down with. You could always live here with your old Da you know. There's plenty of room, and I'd be glad of the companionship. Nice decent boy like him, what more would you want?'

Naomi's stomach jolted as she took in his words. She was quite happy as things were.

After their evening meal she replied to Peter's letter informing him the time of the train she'd be catching to Paddington. She wondered if he lived near her birth mother and wished she'd remembered the address written on the Adoption documents. She spent the next half hour pacing her room, wondering how on earth she could bring the subject up of her birth mother's address. .Then after much thought she decided it would be better all round if she spoke with her father about matters at the last minute, before her trip to London.

Deep down she was frightened of upsetting him. After her mother's death she had stood and watched him remove everything out of her wardrobe. Keeping note of the biscuit tin which held her adoption papers, she was surprised to see him lock it away inside the dressing table. Despite searching for the key on numerous occasions she was puzzled not to have found it.

Naomi caught the early bus home Friday evening. She was not relishing the prospect of bringing up the subject of her adoption papers. Should she ask her father point blank for the address? After all, he could only say yes or no she thought to herself on opening the front door.

As soon as she walked into the hallway she gasped at the sight of her Dad writhing in agony, on the floor.

'Phone the hospital quickly. I think I'm having a heart attack,' he cried, grasping hold of his chest.

Fear suddenly seized her. *Don't take my Dad, God, he's all I've got,* her mind screamed, as she ran out of the house towards the telephone box. She dialled the emergency number, with her mind reeling.

Within minutes an ambulance arrived and Naomi accompanied her father to the Miner's hospital, holding his hand all the way. Everything seemed like a blur to her as the vehicle raced along the roads with its bell ringing non stop.

She waited for what seemed like ages before being called into a side room by the doctor in charge. Her heart was pounding nineteen to the dozen as she sank down into a chair beside his desk.

'Your father has suffered a massive heart attack,' he said, looking at her sympathetically.

Naomi felt the blood drain from her face. Her father was her whole reason for living. Anything or anybody else was secondary. Kind words were all she'd ever known from him. He was one in a million. She felt like screaming at the doctor to make him well, but she managed to keep a tight rein on herself.

'He'll be alright though, won't he?' she cried, twisting the handkerchief in her hand.

'He's over the worst, but not out of the woods yet. Anyway, I think it best if you leave now so he can rest. Ring us in the morning. We'll be in a better position to explain more then.'

A lump rose in her throat as she shook his hand and left the room. 'I'll do anything God, anything,' she whispered, under her breath. 'Please let my Da live.'

As she walked through the long, echoing corridors she tried hard to hold herself together but, as the tears spilled, all thoughts of Peter and her weekend in London were far from her mind.

After a fitful night's sleep Naomi rang the hospital expecting the worst but as soon as the ward sister explained that her father had improved she was elated. Just to be allowed a short visit that afternoon made her feel so much better.

She intended to make her father some Welsh cakes to take with her and, on glancing down at her watch, thoughts of Peter waiting for her to step off the train at Paddington, sprang into her mind. With the worry of her father uppermost in her thoughts she decided it would be best to post a letter off to him explaining what had happened, hoping he would understand the predicament she was in.

Steeling herself as she walked back into the hospital, she quickly made her way to her father's ward, apprehensive as to how she would find him. Once she stepped inside she was overjoyed to see he was sitting up in bed reading a newspaper. 'I thought I'd lost you Da,' she cried, clutching hold of his hand, as relief flooded through her.

Her father dropped the paper then squeezed her hand. 'The doctor's advised me to finish work. The pit's finally taken its toll, but if I take it easy I'll have a few more good years in me yet, cariad.'

'Course you will. It's about time you retired,' she said, trying to make light of the matter. 'Just think, you'll be able to join the Welsh Male Voice Choir, like you always wanted to.'

'Duw, there's a thought now, girl, isn't it?' said her father, with a broad grin on his face.

Naomi's eyes filled. She wondered if he really knew the truth about his condition, or was protecting her as always. As he slid back down on the pillow she could see by the deep lines that etched his face that he had aged ten years over-night. With great effort she gritted her teeth, trying her hardest to be brave. He was her pillar of strength, and always had been. Now she would be there for him.

After several more minutes had gone by a nurse appeared at the foot of the bed. 'I'm afraid that's all the time you have, my lovely. Only we wouldn't want to tire Jack out now, would we?'

Naomi heaved a huge sigh and was reluctant to leave. 'I must go now, Dad. You need your rest,' she said, putting on her raincoat. 'I'll be back to see you tomorrow after work. Oh! I nearly forgot. I've some Welsh cakes in my bag for you.'

Her father's eyes lit up. 'Duw! There's a good girl! Amongst the calamity you still found the time to make your old Da his favourite Welsh cakes,' he said in a voice little more than a whisper. 'By the way don't forget to call in and tell your Aunt Maud about things on the way home. She needs to know,' said her father, winking.

'OK, Dad. I know I'll never hear the end of it if I forget,' she laughed. 'Now you get some shut-eye before they come around with your tea.'

She bent to kiss him goodbye then made her way out of the hospital to catch the bus, which was just pulling into the stop. During the journey Naomi's mind was in a turmoil because she had a deep-seated feeling that, in spite of his optimism, her father did not have long to live. She was always picking up feelings around people and situations and could have done without

34

them at this moment, because more often than not they came true.

As she stepped off the bus she shivered. The cold nip in the air told her that Autumn was well on its way. She could see clouds gathering at the top of the mountains and guessed they were in for a downpour. Suddenly, there was a rumble of thunder and huge spots of rain began to fall so she quickened her step, hoping to save herself from becoming drenched.

On reaching her aunt's house she tapped the gleaming brass door-knocker several times. Her aunt's home was spotless and the windows were always shining from her elbow grease. She had often wondered why her aunt had never married, thinking she would have made someone a good housekeeper.

Her aunt opened the door. 'What's up Naomi? I didn't expect to see you,' she said, grimacing. 'Fetch yourself in out of the rain, now.'

Naomi shook her coat before placing it on the hallstand, and then sat down in an armchair by the window.

'Dad's had a heart attack,' she blurted out, looking at her wistfully.

Her aunt stopped in her tracks. 'Duw! Whatever next? What's going to become of you?' she screeched, throwing her hands in the air.

Naomi looked at her strangely. She had never seen her act in this way. Her spinster aunt was straight-laced, and usually took things in her stride, never panicking.

'There's one thing you must promise me, Naomi,' said her aunt, pacing the room.

'What's that?' Naomi asked, wondering what on earth was coming next.

'I've had suspicions about your Dad's health for some time and if he doesn't pull through from this heart attack I don't want you going down the same route as your birth mother did. She was nothing but a tart!'

Naomi's stomach churned. 'Just how do you know that?'

'It was a well known fact that she was a woman of loose morals,' her aunt retorted, with the air of a disciplined matron. 'I've not many more years left in me, so there'll be nobody to keep an eye on you if you go down the same road as her. It's something my sister and I always dreaded happening.'

Before Naomi could utter another word, a knock on the door broke the tenseness in the room, startling her aunt.

'I'm not expecting anyone,' her aunt grumbled, removing her pinafore. 'Perhaps it's the vicar.'

Naomi raised her eyebrows, feeling glad of the distraction, as she tried to come to terms with what her aunt had said. A minute later she heard her aunt calling and knew by the tone of her voice that she wasn't pleased.

On going to the front door Naomi's heart came up into her mouth when she caught sight of the black Austin car outside, with Peter sitting at the wheel.

Patty, one of Naomi's neighbours, was standing on the front door step talking with her aunt.

Naomi ran out and waved to Peter. She was so pleased to see him.

'I hope you're not going back to an empty house with that young man,' her aunt shouted to her, pulling a face.

'Oh, no,' said Patty, butting in. 'They're coming home with me. My children are around their Nan's for tea so I'll be glad of the company.'

Before Maud could say anything else Patty climbed into the back of the car, making herself comfortable.

After retrieving her coat and handbag from the hallstand Naomi fled from the house, with her aunt on her heels. Just as she was about to clamber into the front seat of the car, her aunt pulled her to one side.

'Take a warning, my girl. Just be careful, or you'll be landing up just like your mother,' she snarled, half frightening her to death.

Naomi gasped, and wondered what on earth her birth mother had done to deserve such a bad reputation.

Naomi turned to wave to her aunt just as Peter was about to drive off but she ran in out of the storm, slamming the door loudly behind her.

Naomi was still reeling with shock and wondered if her aunt's harsh words were spoken because she felt some kind of responsibility towards her. She felt cross, and was certainly not going to be dictated to by anyone, especially now she was a young woman and able to think for herself.

'Mrs Evans saw the ambulance last night and told me you were sure to be at your aunt's so when Peter turned up on your doorstep I came to his rescue and said I'd show him the way,' said Patty, looking very smug in the back seat.

Naomi turned and smiled at her knowingly. Patty was a comparative stranger to her, having only recently moved to the street. She appreciated the fact that she had made the effort to help and knew only too well that her aunt would have prevented her returning to an empty house with Peter in tow.

As Naomi sat back, enjoying the comfort of the leather seats, she directed Peter through the maze of side streets back home. It was the first time she'd ever travelled in a car and she was enjoying every minute of it.

'Fancy coming all this way just for me,' she said, giving a huge sigh.

'I was worried when you didn't turn up so I drove down straight away, taking the Aust Ferry across the

River Severn.'

'There's romantic,' said Patty, smiling.

Peter flashed a grin at Naomi.

When they pulled up outside Patty's house they rushed indoors and, after taking off their coats, settled down in the front parlour while Patty went into the scullery to make some tea.

'It's lifted my spirits being with you,' said Naomi, catching hold of Peter's arm. 'It's been a dreadful twenty-four hours.'

'I understand,' said Peter, looking into her eyes, 'and I think it might be wise to bring our engagement forward considering the circumstances. After all I'm sure your father would feel more relaxed to know you will be in capable hands if anything happens to him.'

Panic surged through Naomi. Suddenly the joy of seeing Peter was overturned by the feeling that she was being pushed into a corner and she had no intention of rushing into things like a fool.

'I...I don't know, Peter,' she said, playing for time. 'I'm only seventeen after all.'

Before Peter had a chance to make the situation even more uncomfortable Patty came back into the room with a tray of tea and made it evident that she'd been listening.

'I was married at your age, with twin daughters, and hard work it was too, believe you me. The only time off I have to myself nowadays is when my mother minds the little ones for a few hours on a Sunday. But that's getting too much for her now she's in her sixties. Can't blame her mind, they're a right handful.'

'I could always baby-sit for you to have a night out,' said Naomi, glad to change the subject. She felt she wanted to repay her kindness and also knew it paid to keep in with the neighbours.

'I might take you up on that,' laughed Patty. 'That

would be a great change from being stuck in every night.'

To Naomi's relief the next hour was spent looking through Patty's photograph album. Peter was polite but looked bored as time went by.

'It's time I was going,' he said, glancing down at his watch. 'I must make a move because I'm on early shift at my father's garage in the morning and it will take me a few hours to drive back home.'

Everyone stood up. 'It's been lovely to see you,' said Naomi, giving his arm a tight squeeze. She liked him a lot, but wished he'd stop pushing things. She fully intended to enjoy herself over the next few years and being tied down to one man all her life didn't appeal to her in the least.

'Don't forget to think over my offer, now. I've seen just the ring you might like,' he said eagerly.

Naomi's heart nearly stopped. 'You must realise that I've got a lot on my mind with my father at the moment, Peter, so I'm not making any plans yet.'

'I understand,' said Peter, looking downcast. 'We'll have a proper chat next time I see you, shall we?'

Naomi nodded and gave him a parting kiss at the door.

'See you next week then,' said Peter, hugging her tightly. 'Perhaps we can visit the hospital together then?'

'To be honest, I'd rather you left things alone until Dad's home. I'd hate to have a bad name for entertaining men friends in an empty house, you know.'

Peter's face fell. 'B..but I wanted to be there for you,' he stammered.

Naomi saw his disappointment. 'Don't worry I shall drop you a line in order to keep you informed about matters.'

His face lit up.

A feeling of guilt swept through Naomi as she waved him off. She wished she'd had the nerve to come clean with him. .

CHAPTER 4

After several weeks of nursing care Jack Williams was well on the road to recovery, and the day of his discharge from hospital was imminent.

Naomi continued writing to Peter, but managed to keep him at arms length as to when he could visit again. At the same time she was attending the Technical College down in Newport, where she was studying English language and shorthand and typing in the hope that it would eventually help her obtain promotion at the foundry. Favouritism was rife at work and she had decided that if her face didn't fit she would seek employment elsewhere.

On the day of the examination at college Naomi tucked her Bible into her bag for some added confidence. She turned to her faith even more now that she was staying in the house on her own and found it a great comfort.

After finishing the exam she gave a huge sigh of relief and couldn't wait to leave the stuffy classroom for the fresh air outside. She was not looking where she was going as she put up the hood on her raincoat, and walked straight into two young men who were talking outside the building.

'I'm awfully sorry,' she said apologetically.

'Don't be, I'm the lucky one,' said the stranger, giving her a wicked smile. It was raining hard and he was holding the collar of his long gabardine raincoat up round his neck, trying to protect a mass of dark curly hair from the storm.

'Anyway,' he said, turning his back on the other man, 'I'm Freddy, and my friend was just leaving.'

His friend looked at him stunned but took the hint and disappeared around the corner into the night.

Naomi looked up at the stranger more closely and

felt strangely attracted to him as she met his dark brown eyes.

'How about a quick coffee in Rabaiotti's before you leave,' he offered with an impish grin.

'The café will be closed by now. Anyway, I have to catch my bus, or I'll be late home.'

'I'll take you to your bus then. That way we can get to know one another better.'

Although totally flabbergasted by his cheek, she thought it would be fun to have someone to accompany her to the bus station.

As they walked down the road together she found her newly found friend easy to talk to and began chatting away as if she'd known him all her life.

'This is as far as I go,' said Naomi walking up to her bus stop. Thanks for your company. I enjoyed our chat.'

The rain began to ease so she took off her rain hood, exposing a mop of long auburn hair.

'I'm partial to redheads so how do you fancy a date next week, then?' he asked, raising his eyebrows.

'Oh, I don't know about that,' said Naomi, grinning. 'Not backward in coming forward are you?' she laughed, toying with the idea in her mind.

'Well, what's there to lose? I can promise you a good time but I'm certainly not the type to be tied down.'

Naomi's eyes lit up. He sounded just the sort of man she was looking for.

'How does Monday evening at seven suit you then?'

'OK. Here's my address,' she said, rummaging in her bag for a pen and paper. 'It's the third terraced house along on the right. You can't miss it.'

'I won't,' he answered, grinning. 'I'll be off now then. I've work in the morning, and the gaffer on the building site won't take it kindly if I'm late.'

With that he turned on his heel and ran up the road, leaving Naomi staring after him. Her heart thudded with excitement. She could hardly believe that she had even contemplated making a date with a complete stranger but had no doubts that she would enjoy his company.

To Naomi's joy her father came home by ambulance the following Monday. She'd managed to take the day off from work, in lieu of pay, and had cleaned the house from top to bottom in readiness for his home coming.

As she helped him inside she was saddened to see that the once broad shouldered man had grown wizened and unsure of himself.

'Sit your-self down now, Da,' she said. 'I've built up a nice fire and we'll have a lovely cup of tea, is it?'

As soon as she'd settled her father in his favourite arm chair with his morning paper she decided to pluck up the courage to tell him about Freddy, living in the hope he wouldn't ask too many questions.

'By the way Dad, I've invited a friend of mine named Freddy round tonight. Do you think you'll be up to visitors?'

Her father peered at her over his horn rimmed spectacles. 'Who's this Freddy then? I thought you were dating Peter?'

'Can't a girl have more than one boyfriend?' she laughed, trying to make light of it, fully aware there was no pulling the wool over her Dad's eyes.

He looked at her thoughtfully, stretching his legs out across the hearth rug. 'Well, I'll soon size this *friend* up when I see him. Anyway, how long have you known this lad?'

She walked over to the pantry and pulled down the cake tin from the shelf, pretending not to have heard him. 'How do you fancy a Welsh cake to go with your tea then Da? They're freshly made this morning,' she said, putting several on a plate in front of him.

'Duw! It's grand to be home again, cariad. The cooking didn't match yours in the hospital,' answered her father, tucking into the cakes.

Naomi smiled at him and hurried out of the room, glad to take refuge in the scullery. There was a chance he might ask her more questions about Freddy and she knew only too well she couldn't possibly tell him the truth. The consequences didn't bear thinking about. Only common tarts picked up men in the neighbourhood, and she had hardly earned herself that name!

Shortly before seven o'clock that night there was a loud knock on the front door. Naomi was dressed in her best frock and briefly glanced in the hall mirror in passing to make sure her hair was just so. On opening the door she gasped in horror at the sight of Freddy who was dressed in a royal blue Teddy Boy jacket and black drain-pipe trousers. She further cringed when her eyes fell upon a pair of bright blue *brothel-creepers* adorning his feet.

Her stomach turned over. During their brief encounter the week before Freddie's clothes had been well hidden underneath his gabardine raincoat. He'd even worn different shoes in the torrential rain too, not the luminous pair that now stood out on the doorstep.

'Well, aren't you going to ask me in then? It's freezing out here.'

'Don't tell my Dad how we met will you? Only he wouldn't approve and I daresay he won't approve of your rig-out either,' she whispered, getting wound up at the thought of it.

'I'll have you know that this is the latest fashion,' Freddy protested, as she propelled him into the living room.

'Th..this is Freddy, Dad,' she stuttered, holding her breath.

Her father's jaw dropped, as she had expected.

'So *you're* Freddy, then?' he said, drawing himself up as if to look a little more imposing. 'Sit yourself down lad, and tell me something about yourself.'

The tone of disapproval showed in his voice and, after a few minutes of stilted conversation, Naomi began to feel totally embarrassed. She'd seen Teddy Boys hanging around street corners and had heard their dress was the latest craze, but it was another thing bringing one home. As word had it nice girls kept away from such boys.

She could tell Freddy was nervous by the way he was shifting around in his seat, and broke into the conversation to try to lighten the tension.

'Well, where are you taking me then?' she asked, with a broad smile.

'To be honest, I can't stop because it's my brother's birthday and we're all going out for a drink,' he said, rising out of his chair. 'I'd forgotten all about it you see.'

She looked at him stunned. How dare he promise her a date then stand her up, she thought to herself, pouting.

'Will we be graced by your presence again, then?' asked her father, as he lit up a cigarette.

'I expect so,' said Freddy, giving him a wry smile. Then, within seconds, he bolted out of the room with a bereft looking Naomi following behind.

'What are you playing at?' she asked, frowning.

'I..it was a last minute arrangement which I couldn't get out of,' he stuttered, his eyes seemingly glued to the pavement. 'I could meet you on Saturday outside the Royce milk bar in Newport around two o'clock though.

You know the one in the High Street that sells the latest American frothy coffee. It's always full of youngsters on the weekends. I enjoy talking with the bikers that congregate outside. I've always set my heart on a motor bike you know, and perhaps one day I'll be the proud owner of one.'

'Is that so?' said Naomi, with a wide grin on her face. 'Well, I suppose I *could* make it around two o'clock, if you're lucky,' she drawled, not wanting to sound eager. 'That is, of course, if I haven't got anything else on,' she added with a mischievous smile.

'That's a date then, and I promise not to break it next time. By the way are you a Catholic by any chance?'

'No I'm not, but what's that got to do with things?'

'Nothing. Just wondered,' he muttered, biting into his bottom lip. 'Well, I'll be seeing you then. Don't be late.'

'Goodnight,' she said, putting her face up to his, living in the hope of a kiss being planted on it.

Her face fell as he left her standing. She stood and watched him turn the corner of the street, not quite knowing what to make of things, but the thrill of the chase excited her. She had every intention of finding out more about the Teddy Boy with the upturned nose and slashed-back hair.

Naomi held her breath as she walked back into the house. 'Well, what did you think of him then, Da?' she asked hesitantly, looking at the frown on her father's face.

'Well, he was certainly an eye opener, and to be perfectly honest not the type of lad I would have chosen for you to be seen with.'

'Still, that's fashion, Dad. You're behind the times you know.'

He grimaced then settled back into his chair,

holding the evening paper in front of him.

Naomi knew he would soon change his mind. She was used to twisting him round her little finger.

On Saturday morning Naomi couldn't wait to finish the household chores before meeting up with Freddy. He'd been on her mind all the week and she'd treated herself to a new outfit especially for the occasion.

'I've left you some faggots and peas cooking on the stove Da, only I'm off down to Newport to see Freddy,' she said, picking up her coat from the hallstand.

'You be careful what you get up to with that lad. He's not of your ilk, do you hear?' said her father as he stoked up the fire. 'And don't be home too late mind,' he called after her. 'Otherwise I'll be coming to fetch you myself.'

'I'm only going to meet him, not running away to Gretna Green!' she retorted in a huff as she closed the door. Buttoning up her coat, she walked purposely up the street intent on having a good time.

When she eventually reached the Royce milk bar she looked through the window but Freddy was nowhere to be seen amongst the crowd of teenagers inside. Suddenly, she began to wonder whether she was doing the right thing or not, since her father's manner towards Freddy was far from ideal. In her eyes he was always a good judge of character. Just as she was about to walk away Freddy turned up looking dressed to kill in his Teddy Boy outfit.

'I thought we'd take a jaunt up the town, first,' he announced, eyeing her up and down. 'Duw, you look fantastic. I'm going to be the envy of all my mates today, you know.'

She had purposely bought something more casual to wear, and hoped her crisp white cotton blouse and flared skirt with stiff petticoats underneath were more to his taste. Obviously it had done the trick and she flushed with the compliment.

'Whereabouts in Newport do you live then? Only I would have liked to have met your family,' she said, feeling a little peeved that he hadn't taken her into the milk bar.

'Well, if you must know, Ma's not keen on me hanging about with a Protestant girl. She's living in the hope that I'll make it back up with my old girlfriend, who was a Catholic.'

Naomi looked at him dumbfounded. She felt a pang of jealousy.

'What's the look for? You can't blame our Mam because we're all staunch Catholics in our family. None of my brothers ever went out with a Proddy. So I'll be in for an ear bashing if she finds out.'

Naomi thought his mother too sanctimonious for her own good. 'I've heard you Catholics stick together,' she said. 'My friend married a Catholic lad and because she wouldn't change her religion the Priest told her that her children would be considered bastards. So where's the sense in that?'

He shrugged his shoulders, then slipped his arm around her waist as they walked in the direction of the shops.

Naomi enjoyed the sensation of his arm about her and kept in step with him as they walked along, looking at what was for sale in the various shop windows.

'Guess what! I'm hoping to see a palmist down Newport with the girls from the office on Monday. Her name's Madam Rhodes and they tell me she's pretty accurate with her predictions, so it should be interesting.'

Freddy's face broke out in a grin. 'You don't believe in that rubbish, do you? She'll probably cast a spell on you and turn you into a toad,' he joked, with a twinkle in his eye.

'Not if I've got anything to do with it,' she giggled. Her heart was racing as he held her hand tightly. He was just what she needed to perk up her life.

By the end of the afternoon, when Freddy took her back to the bus station, she knew she was well and truly smitten with him and was in a quandary about what to tell Peter.

On the bus journey home she decided to change her whole image by tying her curly locks into a pony tail. She had already bought the latest pumps for her feet. There'd be no stopping her now!

On Monday morning before leaving for work Naomi told her father that she may be a little late home that evening as she might have to work overtime. She hated the thought of lying but on no account could she admit to him that she intended to visit a fortune teller, She knew only too well he would have scoffed at the idea.

Rhiannon and Dolly were both secretaries at the Foundry and worked alongside Naomi in the office. They were both big, strapping girls whose sense of humour was second to none. Dolly was hoping for news of a promotion from Madam Rhodes. It was a well known fact that she was up to her neck in debt having just got married whilst Rhiannon, on the other hand, told Naomi that she was just making up the numbers for fun. Naomi had always thought her a dark horse and secretive and somehow knew there was more to her than met the eye.

All afternoon the topic of conversation evolved round the fortune teller. When the foundry's clock struck five the girls darted out from their office in order to catch the early bus into town.

On reaching their destination, the girls hurriedly made their way towards the arcade where Madam Rhode's flat was. And, after climbing up a dark stairway, they knocked on her door.

Within seconds Madam Rhodes herself opened the door and invited them inside. A shudder ran down Naomi's spine as she stepped into the woman's living quarters.

'Well, here goes. There's no changing our minds now,' whispered Dolly, whose eyes darted everywhere.

Rhiannon stood behind the two of them trying to suppress a giggle. Naomi gave her a look fit to kill, worried that they might be thrown out. Although she was apprehensive about hearing her future she needed to know if the woman could tell her anything about her birth mother.

After brushing what Naomi thought might be cat hairs from her black flowing dress, Madam Rhodes looked at all three young women intently.

'I shall read for you first,' she said, pointing to Naomi. 'Your friends can make themselves comfortable on the bench in the hallway,' she added, pointing to the door.

Naomi sat down beside a table in the dimly lit room. The look of the place reminded her of a funeral parlour as it was sparsely furnished and had a strange odour to it.

Madam Rhodes sat on the opposite side of the table and pulled out a pack of playing cards from her pocket. 'Let me see your palms first before you shuffle the cards, my dear,' she said with authority.

Naomi stared hard at the woman and thought she was probably getting on in years by the look of her wispy grey hair and lined face.

After placing her palms on the table in front of her she saw Madam Rhode's eyes narrow.

'Do you realize that you are a sensitive like myself?'

Naomi shook her head and twisted nervously in her seat. She wasn't sure what she meant and didn't intend showing her ignorance.

'A lot happened around you when you were little which completely changed your pathway in life.'

'That's correct,' said Naomi, nodding.

Madam Rhodes continued to stare at her hands and seemed to be looking at the lines beneath her little finger. 'There will be two quiet weddings and you will also conceive a boy and a girl. But one of these you will lose.'

Naomi felt a cold draught blow around her and shivered.

'Nothing to be frightened of, my dear. It's only the spirit people making them-selves known. Shuffle the cards now, please and make a wish.'

Naomi frowned at her as she shuffled, then wished for news of her birth mother.

Madam Rhodes carried on by placing each card down slowly in front of her on the table.

'Men will be your ruination in life if you're not careful, my dear. I see you meeting up with a dark headed man around street corners. He'll be no good to you. Just you wait and see.'

Naomi grimaced as she stared down at the cards and wondered how this woman could see the future in just an ordinary pack of playing cards. She began to feel doubt.

Suddenly, Madam Rhode's eyes darkened.

'What is it? I'd rather know?' asked Naomi, gritting her teeth.

'I can see a prison. It was connected to someone in your past who was up to no good.'

Naomi caught her breath. 'I've no idea who you're talking about. I've always been well brought up and have never mixed with anyone of that calibre.'

'You *will* find out,' Madam Rhodes assured her, as she carried on turning each card.

Naomi sat listening intently.

The woman's face took on a sombre look. 'I can also see a person lying on the floor, left for dead, so I'd be careful of the company you keep if I was you, my girl.'

Naomi froze, holding her hand over her mouth. 'Can't you pick up *anything* good in my future,' she cried, thinking the woman was nothing but a charlatan.

'Well, there is a large sum of money arriving at your door shortly, but it will slip through your fingers like greased lightning.'

'Perhaps it's a rise in wages. It's about time I had one,' she snorted in disbelief.

Madam Rhodes raised her one eyebrow, then picked up the last three cards and sighed. 'I now see a funeral concerning someone near you happening at Easter time.'

Naomi's face fell as her thoughts turned to her father. 'I didn't come here to hear about death,' she snapped, dreading the thought.

'Birth, marriage and death is what life is all about, my girl, so why visit me if you're not prepared to hear about such things? I can only tell you what I see for your future whether it's good or bad,' she said, placing the cards back into her pocket.

'That will be twelve shillings and sixpence, please.'

Naomi gritted her teeth, thinking it was day-light robbery, then she thrust the money begrudgingly into the woman's hand. Gathering herself together she rose from the chair, and hurriedly left the room.

'Ye God's, you look as if you've seen a ghost,' giggled Dolly, grinning.

'I wish I had. It might have been a better experience than listening to Madam Rhode's ramblings. I wouldn't waste my time if I was you.'

Before Rhiannon and Dolly could make any

comment, Naomi ran out of the door, down the stairs and into the street, vowing to herself that she would never return to such a place.

CHAPTER 5

Several weeks later Jack William's began to suffer with re-occurring chest pain. Naomi was worried that something would happen whilst she was in work and dreaded the thought of coming home and finding him dead.

The letters between Naomi and Peter had dwindled and she decided she had to end things between them. She felt guilty but knew his intentions of walking her up the aisle would rob her of the freedom she longed for.

Several days after posting the letter to Peter, Naomi was shocked to receive a reply from him saying that he wanted her to return the cross and chain he'd given her as a present.

'You've got to be joking. You're mine for keeps,' she said, patting the cross and chain which she always wore. She'd never owned anything as expensive and beautiful in all her life and thought it was a cheek of him to ask for it back.

As time went on, Peter never made contact with her again, which left her feeling sheepish about the way she had treated him.

Freddy would call in to see her from time to time but to Naomi's dismay he never stayed long and always had some sort of excuse to tell.

One weekend Patty called at Naomi's house to ask her if she would baby-sit the following Saturday as she had been invited to an engagement party with her husband. Naomi was over the moon at her offer, and the chance of earning a few extra shillings, so she immediately accepted and was looking forward to taking care of her beautiful twin daughters.

Saturday evening soon came around and just as Naomi was making herself comfortable on Patty's settee after putting the girls to bed she heard a knock on the front door. On opening it she was astounded to find Freddy standing outside with a big grin on his face.

'Aren't you going to ask me in then? Only I just bumped into Patty and her old man walking up the street just as I was about to knock your door. She explained to me that you were minding her children and suggested I called in to keep you company.'

Naomi ushered him inside and shut the door behind him, excited at the prospect of having him all to herself, without her father sat in the room beside them.

Freddy whisked her up in his arms. 'Alone at last,' he said, squeezing her tightly. 'Don't you think its best if you check on the children before we *really* get comfy,' he chuckled.

'Good idea,' said Naomi, pulling away from him. She made a quick dash upstairs where she found both girls fast asleep. Then she hurried back down to Freddy who was sprawled out on the settee. The only light was the glow from the fire.

'Shall I put some records on? I daresay Patty won't mind and I know she buys the latest rock and roll songs.'

'Records!' Freddy snorted, looking at her in amazement. You've got to be joking. I haven't come here to sit listening to records when I intend to have my wicked way with you.'

Naomi giggled. 'I might let you kiss me if you're good,' she teased.

'We'll see about that,' drawled Freddy, pulling her down onto the settee.

Before she could answer, his lips were on hers and after several passionate kisses she felt his fingers fumbling with the buttons on her blouse. She flinched, afraid of where it might lead.

'I need you to prove that you love me,' Freddy

urged, holding his hand under her breast. 'Come on now don't be coy. You shouldn't have such a voluptuous figure. It would drive any man to distraction.' He slid his hand through the opening of her blouse. 'There's a good girl,' he whispered. 'You know I love you.'

Frightened of losing him, Naomi yielded but was terrified it would lead to other things. She knew very little about the rudiments of sex. Suddenly, she felt Freddy fumbling with the zip on his trousers and she began to struggle but his strength overpowered her as he forced her down onto the floor. Within seconds he had lifted her skirt and tore at her knickers, ripping them from her. By now she lay stiff with terror and caught her breath as he entered her. Going this far was not what she'd bargained for. 'I love you, I love you,' he kept panting, as he forced himself back and forth on top of her.

With teeth clenched and eyes shut tightly, she let him get on with it, and was relieved when he finally rolled away from her.

On opening her eyes, she pulled a face at him.

'What's the matter with you, woman? You look as if you've committed a murder,' he said, as he zipped up his trousers.

'Well, if you must know I feel like a cheap tart. It's not how I expected sex to be. I wanted to keep myself decent!' she said, quickly pulling up what was left of her torn knickers.

Freddy grinned at her. 'You need to relax more, and then you'll soon learn to enjoy it. Anyway, you're my property now because other men won't want to be handling second-hand goods, you know. And before you mention birth control, I don't intend using anything because it's frowned upon in the Catholic religion.'

Naomi gasped at his choice of words, looking at him

disdainfully.

'I wanted to be a virgin when I got married. Most nice girls are.'

'Bit late for that,' he smirked, putting his coat on. 'Anyway, you gave me the impression that you only wanted fun out of our relationship, so how was I to know you were a virgin?'

'But you said you loved me!' she cried, staring at him in disbelief.

'Well, I knew that would spur you on,' he chortled callously, putting on his jacket.

Naomi's stomach turned over. She felt sick as she stumbled through the darkness to the outside lavatory. How she wished it had never happened. She felt cheated.

When she eventually reappeared in the doorway, Freddy looked set to leave.

'I promised to meet up with the boys for a drink, if I could make it,' he said, looking down at his watch.

'You've had what you came for, so you're going now, is it?' she snapped, angered by it all.

Freddy winked at her then made his way to the door.

After slamming the front door behind him Naomi began to shake. Tears ran down her cheeks at the thought of how he had tricked her into losing what could not be replaced. It was a night she would never, ever forget.

The following Monday Naomi received her exam results through the post. She was thrilled to learn she had passed with flying colours and had won a free scholarship, which meant she would not have to pay for any further tuition at the college. She was over the moon and felt extremely proud of herself. Finding new employment with better wages and prospects were on the agenda at long last.

Freddy was a constant visitor from then on. After downing a few pints at the pub he'd call at the house quite late, more often than not timing it when her father had retired to bed.

Naomi never felt comfortable having sex under her father's roof and was worried that he'd catch them in the act one day. She had become accustomed to a quick kiss and fumble before a quickie on the settee. On more than one occasion, she begged him to be more careful. But more often than not, with beer in his belly, all promises were forgotten, which in time made her cold to his advances.

When Christmas Day came around Naomi was in a state of sheer panic. She had missed a period and was out of her mind with worry.

Freddy appeared at the house shortly before lunch, staying long enough for a festive drink and to collect his present. As soon as he'd had a brief chat with her father he began to leave and Naomi escorted him to the door.

When she was sure they were out of earshot of her father she pulled him to one side on the doorstep. 'I've another little present for you,' she said quietly, catching hold of his hand.

'A quick feel is it?' said Freddy, ever ready for action.

'I'm pregnant,' she blurted out, dreading what his reaction would be.

Freddy's eyes narrowed. The expression on his face spoke volumes. 'You stupid cow,' he uttered with scorn.

'Well, perhaps we can get married. That would solve all our problems, wouldn't it?' begged Naomi, trying to hold back the tears.

'You've got another think coming, my lady,' he

growled, lighting up a cigarette. 'You're a right cold fish compared to other girls I've been with.'

Naomi gasped at the thought of him touching other women. She felt like smacking him across the face.

'What's going to become of me? I can't tell my Dad, it would kill him.'

'Keep your bloody voice down. We don't want everyone knowing about it, do we?' he snarled, looking up and down the street at the passers-by.

Naomi's eyes flashed. It was all she could do to keep a civil tongue in her mouth.

'Don't look at me like that. I'm only in my early twenties, which is far too young to be tied down with a kid.'

Putting her hands on her hips Naomi let rip. 'Is that so? Well, it's your fault, anyway. If you'd used birth control, this would never have happened.'

'Oh! It's my fault now, is it? Don't you think that you should have crossed your legs in the first place, you simple bitch.'

'I wish I'd never met you. You're vile,' she cried, standing back and looking at him with revulsion.

Before he could answer she slammed the door behind him, sliding the bolt home noisily as anger raged through her. It was all she could do to stop herself shouting, 'Who's the daddy then?' through the front room window, when she caught sight of him scurrying away into the distance.

Stunned by his unconcerned manner she sniffed back the tears and returned to the living room, wondering how on earth she was going to hold herself together in front of her father. As well as everything else she'd had a strong feeling that this would be her father's last Christmas and she was determined to make it his best.

By the time Easter came around Naomi's pregnancy

had began to show. She had resorted to wearing baggy clothes in the hope of hiding her shame. All sorts of things ran through her mind and she was frightened as to how and when she was going to give birth without anyone finding out.

She had no idea what to do when the child eventually came into the world and wondered whether she ought to wrap it up and take it to the nearest church for fear of being found out. There was no way her father would accept a bastard child in the house. But despite praying to God for some answers, none came.

Every day Naomi saw that her Dad was becoming decidedly worse. But he surprised her on Easter Sunday by suggesting that they took a slow walk to the cemetery in order to lay flowers on her mother's grave. Naomi made sure she wrapped him up warm in his tweed overcoat and brown plaid scarf before they took a leisurely stroll to the graveyard in the spring sunshine. It pained her to see the sorrow in his face as they arranged the freshly picked daffodils in the pot, and after standing back to admire them they slowly walked back home again, arm in arm. She knew he was nearing the end and choked back her tears.

That night, as she wearily made her way up the stairs, Naomi caught her breath as she felt the baby move. She had pretended for so long that the state she was in wasn't real, but actually feeling the movement brought her sharply to reality. She was at her wit's end and didn't know which way to turn. Tears poured down her cheeks as she flung herself on the bed, muffling her sobs in the pillow.

After tossing and turning for a long time she sat upright in the bed, staring into darkness. For a brief moment she could have sworn she saw the dark figure of a man appear at the bottom of her bed. Fearing that her mind was playing tricks on her she hurriedly slid back down under the bed clothes and stayed there until sleep finally came.

The following morning, Naomi thought it odd not to have heard her father downstairs because he was always an early riser. Flinging on her dressing gown, she rushed into his bedroom to see what was wrong. She recoiled in shock when she found him slumped over the bed with his eyes wide open, staring. She took his pulse. There was nothing.

For several long minutes she stood rooted to the spot, her mind not functioning. Then realization eventually hit her and she began to sob, falling to the floor in a heap, beside herself with grief. 'Why now Da, when I need you so much?' she cried. 'What will I do without you? Perhaps you would have accepted my child after all? I never did ask you and will never know now.'

The next few days seemed like an eternal nightmare for her. Aunt Maud was quick to come over and stay whilst the arrangements for the funeral were being made.

'You look awfully peaky, my girl. Still it's to be understood under the circumstances,' her Aunt commented, as they were leaving the house for the funeral.

Naomi had done her best to pull her swollen stomach into a tight corset, so as not to arouse suspicion, but she found it very hard to sit down as the stays were prodding into her stomach. Despite the April showers she decided to wear her old swagger coat instead of her raincoat, at least it would hide any traces of her pregnancy.

Jack had been an extremely popular man, which was evident by the crowds who attended his funeral. Every moment was like a dreadful nightmare for Naomi. Freddy was nowhere to be seen which didn't help matters. She felt so alone in her grief and found it exceedingly hard to watch her father's coffin being lowered into the ground, knowing full well that she'd never see him again.

After the funeral was over, many of the family and friends came back to the house where Naomi and her aunt had laid out the funeral tea.

Naomi watched in the hallway as her aunt hurried into the scullery whilst she stayed by the front door acknowledging the flow of people who came to show their respects. Amongst them was Naomi's favourite cousin, from away, who couldn't resist the urge to stop and chat for a moment.

'Duw, you've put on some weight, my lovely,' said Jean, raising her eyebrows. 'I believe in keeping trim for my Dylan.'

Naomi swallowed hard. They were the same age and had been firm friends when her mother was alive. She felt tempted to take Jean to one side to tell her about the predicament she was in but thought better of it in case she didn't keep things to herself.

Suddenly, Naomi heard raised voices in the scullery, which was out of earshot from the front room where the mourners had congregated. Both girls looked at each other wide eyed, wondering what all the commotion was about.

'Come on let's have a listen, then,' said Jean, urging Naomi forward.

After closing the living room door behind them, so they could eavesdrop without being noticed, the girls edged towards the green painted scullery door as the loud voices continued.

'I had a feeling you'd show your face, and was keeping a look out for you at May's funeral, but you never appeared, did you! She's managed without knowing you all these years, so why should I tell her about you now?' her aunt was shouting angrily.

Both girls pulled a face at one another, and drew closer to the door.

'I suppose you're right. You'll do her no favours by telling her the truth about her mother, anyway,' said a man's voice, gruffly.

Naomi couldn't make out who he was but noticed that he didn't have a Welsh lilt to his voice.

'Our Aggie's girl told me that Kathy had tried to commit suicide when she was serving a prison term and I believe there was a stink over a book she had written as well.'

Naomi held her hand up to her mouth, lost for words.

'What happened after that?' asked her aunt.

'As far as I know she was let out on parole, and stayed with a friend until things blew over. There was also a rumour floating round that she gave birth to another child before she eventually made a new identity for herself.'

'Nothing would surprise me about that woman,' cried her aunt. 'Anyway, it's time you were going, in case you're seen. I'll keep an eye on things, don't you worry.'

Suddenly the voices went quiet and the girls heard the back door slam. Naomi ran to the side window just in time to see the back of a tall, sleek man with auburn curly hair disappearing through the garden gate.

The cousins looked at each other, aghast. 'What was that all about?' said Jean, raising her eyebrows.

'I'd lay bets it was about my birth mother,' said Naomi, biting into her bottom lip.

'Don't talk so soft,' sneered Jean. 'You always did have a vivid imagination. Still, if I remember rightly our Mam did mention a long time ago that your birth mother was a bad lot. But I never took much notice.'

Naomi stood bolt upright, taking umbrage at her remark. 'Well, I'm determined to find her one day, just you wait and see.'

'You must be daft, that's all I can say. By the sound of things I doubt if she'll do you any favours. Come on, let's get some food down us before we're noticed hanging around,' she urged, pulling a face.

Naomi followed her into the front room and tried her best to mingle with the many mourners who had turned up. Nothing seemed real to her anymore and despite trying to look composed she was relieved when the last couple of mourners drifted away.

Her aunt began gathering up her belongings, ready to leave, and Naomi was sorely tempted to ask her about the visitor in the scullery but she thought twice about it, knowing she might be at the receiving end of her aunt's sharp tongue.

'Keep in touch and look after yourself, my girl. No having boys around and that sort of thing. You know what I mean,' she said, waving her umbrella at her on the front door step.

Naomi nodded, knowing full well it was too late to be warned about such things.

After waving her aunt off she hurried upstairs, relieved to be able to unhook her corset at last. It had been cruelly cutting into her stomach all day. As she was taking the corset off the thought of her adoption papers came into her mind. After hurriedly putting on her pyjamas and dressing gown, she made her way into her late father's bedroom to see if he'd left the key to the dressing table anywhere. Her eyes flitted all around the room until she spied his jacket hanging up behind the bedroom door. On rummaging through the pockets she was relieved to find the key in the breast pocket and as she held the jacket near her face she began to cry.

'You must think me awful, Da, searching for your

keys, but I've got myself into deep trouble and need to find out where my birth mother lives. I know she's got a dreadful reputation but she might find it in her heart to take me and the baby in.'

On opening the drawer where she believed the documents were she was surprised to find it empty. The tin was nowhere to be seen. Her beloved Da had taken the secret of her adoption to his grave. She regretted now that she had not copied down the names and addresses written on the papers and was cross with herself for her stupidity.

Shortly afterwards, Naomi slumped down on the settee with a hot cup of cocoa. She looked down at her bulging stomach, terrified at the thought of what lay ahead of her.

A loud knock on the front door broke into her thoughts. Thinking her aunt might have left something behind she quickly hurried to answer it, and was shocked rigid to find Freddy looking as drunk as a Lord outside.

'So you've eventually shown up like a bad penny then,' she exclaimed, looking at him scornfully. 'Is your conscience pricking you or something, after all this time?'

'I was really sorry to read about your Dad's death in the paper,' Freddy mumbled, stumbling into the hallway. 'Did he leave you much?'

Naomi pulled a face as she smelt the drink on his breath. 'There's only an insurance policy which Dad paid into which should cover the funeral bill and a stone for the grave.' she snapped, closing the door behind him.

'I...I was only thinking that if you'd inherited a couple of bob you might be able to afford an abortion.'

Naomi couldn't believe her ears. 'You've got to be joking,' she shouted, pushing him away from her.

'Anyway, I thought the Catholic Church was against such things?' She was consumed with anger, and wished she'd never laid eyes on him.

'Well, I've no intentions of paying maintenance for a child, so there!'

'It's your child,' she shouted, striking him across the face.

'You bitch,' he snorted, grabbing hold of her hands. 'Try that again and just see what you'll get.'

Naomi's nerves snapped and she began to pummel his chest like a mad woman, infuriated by his behaviour.

Freddie retaliated by punching her in the stomach.

She fell to the ground gasping, and gave him a look fit to kill.

'It was an accident! Just a stupid accident!' he shouted, the colour draining from his face.

Naomi lay on the floor, trembling, rolling in pain. She heard the door slam and after several minutes managed to pull herself up onto the settee. Her heart was breaking and she felt like ending it all.

CHAPTER 6

When Naomi woke up the following morning she felt wretched but, despite feeling ill, she made her way into work knowing that she had no choice in the matter now all the household bills had fallen on her shoulders.

After glancing through the mail in the office she found a large batch of orders and invoices that needed typing and began to work methodically through them as she tried to ignore the rising tide of nausea that threatened to engulf her.

Shortly after lunch a sharp shooting pain shot through her stomach. The girls in the office noticed her wince.

'Whatever's the matter?' asked Dolly frowning. 'You've gone as white as a ghost.'

'It's probably the pasty I ate for lunch,' Naomi mumbled, trying her best to look composed when all the time she was becoming more and more frightened as the pain increased. She knew she dared not tell her workmates about the predicament she was in for fear of the shame and scandal it would cause and it wasn't until another pain seared through her that she guessed she was losing the baby. Terror-stricken she waited until the pain subsided momentarily before gathering up her things.

'I'm going home because I think I'm coming down with food poisoning,' she cried, clutching hold of her stomach.

Dolly looked at her aghast. 'I think that's best under the circumstances. You have gone a funny colour. Don't worry. I'll explain to the boss, when he puts in an appearance, but I doubt whether he'll be pleased, knowing him.'

At that moment Naomi couldn't have cared less but was fully aware that he'd not take too kindly to her finishing work early, when there was so much work to be done.

With great difficulty Naomi boarded the bus and was relieved to find an empty seat. By now she'd come out in a hot sweat and couldn't wait to reach home. Although she tried to remain outwardly calm, she was now trying to fight back the fear that was surging through her soul.

When the bus eventually lurched to a stop near where she lived Naomi hurriedly got off and walked the rest of the way home in comparatively little pain thinking it was a miracle she had made the journey in the first place. After turning the key in the lock she went inside, glad to be out of the way of any prying eyes.

She had hardly got through the door when another stabbing pain gripped her, making her cry out. Petrified, she hung onto the banister waiting for it to subside. It was the worst yet, and she dreaded to think how bad the pains would get.

Shortly after the pain became bearable again she made her way into the living room and, throwing down her coat, she slumped onto the settee. Too frightened to seek any help she rested there for a while hoping the pains would wear off but as time wore on she felt them get stronger and closer together.

The hours went by and darkness started to fall as the night closed in on her. Amidst it all the light went out. The meter was empty and she knew she had given the last of her change to the conductor on the bus. With much effort she dragged herself into the scullery, frantically fumbling around for a candle. She eventually found one which was always kept for emergencies. Her hands reached round for the matches nearby and, after lighting the candle, she knew her time was near as she felt pressure build up within her.

She quickly grabbed a bucket from beneath the sink then snatched a few towels from the back of the door. Just as she placed the candle on the mantelpiece in the living room the pain returned with a vengeance, making her cry out in agony. Beads of perspiration appeared on her brow but, despite it all, she managed to pull herself onto the bucket, knowing her time had come.

'I know I have sinned but please help me, dear God,' she sobbed. The tears ran down her cheeks. Suddenly she felt as if her inside had been ripped open as something gushed from her. She sat in terror, staring through the window into the blackness of the night.

Suddenly, in the candle-light, she could see the image of her father standing before her with out stretched arms. He looked like the dad she knew and loved as a child and wondered whether she was hallucinating or dying in childbirth. The apparition petrified her and she began to weep uncontrollably.

When the pain finally relented she wiped her eyes and after blinking several times all she could see was the candle's flickering flame. Thoroughly exhausted from her ordeal she slowly raised her weary body from the bucket, wiped herself as clean as she could with the towels and collapsed down onto the settee. Her whole body began shaking with shock so she pulled her coat down over her, glad of its warmth, then thankfully slept.

In the light of dawn she awoke and stared at the blood stained bucket and towels before her. She had hoped that the previous night's happenings had been a nightmare and felt like throwing up.

As she rose slowly from the settee her head spun with weakness. She glanced at the time and wondered if one of the girls from the foundry might call in on their way to work. She had to rid the room of all evidence.

Very carefully she lifted the blood stained bucket up and went outside in the back yard to the lavatory. She felt sick as she slowly poured the bucket's contents down into the pan and gasped when she saw a small but perfectly formed foetus amongst the clotted blood. She began crying afresh, knowing full well that she was disposing of the remains of her baby. Then she shuddered as she pulled the lavatory chain. Guilt engulfed her.

As she returned inside, she heard a loud knock on the front door. She panicked and plunged the bucket under the tap, swilling away the bloodstains as best as she could. By now she realized there was no way she would be able to answer the door because she had begun to bleed heavily. She hoped whoever it was wouldn't wander into the back yard to find her.

After bolting the scullery door and drawing the curtains she finally sank down onto the settee, relieved to be safely out of sight. It was then she began to think about the previous night's events, wondering whether or not she'd seen a vision. Perhaps her beloved father had returned to safely take her baby with him to God? She wished she knew and prayed that it might be so.

CHAPTER 7

Naomi decided to return to work the following Monday. She was dreading the thought of how she would explain her absence without a sick note. Her food cupboard was bare and she needed to collect her wages so she'd be able to fund the weekly shop.

Back at her desk Naomi kept up the pretence about having food poisoning and much to her relief nothing more was said about her absence, which pleased her immensely. All day she felt out of sorts and was glad when home-time came around.

Just as she was walking through the gates of the Foundry Naomi had the shock of her life when she found Freddy waiting outside the works. He called over to her in his usual cheeky manner as if nothing had happened.

She felt weak at the knees and was in no mood for an argument so she kept walking towards the bus stop as if he didn't exist. In the mean time Freddy caught up with her. He was full of apologies for his behaviour and swore never to get drunk again.

'I lost our baby and went through hell. A fat lot you care!'

'Good grief,' he moaned, looking at her wide eyed. He put his arm around her shoulder when she began to cry. Then he tried to persuade her to join him for a cup of coffee at a transport café just up the road.

She was feeling extremely vulnerable and was easily taken in by his gift of the gab. So she followed him down to the café like a sheep to the slaughter house.

During the next few days it didn't take very long before Freddy put his next plan into action. He knew Naomi's father's insurance was about to be paid out at any time so he broached the subject very tactfully one evening as they were settling down on the settee.

'I know just the thing that will put some colour back into your cheeks,' said Freddy, giving her a broad smile. If you remember I always longed to have a motor bike and your Dad would have thought it a good idea. Just imagine a trip to the sea-side or the country sitting astride a bike with the wind blowing through our hair. Dew! It would do your health a power of good.'

Naomi's eyes lit up at the thought of it. 'But where on earth are you going to find the money from,' she laughed. 'Thinking of robbing a bank?'

'No,' he said, shaking his head. I was living in the hope that you might be able to lend me some dosh out of your Dad's insurance policy. Don't worry I'll be able to pay you back each month out of my wages.'

Naomi raised her eyebrows in a gesture of uncertainty. What would her Aunt Maud think if she found out? Still, she didn't have to tell her now she wasn't a frequent visitor to her home. The idea of travelling further a field sounded exciting so perhaps the motor bike would be a good investment. After all Freddy was a reformed character since her miscarriage. She mulled things around in her mind. First and foremost the funeral director's bill was to be paid off. Then Freddy's repayments for the bike could be paid to the stone mason each month which would enable her to have a stone on her parent's grave. It all sounded so easy.

By the end of the evening Freddy convinced her that she was doing the right thing. She was like putty in his hands.

As soon as the cheque arrived Freddy was quick to escort Naomi down to Turner Parkes, the general dealer in motor bikes who was situated in Clarence Place, Newport. After browsing around the shop Freddy eventually made up his mind which bike he preferred.

It was a 250cc BSA motor bike and the final bill with insurance, tax and oil came to £182.2s.2d. When Naomi slowly counted the cash sum over to the gentleman serving, his eyes gleamed. It wasn't everyday anyone paid cash for an item in the 1950s because money was scarce.

After the deal was done Naomi walked further down the road in order to settle her account with Albert E Hick's Ltd, who were a well reputed funeral undertakers in Grafton Road. When she left the building she glanced down at the poultry amount of change left in her hand and decided it would be a wise investment to spend her last few shillings on petrol for the bike.

The rest of the weekend was spent touring around the country side on Freddy's new motorbike. Naomi felt on cloud nine, especially when he mentioned they might even get engaged. She had set her mind on a lovely heart shaped ring that she had fancied in Pleasance and Harpers Jewellers the last time she was shopping in Newport and longed for the day he'd propose.

It was high summer and still light in the evenings so they often toured down to the coast. Naomi was in her elements but every time she mentioned a payment for the bike was due. Freddy would plead poverty avoiding the issue. Not wanting to spoil the wonderful time she was having she let things slide.

Then when the nights began to draw in Freddy became more interested in keeping company with the motor bike lads who frequented the Royce Milk Bar instead of calling in to see his girlfriend. By now Naomi had a deep seated feeling that he was playing away with other girls and decided to have things out with him.

One night when he called at the house Naomi

invited him inside with a grim look on her face. Before he could sit down she turned her aggression on him.

'You're over two months in arrears with your payments towards the bike. So what do you intend doing about it? I presume your money is going on floosies and drink when you're out with the motor bike gang?'

His face turned the colour of beetroot.

'Don't keep on. You've had a good time with me haven't you? Anyway, there's not a thing you can do about it because nothing was written down in black and white.'

'I needed that money for my parents gravestone,' she protested.

'Tough, you shouldn't have been so free and easy with your money. Anyway, I'm not stopping because I only came to say I can't be doing with you any longer, now I'm off with the boys,' he yelled, pushing his way past her.

A huge row ensued between them by the front door, with Freddy storming out of the house.

Tears stung her eyes as she slammed the door behind him. She would never forget what he had done and how stupid she had been.

The following Monday a bright yellow card caught her eye in the newsagent's window as she was passing. On closer inspection it read, 'Typist/Telephonist urgently required at Green's Warehouse. Wages: Three pounds, fifteen shillings per week, plus a yearly bonus.' It was just what she was looking for, and on her doorstep too. Turning on her heel she began walking in the direction of the warehouse, hoping that the position was still available.

It was a warm day, with brilliant sunshine, which gave her a spring in her step. She knew she'd be in trouble for not arriving on time at the foundry, but would face that when she came to it. Thoughts of Freddy came into her mind. She immediately felt nauseous with disgust at the way she'd been treated and hoped she would never set eyes on him again.

Green's was a large retailing outlet which was renowned for selling a huge array of fancy goods. And it was just up the road from where she lived. Within minutes of arriving at her destination she was ushered into the manager's office for the interview.

Naomi looked into the face of a well-groomed, middle aged man, with receding hair. He shook hands with her. 'My name's Tony Brain,' he said, directing her to a nearby chair. 'Make yourself comfortable and start by telling me why you've applied for the position on offer.'

Naomi warmed to him, feeling immediately at ease in his presence. 'To be honest, I'm working as a typist telephonist but my wages aren't nearly enough to cover the bills since I have lost both of my parents.'

'I'm sorry to hear that,' he said, looking at her sympathetically. 'Well, let's see what your typing skills are like, shall we?'

Naomi's stomach turned over as he pulled forward a typewriter on his desk and asked her to copy a letter beside the machine. Naomi took a deep breath and was relieved when she was able to finish the task satisfactorily.

'My word, you're fast on the keyboard. Just what we're looking for,' he said, patting her on the shoulder. 'What about your switchboard skills? We badly need someone for relief work when our telephonist is away.'

'I'm PBX trained,' answered Naomi, knowing full well that this skill she had learnt at the foundry would be an asset.

His eyes lit up. 'I've interviewed several people but

none of them have switchboard experience, so that clinches the matter as far as I'm concerned. Welcome to the work force!'

Naomi shook his outstretched hand and couldn't believe her luck. 'I will be expected to give a week's notice at the foundry, but all being well I should be able to start next Monday,' she said, beaming all over her face.

Tony Brain stepped around his desk and ushered her towards the door. 'Splendid!' he said, his face showing as much delight in the appointment as Naomi's. 'By the way, there will be plenty of chances for promotion and, you never know, you could earn a place as my secretary if you work hard enough. I look after my girls well,' he said with a glint in his eye.

Naomi gave him a huge smile, as he held the door open for her to leave, and hurried out of the building feeling over the moon with joy.

When Naomi began working for Green's it wasn't long before she settled into her new routine. It was a welcome change from the foundry. She worked in the chief buyer's office with two sisters, Susan and Maria Jones. They were both pretty girls with dark, shoulder-length hair, who were extremely friendly and easy going.

One lunch time Naomi took over the switchboard duties while Susan and Maria went to the canteen for something to eat. Just as she was settling down in the chair the office door opened and a well built man with a shock of fair hair and piercing grey eyes stood before her. She'd noticed him on several occasions giving her the glad eye as she walked through the warehouse and had overheard that he had recently arrived with his family from Kendal, in Cumbria.

'I'm here to collect the invoices so the boys can

make a start loading up the lorries,' he said, admiring himself in the mirror on the wall.

Naomi handed the invoices over. 'All done and correct,' she said efficiently.

'Thanks, lassie,' he drawled, looking her up and down.

'You're not from these parts are you?' said Naomi, smiling.

'No, My name's Duncan Campbell and I'm originally from the Lake District. Anyway, I was wondering if you'd like to accompany me to the pictures this evening? Only there's a good film on at the Coliseum down in Newport.'

'Duw, you're not short in coming forward are you?' said Naomi, pulling a face.

'That I'm not,' said Duncan, grinning, showing a row of uneven teeth.

Naomi felt a hot flush rise in her cheeks. He'd taken her unawares and she was not sure if she wanted another relationship so soon after Freddy.

'Well, what's it to be then?'

She hung back, trying hard to think of an excuse.

'I won't take no for an answer so I'll expect you to be waiting outside the Post Office in Newport town centre at seven, then,' he said with a commanding air. 'Must dash or the foreman will tear a strip off me for hanging around.'

Before Naomi could reply he strode out of the office leaving her in a quandary. At least he looked well groomed, not rough and ready like Freddy, she thought to herself. So, was it going to be another dull night in with nothing but sad memories to keep her company, or this young upstart who obviously fancied himself but looked like he might be good fun?

Several hours later Naomi stood patiently on the steps of the Post Office. She was wearing her white short-sleeved blouse underneath her navy suit and began to feel cold as she waited. After twenty minutes had gone by and she was just about to leave, Duncan put in an appearance.

'If you'd arrived a minute later I would have been on the next bus home. I'm frozen stiff,' she moaned, rubbing her arms. 'Don't you realise it's bad manners to be late?'

'Sorry honey, I never was a good time-keeper.'

After linking his arm in hers they walked towards the Coliseum Cinema in Clarence Place.

'I'm starving so how do you fancy a hot dog first. There's a little cabin down near the railway bridge on the Caerleon Road that sells them.'

'Oh, I'd like that,' said Naomi, keeping in step with him. She'd had next to nothing for her tea. There wasn't much in the larder owing to the fact that it was coming up to the end of the week.

As they continued walking Naomi began to worry that they might have the bad luck to bump into Freddy. She knew he might be pub-crawling with his brothers at that time of night and hoped and prayed that their paths wouldn't cross. As soon as they found the hot dog stand Naomi stood to one side as Duncan placed his order.

'Off to the pictures, are you?' said the jolly looking lady stallholder, with a broad grin.

'That I am,' said Duncan, slamming his money down on the counter.

As they began to eat their hot dogs Naomi noticed Duncan check the change in his pocket.

'I suggest we skip the pictures, shall we? We've missed the first half and I've less money than I thought in my pocket,' he said, lowering his gaze. 'But you're welcome to come around to our place if you like. My parents should be out tonight at my father's church. Father's a minister you know.'

Naomi looked at him wide eyed. Fancy her going out with a minister's son. Her mother would have been pleased.

Although she was disappointed at missing the film she decided to go along with Duncan's suggestion. They linked arms as they walked back up the road past the Cenotaph and when they reached Newport Bridge they stopped on the way to take a glimpse into the swirling waters of the River Usk.

Naomi began to wonder if she was asking for trouble by visiting an empty house with someone she hardly knew. But naively convinced herself that she would be safe with someone who had been brought up by a man of the cloth.

They eventually stopped walking once they had reached a large semi-detached house which was set back from the main road. Naomi thought it looked quite a prosperous area and wished she'd had the chance to live somewhere similar instead of in a back street terraced cottage.

'Here we are,' announced Duncan, opening the door to number twelve.

Naomi followed him into the house, admiring the beautiful portrait paintings on her way through the hall.

Suddenly, a door opened to the right of her, which made her jump, and a short stubby man with a mop of bright ginger hair appeared. 'And who might you be?' he asked, sternly.

Naomi was startled, and Duncan came forward. 'This is Naomi, one of the office girls, that's all.'

Naomi's eyes flashed at him. He'd made her feel insignificant.

The man looked relieved. 'Well, if that's the case, I'm The Reverend Robert Campbell, Duncan's father and this is my wife Morag,' he said, looking over his shoulder at a short, fair haired, plump lady, who smiled profusely at her.

Morag stepped forward. 'Tonight's church meeting was cancelled. You should have forewarned us that we would be having company, Duncan.'

After shaking hands Naomi was ushered into the lounge where she made herself at home on the leather settee. Her feet sank into the thick carpet beneath her and she thought how fortunate Duncan was to live in such luxurious surroundings. There was a moment of silence before anyone spoke then Duncan's father sat down beside Naomi and started to talk about his church and how he was hoping his son would take up the ministry like himself in the near future.

Naomi was well impressed, and after a brief pause Morag returned to the room carrying a tray of tea and biscuits, which she handed around.

Robert went on to say that his wife had originated from Dundee in Scotland but had moved down to Kendal as a child, and that was where the two of them had first met as next door neighbours.

Naomi felt completely at home in their house, chatting away as if she'd known everyone for years and it wasn't until she heard the grandfather clock in the hall strike ten that she made her apologies and stood up to leave.

'You must come along for tea on Sunday,' Robert announced. 'Morag will bake you one of her special strawberry sponges. And we could perhaps all go to church afterwards.'

Morag nodded. 'It's good to see my only son taking an interest in a lovely lassie like you, instead of flirting around with the wrong kind.' She eyed her son sharply, and Naomi saw Duncan glower at her across the room. Naomi ignored it, happy in the fact that she had created a good impression, and felt quite saddened that the evening had come to a close.

'Lovely to have met you,' said Naomi, turning to them both. 'I've thoroughly enjoyed myself, thank-you.'

'Don't let me down on the weekend, now will you?' said Morag. 'There'll be plenty to eat.'

'I'll be here, don't you worry,' said Naomi, thinking how kind she was.

As Naomi left on Duncan's arm, she wished that she had been brought up in a similar lifestyle. She had often pitied her parents struggling week in and week out in order to keep a roof over their heads. This made her even more determined to better herself, come what may, but not before she had tracked down her birth mother. That took priority over everything.

'I overheard in conversation at work that both of your parents have died, and you live alone. I expect you're a wee bit lonely at times,' Duncan remarked, as they made their way to the bus stop.

'Well, it's not pleasant arriving home to an empty house filled with nothing but memories,' answered Naomi, sighing.

'I'm ready and willing to keep you company, anytime. So don't you forget it.'

Naomi looked up into his eyes, thinking it a kind gesture. Just at that moment the bus pulled into the stop and, before they parted, Duncan gave her a passionate kiss on the mouth in front of everyone in the queue. Naomi felt her colour rise and as she stepped onto the bus she waved him off before taking a seat.

As the bus was pulling away she glanced through the window and was flabbergasted to see Freddy strolling along with his arm around a blonde headed girl on the other side of the road. That won't last long she thought to herself, smugly. She wondered how she could have been so stupid to have courted him in the first place. Her temper began to rise and she felt like banging the window shouting some remark about the money he owed her. But knew it would fall on deaf ears.

The following day when Naomi arrived in work she couldn't wait to tell the girls in the office about her night out with Duncan. 'Guess what?' she exclaimed, 'I spent a fabulous evening last night with Duncan Campbell, from the warehouse.'

She felt the instant unease in the office as both girls looked at her dumb-struck.

'You've never gone out with that Duncan Campbell?' said Sue, pulling a face. He struts around as if he owns the place and there's a darker side to him, mark my words.'

'There's also talk in the warehouse that he's a womaniser and not too fussy either,' grimaced Maria, shaking her head.

'I don't believe you. Not a minister's son. He was a perfect gentleman with me,' said Naomi, feeling peeved. 'Anyway, I've been invited to his house for tea on Sunday. So there!'

Both girls raised their eyebrows but said nothing. With her temper rising Naomi turned her back on them and began working on the filing system. She was angry that her workmates had tried to put a damper on things and put it down to pure jealousy.

The following Sunday afternoon Naomi was enjoying a good soak in the galvanised bath tub when she heard a loud knock on the front door. Stepping out of the bath, she hurriedly dried herself, and wrapped her dressing gown round her. She thought it was probably Patty, her neighbour who had promised to return a cup of sugar she'd borrowed that morning.

On opening the door she caught her breath at the sight of Duncan standing outside.

'You're early. I'm not ready yet,' she said, dragging him inside, in case any of the neighbours spotted her half-naked.

'I can see that,' he jested, raising his eyebrows. He sat down on the settee.

Naomi grinned as Duncan pulled her down beside him. But, before she could even think of resisting, his mouth had quickly met hers, hard and demanding. She snuggled into the warmth of his body then gasped as she felt his hand swiftly slip through the opening of her dressing gown, groping at her breast.

For a moment in time all her inhibitions were lost as she gave in under the strength of his embrace.

'I must have you,' he panted, unzipping his trousers. Within seconds he mounted her as his emotions began to rise. Naomi's body felt alive for the first time ever. Her recollection of experiencing Freddy's wham, bam, thank-you Ma'am excuse for sex instantly disappeared from her mind as her passions arose. Wrapping her legs round his waist, she gasped as he entered her again and again. Thoroughly lost in the emotions that caught her she groaned in contentment after his final thrust, then lay down beside him surprised at how quickly she had responded. She hoped he hadn't considered her cheap and suddenly panicked at the thought that she might have been caught pregnant again.

'We should have been more careful,' she whispered in his ear, knowing full well that he hadn't taken any precautions.

'I thought a girl like you would know all the tricks?' he whispered back.

'There's a cheek,' she snapped, wishing she hadn't given of herself so freely.

'Well, you weren't exactly a virgin, that's for sure! Just how many other men have there been, lassie?'

Naomi's stomach churned. Duncan's ecstatic

embrace instantly turned sour.

'Only one, and he turned out to be one too many.'

'Well, just think, you could have a good little earner living here on your own, and I could be your pimp.'

Naomi couldn't believe her ears. 'How dare you speak to me like that,' she screamed.' What do you take me for?'

Duncan pursed his lips. 'Well, you shouldn't have come to the door with next to nothing on then, should you?'

'But I thought you were a gentleman.' she cried, swallowing hard.

'There's no such thing,' he chortled. His mouth was now turning upwards into a dismissive sneer. 'Now don't tell me you didn't enjoy it?'

Naomi didn't answer. She didn't think it fair for men to be applauded for casual sex, whilst women were classed as whores.

'Come on now, stop day dreaming. Mother's made one of her special strawberry sponges, just for you, and would certainly think it rude if you didn't turn up.'

In her loneliness Naomi turned things around in her mind. She couldn't see the harm in spending some time with his parents when she had nothing else to do. She had begun to hate Sundays on her own since her parents had died and could not bring herself to visit the chapel on the hill anymore knowing full well she'd probably bump into her Aunt Maud. The least her aunt knew about her antics the better. Besides which, she didn't want to let Morag down as she had been so lovely to her on their first meeting.

'I'd hate to disappoint your mother so I'd better get dressed,' she said, a little reluctantly. She wondered whether or not she was doing the right thing now that she had seen another side to Duncan that was not to her liking. He'd made her feel like a cheap tart.

'I've laid a lovely spread out in the dining room. 'Do come through,' said Morag, looking well pleased with herself.

Naomi's face lit up when she saw the array of food on the table. She hadn't eaten as much in ages and made her-self at home with the rest of the family, enjoying the fuss they made of her.

After attending church Naomi lost all track of time when she returned to the Manse for supper. And it was not until she heard the clock chime eleven, that she realised she had missed the last bus. 'Look at the time. I'll have to walk home now,' she said, not looking forward to the prospect. Many of the town's drunks and tramps lurked round late at night looking for rich pickings.

'I wouldn't dream of it. I should have been more observant of the time,' said Morag, looking sorry. 'You're more than welcome to sleep here the night, and I've plenty of freshly ironed nightdresses to hand.'

'Thank you very much, but I wouldn't like to impose…'

'Och, away with ye,' said Morag. 'I'll go and make up a bed in one of the spare bedrooms for you now.' She bustled off through the hallway and up the stairs, leaving Naomi behind with Duncan and Robert who were finishing off their hot chocolate.

After a short while Morag came back into the room and beckoned to Naomi who was more than grateful for her hospitality. After bidding the men goodnight she followed Morag, thinking she was every inch a lady by the way she conducted herself, although she sensed her husband seemed to be of a different calibre.

As Naomi climbed into the four poster bed she stared through the window at the view of the mountains as the full moon caught their majesty. She wished she had a similar view from her own bedroom window instead of back to back terraced cottages.

After pulling the welcoming warmth of the eiderdown round her slim shoulders she snuggled down in the bed and fell asleep within minutes.

Not long afterwards she was awakened by someone shaking her shoulder. She shot bolt upright and was aghast to see Duncan standing by the bed dressed only in his shirt.

'You frightened the life out of me. What's wrong?' she whispered, terrified his parents might wake.

'I want sex, whore, and I want it now,' he snarled, trying his best to force himself into the bed with her.

'You've got to be joking,' she cried, trying desperately to keep her voice quiet, despite her rising anger at being addressed in such a way.

'Get back to your bedroom before anyone hears you,' she said, pulling the bedclothes over her head. She lay stiffly on the edge of the bed. But knew he was still in the room because she could hear his laboured breathing.

Suddenly, she felt a heavy blow to her head from his fist.

'Leave me alone,' she cried, her head reeling with pain. Frightened that he might jump into the bed beside her, she leapt out and tried to make her way to the bathroom where she knew she could safely lock herself in. But Duncan beat her to it and dragged her into a nearby empty box room, flinging her inside. A heavy hand came over her mouth and the force of it thrust her head against the wall.

'Keep quiet or you'll get more of that?' he snarled, his eyes seemingly glazed over in the reflected moonlight.

Naomi looked at him terrified, and as she felt the size of his protruding penis against her she knew that the inevitable was about to happen.

'Duncan please, no...' she whimpered, but it was to no avail. He was like a madman and despite her vain attempts to break free there was no stopping him.

She was raped.

Just as he was pulling away from her, his parents burst into the room. Duncan immediately released his hold on Naomi leaving her to slide to the floor in a dishevelled heap. She quickly covered her face with her hands in embarrassment, and wished the floor would open up and swallow her.

'We heard the rumpus,' shouted Robert, glowering at them. 'This is disgraceful and I want you both out of my house this minute.'

Duncan lunged at his father with clenched fists, pushing him out of the bedroom. A full-scale fight ensued on the landing and Naomi looked on in terror as they fought.

'Stop, right this minute,' Morag shouted at the top of her voice, trying to part the two of them. At the sound of his mother's voice Duncan stopped in his tracks, whilst his father leaned on the wall, gasping for breath.

Still with his penis uncovered, Duncan proceeded to stomp up and down the landing like a spoilt child looking, with eyes like daggers, across at his father.

'Get dressed both of you and never darken my doorway again!' Robert shouted, raising his fist at his son.

'You ought to be ashamed of yourself, you filthy whore,' he cried, pointing his finger at Naomi, with a look of distaste on his face.

'It wasn't my fault,' began Naomi, but her pleas were ignored as Duncan's parents turned from her and left the room.

Within seconds of them leaving, Naomi scrambled to her feet and hurriedly returned to the bedroom where she quickly dressed and gathered up her belongings. She couldn't leave fast enough and thought Duncan deserved a thrashing for what he'd put her through.

After seeing if the coast was clear she made her way down the stairs like a frightened rabbit. Her legs were shaking so badly she worried whether they would support her. She slunk out of the house like a thief.

As she wearily began trudging her way home she heard heavy footsteps running along behind her. Hoping a drunk hadn't latched himself onto her she looked over her shoulder and was horrified to see Duncan trying to catch up with her. He had a small suitcase in his hand.

'Where do you think you're going to?' she asked, eyeing him with alarm.

'Well, to your house of course. Where else is there?'

She bit into her bottom lip, too afraid to argue.

'He's a bloody bastard of a man,' Duncan grunted, wiping blood from his nose.

'Serves you right,' said Naomi, trying to get ahead in the hope of giving him the slip. But as she walked faster he kept in step. She felt desperate as to what to do next knowing full well that behind closed doors she could be raped again.

Just as she turned the key in her lock she barred the doorway. 'I don't want you in my home so find somewhere else to stay,' she cried, hoping the neighbours wouldn't hear.

'Come on now, I'll behave myself. Be reasonable. It's too late to find other accommodation at this time in the morning. Either I sleep on the settee or I shout the place down,' he said, jamming his foot in the doorway.

Naomi cringed at the thought of the neighbours knowing. Quickly she pushed him inside rather than wake the whole street.

CHAPTER 8

As soon as the alarm went off Naomi got up from her bed, heavy-eyed and weary. The horror of the previous night's events whirled round in her mind as she stumbled down the stairs. Just the thought of facing Duncan at this hour in the morning made her cringe. Cursing herself for being stupid enough to let him stay she entered the living room, half hoping he had gone. Her heart sank at the sight of him sprawled out on the settee like the Lord of the Manor.

'Don't think you're staying here all day, boyo! Because you're not,' she snapped, trying her best to look hard-faced.

Duncan sat up rubbing his eyes. 'I've no intentions of working so let me be,' he grumbled, turning away from her.

'Well I want you out of here, pronto. I'd love to be able to stay at home but unlike you I've got household bills to contend with.'

After having a lick and a promise for her morning wash in the scullery she pulled her green floral dress on quickly for fear of Duncan barging in unannounced.

'I'm leaving for work,' she shouted, brushing her hair in the mirror. 'And you make sure you're well and truly gone by the time I return.'

Duncan gave her a look that made her skin crawl. Her mind raced frantically as she hurriedly walked towards her workplace. She sorely wished she'd never got entangled with the likes of him.

'My God you look rough,' said Susan, pulling a face when Naomi arrived in the office.

'Night on the tiles with Duncan was it?' enquired Maria, jokingly.

'Something like that,' Naomi answered, frightened of telling the truth.

'I don't think I saw Duncan in the warehouse as I passed through today but that's not surprising as I've been told how work shy he is,' announced Sue, pursing her lips.

Naomi knew she was trying to goad her into speaking up. She buried her head in her work as if she hadn't heard the remark and for the rest of the day she kept her distance from the girls. On more than one occasion she felt like blurting out everything that had happened but she was afraid of what they would think of her.

She sighed in relief when it was time to go home. Her stomach was crying out for food so she stopped on the way to buy some groceries. She was feeling tired from the lack of sleep and decided to have an early night.

After hanging up her coat she walked into the living room and laid her shopping bag on the table, taking out its contents. Suddenly, something came whizzing across the room and she just managed to duck out of the way. One of her late mother's best bone china tea cups narrowly missed her head, and smashed into tiny fragments on the floor.

'I know you're there,' she shouted, looking towards the scullery door.

Duncan came out with an evil grin on his face. 'You're late. Chatting up men I suppose, you whore,' he snarled.

'I'll thank you to mind your tongue,' she shouted. 'Have you taken leave of your senses or something? Anyway I thought I told you to leave.'

She was shaking inside but tried not to show it. There had to be something the matter with him, she thought to herself, no-one in their right mind would act the way he did. Apprehensive as to what could happen next she stood her ground, watching his every move.

'Just you tell me where else I can go with no money to my name. It's your fault I'm here in the first place.'

Naomi thought she was hearing things. 'How on earth do you make that one out?' she asked, eyeing him strangely.

'Well you shouldn't have tempted me with your body.'

'I've heard it all now,' said Naomi. 'I can't be doing with you around, so I suggest you gather your things and leave,' she cried. 'Look at the mess you've made.'

'I'm staying put and that's that.' Duncan snatched the milk bottle out of the shopping basket and after drinking greedily from it hurled the bottle, still half full of milk, at the wall. The bottle exploded into pieces. Milk splattered everywhere.

Naomi looked on horrified. 'You need locking up,' she cried, clutching her chest. 'Look at the state of my wallpaper.'

She raced out into the scullery for the broom and threatened him with it but he being much stronger wrenched it out of her hand. He gave a deep throated chortle as he threw it on the floor. It made her spine creep.

'It's time you cooked us some tea, isn't it?' he said, giving her a push towards the stove.

By now Naomi was very frightened as to what he would try next. She thought it wise to humour him until she had time to collect her thoughts. 'It's.s.s.sausage and mash,' she stammered and, after clearing up the mess he had made, she began to peel the potatoes. Her hands were shaking.

When the meal was ready she resisted the impulse to throw the plate of food at his head for fear of reprisals. Something to eat was the last thing on her mind as she slumped down in the chair, which was the furthest away from him.

After watching him gorge his meal she hoped and prayed he would leave.

'I enjoyed that. What's for pudding?' he said, smacking his lips.

'You were lucky to get a plate of anything. I've hardly enough to live on as it is. Anyway, you're not in your house now,' she retorted, feeling sick to the stomach with him.

'You know full well I can't go back home, so let's try and make the best of things together, shall we?'

Naomi's jaw dropped. She fought hard to stay calm. 'You've got a nerve. I'm not having the neighbours talking about me, and if my Aunt Maud got to hear about things she'd have a fit.'

'Fuck them all!' Duncan retorted, getting up from his chair.

Naomi stiffened. She wasn't used to hearing language fit for navvies and looked at him in disgust. To think he'd once set her heart racing and now she felt a prisoner in her own home.

'By the way, don't think you're sleeping with me tonight because I've just started my period,' she said, lying through her teeth, hoping he would go somewhere else.

'Good job too,' he said, admiring himself in the mirror. 'I don't intend having kids so I suggest you visit the family planning clinic as soon as possible.'

Naomi caught her breath. 'Decent single girls don't visit such places. They're only for married women and good time girls,' she said, biting her lip nervously.

'Be it on your head then,' Duncan smirked, diving under the covers that were still strewn on the settee from the previous night. 'Goodnight and sweet dreams!'

Naomi left the room and climbed the stairs with a heavy heart. Just as she was about to close the bedroom door she heard a man shouting loudly in the street below and pulled the curtains back to see what was going on. She gasped in horror at the sight of Robert, Duncan's father, standing in the middle of the road with several neighbours looking on. Dumfounded, she quickly called Duncan to come upstairs.

'Couldn't do without me, could you?' he smirked, as he ran into the bedroom.

'You've got to be joking,' she retorted, pulling a face. 'Take a look out of the window. Your father's causing a commotion in the street.' She pointed to where a crowd of people were now standing.

Duncan's mouth dropped at the sight of his father. 'What's the silly bugger doing now,' he growled, looking down at him in contempt.

'Just listen,' said Naomi, putting her ear to the window.

'The wages of sin is death. And there's a scarlet woman cohabiting with my son in that house over there,' The Reverend shouted, pointing over at Naomi's home.

Naomi looked on in disbelief as neighbours clad in their night attire came out on their doorsteps, wondering what the pandemonium was all about.

Robert's voice grew even louder now that he had attracted a large audience. He began to preach out of a Bible about the wages of sin to the gathering as if he was in the pulpit.

Naomi covered her face with her hands, cringing. 'My parents would turn in their grave if they knew this was happening,' she cried, shaking her head.

'Always thought the man had a screw loose,' Duncan snorted. 'He was forever with his head stuck in the Bible and hoped I'd be a lay preacher at some point. Pity he couldn't have spared the time to play football with me instead.'

Naomi was more concerned with the thought of the neighbours knowing her business. She fully expected the news would have spread like wildfire around the neighbourhood by the morning and she dreaded the outcome.

'I'll never be able to hold my head up again now I've been labelled a scarlet woman,' she cried. 'Mud sticks, and there's always someone about who will throw the first stone.'

'Well, there's nothing stopping me staying now everyone knows,' said Duncan, placing his arm round her shoulders.

Naomi cringed and shrugged his arm off demanding he returned downstairs. After the shouting had stopped and the crowd dispersed she undressed and wearily crawled into her bed. She was determined Duncan would not get the better of her so before she went to sleep she thought of a plan to get shot of him, once and for all.

CHAPTER 9

The following morning Naomi scrambled out of bed early and left Duncan sleeping soundly on the settee whilst she crept out of the house. Her first aim was to call at the police station before going to work. As she walked down the street she felt everyone's eyes were upon her as many of the neighbours were busily cleaning their front door steps and window sills. Those that weren't were now pulling back their nets and staring accusingly from their front windows.

Just as she neared the police station she bumped into PC Evans. Being the local Bobby she was well acquainted with him and asked if she could have a word. Drawing him to one side, she explained the predicament she was in and how she was unable to make Duncan leave the house for fear of what he might do. She felt her colour rise as she stared up at the broad shouldered policeman, and could see by the grim look on his face that he didn't hold with such things.

'I remember your parents well. They were respectable people. I'm surprised you've got yourself entangled with some tearaway.'

Naomi flushed with shame and embarrassment, not knowing where to look.

'Never mind,' he said, patting her on the shoulder. 'I'll have that bounder out in no time. Just you wait and see.'

Naomi prayed that it would be so. As they began walking along the street together she noticed several of the neighbours stopped to stare. She felt like screaming at them that it was none of their business but carried on regardless, wishing it was all a bad dream.

Her stomach churned over when she turned the key in the lock and ushered PC Evans into the living room. Duncan was slouched in the armchair, reading the morning newspaper. As he looked up the colour drained from his face.

'What's going on?' he grunted, looking grubby and unshaven.

'This young lady tells me you've overstayed your welcome. I suggest you gather your belongings right now and leave or you'll have me to deal with,' said the officer, with a stern look on his face.

Naomi's heart began to pound, fearing that Duncan might take a swing at her as he shot up out of the chair. She was greatly relieved when he began gathering his things together and made his way towards the door.

'I'm off now,' he snarled, giving her a look fit to kill.

On hearing the door slam behind him she realised that her ordeal was over at last. 'I can't thank you enough for your trouble,' she said to PC Evans, smiling appreciatively at him. 'I don't know how I would have managed without your help.'

'Pity you didn't have some older brothers to stand up for you. I'd heard you'd been left on your own since your parents died. You're easy prey for a bully, like him so don't make the same mistake twice.'

'I won't, don't you worry,' said Naomi, going with him to the door. She watched as the gossips, huddled together in their front porches, and knew by their menacing looks that she was the topic of conversation. As soon as PC Evans left she slammed the door shut, wishing she could move right away from the area. This brought thoughts of her birth mother flooding into her mind again. If only she had some idea of her whereabouts. She needed her so much, it hurt.

Naomi soon regained her confidence as her life returned to normal. She was overjoyed when she'd heard from the foreman in the warehouse that Duncan had been given the sack because of his constant absenteeism, and lateness. How could she have been so blind not to have seen what a bone idle bounder he was? Still, she was well rid of him and hoped he'd never darken her doorway again.

Several weeks later Naomi began to panic when her period failed to appear. As each day went by she grew increasingly concerned that she was probably pregnant again, and was beside herself with worry.

When Lilly, from the accounts department, called at the house one evening Naomi decided to tell her about the predicament she was in. She had heard that she was a trifle lax with her morals so thought she would probably be less inclined to judge.

Naomi looked in awe as Lilly came bouncing into the hallway. With her smart top, flared skirt and pink accessories she looked like someone who had just stepped out of a fashion magazine.

'How do you fancy taking a trip down to the Majestic dance hall in Newport? Only my friend's let me down and I could do with jiving my blues away, see.'

If circumstances had been different Naomi would have loved to have gone with her, but she knew it was pointless to pick up with another lad now she was pregnant, and she wasn't in the humour for dancing anyway.

Lilly made her self comfortable in the armchair. 'Well, get your coat on then or we'll miss the half past bus going down to Newport.'

Naomi hesitated, swallowing hard. 'I don't feel too grand. Do you mind if I give it a miss?'

'Phew, I'm rearing to go,' said Lilly, tightening the pink ribbon on her pony tail. 'Come to think of it you do look a bit peaky. What's troubling you?' she asked, looking questioningly at her.

'Can you keep a secret?' said Naomi, taken aback by Lilly's direct question.

'Course I can. Cross my heart and hope to die if I don't,' Lilly chuckled, lighting up a cigarette.

'I've been feeling quite sick of late and I'm almost sure I'm pregnant.'

Lilly gawped at her for several seconds, mouth wide with shock. 'You're a stupid cow. Fancy getting yourself tied down with a kid when you've got so much going for you. Most of the girls in work think you ought to be on the stage after hearing you singing in the office, and I totally agree with them.'

Naomi slumped down in the armchair, looking mournful. 'Well, it looks as if I'm heading for motherhood instead, and that's supposed to be a full-time commitment.'

'It's never that Duncan Campbell's child is it?' Lilly asked, raising her eyebrows. 'Only the likes of you can do much better than that jerk.'

Naomi nodded, grimacing. 'Well it's happened now, and there's not much I can do about it, is there?'

Lilly pursed her lips. 'Well I do happen to know of a back street abortionist that could help put things right for a couple of quid,' she said, brightly. 'Problem solved.'

Naomi looked at her shocked and thought back to the baby she'd lost. 'I'd never be able to live with my conscience, girl.'

'Bugger the conscience, I say,' blurted Lilly. 'I think it would be wiser if we paid Florrie Morgan a visit tonight. She's an old hand at such things and it shouldn't take too long.'

'If you think I would trust some back street abortionist messing round with my insides you've got another think coming. I've heard all sorts of tales about the damage they can do. And once I heard of a girl who died after having a knitting needle pushed up inside her. I shudder at the thought of it.'

Lilly eyed her sharply. 'Well, the only alternative is to visit the baby clinic then. 'I'll come along for moral support, if you like, but believe you me, if you are expecting to keep this baby it won't be no picnic, I can tell you.'

'It's either that or throw myself in the river,' said Naomi, feeling a surge of fear run through her as she imagined the scene.

'No man's worth that,' cried Lilly, stubbing out her cigarette in the grate. 'Anyway, it's time I was off or I'll miss my bus. See you around ten on the station steps in the morning then, is it? We can always tell the boss that we both had a dental appointment. He's as soft as butter when you get to know him.'

Naomi hesitantly agreed with her plan. Her bottom lip trembled at the thought of walking into such a place, knowing full well that unmarried mothers were frowned down upon. 'I'll be there,' she said, miserably, heaving a huge sigh. 'Now you go off and enjoy yourself while you can.'

'I may be classed as easy game in work but I'm certainly too clever to fall pregnant like you. When the time comes for me to marry I'll make sure I land myself someone half decent, with plenty of money in his back pocket,' she snorted, as she made her way to the door.

After waving Lilly off, Naomi climbed the stairs to bed for an early night, dreading the outcome of the next day.

As she lay in her bed she suddenly thought of Peter and wondered if there was a chance he'd take her on, baby and all. After all, he had the good looks, money and good prospects but after remembering the way she had treated him she thought better of it, knowing full well that he wouldn't want to be saddled with a woman who had spurned him and who was now carrying someone else's child. The fun she yearned for had burned her fingers and she was now getting what she deserved.

After a restless night Naomi met Lilly as arranged. As they made their way to the ante-natal clinic Naomi's stomach was in knots. What if she saw some-one she knew? She'd die of shame.

After taking down her particulars a nurse led Naomi to the lady doctor who took her time looking at her notes.

'I see you're not married,' she said, looking grimly over her horn-rimmed spectacles.

Naomi hung her head, looking ashamed.

'Let's see how far gone you are, then,' said the doctor, pointing to a leatherette couch in the corner of the consulting room.

Naomi held her breath as the doctor prodded inside her.

'I would say you're only in the early stages of pregnancy, so is there any chance you'll get married?'

'The father doesn't know and, even if he did, he wouldn't be the least bit interested,' said Naomi, looking forlorn.

The doctor nodded, then pulled up her chair and began writing some notes. 'We'll arrange for you to stay in an unmarried mothers' home for the confinement, then the necessary papers will be drawn up for the child to be adopted shortly after the birth.'

Naomi looked at her, horrified. 'My baby's certainly not being adopted. I know what that's like and the scar stays with you forever.'

'That's all well and good but what do you intend to live on when you finish work? Fresh air?' said the doctor, looking at her with contempt.

Nothing had prepared Naomi for this. Her mind was in a whirl as she tried to fathom things out.

'Think sensibly!' the doctor snapped, her mouth set in a grim line. 'You've got nothing to offer the child, unless you've family that will help. Anyway, there are plenty of people waiting to adopt, who will give the baby a good home.'

Tears pricked Naomi's eyes. 'I'll do anything to keep my child. Anything,' she cried in desperation. A cold sweat broke out on her forehead.

'I can assure you that many women feel the same way as you do. But most of the men they fall pregnant by are only looking for a good time and want no commitment whatsoever. Maybe this will teach you not to indulge in sexual relations until you're wed. That will be all.' She strode over to the door and opened it. 'The nurse at the desk will give you a card with your next appointment on.'

Naomi looked panic stricken as she stumbled out of the room and into the reception area.

'You look dreadful, lovely. What on earth's happened?' asked Lilly, grabbing hold of her arm.

'They want me to have my baby adopted, but I'm not going to,' Naomi answered fiercely.

'Well, that might be worth a thought. I'd hate to be bearing a child by Duncan. He had a bad name in the warehouse for being an arrogant prig who thought he was better than anyone else. Imagine if you had a son who turned out like that?'

'But I couldn't stand the thought of my child going down the adoption route. I'd never forgive myself,' Naomi sobbed. 'I can't go back into work feeling like this so you best carry on.'

'I'd seriously think about things if I was you, and hope to see you back in work next Monday.' said Lilly, quickening her step towards the bus station.

A thousand worries ran through Naomi's mind during her journey home. She could only think of one other person who might be of help and that was her Aunt Maud.

That evening she dropped her aunt a line asking her to call over when she was able. She needed to see her on her own ground. Just the thought of what she might say half scared her to death, but she knew her late mother's sister might be her only hope.

CHAPTER 10

It was Monday morning and as Naomi walked through the accounts department on her way to the office she had a strange feeling that everyone's eyes were upon her. She quickly glanced down at herself, not seeing anything to warrant it.

'I like your smock,' sniggered Charlie, one of the clerks, leaning against his desk. 'When's it due then?'

Naomi stopped in her tracks, flabbergasted. It was obvious that Lilly had betrayed her trust after promising she would keep things a secret. No-one else could have possibly known.

'I don't know what you're talking about,' she said, trying desperately to keep her composure. 'Anyway Charlie, haven't you anything better to do with your time than to ogle at me?' she snorted, bluffing it out. 'Some of us have *work* to do. Unlike you,' she blustered, barging past him into her office.

Sue and Maria were just settling down at their desks as she walked in. She tried her hardest to look calm although she felt shocked to the core.

Sue glanced up from the switchboard after finishing a call. 'We've heard the second-hand news about the state you're in. Lilly couldn't wait to tell us in the lobby. It's spread through the building like wildfire. What on earth made you confide in the likes of her?'

'I told her in confidence,' said Naomi, trying to fight back the tears that were now welling up in her eyes. 'I never thought for one minute that she'd blab my business to everyone after she promised not to.'

'We warned you Duncan was nothing but trouble but you took no notice. He probably has children all over the show,' said Maria, shaking her head.

Naomi felt every-one was against her. As the anger whelmed up inside her she decided to find Lilly, with the intention of giving her a piece of her mind. 'I'm off to sort that Lilly out once and for all,' she snorted, slamming the office door behind her.

Her rage was beyond control by the time she entered the accounts department, where she saw Lilly laughing and joking with other members of staff.

'I suppose I'm the current topic of conversation,' cried Naomi, her voice rising hysterically.

When she saw Naomi, Lilly jumped a mile and looked up at her sheepishly. The rest of the office workers stopped what they were doing and stared, ready for the unexpected but welcome diversion from their work.

'You deserve a good thrashing for telling everyone I'm pregnant. Some friend you are,' shouted Naomi, looking straight into her eyes.

'And who's going to do it? You!' Lilly scoffed, rising out of her chair and moving around her desk to confront her.

Naomi had the distinct feeling that Lilly was goading her, enjoying the chance to make her feel even more wretched than she already did. But before Lilly could take a step further Naomi slapped her full force across her face, sending her flying to the floor. She was surprised at the strength of her blow but immediately felt much better for it. She'd never resorted to violence before but she was bitterly wounded by her so-called friend's betrayal.

Everyone looked on in amazement as Lilly picked herself up and dusted herself down. 'Alright I deserved that,' she said, rubbing her hand across her reddening cheek, 'but you can expect even worse in the future when that brat grows up with its father's genes in it, mark my words,' she scoffed haughtily.

'I hope you burn in hell,' hissed Naomi, putting her fist up to Lilly's face.

Lilly gawped at her, cowering back.

'Show's over everyone!' shouted Naomi, looking around. 'I've done what I came for.' She left the office, still feeling at fever pitch, but realised that by striking out at Lilly she'd only fuelled more gossip about herself and had probably made matters even worse.

For the rest of the day she was unable to concentrate on her work and was relieved when home time eventually came around. She intended having a quiet evening to herself with her feet up but just as she was turning the key in the front door her Aunt Maud appeared at the gate.

'Thought I'd catch you on your way home from work because I wondered what was up when I received your letter this morning.'

Naomi felt her colour drain away and hoped her aunt wouldn't notice her nervousness. 'Come inside, I'll put the kettle on,' she said, relieved that she'd cleaned and polished the house the previous day.

Aunt Maud sat herself down by the table, eyeing her sharply. 'I'm not bothered about drinking tea. Let's get down to business. You haven't invited me over to talk pleasantries, my girl, and I've heard all about you flaunting yourself about with some lad.'

Naomi looked at her astonished and began to break out in a sweat. It was now or never, she thought to herself. 'Well, the truth is I've been and got myself pregnant,' she blurted out, and waited for all hell to be let loose.

Her aunt's face turned chalk white. 'You're nothing but a shameless hussy. My sister would turn in her grave if she knew of the disgrace you've brought on the family. You're just like your birth mother - no good to man nor beast,' she cried, her eyes getting darker by the minute. 'I'm a big believer in what's in the bone comes out in the flesh, and here's an example of it,' she shouted, flinging her hands in the air.

Speechless, Naomi stared at her. She was amazed that her aunt was so well informed about her birth mother. Despite her aunt blackening her mother's name it made no difference to Naomi's desire to find her at all.

Her aunt eyed her questioningly. 'I take it the baby belongs to the warehouse worker you've been knocking around with.'

'Yes, that's correct but we've split up and it wouldn't worry me if I never saw him again.'

'Had your pleasure and paying for it now my girl, are we?'

Naomi cringed. 'It wasn't quite like that. Anyway, I've been to the mother and baby clinic and they want me to have the baby adopted but I'm determined to keep it and hoped you could help.'

'Help at my age,' shrieked her aunt. 'You've got to be joking. Anyway, I think it would be a good thing if you have the child adopted. Although it will be like history repeating itself,' she added, scornfully.

A look of acute disappointment spread across Naomi's face. 'Well, I intend to keep the baby whatever you say, so there,' she said, trying to blink back the tears.

'Keep it? Keep it?' cried her aunt. 'That's out of the question, my girl. The sooner you grow up and see things for what they are the better. Get your head out of the clouds.'

Naomi was totally unprepared for her aunt's response, and knew full well it was pointless to argue.

Her aunt went on to talk about the rigours of childbirth, making Naomi feel even more miserable.

'How do you know about these things when you haven't brought any children into the world yourself?' she asked, trying her hardest to change the subject.

Her aunt stood up and faced her with her hands on her hips. 'I've spent years helping out at home births, you know, and none of them were bastard babies, like yours.'

Naomi flinched, not knowing where to look. 'What about the Public Assistance board? Do you think they could help me money-wise?' she asked, tongue in cheek.

A deep furrow creased her aunt's brow. 'I wouldn't go down that road if I was you because they would take a dim view of an unmarried mother looking for handouts. Personally I wouldn't be seen dead in a place like that.'

Naomi swallowed hard. All her options had gone. She began to feel panic tearing at her as she realised there was no way out.

'Well, I'm off now to help arrange the flowers in chapel,' said her aunt, standing up to leave. 'So if I were you I'd set the wheels in motion for the child to be adopted. Oh! And I nearly forgot with the shock of it all, here's your mother's biscuit tin.'

Naomi's mouth dropped as her aunt pulled the tin out of her shopping bag. 'Where did that come from?' she asked, quickly taking it from her.

'Your father entrusted it to me before he died because it contained insurance policies and such like. But there's nothing of any consequence left, except for a few receipts and your adoption papers.'

'Thank God for that because I need my adoption papers,' Naomi cried, sighing with relief.

Her aunt raised her eyebrows. 'I hope you're not intending to track down your mother because it's against the law you know, and she wouldn't be the least bit interested, anyway. Why do you think she had you put up for adoption in the first place?'

'I don't know,' said Naomi, looking and feeling

bereft.

'Mark my words, you would have been left in a home if it hadn't been for my sister taking you in,' she snapped, bringing her fist down hard on the table. 'And now you repay her memory by being a wanton harlot.'

Naomi bit hard into her lower lip, wishing the floor would swallow her.

'I can't get over the fact that you're pregnant,' cried her aunt, pulling her gloves over her fingers. 'It's a nasty shock for someone of my age. It could well bring on a heart attack.'

Naomi felt herself quake inside. Guilt was making her feel a thousand times worse. She stepped back for her aunt to leave, relieved the ordeal was over.

As soon as her aunt had left the house Naomi rushed back into the room in order to open the biscuit tin. She took out her adoption forms and sat down on the settee to read them.

She noticed the adoption had been granted eight weeks before her third birthday and tried to imagine how confused she must have felt being handed over to strangers at such a young age. What on earth must her birth mother have been thinking of? Now she'd found out it was against the law to make contact with her she racked her brain as to what to do next.

Her options regarding her unborn child were now disappearing fast. There was no way she could survive without any money coming in. After pondering about it for quite some time she began to realize that she had no other alternative but to try and wheedle her way back into Duncan's favour for her unborn child's sake. Just thinking about it made her feel ill.

CHAPTER 11

'Can you spare us a cup of sugar, asked Patty, thrusting a cup forward as Naomi opened the door.

'God, you gave me a scare. For a minute I thought my aunt had returned.'

'I know the one,' giggled Patty. 'She seemed quite a tyrant when I last met her. What did she want?'

'Oh, nothing much,' said Naomi, brushing it aside. 'Fancy a cup of tea?'

'Don't mind if I do,' said Patty, walking in. 'Only I thought you ought to know there's gossip going round that you're pregnant.'

Naomi looked at her stunned, nearly dropping her cup.

'Is there any truth in the matter, my lovely?' said Patty, peering anxiously at her.

'Who on earth told you?' said Naomi, blushing scarlet.

'Someone from Green's Warehouse was in the paper shop blurting it around. I was told within minutes of them being there and it spread down the street like wildfire, I can tell you.'

'As if I haven't got enough to contend with,' cried Naomi, as she filled the cup with sugar from her bowl. 'Yes, I am pregnant, much the pity,' she sighed, pulling a face.

'Does Duncan know, yet?' asked Patty. 'I presume he's the father.'

'Not yet,' said Naomi, nodding. Just the thought of broaching the subject with him made her feel weak at the knees, let alone the prospect of seeing him again. He could be anywhere for all she knew.

'Why don't you put the baby up for adoption when it's born? Just think, you'll lose all ties with him then,' said Patty, making her-self comfortable on a chair.

'You've got to be joking. No child of mine is going to spend their life wondering what's happened to their natural mother. I was adopted, you know, and it's scarred me for life. Every time I look in the mirror I wonder where my looks come from and whether my birth mother still thinks of me. To be honest, it's a dreadful thing to happen to anyone and my child's certainly not going to experience the trauma I've been put through.'

She couldn't for the life of her understand how people could abandon their child as if they were of little consequence and was angry that anyone else should think her capable of doing so.

Patty looked at her sheepishly. 'I can well remember when a girl I knew from school was taken into an asylum because she was caught pregnant and the unmarried mother's place was full. To top it all, she suffered a nervous breakdown shortly after the baby was taken from her and I did hear she's still in the loony bin, poor girl.'

Naomi looked at her horrified. 'Believe you me, if the authorities told me that I was to be taken into an asylum or unmarried mother's home I'd go into hiding, don't you worry.'

Tears of frustration welled up in her eyes, making her run out into the scullery where she tried to pull herself together. Everything was taking its toll on her nerves making her feel she wanted to scream.

After breathing in several deep breaths to calm herself she hurriedly made the tea and took it through into the living room.

'Thanks love,' said Patty, stretching her hand out for the tea-cup. 'I was wondering whether you ought to confront Duncan's parents with the news of the baby before anyone else tells them. What do you think?'

Naomi's thoughts flashed back to the night when

she was thrown out of their house. She doubted very much they'd want anything to do with her.

'To be honest, I believe they'd never let me inside the door, let alone talk to me,' she sighed, in despair. 'I even had Duncan thrown out of my house by PC Evans so there's not much chance that he will want to come back in a hurry, is there?'

'Like that is it?' said Patty, looking at her thoughtfully. 'So you've caused quite a stink with his family as it is then. But desperate times mean desperate measures and I've got just the idea that might bring you all together,' she said, with a wicked grin on her face.

'I'm all ears,' said Naomi, glad of any help she could find.

'Kids washed and put to bed and the old man is actually minding them for a change,' said Patty, smiling as she made her way through Naomi's front door the next evening. 'Well, I did explain that I had urgent business to attend to,' she said, smugly. 'Come on then, let's get on with it. You might make the front page of the South Wales Argus yet.'

Naomi looked at her, trying to weigh things up in her mind.

'Are you sure you still want to go through with things? I think you're off your rocker wanting that monster back into your life after what you've told me? Still, it's up to you,' said Patty, shrugging her shoulders.

'I know I'm clutching at straws, but anything's better than having to part with my child,' said Naomi, her voice rough with emotion.

Patty raised her eyebrows. 'Well, let's start then. It'll be dark soon enough and I think it best if you put a damp handkerchief over your face in case you breathe in the gas fumes.'

Naomi did as she was told. Her stomach was churning. She was not in favour of Patty's plan. It meant deceiving people but, in the end, she'd managed to convince herself it would be well worth while if the ruse worked.

'Ready then?' asked Patty, her dark eyes fixed on Naomi's.

Naomi nodded, feeling nervous as Patty put things in motion by turning the gas taps full on. She grimaced as the pungent smell of gas filled the rooms, making them a time bomb for a match.

'I won't be long,' said Patty, as she went hurriedly out of the front door, jingling some coins in her hand. 'Let's hope Duncan's parents are at home.'

Naomi stood by the back door gasping for breath and desperately hoped that the phone box would be empty. She stared down at her stomach and prayed she was doing the right thing. There was no going back now.

Within minutes Patty returned, looking triumphant. 'We've done it! The Campbell's are coming, I spun them a yarn by telling them that I'd slipped in and found you flat out on the floor with the gas taps full on,' she announced. 'Quick, let's turn them off because there should be enough of a smell in the house by now.'

Naomi, spluttering her lungs out, ran after her into the yard where both women stood trying to regain their breath.

'What did they have to say then?' asked Naomi, putting her hand up to her mouth.

'Well, to be honest, Duncan's father seemed more concerned in telling me that an attempted suicide is a punishable offence. That seemed a bit stupid to me because it's not as if the victim is going to care a hoot anyway.'

'What about...'

'Ah, yes,' interrupted Patty. 'When I mentioned that you were pregnant by their son they warned me not to breath a word about things because they'd be straight down to see you.'

'Did they now?' said Naomi, smirking. 'Another case of let's have the child adopted out of the way, I expect.'

Several minutes later a feeling of doom spread through the pit of Naomi's stomach when she heard a loud knock on the front door.

'Action stations!' urged Patty. 'Quick, lie down on the settee and pretend to be the dying swan while I answer the door.'

Naomi flopped down, still holding the handkerchief over her nose. At that moment she didn't know whether she'd be able to carry things through. She felt trapped in a situation that was far from the truth and which she didn't really want.

Within seconds The Reverend Robert Campbell and Morag were in the room. As soon as the remains of the gas hit them they began coughing.

'Open all the windows and doors. This woman needs air,' Robert commanded, flinging his arms around. 'This is a dreadful matter. Dreadful! You can be assured that my son will do the right thing by you,' he spluttered, waving his handkerchief about.

Naomi was so relieved to hear those words. Her child was hers to keep at last.

Morag drew up a chair and patted her on the head. 'This mustn't get into the papers because of the position we hold so I think it will be best if we get things sorted with Duncan straight away.'

'Do you know where he's living then?' asked Naomi, purposely avoiding her eyes.

'Back home with us,' butted in The Reverend. 'And believe you me I'll march him into the Registry Office as fast as his legs will take him. It's about time he knuckled down and did something purposeful with his life.'

Patty hovered in the background, not missing a word.

'Yes, dear,' agreed Morag, flatly. 'Well, now this is sorted we have to hurry back home because I'm expecting Duncan to arrive shortly. I think it only fair that we send him straight down to talk things over with you.' Morag looked over at her husband then directed her eyes to the floor.

'I'm so sorry,' said Naomi, knowing full well she looked fit to cry.

'So are we,' said The Reverend, his eyes narrowing.

Naomi felt totally embarrassed by it all and was relieved when Patty showed them out.

After closing the front door behind them Patty, jumped for joy, as she ran back into the room. 'We've pulled it off, my lovely. We've pulled it off,' she shrieked, giving her a hug. 'Bet you never thought we would, did you?'

Realization began to dawn on Naomi. She'd set the ball rolling and would have to face the consequences, dire though they might be. But she didn't care. Her baby's future was safe at last.

Patty glanced down at her watch. 'Is that the time? My David will think I'm lost,' she said, turning towards the door.

Naomi waved her off and went nervously back inside, dreading the thought of having to speak with Duncan again. Choking back the tears, she wondered what fate had in store for her now.

Just as she was thinking of going to bed she heard the knocker come down hard on the front door, making her jump. Squaring her shoulders, she walked down the hallway to answer it and found an angry looking

Duncan standing outside. He arrogantly pushed past her shouting, 'Do you realise I'm being goaded into a shotgun wedding because you've got yourself up the duff? Anyway, how do I know the brat's even mine?'

'I can assure you it is,' Naomi said, standing her ground defiantly.

'Is that so?' he snarled. 'You could have had any amount of men calling since my departure, so why put the blame on me?'

Naomi didn't intend to let him get the upper hand of her and was livid that he'd thought such things. 'It's yours alright, boyo! So you needn't think you can wangle your way out of this one.'

She could tell by the astonished look on his face that her words had set him back.

'Just a minute, I can remember you telling me that you had seen your period the night my father preached to all the neighbours in the street.'

'I only said that because I didn't want sex with you,' she retorted, regretting the fact that she'd lied to him.

'Yet you've changed your mind now and want to marry me. Huh! Pull the other one.'

Naomi's inside squirmed at the thought of it.

'Just give me one good reason why I should get lumbered with you and a kid when I can have my pick of any women?'

Naomi was smouldering but she didn't intend giving in lightly, even if it meant begging him on her knees.

'Well, it's understandable that you need time to come to terms with it,' she said, trying to pacify him. 'But there's a child to consider now.'

He let out a blood curdling laugh. 'To be honest, I don't care what happens to you and your bastard kid. In fact I wish you'd made a better job of things and killed yourself.'

She cringed. It hurt her to think he was so unfeeling

but she was determined he was not going to worm his way out of this if she had anything to do with it.

'I'm off now,' he snarled, making his way to the door. 'Try telling your sob story to one of the other poor buggers who've dipped their wick in you.'

He pushed her aside and stormed out of the house, leaving Naomi shocked to the core.

She was not stupid enough to think she would ever really change him, knowing his track record, but in spite of this she was prepared to make sacrifices and turn a blind eye if he would only make an honest woman of her. As she slumped down on to the settee, praying for her nightmare to end, she suddenly heard a faint mewing outside the back door. On going to investigate she found a tiny black and white kitten clawing at the door. She couldn't believe her eyes and scooped the little mite up into her arms.

'Lost your way my darling? Well, if no-one claims you I shall name you Kim,' she whispered in its ear, taking it inside.

After giving the kitten a saucer of bread and milk she made a makeshift bed in an empty shoe box, where it curled up and fell asleep. She climbed the stairs, with the kitten in the shoe box under her arm, and wondered what would become of her if Duncan refused to face up to his responsibilities. Such a thought didn't bear thinking about.

Several days later, Naomi was greatly relieved when Morag called round to tell her that, despite Duncan's reluctance, she had made a preliminary booking for the wedding to take place at the Newport Registry Office on the 6th December. Morag spoke to her in a very matter of fact way, which made her feel extremely guilty. How she wished she could have been her friend but she was fully aware that Duncan must have blackened her name in order to get out of his duty.

She thought back to when her parents were alive. They had always promised her the best top-hat-and-tail wedding they could possibly afford because she was their only child. It would have certainly broken their hearts to see what had become of her.

In the weeks that followed Duncan kept his distance, only ever setting eyes on Naomi when she called at his house to make sure the wedding plans were still in order.

In front of his parents he was most courteous towards her but in no way was she fooled by his play-acting. For fear of a confrontation, and determined to keep everyone sweet, she endeavoured to heal the rift between the family and herself by agreeing to whatever they had to say.

On one of her visits to their home Naomi was pleased to hear that Duncan's father had found his son employment in another warehouse. She knew it wouldn't last long because of his erratic time keeping and know-it-all attitude but she hoped that once they were married things would be different. He'd have to pull his socks up and work with a child to keep. There'd be no slouching around on the settee all day. She was sure of that.

Naomi was over the moon when Patty offered to lend her a dark brown, three-quarter length jacket and skirt for the wedding because she had nothing appropriate to wear for the occasion. However, as the wedding date drew nearer, she began to think what a farce it was despite being as determined as ever to see it through.

On the day of the wedding Naomi sighed as she watched the rain lash at the windows. She had often dreamed of this day, with all the excitement due to a young bride, and had never thought she would be steeling herself to take her vows with a man she didn't love. Perhaps, she thought to herself, ruefully, he would change with time. But she very much doubted it.

After dusting the front-room in readiness for any guests who might return, Naomi called at the bakers and asked Mr Pugh to put up some freshly baked bread and cakes for the wedding breakfast, paltry though it was. How she wished she could have afforded an iced wedding cake, and all the trimmings.

Shortly after ten o'clock, Patty arrived complete with suit over her arm and a white carnation between her teeth.

Naomi took them off her and put them down on the settee. 'At this moment I feel as if I'm going to the death chamber,' she moaned, shaking her head.

'Duw, we'll have none of that talk now. Hurry up and get dressed before the best man appears.'

Naomi took a deep breath then swiftly climbed the stairs clutching the suit.

When she'd finished dressing she stood back and looked at herself in the mirror. Everything was moving too fast. She felt as if she'd been issued with a prison sentence and felt sorely tempted to run away from it all. But there was nowhere to run to.

'There's nice you look, my lovely,' said Patty, as Naomi came back into the room and gave her a twirl.

'Nice just about sums it up,' Naomi said sadly, trying to button the coat around her protruding stomach. 'No proper reception or honeymoon. There will be nothing to look back on.'

'Well, you didn't expect anything different in the circumstances did you?' said Patty, biting into her bottom lip. 'Anyway, don't you worry about the food, I'll see to that. I'll shovel more coal on the fire as well so the parlour will be cosy and warm on your return. Pity there's no alcohol though. I could do with a nip, just to warm me up. This place is like an icebox.'

Before Naomi could comment, she heard a car draw up outside.

'Quick! Pin my carnation on before I leave,' she cried, beginning to get agitated. 'That'll be Clyde, Duncan's father's friend, outside. At least I'll be leaving in style, not walking.'

Patty quickly pinned the flower onto her lapel, then gave her a hug. 'Good luck, cariad. You'll need it,' she said, looking anxiously at her.

'Well, here goes, I'm off now,' said Naomi, peering nervously outside.

As she climbed into Clyde's car a feeling of dread came over her but she managed to give him a wry smile as she sank down on the seat beside him.

She had met Clyde on several occasions when visiting the Campbell's home and had taken to the chubby-faced, good looking Welshman.

'You don't have to go through with things if you don't want to, you know. I can tell by the look on your face that you're not at all happy.'

'I'm afraid I've no option Clyde, so let's get it over with, shall we?' said Naomi, running her hand over her swollen stomach.

Silence reigned for the rest of the journey until the car pulled to a halt not far from the Registry Office at the bottom of Stow Hill, in the centre of Newport.

'I know there are plenty of young men who would be only too willing to marry a pretty girl like you,' said Clyde, as he helped her out of the car.

'Yes, but not in my condition,' she said, looking at him with watery eyes.

He squeezed her hand and they proceeded to walk into the Registry Office. She was loath to leave his arm when she saw Duncan standing waiting for her, with a ghastly grin on his face.

After acknowledging his parents she took her place

beside her new husband to be. Her mind was racked in torment. As she looked across at the exit door she wondered whether or not to flee. If only her birth mother would miraculously turn up to rescue her - but she was well aware there was no likelihood of that.

As soon as the Registrar appeared the ceremony began. Duncan smiled across at her like a Cheshire cat but Naomi was under no illusion that it was all an act on his part, for everyone else to witness.

When the time came for Naomi to say her vows she doubted very much that she would be able to abide by them, and was greatly relieved when the whole sham was over. But at least her unborn child was safe at last.

Sue and Maria were the only friends she'd invited to the wedding on her side. She had been reluctant to send her aunt an invitation, knowing that she would only be giving the old woman a chance to rub her nose in it even further by refusing to attend.

'There's tea, sandwiches and cakes at the house if anyone would like to come?' she said, looking at all seven people who were present.

Surprisingly, everyone followed her and Duncan home. Patty had built up a lovely blazing fire and was just boiling the kettle in readiness for the guests.

Naomi gazed round the parlour as people tucked into the food. She admired the way Clyde's wife fussed over him with tea and cakes, thinking how fortunate they were to be happily married.

'What a wedding reception,' she whispered to Patty. 'The mood of the moment seems more fitting for a funeral.'

Patty grimaced. 'Well you've accomplished what you wanted my girl. Let's hope things look up for you.'

Naomi nodded and gave a travesty of a smile across the room at Duncan who was sitting with his parents on the settee. She was glad to see they had made things up but wondered how long it would last.

As the last visitor left she noticed that her new husband seemed to be deep in thought.

'Well, that's that. We've made our bed and have to lie on it,' she announced, under no illusion as to what he was thinking.

'That's the very words out of my parents' mouths, and don't I know it,' Duncan exclaimed. 'Still, it's now legal for me to have sex with you at any time. Honour and obey, don't forget.'

Her mind screamed. She wanted nothing of him. Tears flooded her eyes as she looked down at the cheap wedding ring on her finger. She felt more lost and alone than she'd ever been.

CHAPTER 12

During the time leading up to the baby's birth Duncan made Naomi's life pure hell with his possessiveness and perverted sexual demands. Whenever she left the house he accused her of seeing other men behind his back. It all began to wear her down. The spirited person she had once been was turning into a nervous wreck.

As the months went by if Naomi disagreed with Duncan over anything he would throw a tantrum and urinate in the hearth. She thought it an atrocious and filthy practice. It infuriated her to watch and, as the urine splashed and sizzled over the hot coals, Duncan would stand grinning at her like a fool. When in these humours he would try to goad her into repeating obscene language after him as if she was a child. On many an occasion, when she refused to comply with his wishes, he would give her a sharp whack across the back of her head when she least expected it, which more often than not sent her reeling.

By now Naomi was convinced he was insane and could see by the glint in his eyes that he derived a great deal of pleasure out of trying to control and manipulate her. There were brief interludes when Duncan appeared to be acting normally but Naomi was always wary that he might slip back to his 'other self' at a moment's notice.

She also thought it odd when he began hiding himself away in the front-room and, on listening outside the door one day she was amazed to hear him talking in different voices as if play-acting out loud. One day she decided to pluck up the courage to walk in on him, thinking there might be some-one else in the room. To her amazement he angrily turned on her and demanded that, in future, she should knock on the door and wait for him to reply before entering.

Because his behaviour had become so explosive and bizarre Naomi began to fear for her life. She also thought it strange when he began putting on airs and graces, as if he was someone of importance, especially when his parents visited.

One day Naomi decided to have a talk about Duncan's mental health with his mother hoping she could throw some light on the matter.

After taking Morag to one side when she next visited the house Naomi explained to her that she thought her son had some mental health issues because of his 'Jekyll and Hyde' behaviour. His mother pursed her lips and told her in no uncertain terms that she was married to her son for better or worse, and that was all she had to say on the matter. Naomi thought it was a ludicrous reply under the circumstances. She had hoped for some support from Morag at least.

Naomi went into labour shortly after her due date and when the ambulance arrived to collect her she was greatly relieved to be away from the mad house with Duncan and his delusions.

Within an hour of reaching the hospital her labour pains began in earnest and, after what seemed to be an eternity, the cry of a baby cut across her consciousness.

'It's a little boy,' said the midwife, nestling the child in her arms. Naomi looked at him with relief. He was perfect and hers to keep.

Later that evening her heart turned over when she saw Duncan step into the ward. He was just in time to see the nurse place the baby in the cot.

'You've a little boy, Mr Campbell. What do you think of him, then?' asked the nurse, smiling.

Duncan strode over and glanced at the baby, then at the nurse, with a look of disappointment on his face. 'Well, he hasn't got my good looks, has he?' he smirked. 'Still, perhaps the next one will.'

Naomi pulled a face. Her body was still aching from the rigours of childbirth. 'Not if I can help it,' she cried. 'This is the first and last. By the way, I've decided to call him Philip, as you didn't seem interested in choosing a name.'

'After a previous boyfriend, I suppose,' Duncan snorted, screwing up his face.

Naomi ignored his remark. She felt his reaction was unforgivable, considering what she'd just gone through. She had never known such a self-centred bigot. Still, she could do without him now her child was born, but she knew she would have to wait until the time was right before she could put any plan into action.

During her stay at the hospital her mind buzzed with ideas. Duncan had served his purpose and she certainly wasn't going to put up with his insanity for the rest of her life. Meanwhile she enjoyed the company of the other mothers' who all had a tale of some sort to tell about their husbands, but she kept her mouth tightly closed about Duncan and his grotesque ways for fear of being ridiculed. After all, who would have believed her?

Duncan's tantrums, bad language and obscenities suddenly seemed far away. Every time she held Philip in her arms she felt relieved that he had her colouring and looked nothing remotely like his father.

A feeling of impending gloom engulfed her when it was time to return home. She dreaded the thought of having to cope with her husband's tantrums as well as trying to look after a newly born child.

Things soon turned sour when, within a few days of arriving home, Naomi became ill with mastitis. She was so ill the doctor had to be called out and, after he had examined her breasts, he advised her not to breast feed any more because of large lumps that had swollen up underneath her arms.

As soon as the doctor had left the house Duncan came into the room calling Naomi all the swear words he could lay his tongue to because she had exposed her breasts to another man. In order to keep the peace she kept quiet for the sake of the baby. If the truth was known she didn't have the strength left to fight back anymore.

Despite not feeling well she struggled along, caring for Philip and the house as best she could. Duncan never offered to lift a finger and stated it was woman's work if she asked him to do anything to help her.

At the earliest opportunity Naomi visited the local family planning clinic to be fitted for a Dutch cap. She knew if she became pregnant again it would be more difficult for her to leave, and there'd be no hanging around once she'd thought up a plan of action.

Time went by and when Naomi reached her 21st birthday she thought it bizarre to have been living with a baby and a man of many guises. She received a few cards and Duncan's parents gave her a wooden clothes' horse which she was grateful for.

At that time thoughts of her birth mother kept coming into her mind and she wondered if she would have remembered her birthday. She was desperate to hear from her and would have delighted in taking Philip along to see her.

Although Morag had softened in manner since the birth of the baby Naomi still felt there was a distance between them and guessed it was probably because she had trapped her son into a loveless marriage.

One evening Duncan arrived home from work looking cold and miserable. Naomi was aware by the grim look on his face that he'd probably been rubbed up the wrong way or had been disciplined for being lackadaisical as usual. Although the pay at the warehouse was poor Naomi managed to eke out what little Duncan gave her so the debt collector didn't have cause to call. She had once witnessed the bailiffs strip a house in the street of its furniture and didn't intend it happening to her.

'The dinner's on so it won't be long,' she said, quickly bundling Philip into his play pen out of the way.

'What's that bloody cat doing in my chair?' Duncan shouted at her, grabbing hold of the cat.

Before Naomi could answer she looked on in horror as the cat dug its claws into Duncan's hand, making him release her.

'Look what the little bastard's done. I'll get her for that.'

'You leave my cat alone,' Naomi shrieked. It serves you right for being so rough with her.'

As quick as a whippet, Duncan dived after the cat into the scullery and grabbed it by its tail. 'This will teach you,' he snarled, bringing its head crashing down on the stove. Boiling liquid from the steaming saucepan of stew spluttered everywhere. The cat let out a howl of pain.

Naomi couldn't believe her eyes and began to scream hysterically as the cat began to froth at the mouth.

'Give her to me, you evil swine. Let her go.'

'Keep away or you'll have something to complain about too' he snarled, leering at her.

Before she could stop him Duncan kicked open the back door and hurled the cat up the garden path, where it quickly scrambled over the wall out of sight.

'Don't bring any more animals into this house because they'll receive the same treatment, he growled, showing his uneven teeth.

Naomi began pummelling his chest with her fists,

calling him all the names she could lay her tongue to.

A lecherous grin came over his face. 'An angry female always makes me feel sexy,' he chortled, pushing her down onto the cold slab floor.

She tried to stop him but he tore at her underclothes like a demented animal, stifling her screams with his free hand. 'Now take this, you bitch,' he said as he slid inside her. The rape was over in a minute.

'You're a cruel bastard and I detest you,' she cried, between sobs. 'One day I'll leave, just mark my words.'

'Promises, promises,' sneered Duncan, doing up his trousers. 'You'll never be rid of me, my girl. Never! We're chained for life. Talking of chains I've always fancied that cross and chain round your neck. Worth pawning I think.'

'You've got to be joking,' she cried, with clenched teeth, pushing him from her. As she got up from the floor she felt his hand tear the chain from the back of her neck.

'You bloody swine,' she screeched. 'I could kill you without a backward glance. Just you remember that.'

Duncan's lips curled and his eyes rolled. 'That's if I don't get you first!'

A cold shudder went down Naomi's back. He'd unnerved her. She knew he was capable of anything.

The cat never returned. Naomi was deeply upset and her hatred of Duncan grew by the day. His taunting and mental cruelty knew no bounds and the only thing that kept her from losing her sanity was her beloved child.

Christmas day came around and Naomi was happy to spend a pleasant time at her in-laws with Duncan playing the part of the dutiful father and husband. Naomi was fully aware that it was an act as usual and could not understand why Robert and Morag turned a blind eye to his behaviour. She thought it most probable that they didn't want to get involved with their wayward son's antics now that he was well and truly off their hands.

Boxing Day was bitterly cold and snow had begun to fall. After eating some cold meat and fry-up for lunch, Naomi put Philip into his pram to sleep. She proposed calling in on Patty with some sweets for her children, and hoped Duncan wouldn't moan.

'I won't be long. Only popping into Patty's with some little presents for the girls,' she said, as she buttoned up her coat.

'You're always running in there. What's the attraction I'd like to know? Isn't my company good enough for you?'

Naomi didn't answer. She could tell that he was itching for a row. He had always been jealous of her friendship with Patty. At least Naomi thought her friend was fun to be with, unlike Duncan.

'Well, don't be long then. I'll have a snooze and when you return perhaps we could spend the rest of the afternoon in bed?' he said, slumping down on the settee.

Naomi felt her insides squirm, and gave him a look fit to kill. Her days of playing the dutiful wife were wearing extremely thin. Gathering up the presents she quickly left the house, relieved to be away from him.

'There's lovely to see you. Come in out of the cold.' said Patty, welcoming her inside. 'You haven't met my brother Stephen, have you? He's staying with us for a while whilst on shore leave from the Royal Navy.'

Naomi smiled at Stephen as he stepped forward to shake her by the hand. She was quite taken with the good looking, dark headed sailor.

'You must stay and have a drink with us. I've brought some rum off the ship. The real McCoy,' said

Stephen, opening the bottle.

Naomi's eyes lit up. 'Just a small one then,' she said, 'Only I don't drink as a rule. I've only called in with a few sweets for the children.'

'The girls have gone to the pantomime with their father, so I'll leave their presents on the side,' butted in Patty, taking them from her.

Naomi quickly sat down in an armchair near the fire with a large glass of rum held tightly in her hand. After Stephen lit up a cigarette he settled himself down on the settee and began telling the women about his sea-faring stories which had them in fits of laughter. Naomi hadn't laughed so much in a long while and completely lost track of the time.

Suddenly there was a loud pounding on the adjoining wall. She could hear Philip wailing in the background which quickly brought her back to earth.

'I thought Duncan would start,' said Patty, holding her fist up in the air. 'I'm sick to death of hearing you arguing and screaming in there. He's making you an old woman before your time. Anyway, why can't he see to the child?'

Naomi stood up to leave and felt her head reel. 'I must go or there will be blue murder.'

Patty pulled a face. 'You'll be in your grave before long girl if you don't watch it.'

'I know that,' said Naomi, looking glum. She was disappointed by not being able to stay and to have some fun for a change.

Steven and Patty accompanied her to the door then waved her off. As soon as Naomi stepped into the house Duncan jumped out at her from behind the door.

'Having an affair with another man now are we? I saw the bloke on Patty's doorstep,' he snorted, grabbing her arm.

'Yes, and I was enjoying myself for a change,' she

replied. 'Let go of me. You're hurting,' she cried, pulling away from him.

'Is that drink I can smell on your breath?' said Duncan, sniffing at her.

Naomi's whole body stiffened. 'So what if it is?' she said, between clenched teeth. 'It was only a tot of rum that Stephen brought off the ship, and jolly nice it was too,' she said, hiccupping.

'Drunk in the hands of a sailor,' he sneered. 'You'll land up in the fucking gutter one day, my girl.'

'You've got to be joking,' snapped Naomi, picking Philip up out of his pram. She could tell by the look on Duncan's face that the baby's crying was playing on his nerves so she hurried upstairs out of the way to change him.

As soon as she closed the bedroom door she heard Duncan run up the stairs after her.

'I can see that the drink has given you Dutch courage, so I suggest you stay here while you sober up,' he sneered, taking the key out of the door.

She was horrified. 'Open the door this minute. It's freezing in here. There's snow falling outside,' she screamed, rattling the knob.

'I'm off downstairs in the warm. You can now be free to have the rest of the day to sober up on your own and dream about that sailor you're fucking.'

At that moment, Naomi wished him dead. She felt like hammering on the door but knew it would be of no use. Because of the intense cold, she had no option but to climb into bed with Philip. They both lay there, for the rest of the day without any food or drink. This was the final straw as far as Naomi was concerned.

CHAPTER 13

Several days later Naomi bumped into Patty whilst out shopping and, with tears in her eyes, she explained what had happened when she'd returned home on Boxing Day.

'I'd shoot the bugger if I had him,' groaned Patty. 'Anyway, I'm glad I saw you because I'm going to a dance down Newport tonight and could do with some company.'

'You've got to be joking! Can you imagine what Duncan would say? Anyway, I've nothing decent to wear.'

'Don't worry about that. You can always borrow one of my frocks,' urged Patty, with a wicked grin on her face.

Naomi hesitated for a moment mulling things over in her mind.

'Why don't you tell your old man I'm visiting my elderly aunt, like I tell my David? I'll even go as far as to lend him my new cassette player to keep him happy while we're gone. Come on, you could do with some fun.'

'Oh, he'd like that,' said Naomi, warming to the idea. 'I suppose I could always change my clothes in your house and leave the back way, couldn't I?'

'That's my girl. You'll have the time of your life out with me and not before time either.'

Naomi was sorely tempted but she was nervous about telling untruths and afraid that she might be seen. Then her mind strayed back to Boxing Day. What man in his right mind would have done such a thing to his wife and child? They deserved better than him.

As soon as Duncan came in from work Naomi laid their meals out on the table and, with baited breath, blurted out. 'Is there any chance of you minding Philip while I visit Patty's sick aunt with her this evening? She said she'd lend you her new cassette recorder if you want.' She crossed her fingers behind her back.

'If it's one of them new ones just out, you can fly to the moon for all I care.'

Naomi was surprised and relieved that he hadn't kicked up a fuss. She couldn't believe her luck.

At seven o'clock sharp Patty appeared on the doorstep with the recorder tucked under her arm. Duncan's eyes gleamed when he clapped his eyes on it. To Naomi's relief he took it and quickly vanished back inside the house with a huge grin on his face.

'See you later then,' she called, as she left their house and scuttled into Patty's as fast as she could.

After changing into the pretty green dress and stiletto shoes that Patty had laid out for her in the front-room she was raring to go. They both sneaked out the back way and ran up the road in order to catch the bus into Newport.

On arriving in the brightly lit streets of Newport, they caught another bus to the outskirts of the town and got off near the Ringland Club.

'It's supposed to be 'Grab a Granny,' night tonight, laughed Patty, as both women walked quickly through the underpass towards their destination.

Naomi raised her eyebrows. She wondered what she was letting herself in for but now she had come this far there was no turning back.

Her stomach churned over as they walked through the entrance doors. Once inside the dance-hall Naomi could hardly believe her eyes as she gazed in wonderment at the dance band and the glamorous surroundings. Her eyes fell upon a large ball of mirrors hanging from the ceiling which was sending splashes of light around the dance floor as it spun around. She'd never been anywhere like it before and clung onto

Patty's arm as she made her way through the crowds of people stood at the bar ordering drinks.

Within seconds a smartly dressed young man from a nearby table beckoned to them.

'Follow me,' said Patty, with a bright smile on her face. 'This is Frank an old friend of mine.'

By the twinkle in her eye and the way she caught hold of his hand, Naomi had a distinct feeling that there was something more than friendship between them, but she acknowledged the man politely.

'Glad you could make it. I've kept you seats,' said Frank. 'Ted won't be long either.'

'This is Bronwen and Sid,' said Patty, sitting down by a middle-aged couple at the table.

After shaking their hands Naomi took a seat too and then quickly stared across the dance floor to make sure she didn't recognise anyone. When she saw no-one of any consequence she relaxed back into her chair with a sigh of relief.

'What are you drinking?' asked Frank, standing up with a tray in his hand.

'Just a fruit juice please,' said Naomi, not wanting any tell-tale smell of alcohol on her breath when she returned home.

Minutes later as he returned with the drinks she saw a tall, middle-aged man with a mop of brown hair, accompanying him.

'I'm Ted, Frank's brother. Sorry I wasn't here when you arrived. I was talking business at the bar,' he drawled in a husky voice.

Naomi's heart turned over. There was a striking ruggedness about him that attracted her. Despite being the type of man her father would have called a wide-boy, because he was dressed in a black suit, shirt, and white silk tie, she didn't care any more. Duncan could rot in hell.

She smiled at him and before she could sip her drink Ted whisked her up onto the dance-floor. After a few faltering steps she felt as if she was gliding around the floor like an accomplished dancer. She had learnt the rudiments of dancing years ago when she attended the Betty Hutson's school of dancing in Newport. Dancing had always seemed like second nature to her. If only Duncan could see her now, she thought to herself. It was high time she had some fun.

As the evening wore on almost every dance was taken by Ted. In the brief moments when they sat down for a rest they talked and laughed together as if they had known each other all their lives. When the last dance had finished Naomi was reluctant to return home.

'Will you be coming along next week, my lovely?' asked Ted, grinning from ear to ear.

'Just you try stopping me,' she said, laughing.

As Ted caught hold of her hand, she had a feeling there was more to him than met the eye. She didn't care. Their relationship was developing fast and she was enjoying every minute of his attention.

'Back to reality and home for you, my girl,' chimed in Patty, breaking them up. 'Frank's giving us a lift home. He doesn't live far from our place.'

Reluctantly Naomi picked up her jacket and bag and said farewell to everyone.

As they walked through the doors and into the car park Patty whispered into her ear, 'Frank's only a bit of fun you know, so don't broadcast it.'

'It's none of my business what you do,' declared Naomi. 'I'm just glad you fixed me up with Ted, and don't say you didn't. I could tell it was all a put up job.'

'Well, what of it? I could see that Ted couldn't take his eyes off you,' Patty giggled.

'I thought he was lovely but I expect he's married, like they all are,' Naomi groaned, taking one last look back at the club. If she had her way she would have spent more time getting to know all about him but he seemed to have vanished into thin air as soon as she'd left the table.

'Well, take a tip cariad. It's best not to get too involved. Ask no questions and you'll be told no lies.'

'I suppose you're right,' Naomi muttered, glancing down at her wedding ring. Her farce of a marriage was more like a prison sentence than married bliss. She felt like snatching the ring off her finger but thought it a foolhardy thing to do just yet.

On the pretence of visiting Patty's aunt, Naomi lived for her secret Tuesday evening rendezvous with Ted but, as months slowly went by and summer turned into autumn, she knew she was playing a dangerous game. What had begun as a bit of a laugh was now beginning to be serious. She was absolutely besotted by Ted. Whether or not he felt the same way about her she was yet to find out.

Nothing ever held Duncan's interest for long and when he began to tire of using the cassette recorder he grumbled about Naomi's friendship with Patty and expected her to forego her evenings out. She panicked at hearing this and did her best to keep him in a good humour, but it didn't work. He began to smack her around when things didn't suit him, like the time when she found a pile of pornographic magazines strewn all over the place in the spare bedroom. When Naomi confronted him with the matter he banned her from entering the room like a child and put a lock on the door. Shortly afterwards he caught her unawares whilst she was knitting and punched her full force in the back of the head sending her flying off the chair. 'That will teach you not to pry in my room,' he growled, giving her a look fit to kill. She quickly scrambled back to her feet holding her head and was very tempted to stick the bread knife in him. However, she quickly thought twice about the matter because she had no intentions of serving a life sentence for the likes of him. She was certain her day would come and the sooner the better.

One Tuesday evening, as Naomi took off her coat at the club, Ted noticed bruise marks on her arms and demanded to know how they'd got there. It was only then that she blurted out about her husband's Jekyll and Hyde character and the duress she had suffered since their marriage.

Ted's top lip curled and a sudden look of anger came over his face. 'I think that man needs teaching a lesson,' he snorted, punching his fist into his hand. 'Here's my work's telephone number,' he said, reaching for a small scrap of paper from his inside pocket. 'I'm not having my lovely girl treated like that. If you can't get hold of me leave a message with the foreman.'

Naomi tucked the paper into her handbag. She felt somewhat safer now she had the means to contact him. Ted had mentioned in passing that he drove a lorry for a living but there was never any mention of a wife, which she was pleased about. She couldn't even bear the thought of it.

The following week Patty announced she was going away with her husband, David, and the children for a few days, to visit relatives. This left Naomi in a quandary as to how she would meet Ted that Tuesday. She decided to ring him about the change in plans. Luckily for her she was able to make contact as he had just finished for the day and they made arrangements to meet at the bottom of her street the next evening. Naomi knew full well that she was taking a chance by meeting up with him and prayed that no-one would see her.

After putting Philip to bed, she dressed herself up in

the smartest outfit she could find which in no way equalled one of Patty's pretty frocks. She was hoping to sneak down the stairs and escape through the door before Duncan saw her, but he was stood by the door waiting.

Her stomach lurched.

'Where's Patty got to then?' he asked, looking at her straight in the eyes.

'Oh, I've decided to visit a friend this evening for a change because Patty's away,' she answered, hoping he hadn't noticed her discomfort.

'Which friend is that?'

Naomi's stomach turned over. 'You've never met her. It's someone from school,' she said nervously, feeling guilty.

His eyes narrowed. 'Well, you'd better be off then.'

Naomi sighed with relief and went dashing up the road as fast as she could. She was looking forward to some quality time alone with Ted for a change. As she turned the corner her heart leapt for joy at the sight of a blue Morris Minor car with Ted sat at the wheel.

Suddenly she felt nervous, dreading someone might see her. She hung back as she recognised several of the passers-by on the pretence of combing her hair. A few minutes later, when she thought the coast was clear, she made a dive for the car, her head held down.

'Quick, don't hang around or we might be spotted,' she urged Ted, catching hold of his arm.

Ted grinned at her, and started up the engine.

'Where are you taking me then?' she asked, settling herself down comfortably.

'On a mystery trip,' he chuckled. 'Do you like the car? I bought it recently, for a ton, and she drives well too,' he said, looking pleased with himself.

As Ted pulled away neither of them saw Duncan furtively looking round the corner of the street. They were too wrapped up in each other to notice.

After travelling several miles out of the village Ted stopped the car outside a small country pub. Naomi couldn't wait to be in his arms. She ordered a Babycham, thinking it might settle her nerves. Ted whispered sweet nothings in her ear as they cuddled up together in a quiet corner of the pub. Then, when they left after finishing their drinks, he drove to a deserted spot in the woods.

Naomi had taken precautions by inserting her Dutch cap beforehand. Knowing full well she would be like putty in his arms. Within seconds of stopping the car Ted pulled her into the back seat where they lay down together.

His lips sought hers. His kisses were long, demanding and passionate. Naomi's head began to spin and she gave in willingly to the warmth of his embrace, feeling as if she was being swept along on a tidal wave. After their love making was over they cuddled in each other's arms and fell asleep.

It was some time later when Ted lit a cigarette that she awoke and looked at his watch.

'Good God. It's never eleven o'clock?' she gasped. 'We'll have to be going. There'll be murder otherwise.'

The thought of leaving Ted filled her with despair but she knew she had no option and dreaded the thought of arriving home late.

It was well past eleven thirty when Ted dropped her off not far from her home. Naomi ran down the road, surprised not to see Duncan standing on the front door step looking for her. On glancing up at the closed bedroom curtains she presumed he was in bed and hopefully fast asleep. After putting her key into the front door, she took off her shoes and crept inside, relieved to find everywhere in darkness. Stealthily, she made her way up the stairs and peeked in at Philip who was sleeping soundly. Then, just as she turned on her heel to walk across the landing towards the bedroom, the door burst open and Duncan stood in front of her. His eyes glinted maliciously. Naomi's heart came up into her mouth. Her instincts told her he knew what she'd been up to. She was rooted to the spot.

'I always said you were nothing but a fucking whore,' he shouted, grabbing her by the neck.

She screamed as he dragged her inside the bedroom, flinging her down on the bed. Then he bent over her menacingly. 'I didn't believe your tall story so I followed you down the street. Then, lo and behold, I stood back and watched you climb into some fucker's car,' he bellowed, putting his fist underneath her chin. 'Just try and deny it, cow, because I've checked the drawer for your Dutch cap and it's no longer there.'

Naomi was frozen rigid. Her eyes darted frantically, desperately seeking an escape route. But before her mind had chance to whirl into action, Duncan began tearing at her clothes like someone demented. Terrified of what he might do next she tried to push him away, to no avail. She was no match for him.

'Was he as good as me? Was he?' he shouted, pulling his penis out of his pyjamas.

She gritted her teeth and lashed out at him but within seconds he had mounted her.

'Now feel a proper man,' he grunted, lunging at her like some demented animal.

Naomi sobbed continually throughout the ordeal and, when he finally relinquished his hold, she tried to make a run for it only to be dragged back from the door. He grinned as he flung her up against the wall.

'I'll leave for good if you give me some money,' he snarled. 'I've an open invitation up in the Smoke, you know, so why should I stay with the likes of you?'

'You mean London?' she asked, still shaking from

her ordeal. 'How much do you want?' she cried.

'Ten pounds should do it. That will be just enough to get me there, and something to tide me over.'

Ten pounds, she thought, was a small price to pay for her freedom.

'What about your parents? They'll be suspicious when you don't turn up with Philip on Saturday morning. And there's work.'

'You'll think of something, I'm sure. You've been lying to me for ages so you'll have no problem making up another story.'

'I..I..'ll ask Patty,' she stammered, in desperation. Now that her liaison with Ted was out in the open she wanted to be rid of Duncan more than ever. She knew he was capable of anything.

The next day Patty arrived home from her break and after Naomi told her of the previous night's events she willingly lent Naomi £10 from the family's Christmas savings tin.

'I'd do anything to rid you of that tyrant. I can see by the state of your nerves that he's putting you in your grave. All this is bound to affect Philip as well. But I'll expect the money back in weekly instalments because if the old man finds out that I've lent you his precious savings he'll have my guts for garters.'

Naomi couldn't thank her enough and promised she would find the money somehow.

Within seconds of handing the cash over to Duncan he packed his clothes and swaggered out of the doorway, making a grand exit as he left, without even a backward look for his son.

'Glory Alleluia,' Naomi shouted, as she slammed the front door behind him, greatly relieved that he was out of her life at last. She ran into the living room where Philip was playing oblivious to the situation.

'Things are going to be happy from now on in this

house, son,' she said, sweeping the child up in her arms. 'We'll get by just you wait and see, my lad, even if I go without myself. You'll not want I'll make sure of that.'

Philip smiled back at her and she kissed him on his cheek. She sat down by the fire cwtching him in her arms, and felt happier than she'd been for years.

CHAPTER 14

The following morning Naomi wheeled Philip into Patty's kitchen to tell her the latest news. Patty invited her to sit down and handed them each a large slice of toast oozing with margarine.

'I'm free at last,' sighed Naomi, looking elated.

'You're well shot of him too, that's what I think,' said Patty, passing Naomi a huge mug of tea. 'But despite that how do you think you'll be able to pay what you owe now? It'll not be long before Christmas comes round and the old man will be expecting to know where the money is.'

Naomi's stomach lurched. At that moment she didn't have two pennies to call her own.

'Don't worry I'll pay you back every last shilling even if I have to scrub floors.'

'Well, if I was in your shoes I'd seek some advice from a solicitor with regards to a divorce. You've every right now Duncan's buggered off.'

Naomi's eyes lit up. 'Funnily enough I was thinking the same thing myself and might well go down into the town later on. You never know I could land myself a job as well.'

A deep furrow creased Patty's brow. 'Tell me, who's going to mind Philip if you find work? I've enough with looking after my two girls so don't look to me.'

'I'll think of something don't you worry,' said Naomi, confidently. She felt enthusiasm rise in her. A job of work could be the turning point in her life and with Ted by her side she'd be happy enough she told herself.

Later that day Naomi took Philip with her to the solicitors and, after explaining her plight, was delighted to be handed some Legal Aid forms which would help pay towards a separation from her husband. She quickly put the papers into her handbag and thanked the solicitor for all his help. As she left the building she felt on cloud nine. At long last she had set the wheels in motion. Now all she had to do was find herself some type of employment.

On her way home she passed by Mrs Price's grocery shop. She'd heard she gave groceries on tick and decided to give it a try as they had very little food in the pantry.

'Any chance of a few groceries until the weekend, Mrs Price?' she asked, leaving the pushchair by the door.

Mrs Price's large, dark brown eyes looked her up and down. 'Well I can't see that little one go hungry now, can I?' she smirked. 'Anyway, I never ever thought I'd see the day when you'd come in to strap food. Duw, duw.'

Naomi squirmed. She was fully aware that Mrs Price thought she was a cut above everyone else because she owned her own business, but Naomi only ever saw her as a woman with a spiteful streak who looked every bit mutton dressed up as lamb with her bleached blonde hair and tight fitting clothes. She felt like giving her a piece of her mind but clamped her mouth tightly shut, having her eye firmly fixed on a crusty loaf of bread on the other side of the counter.

'A good looking woman like you shouldn't be short of money,' she sneered, leaning over the counter towards her.

'I don't suppose you know of any part-time jobs like cooking, cleaning or sewing?' said Naomi, feeling embarrassed at having to ask.

'They're all taken my girl, but I can easily put you in touch with someone who could help make you a fortune.' A sly smile crept over her lips.

'No thank you I'm not that desperate,' Naomi snapped, knowing full well what she meant.

'Well, you've only got to put a red light up and they'll come flocking. It's better than starving my girl, so let me know if you change your mind,' she cackled.

'I'd rather give it away than stoop that low,' Naomi muttered, rummaging round in her handbag where she found some loose change.

'From what I've heard,' said Mrs Price, 'That's what you've been doing.'

'I've got just enough money to cover the price of a bottle of milk and a loaf, after all, so I won't be wanting any tick from you,' Naomi cried, slamming the change down on the counter.

After snatching a bottle out of the crate beside her and tucking the crusty loaf under her arm she turned on her heel and stormed out of the shop, fuming.

Mrs Price gaped. 'Please your-self, then,' she shouted after her. 'I was only trying to help'

That evening, Naomi did her best to make a soup out of a crumbled Oxo cube and some stale vegetables she had left in the pantry. After slicing two large pieces of bread for Philip and herself, they sat down at the table and ate their meal hungrily.

The cold night air made Naomi shiver as the last of the coal turned to cinders. She decided to have an early night. After bolting the front door she took Philip into her bedroom where they cuddled up together in bed with the stone hot water bottle tucked safely in a towel between them.

Sleep did not come easy to her as she lay worrying about her financial situation. She didn't want to succumb to Mrs Price's offer but knew it might well come to that.

The following morning Naomi was woken early by a heavy knock on the front door. Swinging her legs to the floor she rubbed her eyes then hurried to answer it, thinking it might be Patty. After pulling back the bolt, she was horrified to see Duncan standing outside as large as life.

'What on earth are you doing here?' she cried. 'I thought you'd gone for good.'

Without a word of explanation Duncan pushed rudely past her and ran up the stairs into the bedroom. Naomi followed, in hot pursuit.

'I thought I'd catch you with your lover. Then I'd have all the evidence I need for my divorce,' he snarled, as he looked all round the bedroom. 'And before you mention the money you gave me I've spent it on a nice little whore in Cardiff. And she gave it up a damn sight easier than you, you frigid bitch.'

Naomi put her hand up to her mouth in horror.

'Do you mean to tell me you've spent all that money I gave you on a prostitute. I thought you were off to London?'

'I changed my mind, and very enjoyable it was too. Now where's my bloody breakfast. I'm starving.'

Naomi felt sick to the stomach and stared at him angrily. 'That wasn't the bargain,' she sneered, standing her ground. She was furious to think he had conned her into giving him the money and felt like punching him in the jaw. At that moment she heard the postman deliver something through the door and after gathering Philip in her arms from the bedroom she ran down the stairs to see what it was.

'There's a letter here for you,' she shouted, curious as to whom it was from.

Duncan ran down the stairs two at a time, snatching the letter from her.

'Well, who's it off then?' she asked, trying to read one of the pages over his shoulder.

'See for your-self,' he grunted, pushing it into her

hand.

Naomi's eyes scanned the letter quickly. She began shaking her head. 'So you've lost yet another job for bad time keeping and days off. What's new?' she retorted, throwing it down.

Naomi turned her back on him and began washing and dressing Philip. Up until now Duncan hadn't taken much notice of the child. She was quite used to that, knowing full well he thought him an encumbrance.

After Naomi placed Philip in his playpen she went into the scullery to put the kettle on and found Duncan slicing himself several pieces of bread.

'Don't take it all. We've got to eat as well,' she said, snatching the bread knife from him. 'All I can say is you'd better find the money to pay Patty back, or else. Do you hear?' She held the knife up to his face and although she felt like plunging it into him she thought better of it. Duncan's face hardened. 'I'll find the money don't you worry.'

'Well, make sure you find enough for a sack of coal as well because the coal house is empty, and Philip needs to be warm.'

Duncan quickly disappeared out of the room and within seconds she heard the sound of banging coming from the hallway. She went to investigate and was devastated to see him hammering at the gas meter with one of her late father's old hammers. Before she could stop him a deluge of coins fell out onto the floor.

'You'll get locked up for doing that,' she screamed, 'What ever next! We're in enough mess as it is, and it's all through you.'

A terrible foreboding suddenly flooded through her as he grabbed her handbag from the hallstand in order to fill it with the money.

His face took on a sinister look when he opened up the Legal Aid papers tucked inside.

'So you think you've got the right to divorce me do you? I'll see you in fucking hell first.'

Naomi stepped back as he tore the Legal Aid documents into shreds, flinging them down on the floor. She was ready to run, expecting him to pounce at her, but instead he gathered up some money and left through the front door clutching the bag under his arm.

Her whole body began to shake as she watched him march up the street like someone possessed.

'I hope you get locked up for thieving,' she screamed after him, wishing he'd never return. She felt totally drained and wrung her hands in despair as she walked back inside.

Even if she had managed to find a sitter for Philip her hopes of seeing Ted at the club that evening now seemed remote. If only she had somewhere to escape to. She would be gone without a backward look.

Naomi was in the process of peeling some potatoes in order to stretch what was left of the previous evening's soup when Duncan showed his face round the door.

'When I went to fetch a gallon of paraffin for the heater I saw Patty trotting up the street and in no uncertain terms told her that you won't be accompanying her to visit her sick aunt anymore. Sick aunt my arse!' he sniggered.

'What have you done with all the money from the gas meter then?' Naomi snapped, snatching the can from his hand.

'I gave it to Patty as a first instalment.'

Naomi looked at him wide eyed. She thought he might possibly be trying to make amends but it was too late as far as she was concerned.

'Don't keep on because I'll get things sorted when I take Philip round to see my parents as usual on Saturday. I intend sucking up to my father for some money. I can always say it's for Philip. He might cough up then.'

Naomi looked at him in disgust. 'Well, you can go on your own because I'm not pretending to play happy families when it suits you,' she said, storming out into the scullery. She felt unbearably alone and wished she had a mother to run to.

Later on that evening, just after Naomi had settled Philip down for the night, she heard the sound of a car horn beeping outside and hurried into the front room to look through the window. She knew full well that Patty would have told Ted about everything when she saw him at the club and wondered whether or not it was him.

'Expecting a visitor?' asked Duncan, peering over her shoulder.

'I don't see if it's any of your business now I've filed for a separation,' she snorted, with a brave show of defiance.

'Don't talk daft. I've ripped the papers up now. Anyway, I bet that's your boyfriend wondering whether you're going out to play,' he taunted, as he grabbed his overcoat from the hallstand.

'Where are you off to?' she cried, following him.

'I'm off to tell your boyfriend that we are making another go of things,' he shouted, slamming the door behind him. 'Well, we are aren't we?'

Naomi couldn't believe her ears and watched him run down the street as if a band of thieves were after him. Her thoughts whirled as to what could have been happening outside. After she had been staring through the window for several long minutes Duncan appeared in the doorway breathing heavily and with blood dripping down his face. He looked panic-stricken, and bolted the front door.

'I stopped your lover's car and told him we were

back together, and for him to butt out,' he grunted, panting for breath, 'but the fucking bastard opened the car door and dived straight on top of me saying he was going to pay me back for all the bruises I'd given you. He caught me with a right hook but tripped on the rough ground so I got away.'

Before Naomi could answer, the sound of fists pounding on the door made her jump. 'You deserve all you've got and more,' she said, sliding the bolt back, contemptuously.

Duncan's eyes darted frantically as he tried to make a run for it but as he reached the living room Ted was behind him and grabbed him by the scruff of the neck.

'You're only fit to hit women so how do you like this then, you yellow-bellied bastard?' shouted Ted, smacking him around all four corners of the room.

Naomi stood with her hands over her face until she heard a loud thud. It was the sound of Duncan crashing to the floor in a dishevelled heap.

The noise of the fighting brought Patty's husband to the back door. 'I've heard enough noise to wake the dead, and I've children asleep. What's going on here then?' he said, pushing his way in. He gasped at the sight of Duncan writhing in agony on the floor. 'I'll get the police to you lot if this noise continues,' he threatened. 'I've just about had enough.'

Ted eyed him warily. 'Well, he needed a warning, and I've given him one.'

'About time too,' said David. 'He deserves everything he gets, that man, but let me tell you he's not worth going to jail for.'

'I'm well aware of that,' grunted Ted, making his way out.

Naomi ran after him like a frightened puppy. 'I'm terrified of what he will do now,' she cried, clutching onto his arm. 'Duncan will have his own back if I know him.'

'Don't worry. We'll have you out of here in no time. Just make sure you have your bags packed by eleven on Saturday morning. I've found you a hiding place with accommodation at my friend's pub near the dock area in Cardiff. It's free bed and board if you're willing to help behind the bar. I know you'll be safe there.'

Naomi couldn't believe her ears. She had an escape route at last! 'You're the answer to my prayers,' she said, giving Ted a huge hug.

'I must fly. I don't need the coppers sniffing around. I'll pick you up Saturday so be ready.'

Ted disappeared into the darkness of the night leaving an anxious looking Naomi behind. She stepped back into the house worried as to what Duncan might do next. She ran up the stairs to check on Philip and was shocked to find him still sleeping despite the racket that had gone on.

Just as she stepped out of the room Duncan, still covered in blood, was behind her and without any warning threw her roughly against Philip's bedroom door, breaking the door knob. Naomi winced with the pain as it stuck into her back. But before she could begin to think of fighting him off he pressed his body into hers and she instinctively knew he was about to rape her.

'Not this time, my lovely,' she sneered, kneeing him hard in the crutch. 'Your days are numbered.'

Moaning he fell to the ground like a sack of potatoes. Naomi fled for her life, out of the house, to Patty's. She began hammering the door with her fists, frightened to death that Duncan might have followed her.

'Good God! I thought it was the law at the door,' said Patty, looking flustered. 'We'll go into the front room so the old man doesn't hear. He's in a foul mood.

150

I've only just arrived home from the club and heard about the ructions at your house.'

'On top of Ted and Duncan fighting, Duncan's just tried to rape me so I ran for my life,' said Naomi, quickly stepping inside.

'Mark my words you're best rid of him, or you'll be in your box, my girl.'

'Well, let me tell you, Ted has offered to take me down to Cardiff where I can have bed and board for working in a pub down there, so I'm off on Saturday.'

Before Patty could answer they both looked at each other in alarm when they heard Duncan shouting at the top of his voice in the street.

'*Naomi*, if you don't come inside right now, I shall take Philip out of his cot and walk him barefooted on the pavement in the freezing cold until you do,' he bawled, for all to hear.

Naomi's hand flew to her mouth. 'You don't think he'd stoop so low as to do that to his own son, do you?' she said, clutching at her chest. 'It's bitter out there.'

'Take no notice. It's only idle threats,' cried Patty, turning her nose up.

Within minutes they heard the sound of Duncan's voice shouting Naomi's name again, and both women looked aghast when they saw little Philip being dragged down the street bare-footed in his pyjamas, whilst a bitterly cold north easterly wind blew.

Panic stricken, Naomi ran out of the front door towards her son, lifting the shivering child up in her arms. She broke down into a torrent of tears. 'He could well catch pneumonia in this weather, after coming out of a warm cot. I hate you more than you'll ever know,' she screamed at Duncan as she took the shivering child back inside.

A sly smile came over Duncan's mouth as he followed them into the house and closed the door.

CHAPTER 15

The next morning Naomi woke early, after spending a restless night on the couch. She pulled back the curtains and was flabbergasted to see Patty's face pressed up against the living room window.

'What's wrong with the front door?' she asked, as she quickly ushered Patty inside. 'Don't tell me your husband has forbidden you to visit after the shenanigans last night.'

'Don't talk so daft. He wouldn't do that if he knows what's good for him. I'd cut off his rations,' she said, laughing. 'Anyway, thank God you're still in the land of the living. I thought I'd have found you dead on the floor. I've been mulling things over in my mind all night and think it would be best if you pay a visit to the Children's Welfare Officer about leaving Philip before you depart. If it's only to inform them about the situation you're in. Don't worry about dragging him into town with you. He'd be better off in the warm, playing with my girls.'

Naomi could see it made sense and was hoping to be there and back before Duncan got out of bed. She ran up the stairs for Philip and handed him over to Patty then hurriedly put her coat on and went up the road to the bus stop, arriving just as the bus was pulling in.

After a bumpy journey she jumped off at the stop near the Children's Welfare Office. Her mind was in a whirl but now she'd come this far she wasn't going back.

As she walked up to the reception desk she smiled at the girl behind the counter. 'I'm hoping for some advice concerning my son,' she said, feeling her stomach churn.

The girl nodded and took down a few particulars from her then disappeared from view. Within a few minutes she reappeared and beckoned Naomi into a small office where a middle-aged, grey haired man sat thumbing through some paper work on his desk.

'My name's Parry,' he announced, shaking hands with her. 'So, what is it you've come about?'

Naomi unfastened her coat and sat down facing him, not knowing where to begin. 'I was hoping you could give me some advice regarding my son.'

'Take your time now,' said Mr Parry, staring at her over his half-eye spectacles.

After taking in several deep breaths, Naomi blurted out a shortened version of all that had happened in recent weeks, up until the present day.

'Surely there's somewhere else you could seek refuge, other than a public house?'

'Not really,' answered Naomi, 'I've no family you see. I need to earn some money to help pay the bills, which are mounting up every day.'

'I expect you're aware that the law's nearly always on the mother's side but who's to say Duncan will vacate the property after you're gone?' Mr Parry raised his eyebrows questioningly. And is the child safe with him?'

'Well, he's never as much as washed up a cup and saucer in his life leave alone looked after a child. But one things certain, he will run back home to his mother and Philip will be in safe hands with her.'

'Now let me get things straight,' said Mr Parry, standing up. 'You're intending to leave your husband and abandon your child in order to take refuge in a public house?'

'That's correct,' said Naomi, heaving a huge sigh.

'Tell me,' he said, rubbing his chin, 'is there another man involved in all of this?'

Naomi's face turned the colour of beetroot. 'Well yes, I have met someone else.'

Mr Parry looked at her disapprovingly. 'This puts a different light on the matter. You must keep me informed as to what is happening and when you intend to return home. That's if you intend doing so.'

'As soon as Duncan has vacated the house for good my neighbour will contact me, and I'll be free to return then,' said Naomi, rising out of her seat.

Mr Parry took her address and noted on his pad several things she had mentioned, before escorting her to the door.

She couldn't wait to leave the place because she was worried that Duncan might have woken up in her absence. They shook hands by the door and a dejected looking Naomi left the building with a heavy heart. Leaving Philip in order to regain her freedom was a price she knew she would have to pay. It would be the hardest thing she had ever done and she prayed to God that He would see her through.

After collecting Philip from Patty, she entered the house and cringed at the sight of Duncan having a wash in the sink. She pretended she'd been to the shop but he gave her a sly look as if he didn't believe her. His face looked battered and bruised but she felt no remorse. Before the weekend was over he would learn that his emotional blackmail was useless.

Shortly after ten o'clock on the Saturday Duncan changed into his best clothes in readiness to take Philip to his parent's house.

Naomi was already a bag of nerves at the thought of parting with her son but she tried her hardest not to show it, for fear of being found out.

'We're going now,' shouted Duncan. 'Sure you don't want to join us?'

'No I've too much to do,' said Naomi, trying to fight back the tears. After hugging Philip tightly, she placed him into his pushchair. 'Keep him wrapped up warm mind, because the wind is bitter cold,' she said, tucking a thick plaid blanket over the little one's legs. This was the moment she had dreaded, and she swallowed down the hard lump in her throat.

After waving her son off Naomi went back inside the house and broke down into sobs. With tears running down her face she packed her case. As soon as she closed the lid she heard someone knocking at the front door.

'It's only me,' shouted Patty through the letter box. 'Hurry up I'm freezing to death out here.'

Naomi answered the door, glad to see her friend before she left. 'What is it?' she asked, looking at her expectantly.

'I've noticed you haven't got a warm coat to your name so I decided to give you one of mine.'

Naomi's eyes stared down at the beautiful fur coat clutched in her arms. 'I couldn't take that,' she protested, looking at her perplexed.

'Yes you can, cariad,' cried Patty, pushing the coat into her arms. She looked at her watch. 'You haven't much time, so I wish you all the best and don't forget to keep in touch. Don't you worry now I'll keep my eyes open as to what might be going on.'

Naomi put the coat round her shoulders and gave Patty a hug. 'I'll never forget all you've done for me and as soon as I earn any money I'll send it on in order to clear the debt I owe you.'

'I would appreciate that,' said Patty. 'By the way, are you leaving a "Dear John" note behind when you leave?'

'Good God! It had never entered my head. But he doesn't deserve even that.'

'Must fly,' said Patty as she flung her arms around her. 'I've shopping to do. So take care now and good luck.'

Within seconds of Patty disappearing up the street Naomi saw Ted pull to a halt outside the house. She gave him a huge smile and then dashed inside to gather up her things. This was it. There was no going back now.

Excitement at escaping and guilt for leaving Philip flowed through her veins in equal measure as she clambered into the passenger seat beside Ted.

'You all set now?' he asked, smiling at her.

'Yes,' said Naomi, triumphantly. 'Let's get the hell out of here before it's too late.'

CHAPTER 16

Naomi stared all round her as Ted pulled the car to a halt outside The Ship Inn. She knew she was in the Dockland area of Cardiff because the sound of fog-horns greeted her as she stepped from the car, clutching her small case.

Before she could take a good look at the place Ted ushered her through the door of the pub. The pungent smell of beer hit her as soon as she stepped inside. A stout middle aged man with dark curly hair came forward to greet them.'I'm Jim,' he said. 'So glad you've arrived because the lunch time rush is about to start and it will be all hands on deck then.'

Naomi quickly shook his outstretched hand, and swallowed hard, wondering what was in store for her.

'Follow me and I'll take you into the living quarters up-stairs, so you can get acquainted with the place,' said Jim, smiling.

After climbing the stairs they entered a large room which was full of clutter. Slumped in an armchair near a roaring fire was a young, freckle-faced woman with a mop of unruly corn coloured hair that looked as if it hadn't been combed in days. Her green eyes narrowed as they walked in. She took several swigs from a well filled brandy glass before speaking.

'The top of the morning to you,' she said, hiccupping.

'This is Alice, the wife,' said Jim, looking a little shamefaced. 'She's in love with the brandy bottle, as you can see.' He pointed to the half empty bottle of spirits standing on the floor.

Naomi nodded, at a loss how to answer. It was plain to see the woman was completely drunk.

'Hey up!' Jim called. 'Here comes our little Bess. Coming to give your Dad a big kiss, is it?'

A small child with long, dark, curly hair came bounding across the room and threw herself into his arms.

Naomi smiled at her. 'Hello there,' she said, thinking how like her father she was.

'Go and play like a good girl, then,' said Jim, putting her down. 'I've business to discuss.'

Bess picked up her doll and ran out of the room with a mischievous grin on her face.

'Well, you can see the predicament I'm in, can't you?' said Jim, throwing his arms in the air. 'Unfortunately my wife is incapable of doing much work because more often than not she takes to the bottle behind my back. On top of it all I've just found out that my daughter, Wendy, is six months pregnant by some loser who frequents the place. It all means extra work for me.'

'I'm not frightened of hard work,' said Naomi, 'but I think it's only fair to tell you I've never pulled pints in a public house before.'

'Don't you worry about that. We'll have you sorted out in no time,' said Jim, smiling. 'Anyway, it's time you unpacked, so I'll take you up to our Wendy's room. You'll be sharing with her.'

'And it's time I was off,' butted in Ted. 'The lorry won't load itself with shale, will it?'

Naomi mentally steeled herself as she followed him to the door.

'You'll be fine my lovely, don't you worry. I'll call in from time to time,' he said, giving her a quick peck on the cheek.

'See you Jim, Take care of her, butty. She's had a rough time.' And with that he disappeared out of the door.

Naomi gave him a long lingering look as he left, then followed Jim up another set of dimly lit stairs into

Wendy's bedroom. She was glad to be left alone to unpack her belongings and, after hanging up a few simple clothes in the wardrobe, she looked into the dressing table mirror to make sure she was tidy.

Everything was happening so quickly and she was already missing Philip but she knew she had done the best she could in the circumstances.

She glanced at the used cups and saucers that were strewn on the bedside cabinet and moved them aside to make room for a photograph of her child. A lump formed in her throat but she'd come this far and was determined to see things through, until they could be reunited.

Swinging her bag over her right arm she left the room to begin work, knowing that keeping herself busy would help lessen the pain.

Teddy Boys, sea faring men and the like all looked up from what they were doing when Naomi made her appearance in the bar. On seeing her Jim immediately put his arm around her shoulder and began to introduce her to the customers. She could smell the liquor and tobacco on his breath and flinched when he squeezed her arm.

'You'll have to get used to that kind of thing in here, my girl,' he said, giving her a deep throated laugh.

Naomi smiled, then carefully watched Jim as he showed her how to pull a good pint of beer without any waste. In no time at all she was left to fend for herself. Just as she was totting up the first round of drinks in her head Wendy appeared on the scene dressed in a plain pink smock and black skirt. Naomi guessed she was in her late teens and immediately took a liking to her. She was glad of her company, but there was little time to talk as a steady flow of customers lined up at the bar.

Trade was brisk all day and evening and it wasn't

until last orders were called that Naomi was able to relax a little. After making sure the premises were clean and tidy Wendy took her into the kitchen, where they enjoyed a well earned cup of tea and some buttered toast before wearily climbing the stairs to bed.

Naomi tossed and turned on her unfamiliar mattress, longing to know how Philip was faring without her. In the end she eventually fell into a fitful sleep, and before she knew it the alarm clock woke her up.

Knowing her first week's wages were already spoken for twice over she decided to post Patty some money to pay off some of Duncan's debt. She couldn't leave her friend short after she'd been kind enough to lend her the money in the first place. So she wrote her a letter stating she'd pay the rest of what she owed as soon as she could, and asked her for any news of Philip and Duncan.

By return of post Naomi received a brief note telling her that Patty had seen Philip being wheeled in his pushchair by Duncan's mother. But she was under the impression that Duncan was still living in the matrimonial home because she had heard him on several occasions using the outside lavatory.

Naomi was annoyed that Duncan hadn't budged and thought he had a cheek staying put under her roof now she had deserted him. It left her in a quandary as to what to do next. One thing was sure, she'd never return as things were.

In no time at all Naomi took to the work in the bar, and loved mixing with the constant flow of people who seemed to come from all walks of life. The Beatles' latest hits were always blaring on the jukebox which helped to keep her spirits high. *I Want to Hold Your Hand* was played over and over until she knew every word by heart.

Every day, like clockwork, the same prostitutes

gathered in the far corner of the bar ready to ply their trade with any man who was seeking sexual favours. The sounds of their voices shouting, 'Do you fancy some fun, my lovely?' rang in Naomi's ears as she served them drinks. As time went by she made friends with several of the girls. There was one in particular by the name of Lola, who was held in high esteem by the other women. She stood out from the rest with her long blonde hair, expensive perfume and black fish-net stockings.

One evening when Lola was waiting for a boat to dock, she sat by the bar talking to Naomi about her life as a prostitute. She boasted that she was able to drive through the dock gates at any time of the day or night without being stopped because she was able to bribe whoever was on duty with whisky and cigarettes.

It was common knowledge in the pub that Lola was notorious amongst the other prostitutes for her antics. Many a captain from on board ship delighted in her company and it was a known fact that she always made sure she plied her wares with a high ranking officer so that she could get a pass to go on board in case the police turned up.

Lola carried on talking about the money she could earn selling her body and how the drink flowed all night on board ship. She made it sound like a good life but, despite all this, Naomi could not see herself dressed in a leopard skin coat, like most of the girls wore, with a chain dangling round her ankle, making it obvious what she did for a living.

'That's all very well, but what about the poor prostitute that was murdered recently after climbing into some man's car down in Bute Street? Doesn't that frighten you?' said Naomi, pulling a face.

'When your number's up that's it,' chuckled Lola. 'Anyway, the good Lord won't want me up there,' she said, raising her glass of beer.

'I know it's the oldest profession in the world but what made you go down that road in the first place?' Naomi asked, full of curiosity.

'My mother was on the game, bless her cotton socks, and one day it came to light that she got up the duff for me whilst on a German boat. So I suppose you could say it runs in the family, see.'

Naomi nodded, admiring her honesty. At that moment a taxi driver walked in and beckoned to Lola.

'Me and the girls are ready and waiting, my lovely,' she shouted to him in a broad Welsh accent.

'Why not come along? It's nearly closing time. I'll make sure you don't sell your body to a cabin boy or such like. Lola's always around to keep an eye on her girls.'

Naomi couldn't believe her ears. 'I'd rather starve than sell my body, thank-you! Anyway knowing my luck I'd be shanghaied off somewhere and never be seen again,' she grimaced.

'Please your-self then' said Lola, jumping off her stool. 'But you know where we are if you ever change your mind. Duw, I'd soon teach you the ropes, girl.' With a sweep of her hand she beckoned to the other ladies of the night and within seconds they had all followed her through the door.

Naomi felt a surge of excitement every time Ted showed his face but, more often than not, after downing a pint of ale he made an excuse to leave. She was disappointed with his behaviour but accepted his terms rather than be without him.

Naomi soon realised that she'd made the right decision not to have taken Philip with her because as young as she was little Bess swore like a trooper and had a temper to match. She wouldn't have wanted her behaviour rubbing off on her son and prayed for the day when she could return home to him.

In no time at all her self-esteem quickly returned when many of the punters sounded her out for a date. She enjoyed their banter but was determined to remain faithful to Ted, hoping that some day they would be able to make a go of things together. She had found it odd that he never spoke much about his home life. Whenever she brought the subject up he'd given her the impression that he was single and moved around with his job, which more often than not satisfied her curiosity.

One evening Jim threw the evening newspaper down on the counter pointing out the personal column to Naomi.

It said, "Naomi, Philip ill. Make contact. Duncan." She was panic-stricken and called up the stairs asking Wendy to take over while she made a phone call to Duncan's parents' house.

Wendy appeared looking very pregnant underneath her floral smock top. 'What's the matter? I thought the pub was on fire,' she jested.

'I won't be long,' said Naomi, clenching her teeth. 'It's Philip. He's ill.'

After dialling the number she held her breath. Her mind was in a turmoil as to who would answer. She flinched at the sound of Duncan's voice on the other end of the line.

'What's happened to Philip?' she cried, biting into her bottom lip.

'If you must know, he's ill with bronchitis. But a fat lot you care.'

She was filled with alarm. 'Hark who's talking. I don't suppose walking my son up and down the street in the freezing cold night air helped his chest, did it?' she retorted, frostily.

'That's rich coming from my *wife*, who literally abandoned her kid in order to live with her lover.'

Naomi was seething. 'If you must know I'm not living with anyone. The only way I could pay off your debts and be rid of you was to find a job with living accommodation in a public house.'

'Where you can have your choice of men every night as well I expect,' Duncan sneered.

Naomi felt her temper rise. 'I happened to have seen the Child Welfare Officer before I left and explained that I'd return as soon as you leave the property.'

'Is that so?' said Duncan, changing his tone. 'Well, if you give me your phone number I can keep you informed about everything.'

Longing to know how her child was she quickly read the number out to him from the dial on the phone, surprised he had turned affable all of a sudden. 'You will ring me won't you?' she almost begged, letting her emotions rule her. Her heart sank as the telephone line went dead.

On her return to the bar she noticed Wendy was discreetly talking to the father of her unborn child. She could see Jim watching them out of the corner of his eye and she sensed a row brewing.

Within the hour the main doors swung open and in flooded a group of tough-looking men who looked as if they were from a Greek ship that had docked that night. She could tell by their stance that they were already well-oiled and knowing how impatient they could be she worked busily beside Jim so there'd be no complaints from the customers about waiting.

After looking up from pouring a round of drinks Naomi was flabbergasted to see Duncan leering at her from the other side of the bar.

'Well, well,' he said, looking around. 'Haven't we come down in the world, my darling?'

'Just tell me how Philip is,' she said, sticking her chin out defiantly. 'There was no need for you to slam the phone down on me.'

He beckoned with his finger and she bent towards him knowing she would not have heard what he had to say amidst the noise of the jukebox.

'I've just come to tell you that you'll never ever see your son again. I'll make sure of that, you whore,' he sneered, grabbing her arm.

Within seconds Jim was beside Duncan holding him in an arm lock. 'Leave my staff alone you shit-house,' he roared, physically dragging him towards the exit.

Naomi watched with an open mouth as Jim proceeded to push Duncan out on to the street. Then with one hard shove from Jim she saw Duncan fall headlong into the gutter.

'Stay away from my pub or you'll have more than being thrown out on your arse, boyo. Just you think yourself bloody lucky.'

Leaving a bedraggled looking Duncan lying on the ground, Jim stormed back inside, slapping his hands together.

'Thanks Jim! That was my husband and things would have taken a turn for the worse if you hadn't intervened,' she said, clutching at her chest.

'Not in my pub it won't,' said Jim. 'I guessed it was your hubby, so let's say he's got his just desserts. I was aiming for a row with my Wendy's fellah but your old man copped it in the neck instead.'

Naomi could feel her whole body shaking but she felt relieved that there had been someone around who would stick up for her for a change. She thought herself a fool for giving the pub's telephone number to her husband and wondered if he was only using Philip as a ploy to track her down.

CHAPTER 17

It was Christmas day and the Ship Inn was crowded with people standing three deep at the bar. The jukebox was blaring out Christmas carols and everyone seemed to be in high spirits.

Jim and Naomi were busily serving drinks when the sound of the phone ringing sent Naomi hurrying towards it. She lived in the hope it might be Patty with news from the home front.

'Speak up will you, only I can't hear anything with the din going on in this place,' she shouted, getting agitated.

'It's Patty. Merry Christmas! I'm just ringing to tell you that Duncan's left the house for good and he's given me the key,' she shouted back. 'By the way, he told me Philip is much better and he intends to return him to you in the New Year.'

Naomi's heart soared. 'That's wonderful news. There is a God after all. Thanks ever so much for ringing but I can't stop now. I'm up to my neck serving customers. Hope to see you soon.'

As soon as she returned to the bar a crowd of people surged in demanding drinks. She was saddened not to see Ted amongst them and thought he would at least have turned up to see her.

Well after last orders were called Naomi ushered the last of the customers through the door before finally locking up. Her stomach was rumbling in anticipation of her Christmas lunch. After stacking the chairs while Wendy and Jim cleared the glasses, she left them to cash up. She knew that the takings had been good seeing it was Christmas and was looking forward to putting her feet up for the rest of the day but as she climbed the stairs she thought it strange not to smell the Christmas roast. She feared the worst.

As soon as she walked into the living quarters she gasped at the sight of Alice slumped in the chair in a drunken stupor. She rushed into the kitchen and felt angry when her eyes lit upon the uncooked bird lying half stuffed beside the sink. How could Alice have drunk herself silly first thing in the morning when people were relying on her to do the cooking?' she muttered to herself under her breath.

At that moment Bess came rushing in to show her one of the dolls she'd received for Christmas. Naomi gave her a hug, feeling sorry that the child was having to spend Christmas Day alone with her drunken mother.

'I'm hungry,' Bess cried, with a look of despair on her face. 'Where's my dinner?'

Naomi picked her up and, as she held her in her arms, tears came to her eyes as she thought of her own child. At that moment she was sorely tempted to telephone to ask about Philip but she knew only too well that she would have to face the wrath of her mother-in-law, or even worse, Duncan.

'Go and play with your dollies now, my darling. I'll see if I can rustle us up something to eat.'

On looking over the pantry shelves it was obvious that Alice had omitted to buy extra food in for Christmas. Naomi was fuming as she took down a lone tin of corned beef in order to make some sandwiches. She was disgusted that Alice could be so lax.

Several minutes later Jim and Wendy came wearily into the room and stopped in their tracks at the sight of Alice.

'Don't tell me there's no Christmas dinner for us?' Jim shouted, throwing the takings onto the chair.

'I'm afraid not,' replied Naomi. 'It's corned beef sandwiches all round,' she said, pushing a dinner plate full of sandwiches across the table towards him.

'This is the final straw. We can't go on like this. I

need someone reliable to take over and manage the bar full-time so I can keep my eye on other matters. How do you fancy the job, Naomi? You're a good worker and I'll up your wages.'

Naomi stared at him in disbelief, taken aback by his offer. She was sorely tempted. During the weeks she'd lived there Jim had made her feel like one of the family and she knew she was safe while he was around.

'Believe you me if I didn't have a child I would have jumped at the offer but, to be perfectly honest, I must go home soon. Patty rang earlier to say Duncan has at last left the house and I don't want to risk losing my son.'

'You could have gone far in the pub trade, my lovely, with your looks and personality,' said Jim, as he gorged into his sandwich.

Naomi knew only too well that she would sorely miss the steady weekly wage but was relieved to think that the money had helped pay Duncan's debt off.

Jim looked disappointed. 'We'll say no more about the matter now. I can see how you're placed. Great pity though.'

'Well it's not too late for me to finish stuffing the bird and I'm sure I can sort out a few vegetables to go with it in time for supper,' said Naomi, rising from her chair, feeling awful at having to let him down.

'You get on with it, girl. Better a late Christmas dinner than nothing at all. And as soon as you've finished we'll all have a toast to Christmas.'

'And pull some crackers,' chuckled Bess, who was trying her hardest to climb onto Wendy's lap.

Naomi smiled then went into the kitchen and hurriedly finished preparations for the meal. After closing the oven door on the bird and opening a few tins of vegetables she returned to the living room where Jim handed her a large glass of sherry. She stood beside

Wendy and Bess and they all held their glasses up wishing each other a Happy Christmas.

Then Jim surprised her by putting his arm around her. 'It's been a pleasure knowing you, my lovely. To be honest I don't know what I would have done without your help.'

Naomi's eyes filled. 'You're welcome,' she said, trying her best to smile. 'Believe you me this will be a Christmas that will stay in my memory forever.'

CHAPTER 18

After Christmas Naomi made a telephone call to Mr Parry, the Children's Welfare Officer, to explain the state of affairs and he made her an appointment for the following day at eleven sharp for the hand over of her son.

Naomi was frightened to death at the thought of meeting up with Duncan again but overjoyed at the prospect of seeing her child.

She packed her case, tearfully said her goodbyes to everyone and caught the bus back home, where she made her way purposefully to the Child Welfare Office. It was a cold frosty morning and Naomi was very glad to have put on the fur coat that Patty had given her.

As she walked up the steps to the office she looked up to see Duncan strutting through Mr Parry's door holding Philip's hand, just as if he owned the place.

She leapt at the sight of her son and was saddened to see him looking so pale.

'It's Mammy, darling, I'm back,' she cried, weeping with joy.

Philip ran into her arms. As Duncan passed over his carrier bag of clothes she gritted her teeth.

'Fur coat, no drawers is it?' he whispered in her ear, raising his eyebrows.

Naomi gave him a look fit to kill.

'Right, let's get down to business,' said Mr Parry, shuffling the papers in front of him. 'If it's agreeable to both of you I have suggested Duncan continues to have access to Philip at weekends, say perhaps a few hours on Saturdays, until something is finalized properly with the courts.'

Naomi cringed at the thought. No way was she ever going to have Duncan darken her doorway again. If it was left to her he'd never see Philip but she had no intentions of spiting her mother-in-law for her son's sins so she reluctantly agreed to the situation.

After Mr Parry had finished documenting the details on paper he stood up to shake Duncan by the hand, then opened the door for him.

'Well, I've places to go and people to meet,' Duncan said, making a grand gesture of waving goodbye to Philip.

Naomi stood and stared at him. She knew him of old. He was all show and his talk was cheap as far as she was concerned.

As soon as he'd left the room Naomi made herself comfortable on a chair, with Philip sat on her lap. 'I hope you don't mind me staying a few minutes more,' she said, smiling at Mr Parry. 'Only I'd like to bet Duncan has something up his sleeve. He was far too agreeable about the whole thing for my liking.'

'I can run you home if you're nervous of bumping into him. I have to make a call somewhere near your address,' offered Mr Parry, looking down at his watch.

'That's extremely kind of you,' said Naomi, sighing with relief. She picked up the brown carrier bag and quietly followed Mr Parry out of the building holding Philip's hand tightly. 'We're having a ride home in a motor car, Philip. Duw, isn't that posh?'

Philip looked up at his mother with his deep blue eyes and smiled. She almost wept at the thought of what she must have put her child through by her absence and thanked God that they were together once more.

After her lift home Naomi looked around and noticed several of the neighbours gathering together. She could tell by their grimaces that they were talking about her. She was sick to the teeth of being judged. But she held her head high.

As soon as she walked into the house she was greeted by an obnoxious smell. She went from room to room and was shocked at the filth Duncan had left behind. The stench hit her even more when she entered the kitchen where there were piles of dirty dishes, covered in mould. She was amazed that Duncan could have lived amongst it all knowing full well that his son would, in time, return to such a gruesome mess.

'I must light a fire first, Philip, because it's freezing in here, but we'll soon have it warm and cosy, my boy.'

Philip ran to the coalhouse outside and poked his head around the door. 'No coal, Mam,' he shouted.

'Don't worry, son, I'll scrape something up. Come on in out of the cold and play with your toys,' she urged, placing down a box of toy soldiers in front of him. She'd bought them as a present for Christmas, and the delight in his eyes shone as he opened the box.

Taking off her coat, she took her pinafore from behind the door and began clearing out the grate.

Philip watched his mother's every move as she did her best to make a fire out of the few cinders that were left, topping it up with a shovel full of small coal scraped from the corners of the coal house. Within minutes of the fire catching Naomi put some money in the dented gas meter and boiled the kettle so she could wash up the putrid smelling plates and cups that were littered everywhere. Once this was done she opened the pantry hoping to find something for their lunch but was presented with an empty cereal packet lying on the top shelf. She was fuming, remembering that when she had left all those weeks ago there was at least a supply of basic food.

Suddenly there was a rap on the front door and on opening it she was thrilled to see Patty standing outside, waving the house key in her hand.

'Can't stop long because the old man is home

minding the girls. But I thought you'd better have the key now that the tyrant's left, and I've a small bar of chocolate for Philip,' she cried, gleefully. The two women quickly hugged each other. 'Just came to tell you that you're famous. The neighbours have named you after Christine Keeler. I expect you've heard the recent scandal about her in the newspapers?'

'Too right I have, but I can assure you I'm no call girl,' Naomi retorted.

'It's a known fact that the valley people tittle-tattle and with a juicy bit of gossip like you clearing off into the wild blue yonder without your child, what do you expect, cariad?'

Naomi's face coloured. 'Christine Keeler is it? Huh! I wish I had her money because I don't know how we're going to manage now I'm out of work. We won't get fat on what's left in my purse but at least I managed to pay off your debt,' she said, sighing.

'Thank God you did because my David would have had a fit if he'd found out. Anyway, why don't you get yourself straight down to the National Assistance Board before they close for the day. They'll have to give you something, especially where a small child is concerned.'

Naomi looked at her horrified. 'I thought such places were only for down and outs, like tramps,' she grimaced.

'Well, you haven't much option, have you, my lovely? But, whatever you do don't wear your fur coat down there because you might have it ripped off your shoulders by the likes of them that frequent the place.'

'I won't. Don't you worry,' said Naomi, pulling a face. She dreaded the thought of ever having to resort to such things. But knew she had no option.

'It's a pity Ted can't help you out. Come to think of it I haven't seen him up the club lately,' Patty added.

'Perhaps he's ill or something? Anyway, I'm too independent to ask him for money.'

'He'll turn up like a bad penny, just you wait and see,' said Patty, grinning. 'I must dash because the old man will only grumble. I'm supposed to be up the shop buying a packet of Woodbines for him. He gets a cob on if he hasn't a fag.'

Naomi hurried back inside and put on her shabby navy-blue hooded raincoat. After wiping Philip's face clean she put him into his pushchair, tucking a warm blanket round his legs.

As she walked up the street she was conscious that every head turned in her direction. It made her feel awkward but she was determined to keep a firm grip on herself and held her head up high. She wondered what stories Duncan had told them knowing full well he would have painted her black and himself as white as snow.

After a long trudge in the bitterly cold wind she joined the long queue inside the Assistance Board office, feeling degraded and ashamed at having to do so. However she was glad of the warmth, as her hands and feet were perished. Naomi stared at the other people in the queue and wondered what had brought them to such a bleak place. The man in front of her had grey tousled hair and was dressed in a dirty black overcoat that looked two sizes too big on him. She could smell his body odour, which hung in the air, and was relieved when her name was eventually called.

A stern looking middle aged man with horn-rimmed glasses interviewed her. After explaining her circumstances she was told that she would have to wait for an official visit at her home from one of their officers before she could be considered for payment.

'Duw, what are you talking about? We've no food in the house and there's no coal either,' she exclaimed, panicking.

'You could be living in Buckingham Palace for all we know,' the man said, bluntly. 'So expect someone to call Monday morning.'

Naomi's mouth fell open in shock. She thought the man obnoxious. Just as she turned on her heel to leave, she bumped into a grubby looking tramp who had a piece of sacking tied over his shoulder for warmth. He gave her a wink whereupon she dashed out of the place pushing the pushchair as quickly as her legs would carry her.

On her way home she stopped at the corner shop and looked in her purse. The few shillings she had left would just about cover a small loaf of bread, margarine, and a bottle of milk. .

As soon as they arrived at the house Naomi shovelled the last of the small coal onto the fire and spread margarine on several rounds of bread for their tea.

After going upstairs to change the sheets she noticed the spare room door was open and went inside. Much to her surprise Duncan had cleared the room of his pornographic magazines which had left the room bare.

After reading Philip a bedtime story she put him to bed with a fresh hot water bottle wrapped up in a towel, then went downstairs to sit by what was left of the fire to finish some knitting she'd found in the drawer.

She laid the work out in front of her and looked at it with pride. She'd often knitted Philip coats, hats and jumpers out of skeins of wool she'd bought on the weekly at the wool shop down the road. At least she could say her son never lacked for warm clothes and was always turned out smartly.

She sighed as she sank down in the chair, glad to be back in her own home. The freedom she longed for more than anything else was now hers. She began humming to the wireless, as she worked away at the knitting pattern and began to wonder what had become of Ted. As her eyes began to close with tiredness the back door creaked open and she nearly fell out of the chair with shock when she saw Duncan standing in the doorway.

'You never were one to lock your back door at night, were you?' he sneered, stepping into the room.

Her heart was in her mouth as he lunged towards her. 'What do you want?' she screamed, trying to back away from him.

'I need a signed declaration from you stating you've committed adultery and who with. My name's not being dragged through the mud because of you.'

'You've got to be joking,' she cried. 'I'm not admitting to anything of the sort.'

Before she could move he placed his hands round her throat and, as his grip tightened, she thought her end had come. A weak cry came from her lips as his hands gripped even tighter.

'I'll do anything. Anything,' she croaked.

He released his grip and took out of his pocket a pen and some paper, laying them down in front of her.

Coughing and spluttering, Naomi signed the declaration of adultery, frightened to death what might happen if she didn't comply with his wishes.

Duncan quickly snatched the paper from her. 'That lets me off the hook and spares my parents the humiliation of seeing my name dragged through the mud. I knew you'd come to your senses in the end.'

She was shaking from head to foot. Her eyes were those of a frightened animal.

'I'm off now to shag my new girl-friend,' he said, smirking at her.

'The best of luck to her,' spluttered Naomi hoarsely.

'Well, I wouldn't touch you with a barge pole. I

don't know where you've been,' he yelled, as he shut the back door behind him.

Naomi flinched as she heard the door slam, and ran to bolt it. She clutched at her neck and knew only too well that Duncan would have killed her in cold blood if she hadn't succumbed to his wishes.

CHAPTER 19

After a sleepless night Naomi emerged from her bedroom looking like death warmed up. She thought back to the previous nights events and thanked God she was still around to tell the tale. One thing was for sure, she would never again forget to bolt the back door.

It was a dark dreary morning and within minutes of her turning on the electricity the meter ran out of money. Her heart plummeted. She didn't have a penny piece to her name.

After setting the fire with a few sticks of wood and some cinders she soon had a cheerful blaze going. She got Philip up from his bed and put the last crust of buttered bread in front of him.

'Eat it all up. There's a good boy,' she said, watching her son as he ate it hungrily. Pangs of hunger dug into her stomach and for one fleeting moment she wondered whether she ought to resort to contacting Lola at the Ship Inn. But just the thought of strange men seeking sexual satisfaction with her made her feel sick.

Thoughts of her birth mother returned. For all she knew she might have been killed in the Blitz that had affected London so badly. But deep down inside her she had a strong feeling that she was still alive.

Her thoughts then turned to Ted. Perhaps he would appear, like a knight in shining armour, to rescue her from all this. Her heart ached for him and she wondered if he would ever return.

Shortly before lunch time there was a loud knock on the front door. Her mind whirled frantically as she dreaded the thought that it could be Duncan. She peeped through the front room window and was relieved to see Patty outside with a raincoat pulled over her shoulders. She quickly opened the door and Patty rushed inside.

'The old man's gone down to visit his mother in Ty-Coch with the girls, so how do you fancy sharing some Sunday lunch with me? I've plenty to spare.'

Naomi was thrilled to bits and without being asked twice she quickly collected Philip and followed Patty into her house. 'You're an angel in disguise,' she cried. 'The Assistance Board aren't calling until tomorrow and our cupboards are bare.'

'Duw! We can't have that. Not to worry, I've roasted a lovely piece of Welsh lamb from the Farmers' Market. I hope you both like mushy peas and cabbage, only it's a favourite of ours.'

'It smells wonderful,' sighed Naomi, as the aroma of roast lamb wafted under her nose.

Naomi and Philip's mouths drooled as the meal was put before them and within seconds they tucked into the roast dinner like famished vultures.

After clearing away the empty plates, Patty came in with fruit dishes piled high with stewed apple and custard. 'Get that down you now before the custard grows cold,' she said, quickly tucking into hers.

'Believe you me, this is a meal fit for a queen,' sighed Naomi, patting her stomach. 'I don't know where we would have been without you.'

Patty smiled. 'I'd rather do you a good turn than a bad one, my girl. I know you would have done the same for me. Anyway, I can sense there's something on your mind so we'll leave Philip tucked up in here for his afternoon nap while we wash up the dishes in the scullery, is it?'

Naomi nodded and gathered up the empty dishes from the table. As soon as she was out of earshot of her son she told her friend all about the previous night's events.

Patty's jaw dropped as she listened to her. 'You

179

should have called the local bobby. He'd have sorted him out,' she cried, grimacing in horror.

'I didn't have the chance. It was all over in no time but I'm wondering what Ted will say about the matter now I've named him as an adulterer.'

'Bugger Ted. It's not that you've seen him much since he's had his oats from you, is it? Anyway, I'm wondering whether you should walk away before you get hurt.'

'But I love him,' Naomi declared, colouring up.

'Well, if that's the case why don't you join me up the club this Tuesday evening? And If Ted's turns up you'll be able to sort things out one way or the other.'

Naomi could see the sense of that and quickly grasped onto the idea. 'The only problem is I've Philip to take care of and we haven't even enough money for food and electric, leave alone the bus fare up the club,' she said sadly.

'Don't you worry about that, my girl' said Patty, digging into her handbag. 'Here's a few bob to tide you over, and I don't want it back either.'

Naomi thanked her profusely, then put the money into her pocket a bit sheepishly. She hated being so poverty-stricken but consoled herself that at least now they would not have to spend their evening sitting in the dark, with candles.

'I've just thought. Why don't you bring Philip in for a sleep over with the girls on Tuesday evening? My David won't say anything if I tell him it's just the one off.'

'That's a wonderful idea,' said Naomi, her eyes lighting up. 'I can't wait to see Ted again.'

'I wouldn't pin all your hopes on him if I was you. He seems to be like the elusive pimpernel.'

Naomi knew Patty was saying the hard truth, but it wasn't what she wanted to hear. Although she had

Philip to keep her company she longed to be in Ted's arms.

Early the next morning a grim looking, middle aged Public Assistance woman called at the house. She was dressed in a thick tweed coat and wore lace up shoes which she wiped firmly on the mat as she came inside.

Naomi's face looked glum at the thought of the woman poking her nose around the place.

'Well, don't look like that girl. I'm here to see if you're cohabiting before we can even discuss the case,' she said sharply, looking down her nose at her.

'Chance would be a fine thing,' Naomi muttered under her breath.

'What was that?' asked the woman sternly, as she began to climb the stairs.

'Nothing,' said Naomi, coughing in the pretence of clearing her throat.

As they entered her son's room she held up the bedding from his cot. 'I badly need a bed and blankets for my boy. He has to sleep with me because the cot's too small for him,' she said, standing back for the woman to have a clear look into the sparsely furnished box room. 'Even the handle on the door is broken in here, and it wasn't of my doing.'

Her mind went back to the time when Duncan had fought with her at the top of the stairs.

'I can't help you with household repairs,' snapped the woman. Her eyes darted around, taking stock of everything. 'I shall have to take this up with my superiors because we have a tight budget to adhere to.'

'Well, we can't go on existing without any money,' Naomi grumbled, staring at her.

'You should never have got yourself like this in the first place then, should you?' the woman replied scornfully.

Naomi couldn't believe her ears. She continued to

follow the woman into each room. After a thorough search of the house the woman stopped at the bottom of the stairs to scribble some notes down on a pad. 'You'll be hearing from us shortly. If there are any changes in your circumstances you must contact us immediately,' she stated, putting her nose in the air.

Naomi nodded and showed her to the door, then watched in silence as she marched out of the house in a manner which would have done credit to an officer from the Gestapo. Feeling humiliated from it all she closed the door after her, feeling like a beggar.

The following day Naomi was relieved to receive a weekly order book and a cheque for two pounds five shillings towards a new bed for Philip. She had become used to managing on next to nothing over the years and was determined to put every penny to good use.

After cashing her weekly amount of money she bought some badly needed groceries, a piece of scrag-end from the butcher, and some vegetables. She intended making a huge pot of stew as soon as she arrived home and licked her lips at the thought of it.

Just as she was turning the corner of the street she saw the coal man at her door and paid him for a hundred-weight of coal. She knew that with care it would last them all week. She hurriedly ushered him inside to where the coal bunker was. And as he tossed the sack of coal off his back Philip looked on in awe.

Although things had begun shaping up for her, her nerves had been in tatters since Duncan's last visit. She had the habit of jumping at every noise, thinking that he might have forced entry or was hiding somewhere. This inbuilt fear of him ran so deep she was convinced it would remain with her for the rest of her days. Her mind had become blighted by the debauchery he had imposed on her, which had turned her into a shadow of her former self.

Shortly after lunch time Patty called with a pretty pink crimplene shift dress in her hand. 'I thought this might come in handy for you to wear tonight. It doesn't fit me anymore now I've put on weight.'

Naomi took one look at it and shrieked with delight. She hoped that one day she'd be able to repay her friend for all her kindness.

That evening, after dropping Philip off with David, she and Patty made their way to the club. Naomi couldn't get there quickly enough because she had a strong feeling that Ted would be there. She felt like the cat's whiskers in her new dress and when she and Patty walked into the dance hall the band struck up to play a tune.

Naomi stood looking eagerly for Ted and gasped when she saw him coming towards her across the dance floor. He held out his arms as she ran up to him. She was almost free now so she couldn't have cared a damn about who saw them.

'I've missed you so much, Princess, and was hoping you'd be here tonight. Jim rang me to say you'd left the pub but I wasn't sure whether you'd returned home or not.'

Naomi hung onto his every word and revelled in his embrace, looking up into his eyes adoringly. As he held her tightly there was no doubt in her mind that he was the man for her.

They sat down at the table with Patty, and Naomi acknowledged the other couple, Bronwen and Sid. Sid appeared the worst for drink but she ignored it. After all she was here to enjoy herself with the love of her life, not concern herself with other people.

Ted went to the bar for a round of drinks. Then Patty took off her coat and made her way onto the dance floor with Frank as if she didn't have a moment to waste. Within seconds of them leaving the table

Naomi noticed that Bronwen exchanged glances with Sid before making excuses to visit the Ladies room.

Naomi couldn't wait for Ted to hurry back with the drinks and noticed that he was in deep conversation with two other men, whom she thought looked to be on the rough side. All of a sudden Sid broke into her thoughts by beckoning to her with his forefinger. Naomi bent closer so she could hear him speak above the sound of the music.

'I think it's about time a nice girl like you found out the truth about Ted, b.b.before it's too late,' he slurred, with desperation in his voice.

'What on earth are you talking about?' she asked, supposing it was the drink talking.

'Take a warning now there's no one around,' he said, hiccupping. 'You're keeping company with a married man who's recently been released from prison after serving a seven year jail sentence for almost killing a man.'

Naomi's stomach lurched. She looked at him stupefied. 'Don't be so daft. You've had too much to drink, you silly old fool.'

A sly grin crept over his face. 'I guessed you didn't know. b..because it's not something he'd brag about, is it?'

At that moment Ted turned up with the tray of drinks and Sid quickly jerked back in his seat, like a rat retreating into a hole.

Although shaken by what Sid had divulged, Naomi tried to remain composed in front of Ted, who was busily placing the drinks on the table. But the seeds of doubt had been planted and she began to wonder whether there was an element of truth in it after all. Worry and curiosity overwhelmed her as she sat sipping her fruit juice.

'You look as though you've seen a ghost,' Ted

teased, nudging her. 'Let's put some colour back in those cheeks with the next quickstep, is it?'

Before she could raise any objections Ted whisked her up from her chair. Her mind was racing frantically as they began to dance. What if Sid was telling the truth she thought to herself, not relishing the prospect that he was.

'What's the matter, Princess? You look miles away,' asked Ted, squeezing her hand.

'I'd like to leave early if it's alright with you,' she said, swallowing hard. 'I need to have a talk.'

'That's fine by me,' said Ted, his eyes twinkling. Then within seconds of the dance finishing they left the dance floor.

'I'm leaving now,' said Naomi, picking up her handbag from the table.

'There's a pity,' said Sid, looking slyly over at her. 'Better things to do, is it?'

Naomi could hardly bring herself to look at him and turned her attention to Patty, who was busily talking with Frank. 'I'm off now but I'll see you later. I need to have a chat with Ted,' she said, finding it hard to raise a smile.

'Enjoy yourselves then,' said Patty giving her a huge grin. 'Don't do anything that I wouldn't do,' she laughed, waving her off.

Having sex was the furthest thing from Naomi's mind. It was make or break time as far as she was concerned.

Once they were out in the car park Naomi climbed into Ted's car, her stomach churning. What if Sid had been spinning a yarn? All manner of thoughts ran through her mind.

'I know there's something the matter because you're not your normal cheery self. Is it because I haven't been down to see you lately? Only things have been awkward you see,' said Ted, trying to put his arm around her shoulder.

Naomi pushed him away.

'What's wrong, my lovely?' he asked, eyes wide.

'I've recently heard that you're a married man and have served a prison sentence for grievous bodily harm,' she blurted out.

There was a frosty silence as the clanger dropped. Naomi gritted her teeth as she waited for an answer.

'Who told you these things?' he asked, his face flaming angrily.

'That's for me to know and you to find out,' she snapped. 'I just want to know if it's true?' she demanded, banging the dashboard with her fist.

'I bet you a pound to a penny that pissed up Sid told you. He never could keep his mouth shut about anything. He's for it, I can tell you. And if you must know I'm married in name only because my wife befriended a local farmer when I was banged up for something I wasn't guilty of.'

Naomi forced herself to meet his eyes. 'Now let's get things straight, shall we? You don't sleep with your wife and you were put away for something you didn't do. Credit me with some sense, will you?' she cried, angrily. 'Anyway, why didn't you come clean about things before? You ought to have known that the truth would have come out at some time or another. It always does.'

Ted sat in silence for a minute looking at her sheepishly, whilst Naomi sat wringing her hands.

'To be perfectly honest, I couldn't stand the thought of losing you. You're the best thing that has happened to me since I left the Scrubs and I'm sorry if I haven't been around of late but I've had a lot of business to attend to.'

'Perhaps it's best I don't know about your business,'

she snorted, getting more angry by the minute. 'Is that the reason you hardly ever visited me when I was working down in Cardiff?' she cried, her eyes filling up with tears.

'Come on now, girl. Don't fret. I may have been a Jack the Lad in the past but that's all over now. Surely you can give me another chance. I helped you get rid of your old man, didn't I? And found you a place to live? That's got to be worth something,' he said, taking her hand.

Naomi tossed things over in her mind. She knew, deep down, she would be a fool to stick with him but she yearned for his love and, with a resigned sigh, fell into his arms.

'I love you and would never do anything to upset you, my darling,' he whispered in her ear.

CHAPTER 20

The following day Naomi received a letter from Duncan's solicitor stating that she would shortly be receiving a visit from an investigator as she had written an admission of her guilt regarding her adultery. It carried on to say that if she didn't oppose the divorce proceedings she would be granted custody of Philip.

Naomi was fully aware that she could hang Duncan by telling the court about the mental and physical cruelty he had inflicted upon her but because everything had happened behind closed doors with no witnesses she knew it was only her word against his. After much thought she telephoned his solicitors stating that she didn't intend to fight back because she wasn't taking the chance of losing her beloved son.

She felt evil about it all and screwed the letter up in her fist, seething to think that her husband had held the upper hand over her. But she was prepared to admit to anything so she could keep her child and thought it was well worth having her name dragged through the mud.

Several months later the divorce was finally granted. It was published in the local newspaper along with several other divorces in the area. It stated that Duncan had dissolved the marriage on the grounds of her adultery, naming Ted as the co-respondent.

Not long after that tongues began to wag in the street. Some of the neighbours, when passing her, looked at Naomi in disgust, as if she had the plague. To be divorced held a stigma in the valleys, making Naomi feel like a social outcast which did nothing for her self-esteem.

Shortly afterwards Naomi received a letter from the courts which stated that she had been awarded the sum of twelve shillings and sixpence in maintenance for Philip each month. This was a pittance as far as she was concerned but she knew, and delighted in the fact, that Duncan wasn't able to wriggle out of paying for his child as he would have if he'd had half a chance.

As she read down the document further her attention was drawn to a statement declaring that Duncan was to have reasonable access to Philip. Just the thought of him knocking her door every week was something she dreaded but she had a feeling it wouldn't last long, knowing Duncan as she did.

After making initial contact with Philip, and much to Naomi's relief, the visits stopped. Neither Duncan nor any of his family made any contact at all. As time went on there was not even a birthday or Christmas card sent to the child. It was as if he had ceased to exist.

Ted carried on visiting Naomi a few times a week but they rarely went out together. She felt plagued with a mixture of emotions knowing she had now become the *other woman.* She was saddened when there was no more mention of Ted divorcing his wife. Her name was never brought up and, for fear of losing him, she let the matter rest.

On the odd occasion Philip would come in contact with Ted but his visits were nearly always past the boy's bedtime so Naomi never felt she had to explain that he was anything more than a friend.

One evening Naomi decided to raise the subject of her adoption with Ted. As the years went on she'd found that the longing to search for her birth mother was always on her mind, like an underwater current.

'Did I ever mention that I was adopted?' she said, just as they were settling down together on the settee.

'I believe you did at some point. What of it?' asked Ted, staring into her eyes.

'Well, I was wondering whether you'd be interested in helping me search for my natural mother. The thought of her keeps coming up in my mind all the time and despite it being against the law I won't be able to rest until I find her.'

'What on earth do you want to do that for? You've always got me, my lovely.'

'Unless you've been through the adoption issue yourself you cannot possibly understand how it feels not to have known your roots,' she retorted, angered by his answer. She knew he didn't have a clue as to how she felt. It was beyond his comprehension.

'The way I look at it, I think the woman's made it plain enough that she didn't want you around. Otherwise why would she have had you adopted in the first place?' Ted pointed out.

His words hurt Naomi to the quick. She was tired of being knocked back time after time, and longed for someone to give her some support. 'Well, talking of getting shot of people, what's happening about your wife?' she cried, her eyes blazing.

Ted took a deep breath. 'Just you take my advice and let sleeping dogs lie where that's concerned,' he said, raising his voice. 'The times not right yet.'

'I'm sick to death of hearing that. So when is it going to be right, then?' she retorted, looking daggers at him.

'When I say so,' he snorted, pulling himself up from the settee. 'I'm off before I lose my temper with you.'

Naomi looked at him in shock and watched silently as he strode out of the house, like a man with a flea in his ear. She was sick of playing second fiddle and believed honesty and trust were vital in a relationship such as theirs. As long as he was married to another woman there could be no honesty as far as she was concerned. Also no future!

The next time Ted arrived at the door he was dressed in his best suit, black shirt and white tie. He surprised Naomi by suggesting that they went out for an evening to a nightclub in Cardiff. She jumped at the chance and, after arranging for Patty to keep an eye on Philip, she ran up the stairs to get changed.

The night club was bustling with people and the size of the place took Naomi's breath away. As she focused on the expensive looking outfits some of the women were wearing she wished she'd been able to dress in something more elegant but every penny was taken by the housekeeping bills and clothes for Philip now that he had grown into such a tall lad.

Ted ushered her to a table near the bar where she was introduced to a middle aged couple named Megan and Joe. They both looked at Naomi in surprise.

After shaking hands and loosening her coat, Naomi made herself comfortable on a seat alongside them while Ted went to the bar for some drinks. Naomi had asked for her usual pineapple juice but she noticed that everyone on the table seemed to be drinking shorts, and they were all well oiled.

When Ted returned he was accompanied by some other people. Naomi smiled at them and thought they were about the same age as herself. The man looked to be quite well off with his expensive looking suit and gold rings. A pretty young woman, with long black wavy hair, hung on his arm.

'This is Reg and Carol friends of mine,' announced Ted, beaming all over his face. 'And this is my friend, Naomi.'

All eyes focused on her.

'We've heard a lot about you,' said Carol, smiling. 'It's lovely to meet you at long last.'

That pleased Naomi as she wasn't sure that anyone in the company was aware of her relationship with Ted. As the evening wore on she felt more at ease as she joined in with the conversation. But before the night was over Ted stood up with the other men and finished his drink. 'See you later, sweetheart. Only I've business to see to. I've left some money behind the bar. So make sure you enjoy yourselves, ladies.' He winked at Naomi and, without further ado, the three men disappeared through the exit leaving a bewildered looking Naomi staring after them.

'Tell us about yourself, then,' said Megan, sipping at a large brandy. 'I'm Joe's fancy piece, you know, and have been for years.'

Naomi was amazed that she should admit such a thing to a comparative stranger, and just smiled.

'There's not much to tell really,' she said, spluttering over her drink. 'No doubt you all know about my relationship with Ted and, talking of the devil, where has he sneaked off to, may I ask?'

Carol ran her long painted nails through her hair, giggling. 'It's a renowned fact that the men are always out on business, or didn't you know? And we always back up their whereabouts come what may. Do you follow?'

'Business? What are you talking about?' asked Naomi, looking confused. She was positively bristling at being left behind.

'My, you are naïve,' said Megan smiling. 'I thought you would have figured things out by now, being a gangster's moll.'

The colour drained from Naomi's face. She couldn't believe her ears.

'Forget I said it,' announced Megan, leaning back in her chair. 'I can tell by the look on your face that you didn't know. Just remember it doesn't pay to ask questions where Ted's concerned. He's the type that will turn nasty at the drop of a hat.'

Naomi sat looking stupefied. She felt distinctly unsettled. What type of gangster was she going out with? And how many more sides were there to the man? she wondered, her heart thumping wildly. She had certainly fallen out of the frying pan into the fire.

CHAPTER 21

Early the next morning as Naomi was sweeping the front door step a young gypsy girl with long flowing dark hair and an abundance of gold rings on her fingers approached her.

'I can see that you've suffered much heartache and if you buy a bunch of my lovely flowers I'll tell your fortune for you.'

'How much are they?' Naomi asked, immediately interested.

'Half a crown to you, my girl, and that's cheap,' said the gypsy, thrusting a bunch of assorted flowers in front of her face. 'You should always cross a gypsies' palm with silver you know.'

Naomi immediately went inside and rummaged about in her purse. 'I've only a two shilling piece. Will that do?' she shouted down the hallway, hoping to barter with her.

The gypsy girl pursed her lips. 'You drive a hard bargain missus, but I suppose it will.'

After exchanging the flowers for the money she began staring deeply into Naomi's eyes. 'You'll be offered work soon, which will help money-wise and I can also tell by your eyes that you are psychic, like myself.'

Naomi had a job to stop herself from smiling thinking it a tall story but she let the gypsy girl carry on, living in the hope she might bring something up about her birth mother.

'I can sense you don't believe me so try reading the tea leaves one day for your friends. You may be in for a surprise. Just drain the cup of the dregs then swish it around three times towards you before emptying it out, but never read your own cup because it's bad luck.'

Naomi stared at her in silence taking it all in. Then

the gypsies' face grimaced. 'I can see danger around you concerning a married man. I'd be very careful if I were you, my dear.'

Naomi nearly choked. 'What sort of danger?'

'That I can't tell you, but take the gypsy warning to be true.'

Naomi gaped at her thinking it was a bold statement to make.

'I must be on my way now, dear, so *do* take care.' With a swish of her colourful skirt, the gypsy girl turned on her heel and crossed to the other side of the street, leaving Naomi pondering over what she'd said.

During the following months Patty's husband left his employment in the carpentry shop to work at the newly opened Spencer Steel Works in Newport. Good money was to be made there by working shifts. But to Naomi's dismay, Patty and her family decided to move down to Newport because they had been offered a reasonable priced property near the works.

Naomi felt completely lost without Patty to talk to but within a couple of weeks new neighbours moved into her old house. Houses didn't stay empty for long in the valleys. As soon as one became vacant it was snapped up.

Early one morning, just as Naomi was pegging out the washing, a short tubby little woman with dark hair cut into a bob beckoned to her over the garden wall.

'Hello, I'm Morfydd. My family and I have come down from Merthyr and to tell the truth I haven't got the house in order yet otherwise I would have invited you round for a cup of tea,' she said, with a beaming smile.

Naomi stared at the pretty looking woman guessing that she was probably well into her thirties.

'My name's Naomi and no doubt you'll have heard

me mentioned by the gossips in the street. But I'm not all bad you know,' she laughed.

'Yes, I did hear some tittle tattle, but always remember while they're talking about you they're leaving someone else alone,' said Morfydd, grinning. 'Anyway, I don't suppose you know of anyone who'd be interested in cooking lunch for my kids and tidying up round the house from Monday to Friday each week? Only I promised to help my sister out in one of the market cafés down in Newport for a few hours a day. My Evan had an accident down the pit so he's only able to do occasional light work. And with two boys growing up and a six year old daughter to contend with, duw, it's becoming harder by the day to make ends meet.'

'I'd be only too willing to help,' said Naomi, jumping at the idea. 'That's as long as I can bring my Philip along with me.'

'Of course you can,' said Morfydd. 'Call in tomorrow before eleven o'clock and I'll show you what needs doing. I'll only be able to give you a couple of bob though but you'll both be welcome to help yourselves to a cooked meal with the young 'uns.'

Naomi couldn't believe her ears and thought back to the gypsies' predictions. She hadn't expected a job to fall into her lap as easy as that and decided there and then to put the extra few shillings down on a new winter coat for Philip.

After finishing her first shift at Morfydd's Naomi found an invitation pushed through her door for Lucy Lewis's birthday party at four o'clock. She was surprised to have received an invite because the Lewis family were recent newcomers to the street. She thought it a lovely opportunity for Philip to mix with the other children and searched through the drawers for a clean shirt and trousers for him.

As the clock struck four Naomi took Philip across the road to the party. Within seconds of her knocking the door it was answered by a tall dark headed woman who invited her inside. 'Well, hullo there, do come in. I'm Lucy's mother and my name's Diane.'

Naomi smiled at her and sat gratefully on a chair that was offered to her in the front room whilst Philip was taken into the other room where the tea party was laid out.

She looked around and acknowledged two other people who were sitting on the settee, and strangers to her. She admired the furnishings which she thought would have put her place to shame. Her mouth watered as her eyes fell upon a huge plate of sandwiches and an assortment of home-made cakes which were laid on the coffee table.

'Help yourself to whatever you want,' said Diane, passing some china plates round. 'The children are in the capable hands of my parents so we'll have a chance of some quiet in here for a while.'

Naomi sat back in her chair, conscious that everyone's eyes were upon her, and wondered if her reputation had gone before her, like it always had.

'I've recently moved from the Canton area of Cardiff to live here and thought it would be nice to make acquaintance with the neighbours,' said Diane sweetly. 'This is Emily and Kathleen, my twin sisters,' she continued. 'Eat up there's plenty to be had.'

Naomi smiled at the twins, thinking they looked nothing alike, then took a few sandwiches and sipped her tea appreciatively, wishing she'd changed into something smarter than her everyday clothes.

'Is it true that you're the talk of the street?' blurted out Kathleen, a sly smile spreading across her face.

Naomi gave her a stern look and noticed Emily avoiding her gaze, as if embarrassed.

'It's a pity the neighbours have nothing better to do than gossip,' she said, bluntly, eyeing the girl with dislike.

'I say, did anyone buy a posy from the gypsy that called the other day?' Diane butted in. 'I wouldn't open the door when I saw who it was through the window. I've always been frightened of gypsies.'

'Is that so?' said Naomi, relieved to be able to steer the subject away from herself. 'She read my fortune you know and she told me that I had the gift myself and should try it out by reading tea-cups.'

All eyes were upon her.

'Never,' said Diane, pushing her empty tea-cup into her hand. 'Tell us what you see in there then.'

Everyone in the room pricked up their ears.

'By rights you're supposed to swish the tea that's left in the cup three times towards you, before pouring the dregs out,' Naomi spoke up feeling embarrassed at being put on the spot.

'There I've done it,' said Diane, pouring what was left of the tea in the cup out. 'Tell us what you see then,' she urged, her eyes looking wide with interest.

Naomi gazed into the cup and at first couldn't make head nor tail of the mass of tea leaves that were in there, until she held the cup further away from her face.

'I can see what looks like a car accident,' she said, turning the cup slowly around. In her mind's eye she saw what she thought to be a young man holding his head. 'I can see a man holding his head as if he's in pain. It's as plain as day.'

'No one I know owns a car. You'll be telling me next that I'm going to win the pools,' Diane giggled.

'Well, there's blood everywhere and I feel it's something to do with someone concerning you, so don't mock,' said Naomi, her eyes flashing.

'I think you're letting your imagination run wild.

None of it ties in with me,' said Diane, shaking her head.

Before Naomi could carry on the front room door burst open and everyone jumped as the children barged in.

'Thanks for the entertainment, gruesome as it was. I think that will be all for now,' smirked Kathleen, sniggering. 'Perhaps you'll be able to forecast brighter news next time.'

Naomi didn't argue. She was too shocked by what she'd seen, knowing full well it wasn't just a figment of her imagination.

A loud hammering on the front door woke Naomi early the following morning and, after throwing her dressing gown round her shoulders, she pulled back the door and was shocked to find Diane standing outside looking in a dreadful state.

'What on earth's the matter? You look awful,' she said, ushering her inside.

'My cousin's been badly injured in a road accident. Just like you described,' Diane sobbed. 'The car he was travelling in hit a pot hole as he was coming back from a night club. He has extensive head injuries.'

Naomi put her hand up to her mouth, totally flabbergasted.

'He'll be alright won't he? Say he will,' Diane said, almost begging.

Naomi wasn't happy that she was willing to hang on to her every word so just nodded, living in the hope that it would bring her some comfort. She was amazed at the accuracy of her prediction and within a few hours of Diane's visit, the news of Naomi's clairvoyance spread like wildfire down the street.

During the next few weeks, despite making light of the matter, a constant flow of people knocked at Naomi's door hoping that she would be able to predict their future. Apart from several of the churchgoers' labelling her as a witch, she was amazed at how popular she had become all of a sudden.

One afternoon just as Naomi and Philip were turning into the house after working at Morfydd's Naomi saw an old school friend walking down the street and called out to her. 'Well, Sarah Thomas! You were the last person I expected to see in this neck of the woods. You're still as trim as ever. Anyway, what are you up to these days?'

Sarah gave her a huge grin. 'I'm working shifts as a clippie on the buses. Good fun the lads are too. What about you?'

'Well, at the moment I'm reading tea-leaves for people, amongst other things. Would you believe it?'

'There was never a dull moment with you around,' laughed Sarah, running her fingers through her long black hair. 'What does you're husband have to say about that, then?'

'To be honest, I'm divorced and it's a long story which I'd rather not talk about.'

'I've never met anyone who's been divorced before. You always did like to be different. Anyway, who's the little chap, then?' Sarah asked, tweaking one of Philip's curls.

'This is my son, Philip, and he'll be starting school soon.'

Sarah bent down and patted the little lad on top of his head. 'You have got your hands full, haven't you? Do tell me more about your tea leaf reading. I've always been fascinated by such things.'

'Well, It all started when I predicted an accident that happened and it snowballed from there. I don't charge mind because it started off as being a bit of fun but I can actually see things happening in the cups you know.'

Sarah raised her eyebrows. 'Well, seeing as you're interested in that sort of thing, how do you fancy accompanying me up to the Spiritualist church down in Newport. One of the drivers on the buses told me there's a good medium speaking there tonight, and I didn't fancy going on my own.'

Naomi looked at her in surprise. 'I thought such things only went on in people's houses for fear of reprisals from the chapel ministers?'

'No, that's long gone now. Go on, say you'll come.'

'I'd love to,' said Naomi, excitedly, hoping there would be a chance of finding out something about her birth mother.

'Well, just make sure you're on the six o'clock bus into Newport and I'll meet you at the other end, is it?'

'Try stopping me,' laughed Naomi. 'Wild horses wouldn't keep me away. I'm really intrigued.'

On her return home she saw Diane cleaning her windows and ran over to her. 'Could you mind Philip tonight for a while? Only I've promised to go down to the Spiritualist church in Newport with an old friend of mine. We shouldn't be too long.'

Diane looked at her horrified. 'I wouldn't have the nerve to enter one of those places if you paid me. Anyway, if I keep an eye on Philip perhaps you'd be kind enough to read my cup for me again. But what if Ted appears on the scene? Am I to say anything to him?'

'Not on your Nellie,' said Naomi, shaking her head. 'He's not keen on me reading the tea leaves as it is, so don't you dare breathe a word to him or he'll have my guts for garters.'

'You're secret's safe with me,' laughed Diane, giving her a broad grin. 'You can bring young Philip over as soon as you're ready.'

Naomi thanked her profusely. She was thoroughly

looking forward to her evening out. Her trips with Ted had been few and far between of late.

When the bus eventually pulled into Newport town centre the two girls met up and made their way through the streets towards Charles' Street. After linking arms they slowly trudged up the steep hill towards the church. Both women were out of puff by the time they were near the top of the hill and stopped momentarily to regain their breath. Naomi didn't have the slightest clue as to what to expect but hoped she'd receive a message of some sort before the service finished.

'Well, it's now or never,' said Sarah, stepping inside the church. 'Come on then. There's nothing to be frightened of,' she urged Naomi, tugging at her arm.

Naomi followed her inside and stared around. She didn't think the building looked any different to the Welsh Baptist chapel she'd attended in her teens.

'I want to sit near the back,' said Sarah, 'so I can see everything that goes on.'

'More likely to make a quick exit, if needed,' whispered Naomi, grinning at her.

After they'd made themselves comfortable on the pew Naomi stared around at the congregation and was surprised to see people who looked to have come from all walks of life sitting there.

The service began with a hymn and both girls stood up to join in the singing. Then, after a prayer was said, a smartly dressed middle aged lady stepped up onto the rostrum, introducing herself as the resident medium. All eyes were upon her as she gave an introductory talk. She then went on to explain that life on earth was a school of learning and a medium was likened to being a radio transmitter, connected between two planes of existence, which enabled people like herself to pass messages from loved ones to people on the earth plane via the help of her spirit guide.

Sarah and Naomi sat transfixed to their seats, digesting her every word. And when the medium began to communicate with the spirit world Naomi prayed that she would call on her and nearly jumped out of her skin when she directed her hand towards Sarah.

'I have a young man who tells me that he died in a motor bike accident. I'm hearing the name of Tom. Can you place him please?'

Naomi could see her friend was startled and gave her a nudge.

'Yes, I can place him,' Sarah said, catching her breath.

'He's saying that he drove into a lorry and was killed instantly.'

Naomi watched her friend closely waiting to see her reaction.

'That's correct,' said Sarah, her eyes filling up. 'He was a friend of mine who was an atheist. We'd often had heated discussions about the after-life and he promised to make contact with me if he went over first, so he could tell me if people's souls lived on.'

The medium smiled at her. 'Well he knows different now, he's saying.'

Sarah thanked her for the message and Naomi could see by the look in her eyes that she was greatly moved.

After giving several more messages to various people in the congregation the medium finished speaking. Then the final hymn was sung and the meeting ended with a prayer before everyone left to go their separate ways.

Naomi linked arms with Sarah as they stepped out of the church. 'I was really disappointed not to have had a message. Still, there's always another week, isn't there.'

'Well, to be honest, I'm flabbergasted about it all. Tom and I were great pals and I can remember what happened as if it was yesterday. I was riding pillion on my boyfriend's bike and saw everything. It was dark and the rain was lashing down in sheets. It must have been all over in a couple of seconds,' said Sarah, sadly.

Naomi looked at her friend shocked. She was quite taken aback by it all and would certainly be returning.

During the months that followed, Naomi and Sarah became extremely interested in Spiritualism and were regular visitors to the church. The services became a lifeline to Naomi and it helped her renew her faith in God.

CHAPTER 22

When Philip was five he began his schooling. Naomi felt extremely lonely without him during the day but was glad to see he was enjoying himself and making new friends.

One morning, after dropping Philip outside the school, she bumped into a friend of her Aunt Maud's who told her that her aunt was very ill in hospital, with cancer. Naomi was shocked and, although she was aware that her aunt wanted nothing more to do with her because of the way she had conducted herself she decided to pluck up the courage to visit her. She felt she owed her that at least.

After finishing her chores at Morfydd's Naomi caught the bus to the hospital, armed with a bunch of flowers.

On arriving there she was shown into a sideward and told by the sister not to stay long because her aunt was extremely weak.

Naomi was relieved to see there were no other visitors around so pulled up a chair beside the bed. Her aunt seemed to be asleep and Naomi was saddened to see how ill she looked. She wished she'd patched things up with her instead of foolishly keeping away, but she had been too ashamed and frightened to make the first move.

After placing the flowers on the locker, she noticed her aunt's eyelids flicker and bent over her in order to make her presence known. 'Hullo, Aunt Maud. How are you?' she asked, with trepidation, hoping her aunt wouldn't shy away from speaking to her.

Her aunt reciprocated by opening her eyes and giving her a weak smile. 'I'm glad you're here because there's something you should know before I die,' she whispered in a croaky voice.

'What is it?' asked Naomi, catching hold of her hand.

'The man named on your birth certificate is not your real father. But money was passed to our May after she'd adopted you during the war years - from your birth father's family. They wanted it all hushed up. Good family they were see, and they didn't want it to be known that their son had got entangled with the likes of your birth mother.'

'Is that so?' said Naomi, taking her every word in.

The old woman took a deep breath. 'Although your mother was married at the time she liked the men and before clearing off with one of them she left you behind in a home.'

Naomi gaped at her in amazement. She felt her aunt's hand tighten round hers, as she drew herself up in the bed. 'God knows what would have happened if my sister hadn't taken you in. Your birth mother was a bad lot and if she's fortunate enough to be buried in a Christian graveyard may God bless her soul and forgive her for her sins.' Her voice began to trail off.

Naomi clutched at her chest, shocked rigid. There were so many questions she needed to ask her aunt about things but she could tell by her laboured breathing that she wasn't up to it.

'I must ask you to leave now, because it's time for your aunt's medication,' said the staff nurse beckoning to her. 'Perhaps it would be best if you rang the hospital in the morning to see how things are.'

Naomi rose from her chair with a heavy heart. Her head was reeling as she thought over her aunt's words, and she hoped she would find out some more information the following day.

The next morning Naomi telephoned the hospital asking how her aunt was. She was devastated to hear that she had passed away during the early hours of the morning.

Feeling an outcast, as she had done so for many years, she thought it best not to attend her funeral for fear of reprisals from other members of the family. She would have found that hard to deal with. The picture of her birth mother was becoming all too clear in her mind and she began to realise why so many people had shunned away from talking about the subject. Despite it all she was just as determined as ever to seek her out one day so she could lay the ghost to rest.

The next day Joe and Megan turned up unexpectedly at the door shortly after Naomi had put Philip to bed.

'It's so nice to see you. I was just about to put the kettle on,' Naomi said, ushering them inside.

'In actual fact we called on the off chance that you might fancy having a drink with us at your local. Only Joe's got business there and I don't fancy sitting on my own in a strange pub, like a lemon,' Megan said, pulling a face.

'I'd be delighted to. I could do with being cheered up but I'll have to clear things with my neighbour first to see if she will keep an eye on my little boy.'

As soon as Diane arrived Naomi changed into her tidy clothes and, after giving her rich auburn curls a quick brush, she left the house looking forward to a chat with her friends.

Once they were inside the pub Naomi and Megan found seats near the piano, while Joe went over to fetch the drinks from a crowded bar.

'Sure you only want a pineapple juice?' asked Megan. 'I'm paying for the round, not Joe.'

'No that will do nicely thank you,' said Naomi. 'I was never one for shorts but I'm curious to know, if Joe's your man-friend how come you're paying for the drinks?'

'Well, I'm the one with the money, see. I'm a rich widow and all that. Still, he's good fun to be with so I don't mind.'

Naomi looked at her dumbstruck, wondering what a fashionably dressed woman like Megan saw in Joe. He was only a puny man, half her size and with no looks to speak of.

Just as the pianist struck up a tune Joe appeared with a tray of drinks. 'I'm off to have a chat with an old crony of mine. Won't be long, girls,' he said, grinning like a Cheshire cat.

'That means the duration,' sighed Megan, giving him a black look. 'He's always up to something, that man. Wheeler-dealer should have been his middle name.'

'How long has he been friendly with Ted then?' asked Naomi, hoping to glean some information from her.

'He and Joe were in the Marines together during the last war, where they had a fine time by all accounts. I don't ask what goes on between them because it's best to let sleeping dogs lie as far as those two buggers are concerned,' she replied, grimacing.

Naomi thought it wise not to comment so changed the subject to other things. If the truth was known she was having second thoughts about Ted but was at a loss as how to end the relationship.

Later in the evening the rear door of the lounge opened and Joe came back inside looking half cut. With a glass of whisky in his hand, he plonked himself beside Megan trying his hardest to sit up straight in his seat.

Megan and Naomi left him to it while they gave a rendering of *I'll take you home again Kathleen*, at the piano. Everyone clapped them and Naomi felt elated. It was the best night out she'd had in ages.

When they returned to their seats, they found Joe sprawled in his chair, looking as if he was about to fall asleep.

'Why don't you both come back to the house for a night cap? I'd be glad of the company and might even read your tea cup, Joe,' giggled Naomi.

'So you're a witch, then? I would never have thought it,' said Joe, swaying as he got out of his chair.

'There's nothing I'd like better than to hear his future,' laughed Megan. It should prove interesting.'

The three of them traipsed arm in arm down the back streets together and, on reaching her front door, Naomi was relieved not to see Ted's car parked outside. She thought he might well have caught her out and knew he wouldn't have approved, being the possessive man he was.

On stepping inside Naomi could see by the frightened look on Diane's face that something was up.

'What's the matter, girl?' she asked, hoping that Philip hadn't played her up.

'Well, I never heard a peep out of your lad, but I'm sure your house is haunted. I kept hearing strange noises, like some-one walking the stairs.' she said, shuddering.

'Duw!' said Naomi, looking flustered. She didn't want to elaborate as she had often heard the same thing but tried to make light of the matter fearing she would lose her sitter. Before she could say another word Diane ran out of the door as if the devil himself was behind her, leaving Naomi standing in the doorway open mouthed.

After closing the door behind her she took Megan and Joe into the kitchen where the remains of a blazing fire still glowed. They both sat warming their hands whilst Naomi hurried into the scullery to make a pot of tea.

A few minutes later she returned with a tray of tea and custard cream biscuits. And it wasn't long before Joe waved his cup in the air giggling like a fool. 'Come on then, girl. Let's see what you're made of!'

Naomi sat beside him on the settee, while Megan sat in the armchair, trying to stifle her giggles.

'Swill your cup round three times towards you then pour out the remaining dregs into the saucer, please,' said Naomi, trying her best to look serious despite his larking around.

Joe did as he was told then put the cup into her hand. 'Am I going to win on the gee-gees this week?' he cried, grinning all over his face. 'They used to burn people like you at the stake, you know.'

'Is that so?' said Naomi, trying her hardest to concentrate on what she was doing. For a second the lights flickered.

'My God, what was that?' cried Megan, looking all round her.

'Nothing to worry about, it's only my spirit friends telling me they're near.'

Joe burst out laughing, and quickly lit up a cigarette, whilst Megan's face went chalk white.

'I can see a dark headed man handing you some cards Joe, so I suggest you watch your step in work.'

'Never mind about cards, girl. Might it be a fat juicy cheque being handed to me by the Bookies?'

Naomi and Megan broke down into fits of laughter and weren't aware of the front door opening. As Naomi stared once more into the cup everyone jumped as Ted, with a face like thunder, flung the living room door wide open.

'Been having a good time at the pub, have we? I've heard all about you making an exhibition of yourself singing,' he shouted, bringing his fist down onto the living room table.

Before Naomi could answer, Megan immediately jumped out of her chair to her defence. 'What of it? The girl was doing no harm.'

Without any warning Ted stepped towards Megan and smacked her across the face with the back of his hand. The force of his blow sent her tea-cup flying, and she fell sprawling onto the floor.

Joe did his best to intervene but was no match for Ted who was twice his size.

'Leave well alone,' growled Ted, like a demented hound.

Megan pulled herself up from the ground, holding her jaw.

'We've done nothing wrong,' spluttered Naomi in a hoarse voice.

Pushing Megan aside Ted turned towards Naomi, pointing his car keys at her.

Fear gripped at the pit of her stomach.

'You don't ever frequent public houses unless you're with me or I'll kill you stone dead.' Screwing up his face in fury he suddenly leapt towards her.

Naomi let out one almighty scream, and ran through the back door, terrified. In fright she jumped over the garden gate like an experienced hurdler, then continued running like a frightened rabbit through the dimly lit streets looking for refuge.

Her lungs began to feel as if they were going to burst any minute so she stopped to take shelter in a shop doorway. Panting for breath she suddenly thought of her son asleep in bed and gasped. She was scared of what could be happening in her absence. After regaining her breath she made her way back home. A bitter wind had risen and by the time she reached the corner of the street she was chilled to the bone.

Her eyes searched the area for Ted's car but, much to her relief, it was nowhere to be seen.

At the front door she stiffened at the sight of broken glass strewn all over her front doorstep. She felt for the spare key that was dangling on a piece of string inside the letter box, and opened the door, fearing the worst. In a panic she ran up the stairs afraid that Ted might be lurking in the shadows. For some unknown reason she'd always been fearful every time she looked into the blackness at the turn of the staircase, feeling someone was watching her. Choked with fear she opened her son's bedroom door and fell to her knees, thanking God that he was fast asleep.

After several minutes of hearing no movement downstairs she stealthily crept down, fully expecting Ted to jump out at her, but the room was just as she'd left it with the smashed pieces of the cup lying on the floor.

She slumped down on the kitchen chair, dazed with shock. She wanted to be rid of Ted now he had shown her his true colours but she was fully aware how dangerous a task it would be to accomplish.

Early the following morning Megan appeared on the doorstep sporting a huge bruise down the side of her face. 'Thank God you're still in one piece,' she said. 'I had visions of you being laid out in a mortuary. Ted meant business you know. He's known for being dangerous when roused and in drink.'

'What happened out the front?' asked Naomi pointing to the broken glass. 'I'll have to sweep it up shortly, before anyone cuts themselves,' she said, kicking it to one side with her foot.

'It was a dreadful shindig,' said Megan walking inside. 'Joe tried to make a getaway, like you, but Ted caught up with him and smashed the empty milk bottle from the front door step over his head. Then, not content with that he punched him in the jaw breaking Joe's false teeth.'

Naomi's eyes were as big as saucers. 'Why on earth didn't you call the police?'

'He's not the sort of man you snitch on without repercussions. Believe me I know him of old. Anyway, wait until my family see the state of my face. I don't know how on earth I'm going to explain it away.'

Naomi grimaced. 'Thank God Joe drew him out of the house. It doesn't bear thinking about what could have happened. And I'd love to know who tipped him off about us being in the pub.'

'Well, what of it?' said Megan, peevishly. 'He'd no right to do what he did. It's not as if we were up to anything.'

'This is the final straw for me, you know,' said Naomi, sticking her chin out forcefully. 'It's time he and I parted company.'

'He's bad news, so you be careful, my girl,' Megan cried, shaking her head.

'One thing's for sure, Megan, he's not going to rule me any longer. I fully intend giving him his marching orders, in no uncertain terms, when he calls round tonight.'

'Have you gone off your rocker, girl? It won't be as easy as that, I can tell you, especially if he's got the whisky in him.'

Naomi didn't care. She made her mind up that she would be rid of Ted that night, without a doubt, come hell or high water.

Shortly after putting her son to bed she heard Ted's key turn in the lock and ran to the hallway to greet him, with her hands on her hips. She uttered a quick prayer as he came in through the door.

'What are we doing waiting in the hall for? Thinking of doing a runner again?' he jested, smiling all over his face.

'To be perfectly honest I was horrified at your

performance last night so I think it's best if I have my key back. I've had my fill of being told what to do by a married man.'

'Is that so?' Ted sneered, raising his eyebrows. A deathly silence enveloped the hall as Ted stood silently nodding.

Naomi could feel a cold sweat breaking out on her brow as she waited for his response. Her heart was beating nineteen to the dozen.

Ted's eyes narrowed. 'Well, if that's the way you want things, so be it,' he snapped, throwing the key in the air towards her.

Naomi snatched it quickly, and was amazed when he quietly turned on his heel out of the door. She couldn't believe her eyes and hadn't expected things to go so smoothly.

She heard his car pull away. There was no turning back now. But she felt it had all been too easy somehow.

CHAPTER 23

After Naomi had finished her chores at Morfydd's she hurried home with the intentions of making a cheese and onion pie before collecting Philip from school. Just as she was preparing the potatoes a loud knock on the front door startled her. She wasn't expecting visitors so glanced through the front room window and was delighted to see Carol, Reg's wife, standing outside looking more than a little pregnant.

'There's wonderful to see you. I never noticed you were pregnant last time I saw you, when I was out shopping with Philip in Newport.'

'I was probably wearing my swagger coat which hides a multitude of sins,' laughed Carol. 'Anyway, I've only a few weeks to go and needed to speak to you about something.'

'Well, lay yourself out on the settee and I'll make you a nice cup of tea,' said Naomi, fussing over her like a mother hen. 'You won't get much chance to rest after the baby's born.'

Carol did as she was told and took a huge sigh. 'I wasn't certain where you lived otherwise I would have visited before. Then I found out from Megan that you have been having trouble and she gave me your address. Only my Reg told me this morning that you've finished with Ted and I thought it only right to warn you what you could be in for.'

Naomi pulled a face. 'What do you mean *in* for? He gave me back his key and left without a backward glance.'

Carol's face took on a grim look. 'He's as sly as a fox, that one,' she warned, rolling her eyes. 'Reg and I have known him much longer than you and to be truthful he's got too much on my Reg for them to break company.'

'Never!' said Naomi, looking concerned. 'Well, he's got nothing on me and I'd call for the police if there were any shenanigans.'

'The police won't worry him,' cried Carol, pulling a face. 'Just you be careful, and watch your back.'

Naomi accepted what she was saying. She knew what an idiot she had been by going out with Ted in the first place. At the first hint of danger she intended to up sticks and leave but she hoped it wouldn't come to that.

'Thanks for the advice. By the way, before I forget, I've some wool going spare so how would you like me to make the baby some matinee jackets?' she asked, going over to the Welsh dresser.

Before Carol could answer there was a knock on the front door. Carol quickly heaved herself off the settee onto her feet. 'What if it's Ted?'

'Don't talk so daft. It's most probably my next door neighbour wanting to borrow something.'

Carol raised her eyebrows, and backed into the corner looking worried.

As she opened the door Naomi gasped at the sight of Ted standing there, one foot firmly planted on the step.

'What do you want?' she asked, trying hard not to show her fear.

'Aren't you going to ask me in then?' he said with a sly look on his face.

Her stomach lurched as she smelt the stench of drink on his breath.

'I believe I've left my navy donkey jacket behind. I can't find it anywhere.'

'I haven't seen it but I'll go inside and check for you,' said Naomi, trying hard not to antagonise him.

His shifty eyes narrowed in anger as she walked down the hall. Just as she entered the living room a blow from his fist sent her flying across the room.

Naomi began to scream at the top of her voice, and

she tried to scramble on all fours into the scullery, hoping to escape through the back door. But before she could get there Ted kicked her down onto the paved stone floor and began beating her with his clenched fists.

'Stop it. Stop it,' she cried, clawing desperately at the door like a trapped animal.

'Let me instil this into your brain, my lovely. If I can't have you, no-one else will. Do you hear?' growled Ted, in a low menacing tone.

In the frenzy of the moment he failed to see an ashen-faced Carol clinging onto the back of the chair in the corner of the living room.

Naomi was terrified but before she could plead with him any more Ted grabbed her by the throat and slammed her up against the scullery wall.

'Have you any last wishes?' he whispered in her ear, as he drew a knife from his inside jacket pocket. For a second their eyes locked.

Naomi's heart began beating twenty to the dozen. She was in no doubt that she was about to die. As she felt the sharp edge of the blade penetrate her skin her face contorted in terror.

'Stop! It's all been a mistake. I want you back. I didn't mean the things I said,' she cried, petrified. 'I saw Reg and told him so.'

Suddenly there was a blood curdling scream from Carol who was hunched up in the corner. Ted spun on his heel and let go of Naomi, then made a quick exit through the door.

Naomi fell in a heap on the floor.

Carol took to her heels and ran up the road looking for help but the shock of it all had been too much for her. She was struck dumb. As she reached the grocers, at the top of the street, Mark, the owner could see the state she was in and made her sit down on a chair. After giving her a sweet cup of tea she managed to say, 'I think my friend's been murdered.'

Mark called to his wife, Gwyneth, to take over serving saying there had been an emergency. The grocer's wife came rushing into the shop and wanted to know more about things but Mark left her to serve the waiting customers without a word of explanation.

Carol was fully aware that the slim shouldered grocer would be no match for Ted and hoped he would be well and truly gone from the scene when they arrived.

After cautiously opening the front door Carol and Mark stopped in their tracks at the sight of Naomi's body lying on the scullery floor.

'The bastard's killed her,' yelled Carol, wringing her hands in despair.

'I'm having no part of this,' cried the grocer, stepping back horrified. 'I've heard all about the man she's involved with.'

'I don't believe I'm hearing this. We just can't leave her here,' groaned Carol, who looked about to faint.

'She's asked for all she got, if the truth was known, getting mixed up with the likes of him. She's been the talk of the neighbourhood for years, you know.'

'Shush!' cried Carol, bending over Naomi's body. 'I'm sure I saw her breathe. I've got smelling salts in my bag.'

After rummaging for the salts Carol waved them under Naomi's nose and within seconds she sighed with relief as Naomi began to come around.

'My God I thought my end had come,' Naomi sobbed, clutching at her blood stained throat.

'It's a wonder I didn't have this baby right here on the spot,' cried Carol. 'I thought Ted had killed you.'

'Let's get her up on her feet,' said Mark, looking relieved. 'We'll lay you on the settee, is it?'

Naomi nodded, gingerly hanging onto Carol. 'I must have passed out with shock. Anyway, where's Ted gone? My Philip needs collecting from school and Ted might try and snatch him.'

'You're in no fit state to pick the boy up. I'll do it and I think it's best if you come back to my house because Ted might still be hanging about,' urged Carol, as she picked up her car keys from the table.

Mark took her to the door and explained the quickest way to drive to the school. So Carol jumped in the driving seat of her Triumph Herald and drove like a maniac up the road.

Despite her spinning head Naomi managed to make it into the scullery where she did her best to wipe all traces of blood from her face and neck with a wet flannel. Whilst Mark paced the room, keeping an eye open for Ted.

Naomi felt slightly better after her cold wash and went back into the living room, slumping down on the nearest chair.

Mark looked across the room at her, shaking his head. 'Duw! You sure choose the bounders, don't you?' he exclaimed. 'It was common knowledge that your ex-husband was playing around down in Cardiff when you were married. To be honest, I never liked the man and wouldn't have trusted *him* with my dog.'

'Well, you always find out these things when it's too late,' Naomi nodded feebly. 'Still, this has taught me a lesson. I'm never bothering with men again.'

'I've heard that one before,' chuckled Mark, trying his best to cheer her up.

Naomi was glad he had stayed with her because she was terrified of Ted returning. She touched her neck with her fingers and could feel the wound from the knife was still bleeding. She had never been so close to death before and knew she was lucky to be alive.

As Carol was parking the car on the road near the school her stomach lurched as she spied Ted waiting in a nearby shop doorway. She was taking no chances and hurried over to the school gates just as the children were making their way out.

Carol knew Ted had the advantage because Philip hardly knew her and she hoped with all her heart that she would be able to get to him first. Suddenly she noticed Philip ambling along and hurriedly went up to him to introduce herself.

'Remember me? I'm your mother's friend, Carol. She's not well and she's asked me to collect you,' she said, taking hold of the child's hand.

Philip stared at her and hung back. Carol could see he was hesitant but knew there was no time to delay. Glancing across the road she saw that Ted had disappeared from the shop doorway. She began to panic.

'I've got a lovely car but we have to be quick,' urged Carol, looking all around her.

'I want my Mammy,' cried Philip, standing his ground.

'Listen, there's a bad man after us so we have to hurry,' she implored, pulling the child along the pavement beside her. With a look of reluctance on his face Philip did as he was told. But when Carol bundled him into the front of the car and pushed some sweets into his hand their friendship was clinched.

Carol started up the car and drove as fast as she could through the streets until she was forced to slow down at a junction. Looking into her mirror her eyes rounded with fear at the sight of Ted's car following closely behind. As she continued driving she could feel beads of sweat breaking out on her forehead as he tried to overtake her. Just at that moment, as if out of nowhere, a lorry pulled out of a side street and shot in front of Ted barring his way.

'Yes,' cried Carol triumphantly, watching the incident in the rear view mirror. Then her mouth fell as she saw Ted jump out of his car and drag the driver from his cab, punching him to the ground. This hold up was all she needed. With Lady Luck on her side she put her foot down and quickly arrived outside Naomi's house. Pushing past Mark at the door she called for Naomi to gather her things as there was no time to lose.

Naomi did as she was told and stumbled into the back of the car clutching a flannel to her neck.

Philip turned to look at her. 'What's wrong, Mammy? Why is your neck bleeding?' he asked, looking worried.

'I fell in the scullery, that's all,' said Naomi, trying her best to make it appear that everything was alright.

Mark was pacing the pavement outside the house keeping a look out for Ted. Naomi thanked him for his kindness then waved to him as the car began to disappear up the street.

Carol drove back to Cardiff as if Old Nick himself was after her, while Naomi sat with her arm around Philip, nursing her cuts and bruises.

Half way through the journey Carol turned on the radio just in time to hear a commentator speak about a dreadful disaster that had happened south of Merthyr Tydfil in a village called Aberfan. After several days of heavy rain a coal tip had slipped down a mountain engulfing a farm, several houses and a school. Hundreds had been killed.

'Hearing that makes what happened to me seem quite paltry,' cried Naomi, as her eyes began to flood with tears.'

Carol agreed with her and drove the rest of the journey in silence.

At long last they came to a stop outside a semi-detached house on the outskirts of Cardiff.

Carol led Naomi and her son inside and was astounded to see Reg looking in a dreadful state in the kitchen. She quickly ushered Philip out the garden to play knowing full well that he was listening to their every word.

'That bastard Ted came down the works after me, swinging an iron bar in his hand. So what's been going on may I ask?' he snorted, looking angrily at his wife.

'Naomi was about to have her throat slit by Ted. She had to tell him something to stop him. I was there and heard it all,' cried Carol. 'It's a wonder I didn't have the little 'un on the spot.'

'Well, it took three men to get that bastard off me and I can generally handle myself well. He was like a madman and kept shouting that Naomi had told *me* to tell him that she wanted to make things up with him. I didn't have a clue as to what he was on about. '

'I never dreamed he would go after you,' said Naomi, feeling choked.

Carol put the kettle on and made them all tea. The warmth of the drink did nothing to ease Naomi's inner turmoil. She was safe for the time being but dreaded the thought of returning home.

When she woke the following morning memories of the previous days events flooded through her mind. Although feeling rested she still ached all over and was surprised no bones had been broken.

She got up from the bed and looked aghast at the sight of her black eye in the dressing table mirror. Her thin frail body was covered in bruises but despite this she knew she was lucky to be alive.

'Breakfast is ready,' said Carol, poking her head round the door. 'Only Philip's already had his breakfast and has gone next door to play with their young lad, so we've time to talk.'

'How are you feeling?' Naomi asked her, thinking Carol looked awfully pale.

'I'm still in a state of shock, but never mind. Hurry up downstairs because my Reg is busy cooking bacon and egg for us all.'

Naomi was not used to eating breakfast although she always made sure Philip had something substantial inside him before he went to school. To be waited on for a change would be heaven, she thought to herself as she washed and dressed.

'My God, there's a lovely shiner,' said Reg when Naomi sat down at the breakfast table. 'You're lucky to be in the land of the living my girl.'

Naomi nodded. 'For one minute I thought the nightmare that Ted often spoke about was about to come true.'

Reg passed her breakfast across the table to her. 'What nightmare's that then?'

'Well Ted and another man were supposedly disposing of a woman's body in some woods where he once lived. Apparently, this dream always came back to haunt him and he truly believed that it was a premonition of something that was yet to happen.'

Reg roared with laughter. 'That man's not frightened of anything. I expect he said that just to wind you up.'

Naomi pulled a face. 'Maybe so, but it got me thinking that something horrible might happen to either me or his wife. I feel so sorry for the poor wretch having to live with him.'

'It's a bit late for that now. You shouldn't have got caught up with Ted in the first place, should you?' Reg retorted.

Naomi was fully aware she had made an incredible mess of her life and desperately wanted to turn it around from then on, for Philip's sake as well as her own.

The following day Carol's mother arrived to stay for the confinement. Naomi knew they'd have precious little room for her and Philip so, after enjoying Sunday lunch together, Reg and Carol drove them both home.

Her nerves jangled as she walked in through the front door with Philip. The house didn't hold happy memories for her. One day when she'd saved enough money she intended having an electric light fitted on the landing, because she loathed treading the stairs in the dark. The smell of rising damp, a galvanised bath and an outside lavatory were the hardships of living in the back streets but a life far away from this and living with her birth mother was her dearest wish, if only it could come true. In her mind she envisaged a fairy-tale existence with the woman she so longed to meet. She wished with all her heart that some day she'd find her, despite everything her aunt had said.

How was she going to live in the house without fearing the next knock at the door she wondered to herself? After mulling things over in her mind she decided to seek advice from a solicitor, and quickly.

The next day Naomi contacted Megan in order to find out Ted's address. Then after she dropped Philip off at school she caught the bus into town. She was surprised to get an appointment with a solicitor within the hour and, with her stomach in knots, she sat down opposite a young, well groomed man who listened intently to her tale.

From time to time he looked at her gravely and began to scribble notes on a pad.

'Ted wants to own me body and soul, you see,' she said, wringing her hands. 'But I'm terrified to walk the streets as things are.'

The solicitor looked sympathetically at her. 'Well, as you don't wish to proffer charges because of what might happen to the other people involved the only alternative is to send this man a letter stating that if he continues to pester you he could well be in line for a prison sentence, taking into consideration his previous record.'

Naomi's face lit up. 'Thank God something is being done at long last,' she sighed. She rose to her feet, feeling much relieved, and after shaking hands on the matter she returned home hoping that the solicitor's measures would prove successful.

CHAPTER 24

Life improved for Naomi over the next few months and, much to her relief, Ted was nowhere to be seen. There was no more looking over her shoulder in fear anymore. She felt as free as a bird.

One afternoon while Naomi was shopping at the grocers, Mark, the owner approached her and offered her a job as counter assistant. One of his girls had left suddenly due to ill health.

Naomi looked at him dumbstruck. She was quite taken aback.

'Well, what have you got to say for yourself then? Only I need someone to start as soon as possible and as you only live round the corner you could fall out of bed and into work. And if it's little Philip you're worrying about my Gwyneth can collect him from school with our little one. They'll be able to play in the back room until you finish your shift. The same will apply to school holidays as well.'

Naomi couldn't believe her luck. At long last she wouldn't have to rely on meagre handouts from the government.

'Yes, I'd be delighted to work for you but I'll have to give my notice to Morfydd down the street first. I do a few hours a week cooking and cleaning for her, you see, but this is more permanent which is just what I was hoping to find.'

After telling Morfydd about her new job offer Naomi carried on working until the weekend. Morfydd told her she was sorry to see her leave as the children were quite taken with her but she understood and would have done the same if she had been in her place.

On her first day at the grocers Naomi was introduced to Mrs Jenkins, Mark's other shop assistant, who was a buxom woman with a ready smile and greying hair arranged in a bun at the top of her head.

'Mrs Jenkins will show you the ropes. You'll be working alongside her most of the time which will give me chance to see to some other business I've got in hand.'

Within a matter of minutes Naomi had served her first customer with a few slices of bacon and half a dozen eggs. She was surprised at how under Mrs Jenkins' watchful eyes she had mastered the bacon machine without taking off any of her fingers.

As the hours went by she noticed a few of the older neighbours raise eyebrows in disapproval when they saw her standing behind the counter but she carried on, trying her hardest not to take any notice and wishing she could live her reputation down.

One evening Naomi was surprised to find Emily, Diane's sister, on her doorstep looking like a frightened mouse.

'I've something on my mind I've been longing to share with you because I'm not allowed to bring the subject up at home, and I know you of all people would understand,' she said, with some urgency in her voice.

Naomi could tell by her furrowed brow she was troubled and ushered her inside.

Emily perched herself on the edge of the settee, twisting her hands together, looking nervous.

'What can I do for you, Emily?' said Naomi, looking concerned.

'I need to speak with you because I've a secret I think you should know.'

Naomi nodded, wondering what on earth she was going to tell her next.

'Well, I also had a baby about the same time as you,' Emily blurted out, 'only my parents wouldn't let me keep it. They insisted that I should be sent away to a home for unmarried mothers so as not to create a scandal.'

Naomi stared at her dumbfound.

'I needed to get if off my chest before I explode, and knew you wouldn't think badly of me like other people would have.' Her eyes filled with tears as she bit into her bottom lip. 'I think it's dreadful how everyone talks about you when they've probably got skeletons in their own cupboards.'

'Rest assured whatever you tell me won't go any further. Anyway, what was it like in the unmarried mothers' home? I was also offered the chance of going into one.'

Emily pulled a face and shuffled around on the settee. 'Think yourself lucky that you didn't because it was only a step away from the workhouse. I'll never forget what went on there for as long as I live.'

'Why was that?' Naomi asked.

'Every day from dawn to dusk, me and the other unmarried mothers were made to clean the huge old mansion house that housed us - brushing, mopping, dusting, scrubbing and polishing, until we were all totally exhausted. It was part of our punishment, you see.'

Naomi raised her eyebrows in horror as the expression on Emily's face grew more tragic.

'The worst thing of all was that the villagers shunned us, even though some of the girls took to wearing cheap Woolworth's wedding rings. They still somehow knew where we were from and every one of us was treated with contempt.'

Naomi shook her head in disbelief and watched silently as Emily paused to take a deep breath.

'Apart from buying some sweets from the village shop the only outing we ever had was a weekly visit to the local church on a Sunday. Even then we were made to sit in the back row and forced to listen to sermons directed at us. It was drummed into our brains that when a child is conceived in lust you are a sinner in the sight of God. Then, more often than not, the parishioners would turn around to stare at us in our smocks, making us feel utterly worthless. It was common knowledge that many a girl had tried to commit suicide while staying at the home. That was why we were all monitored so closely by the staff I expect.' Emily broke down in tears.

Naomi rose to her feet and put her arm round the girl's shoulder. She felt so sorry for her and knew only too well the same thing would have happened to her if she hadn't gone through with her marriage to Duncan.

'We were locked in after six you know, just like prisoners,' Emily went on, with a glazed look in her eyes, 'and our only luxury was to be able to tune into Radio Luxembourg at night. It was a horrendous place.'

'What happened when you had the baby, then?' asked Naomi, tentatively.

Emily's face dropped. 'That was the biggest nightmare of all. After a dreadful, long labour I gave birth to a baby boy. He was beautiful and I named him Morgan. But it wasn't long before the delivery nurse took him from me. She said that by having my baby adopted I was saving my family from shame and doing something wonderful for the child. It was like experiencing a birth and bereavement at the same time, I can tell you,' she sobbed, almost choking on her words. 'Come to think of it I don't even remember signing any documents. Everything seemed a blur from then on.'

'May I ask what happened to the father of the child, or is that too personal?'

'Huh! I never did set eyes on him after he found out I was in the family way.'

'That's men for you,' cried Naomi, gritting her teeth

in anger.

'You won't tell anyone my secret, will you?' begged Emily, wiping her eyes with a handkerchief. 'The feeling of pain never leaves me you know. I have a deep emotional tear inside and feel that my life is not worth living now that Morgan is gone.'

'There now, my lovely! Perhaps one day Morgan might seek you out. I was adopted as well and I always hang on to the hope that I'll find my birth mother one day. And you must do the same about little Morgan.'

Naomi's few words seemed to cheer Emily and after standing up and wiping her eyes again she gave her a huge hug before taking her leave, looking marginally brighter than when she'd arrived.

Just as Naomi was about to close the door behind her she saw her friend, Sarah, still clad in her bus conductress outfit making her way to the house.

'I'm glad I've caught you home. I've had a brainwave I think you might be interested in,' said Sarah, hurrying inside.

'You look like a drowned rat,' said Naomi, pulling a face. 'Let's have your jacket off before you catch your death of cold.' She took it off her friend's shoulders and draped it on the clothes horse near the fire.

'Come on then, let's be having it. What's this brainwave all about?'

'Well, one of the girls in work told me that she used the Ouija board for contacting spirits, so I borrowed it off her and thought perhaps we should give it a try. It might help you to find out where your birth mother is living.'

Naomi raised her eyebrows, feeling dubious. 'I've never heard anything so daft in all my days. How on earth do you think some board is going to talk?'

'Let's try it and see. All you have to do is to write out the alphabet on pieces of paper then place them round the table. After that you put an upturned glass in the middle with the words yes and no either side of it. It's as simple as that!'

'Then what?' asked Naomi, looking mystified.

'We put our fingers on the upturned glass and ask it questions.'

'You've got to be off your rocker, Sarah, if you expect me to believe that. Perhaps your friend had taken a drink or something,' she chuckled.

Sarah flashed her deep blue eyes at her and got off her chair. 'Give me a pen and some paper then, and I'll show you,' she said, sharply.

'I've got to see this,' said Naomi with glee, handing her a pen and writing pad from the drawer.

She watched in silence as Sarah wrote the alphabet on small pieces of paper, then placed each piece in a circle around the coffee table.

'Where's the glass then? It won't work without that you know.'

Naomi rummaged around in the Welsh dresser and took out a glass. 'Will this do, then?' she asked, stifling a giggle. 'Our Mam kept it for best occasions, but it was hardly ever used.'

Sarah smiled at her then took the glass and placed it upside down in the middle of the printed letters.

'Is that all?' said Naomi. 'I would have thought the spirits might have wanted some sherry or something poured in it first.'

'Stop your messing now and put your forefinger on the bottom of the glass like I'm doing and don't for heaven's sake keep giggling or it won't work.'

Naomi gave her a salute and crouched down on the floor opposite her friend, trying her hardest to keep a straight face.

'Is there anybody there?' cried Sarah, in a loud melodious voice.

Within seconds the glass began to move, taking their fingers with it. Both women looked across at each other startled.

'You did that,' accused Sarah, glaring at Naomi.

'No I didn't! I thought it was you playing silly beggars, to be truthful,' Naomi groaned, not believing what she'd just witnessed. Suddenly she felt the temperature fall in the room and the glass began to move again. This time it spelled out the name of Bethan.

'What about Bethan?' Sarah asked, with her eyes nearly popping out of her head.

Holding her breath Naomi watched the glass spin around the table. She read out each letter it touched. 'Died with consumption' was spelled out.

'I don't like this one bit. It's far too creepy for me,' cried Sarah, pulling a face.

'Let's pack things in,' said Naomi, shuddering. 'I'm sure there's some kind of presence here. It's as if someone has just walked over my grave.'

With their fingers still on the stem of the glass both women looked petrified as it took off at a great speed, knocking the pieces of paper off the edges of the table. They quickly removed their fingers and screamed as the glass spiralled off on its own, smashing itself against the wall and sending splinters of glass flying everywhere.

Sarah and Naomi clung to each other shaking. Then the lights dimmed and, for a second, Naomi thought she saw the figure of a middle-aged woman with a Welsh shawl draped around her shoulders, disappear down the hallway.

'D..Did you just see what I saw?' she gasped, clutching her friend's arm.

Sarah nodded. 'I'll never be able to sleep tonight after this,' she moaned. 'This house has always given me the creeps, even more so now.'

Naomi looked at her, knowing full well what she meant. Apart from the noises that she couldn't account for she often had the feeling that she was being watched, and put it down to her nerves.

'I think it's best we say the Lord's Prayer together, don't you?' Naomi suggested, feeling as if the devil himself was after her.

Sarah agreed and as both girls knelt beside one another in prayer Naomi began to feel much better.

'I suggest you tell your friend that she's dabbling around with something she knows nothing about and to be extremely careful. Don't you think so?'

'I expect you're right,' agreed Sarah, getting up from the floor. 'I've heard that you can pick up entities from a low plane of existence.'

Naomi shuddered. 'How do you fancy staying the night? You've probably missed the last bus home by now,' she said, staring up at the clock on the mantelpiece.

'If you think I'm sleeping here after all I've just witnessed you've got another think coming. I'd rather walk home and get drenched, thank you,' said Sarah, reaching for her coat.

After waving her friend off, Naomi cleared the room of broken glass and made her way to bed. She hoped the woman dressed in the Welsh shawl wouldn't show herself again but, as she stepped onto the landing, she felt just as if she was being watched.

All night long Naomi tossed and turned in the bed. She had dreadful ear-ache and was sure she was suffering with an abscess, to which she was prone. In the early hours of the morning she cried out in pain as it broke then, with the pain relieved, she curled up in the bed pulling the eiderdown over her head for warmth.

The following day she felt loath to get herself ready

for work but knew that she couldn't afford to stay at home. She found it exceedingly hard managing on her own and had often wished she had a man's wage coming in. However, after giving Philip his breakfast she took him to school before making her way to work, anticipating just another ordinary day.

CHAPTER 25

Half an hour or so later Naomi entered the grocers and, after putting on her overall, began to clean and stack the shelves with Mrs Jenkins.

'You don't look at all well this morning,' said Mrs Jenkins, looking concerned.

'I was awake most of the night with ear-ache and prior to that a friend had called round suggesting we try the Ouija Board game. It frightened the life out of me.'

'Why was that?' asked Mrs Jenkins, raising her eyebrows.

'Well, I didn't believe it would work until someone by the name of Bethan decided to come through and scared the living day lights out of us. I was convinced I saw an image of this Bethan with a Welsh shawl wrapped round her, but I think my imagination must have run riot.'

Mrs Jenkin's jaw dropped. 'My God, that must have been Bethan Jones who lived in your house many moons ago. I believe it was a tiny cottage then and talk had it that she died from consumption.'

Naomi felt her hair stand on end.

'You must realize that spirits often return to where they once lived because they cannot understand why strange people are occupying what was once theirs. I suggest if you see Bethan again you speak with her and tell her to find her way to God. You can always cleanse your house by preparing some holy water. It doesn't have to come from a church. Just place a bowl of water somewhere in the sun and make the sign of the cross three times over it, then sprinkle it around the house,' prattled on Mrs Jenkins, as if she was an authority on such things. 'That should do the trick.'

Naomi was surprised she was so knowledgeable in these matters but she had no intention of calling Bethan up again just to see if it worked. Before she could make any further comment Mark walked into the shop looking debonair in his best tweed jacket and flat cap. After putting his cap down on the counter he beckoned Mrs Jenkins and Naomi towards him with a huge smile on his face.

'You look well pleased with yourself, boyo.' exclaimed Mrs Jenkins, rubbing her hands together from the cold. 'Something to do with money is it?'

'You could say that,' said Mark, puffing out his chest. 'I've just sold the shop for a tidy sum which means I'll be able to open bigger premises with my brother Paul in Merthyr now. My Gwyneth will be pleased.'

Mrs Jenkins face fell. 'What about our jobs? I can't afford to be out of work, what with my Idris laid low with his back from an accident at the pit.'

Naomi stood in the background looking fraught. It was news she could well have done without now that she was just getting on her feet.

'Well, it's up to the new owners if they keep you on. I've sold the premises, just as it stands, to Rosie and Taffy Jones who own a large boarding house and transport café down in Pillgwenlly, Newport.'

'Oh aye, I've heard of Rosie Jones,' exclaimed Mrs Jenkins, with mouth agape. 'She's quite a rum character by all accounts.'

'You've got the one,' nodded Mark, grinning. 'She's coming down to inspect the shop and living quarters this afternoon so you'd better make sure things are up to scratch.' With a clap of his hands he turned on his heel and disappeared into the living quarters leaving the two women staring at each other in shock.

'What's this Rosie like then, Mrs Jenkins?' asked Naomi, looking alarmed.

'You wouldn't want to know,' said Mrs Jenkins,

rolling her eyes. 'Put it this way, she's not a person to be crossed. Even I wouldn't get on the wrong side of her. She also swears like a navvy, you know.'

'Sounds worse by the minute,' said Naomi, grimacing. 'Anyway, what do you think our chances are at being kept on?'

'Let's just say, if she finds out about your reputation with men, I don't fancy your prospects. She won't want you sniffing around her old man.'

'As if I would,' scoffed Naomi, taking offence at the remark. 'I've had my fill of married men.'

Shortly after lunch the shop door bell rang and in walked a smart young woman dressed in a fur coat, with an abundance of gold jewellery around her neck. Naomi stood, eyeing her up and down. It was a working class area and people dressed such as she was were rarely seen shopping in a back street grocery shop.

The young woman's dark eyes began darting around all four corners of the shop, as if inspecting everything.

'Can I help you?' asked Naomi, stepping forward.

'I'm Rosie, the new owner,' announced the woman, turning towards her.

Naomi gulped. 'Pleased to meet you I'm sure.' She was mesmerized to see the amount of gold rings on the woman's fingers as she held her hand out to her.

'What on earth are you doing with that cotton wool hanging out of your ear, girl?' shrieked Rosie, pulling a face.

Naomi was taken aback by the sound of her melodious voice as it rang around the shop like a resounding bell. 'I've been suffering with dreadful ear-ache all night from an abscess and decided to use the cotton wool to help keep out the cold.'

Rosie nodded. Then she tossed her long red hair over her shoulders as she walked behind the counter.

'This will be the first bleeding thing to go,' she said bluntly, glaring down at the wooden till. 'I'll have a new one installed which has a proper till roll that can be checked every night in case there are discrepancies.'

Naomi winced at her language and took umbrage at her remark about checking the till because she had never stolen a penny in her life, and she doubted Mrs Jenkins had either being a pillar of the community. At that moment several customers arrived. Naomi and Mrs Jenkins were quick to attend to them. By the time they were served Rosie emerged from the living quarters beckoning the two women towards her.

Naomi stood silently, staring into her face, fully expecting her cards.

'Not many girls would turn up for work after a night of earache, so I've decided to keep you on for the time being to see how you shape up, despite the gossip I've heard.'

Naomi's cheeks coloured. 'Thank you very much, Rosie,' she said, feeling relieved. 'I can assure you that I'm always punctual and willing.'

Rosie raised one eyebrow then turned her attention to Mrs Jenkins who was busy at the counter, filling up blue paper bags with sugar. 'I will need you to stay and teach me the ropes as you are an old hand on the job, Mrs Jenkins. But be warned, there's not much I don't understand about business and no one has ever dared pull a fast one on me.'

Mrs Jenkins's gave a huge sigh of relief on hearing the news, and thanked Rosie profusely.

Several minutes later both women turned to wave goodbye to Rosie who strode out of the shop looking like a fashion model on a catwalk.

'Put the kettle on, Naomi. I could do with a cuppa after all that,' said Mrs Jenkins. 'Believe you me, our quiet little grocery shop will never be the same again.'

During the next few months Naomi got used to Rosie's different humours and learned that under her tough exterior lay a heart of gold. What touched her most of all was that Rosie took a shine to Philip. She often gave him small chores to do when he returned to the shop after school, for which she would give him a small treat.

Rosie's husband, Taffy, seldom served in the shop because he was busy keeping their café running. He was a well built, jovial man whose eyes always lit up when Rosie was around. It was common knowledge in the neighbourhood that they made a good team.

One morning, shortly before lunch time, Naomi felt distinctly ill and, without any warning, fainted just as she was in the process of serving a customer. Within seconds Rosie came to her rescue and carried her into her living quarters where she held smelling salts under her nose.

'I hope you're not in the bloody family way. Only I can't have my staff falling ill,' Rosie exclaimed, as Naomi began to stir.

'You've got to be joking,' Naomi said, grimacing. 'I don't have a boyfriend and rarely go out in the evenings. To be honest, I can't remember when I last had a square meal because as long as the bills are paid and Philip has a full stomach that's all I care about.'

'Well, we'll soon change things. Mrs Thomas, serve us up another dinner! Naomi could do with a good meal inside her,' she bellowed through the kitchen doorway.

Naomi's mouth watered as she watched Mrs Thomas pour rich brown gravy over a mound of creamed potatoes, vegetables and meat. She had grown fond of the middle aged lady who came in to clean and cook each day, often chatting with her when the shop was quiet. She was a hard worker and was known for her beautiful singing voice, especially when she performed at the miners' Christmas concerts.

As Naomi was finishing her meal Rosie returned to the kitchen.

'I want you to find yourself a sitter for that son of yours on Saturday night because you and I are going to paint the town red, girl.'

'Where are we going, then?' asked Naomi, looking up from her plate in surprise.

'For a night out that you'll never forget, so make sure you have your best clobber on.'

Naomi knew not to argue and began to look forward to the outing, despite having nothing special to wear.

Saturday evening soon came and, after arranging with Diane to keep an eye on Philip, Naomi slipped into a black shift dress that she'd bought especially for the occasion. On looking in the mirror at herself she was well pleased with the way she looked. Then, as soon as she heard Taffy's car pull up outside, she swaggered to the door draping her black jacket over her shoulders.

Naomi instantly felt dowdy at the sight of Rosie, who was dressed up to the nines in a stunning red sequined dress, but she was so excited she soon got over it.

'Come on, girl. Let's get going and show them what we're made of,' Rosie laughed, ushering her into the back of the car.

After travelling down the valley roads for some time they reached Newport and, in the blackness of the night, Naomi could just about make out George Street Bridge in the distance. Shortly after crossing the bridge the car came to a halt outside a club near the corner of the street.

Rosie and Naomi pushed their way through the small crowd of people outside, then made a grand entrance into the club. Within seconds of them bagging their seats several men pulled up chairs, clambering over each other to buy the girls a drink. It became apparent that Rosie was well known in the town by the way people shouted out her name.

'Well, what are you drinking then, girls?' asked one of the men, digging deep into his trouser pocket.

'I'll have a pineapple juice please,' answered Naomi, amazed at the welcome they'd received.

Rosie shrieked with laughter. 'You'll have no such thing. My friend and I will have a brandy and lemonade please, and not one of those bloody little piddling drinks either. Make it doubles!'

The tall, red headed man winked at her. 'OK Sis. I'll be back in a flash.'

Naomi could see the likeness between them and wished she'd been fortunate enough to have a brother to stick up for her. Perhaps many of the misfortunes that beset her wouldn't have happened if she had.

As they began to sip their drinks the band began to play *Running Bear* and Rosie waved over to the good looking, dark headed man who was playing the drums.

'This one's for you, Rosie. Glad to see you're back in town,' he shouted into his microphone.

Rosie and Naomi exchanged glances, then both women took to the floor, rhythmically moving to the music for all they were worth, and it wasn't long before they were swept off their feet by eager partners.

After several dances Naomi and Rosie eventually sat down to catch their breath and start on the drinks that were lined up on the table.

Naomi was in her element and although the brandy tasted like poison to her she was thirsty and gulped it down as if it was lemonade.

'That's right, get them pissing down you, girl.' Rosie teased.

Then within minutes she dragged her up on the

dance floor again.

By the end of the evening Naomi had lost count of how many glasses of brandy she'd drunk and her head was beginning to reel. She was relieved when she heard the sound of the bell ringing behind the bar and wanted nothing more than to go home to bed.

Rosie picked up their belongings then ushered her out into the foyer. 'I won't be long. Just calling a taxi, so wait by this pillar,' she said, as she tried to prop Naomi up against it.

Naomi leant against the marble pillar, glad of its support, but within seconds she felt herself slide down to the floor in a crumpled heap. After that she could vaguely remember being carried out of the club and into the back of a car with her head thumping as if she'd been struck by a sledgehammer.

When she finally came around she found herself back home stretched out on the settee with Rosie sitting beside her.

'You want to take more water with it next time,' joked a dark headed stranger standing by the fireplace.

'Who are you?' asked Naomi, looking perplexed.

'I'm Charlie, the taxi driver who picked you up from the floor in the club. Or don't you remember?' he chuckled.

'I don't generally drink. It was Rosie's fault,' she wailed, holding onto her head.

'It's not my fault you can't hold your bloody liquor,' Rosie retorted, throwing her head back and laughing.

'I'm off before a full scale row ensues,' chuckled Charlie, winking at them both.

'So am I,' ranted Rosie. 'Otherwise my old man will think I've done a runner. I've checked on Philip and he's sound asleep, so there's nothing to worry about.'

After making sure Naomi was comfortable Rosie

left, leaving her to sleep things off on the settee. Within seconds she was in dreamland.

On her arrival in work on Monday morning Naomi saw Mrs Lewis, one of the local gossips, idly propping up the counter while Mrs Jenkins made up her grocery order. Naomi went into the back of the shop where her overall was hanging. She was still in earshot of what was being said.

'Duw! I'm glad to be able to say that I'm proud of my daughters. They both married good reliable Welshmen, you know, not like some we can mention. Man mad she is, and not too fussy either.'

'Is that so?' said Mrs Jenkins, packing the groceries into her bag.

'Do you know what? I actually saw her being carried out of a taxi at the weekend, too drunk to stand, and the taxi driver stayed a while too. Still, there's no accounting for taste, is there?'

Naomi bit into her lip, tempted to respond, but thought better of it when she saw Rosie appear in the shop.

'What's the matter with you, girl? You look as if you've lost a pissing pound and found sixpence?'

'It's the likes of her slandering me off again, Rosie.' Naomi pointed to Mrs Lewis as she was leaving the shop with bags fully laden with groceries.

'She spends well, so take no notice, cock. Perhaps she's nothing better to do.'

'Half the people who talk about me haven't a clue what hardships I've suffered, so what qualifies them to sit in judgement?'

'You're right there. They want to be bloody thankful your misfortunes never arrived on their doorsteps,' ranted Rosie, who looked genuinely concerned. 'Well, never mind. I've got some news to cheer you up, girl. Remember Charlie, the taxi driver who brought you home on Saturday night? Well, he's calling in the shop some time today to arrange a date with you.'

Naomi's eyes sparkled. She suspected Rosie might have had a hand in the matter. Her day had taken an about turn and was looking good already.

CHAPTER 26

Naomi asked herself should she take a chance by accepting a date with Charlie or not? And, with her track record, would it be worth taking the risk of getting entangled with another man? She drew a deep breath as she mulled things round in her mind. On the other hand did she really want to remain lonely all her life, especially in years to come, when Philip had flown the nest? To be left all alone trying to scrape by on a meagre income was the last thing she wanted to look forward to.

'I suppose I could do with a good night out with Charlie, Rosie,' she called across the counter to her.

'That's my girl,' said Rosie, nodding approvingly. 'Now let's get stuck into sorting out some of these grocery deliveries, shall we?'

Several hours later Rosie gave Naomi a quick nudge. 'Here's Charlie boy,' she whispered, grinning all over her face. 'If he asks you for a date, no excuses mind and if Diane's not available to keep an eye on Philip, *I will*!'

'I just called in to see if you'd fancy a night out at the Labour club down in Newport tonight?' asked Charlie, with a glint in his deep brown eyes.

Naomi could feel her colour rising and had a job to keep a straight face. She could only just remember what Charlie looked like but was quite taken by his good looks.

She heard the lilt of his Welsh accent. He looked like a true Welshman, short in stature with dark hair, just like her late father, she thought with a pang.

'I could do with a good night out,' she said, enthusiastically. 'But before I accept are you married by any chance?'

Charlie gaped at her in amazement. 'Now do I look

as if I am?' he jested. 'I'll take that as a yes, then. The show begins at seven thirty so I'll pick you up around seven at your house, is it? I remember the place well, after carrying you in after your night on the town.'

Naomi looked at him sheepishly and grinned. 'You don't hang about do you?' she smirked.

'What's the point?' laughed Charlie, giving her a wink.

Before Naomi could say anymore Charlie sauntered out of the shop, looking as if he'd conquered Everest.

That night, as soon as Naomi heard the sound of a horn blaring outside, she grabbed her jacket and handbag before dashing out of the house. She was bowled over at the sight of a stunning white Zephyr car parked outside with Charlie sitting at the wheel. It amused her to see he was wearing a brightly coloured, paisley patterned shirt. The first words out of her late mother's mouth would have been, 'Duw, he's a proper valley boy, cariad! He likes his colours.' She could also imagine her mother giving him her seal of approval.

As she climbed into the car beside him she was aware of several neighbours having a good gawk at her from across the road so when Charlie turned the ignition on and slowly drove down the street Naomi made a point of waving to them with a wicked smile on her face, knowing it would be all round the neighbourhood like lightning.

'Glad you could make it,' said Charlie, giving her a wolf whistle as he feasted his eyes on her mini-skirt.

'Keep your eyes on the road, boyo. I want to arrive in one piece, you know.'

Charlie grinned and put his foot down on the throttle.

In no time at all they arrived outside the club and walked inside, arm in arm, as if they were an old married couple.

'What's your poison?' asked Charlie, grinning. 'Only I don't intend having to carry you out on my arm dead drunk again. What about a Babycham?'

'I'll give it a try,' said Naomi, smiling. She felt at ease with him and relaxed back in her chair.

During the course of the evening Charlie told her that he was once married but whilst he was working away the window cleaner took a shine to his wife and that was the end of things.

Naomi looked at him in amusement. Because of the grin on his face she had no idea whether he was joking or not.

After the artistes had finished their acts Charlie swept Naomi up onto the dance floor. It was crowded but they found a space and began to jive. She was in her element and danced the night away, barely stopping for a breather.

During the journey home Naomi decided to find out more about Charlie. With her track record she could have been cavorting with a serial killer for all she knew. She had also noticed that he could hold his drink well and had a strange feeling he'd had led quite a chequered past.

'How long have you worked on the taxis then, Charlie?'

He looked at her with a glint in his eyes. 'It seems like ages now. But I gave in my notice last week. I'm planning to leave soon to work in the building trade up in the north of England, where there's more money to be made.'

Naomi's heart turned over. It was just her luck.

'Anyway, before I go how do you fancy accompanying me up to the Rhondda valley at the weekend? I need to make peace with the old man and could do with some support.'

'I find it odd that you need support to see your own father,' said Naomi, rubbing her chin.

'It's a long story which I don't really want to go into,' said Charlie, heaving a huge sigh.

Naomi thought it best not to ask any more. 'I've got a young son you know, so I can't just flit off at a moment's notice.'

'That's OK by me. Bring him along. The more the merrier. Shall we say around ten o'clock Saturday morning then?'

I'll look forward to it,' said Naomi, her eyes twinkling.

As they drew nearer home she began to feel nervous and wondered whether he would be expecting her to be "accommodating" on their first date. Charlie grinned, as if he was reading her mind, but as soon as they arrived outside her home she was surprised and relieved when he only gave her a polite peck on the cheek before she stepped out of the car.

'Thanks for a good evening, Charlie. I'll look forward to Saturday,' she said, blowing him a kiss.

As she waved him off she was upset to think he was leaving the area now she had taken such a liking to him.

When Charlie arrived outside on Saturday morning Naomi quickly bundled Philip into the back of his car after introducing him. She glanced up at the gathering rain clouds and hoped the day would brighten up.

Philip's eyes were everywhere as he looked round the inside of the spotlessly clean vehicle and, as soon as Charlie started up the engine, he grinned at his mother in delight.

Naomi was wearing her conventional navy two-piece suit that she kept for special occasions and thought Charlie looked the business dressed in a crisp white open necked shirt, black trousers and jacket.

'My word we do look smart today,' she jested, pulling a face. 'And there's not a hair out of place.

'Well, if you must know I'm hoping to impress the old man. He hasn't seen me for ages, which is something I feel dreadful about. That's why I was hoping you'd come along.'

'So you think I'll give you Dutch courage then?' said Naomi, laughing.

Charlie nodded sheepishly. 'I need to make my peace with Da before he dies, you see,' he admitted, looking somewhat ashamed.

'Duw, I'm glad to be of some use then.' Naomi remarked coolly, wondering what she was letting herself in for.

Silence reigned as they sped down the road towards the Rhondda. During the journey rain clouds formed like huge dark curtains around the mountain tops and, within minutes, a deluge of rain lashed down onto the windscreen making it difficult for Charlie to drive. When the sun eventually appeared through the clouds in the distance Naomi could see several rows of small cottages.

'We're nearly there,' said Charlie, biting into his lip. 'Don't expect a palace, mind. Mam did her best with Dad's money from working down the pit but when she died it nearly put paid to the old man. As a child the only big treat I can ever remember was when we went away on miners' fortnight at the end of July. We stayed in a gas lit caravan down in Porthcawl. Duw! We had some fun when us kids scrambled on the beach with our buckets and spades. Those were the days! Not a penny to scratch your arse with but the camaraderie amongst the other families was second to none. They used to say that the air down Porthcawl was better than the Costa Brava, because it helped to empty the coal dust from the miners' lungs.' His eyes filled up. 'I broke the old man's heart you know by not marrying a Welsh girl. I went off with someone from up north a few years back and after a huge family row I never stepped into the house again.'

Naomi's heart sank. She was miffed to think she had got embroiled with yet another married man but thought it best not to comment with Philip within earshot.

'Here we are,' cried Charlie, bringing the car to a halt. 'Come on Philip, out you come.'

'I do like your Zephyr, Charlie. Can't I stay and mind it?' Philip asked, with a cheeky look on his face.

'Another time maybe, son,' said Charlie, smiling as the boy ran to his side. This pleased Naomi. It made her happy to see that Charlie was taking an interest in Philip, which was more than Duncan or Ted had ever bothered to do.

Naomi was glad to stretch her legs and smiled down at several small children playing hopscotch at the side of the road where sheep and children intermingled. Several women, dressed with three-cornered Welsh shawls around their shoulders, were keeping a watchful eye on the children as they played. As Naomi passed by she caught sight of a tiny baby tucked safely into one of the women's shawls, suckling at her breast.

'Bore da,' said one woman, smiling.

Charlie immediately spoke back to her in Welsh, and a broad beam came over her face.

'This place used to be a thriving community, you know,' said Charlie. 'Before the pits were closed down.' He shook his head.

'There's a shame,' said Naomi, looking at the surrounding scenery.

'The place reeks of poverty since they did that. Coal was once considered as King, you know.'

Naomi's eyes caught sight of an old neglected

mineshaft lower down in the valley and, for one brief moment in her mind's eye, she could see the images of miners hacking out the coal with their pickaxes. For a second she was convinced that she heard the sound of the men singing in the background as they toiled, and was almost moved to tears.

Charlie suddenly took hold of her arm and she jumped.

'Duw, girl, you were miles away then,' he said, giving her arm a tight squeeze. 'We're here now.'

'I went back in time, you know. The spirits of the miners are still there, see.'

'You feel it too,' said Charlie. 'It's magnificent, isn't it?'

Philip looked at them both in bewilderment.

'Come on, Philip. Let's go and meet Charlie's Da,' said Naomi, putting her arm round him.

Charlie brought the solid brass knocker down on the door and within seconds it was opened by an elderly man who looked to be small in build like Charlie, but he had very little hair left on his head.

'Is that you, our Charlie? I can't see very well. Is it really you?' the old man cried, tears washing his eyes.

'Aye, it's me alright, Da. How are you?'

A lump came into Naomi's throat as she watched the two men embrace. When Charlie's father eventually released his grip Charlie introduced Naomi and Philip as they made their way in through the door.

She took to the old man immediately and shook his hand. When she stepped into the living room, she couldn't help but notice how sparsely furnished it was. There was a welcoming fire in the grate and as Charlie's father sat down in the wooden rocking chair a side door suddenly burst open and a small dark headed boy came hurtling through, flinging out his arms to Charlie.

251

'This is Elwyn, my sister's son,' Charlie announced proudly, lifting the boy in the air. 'My, you've grown, bach!'

'He's starting school shortly, aren't you, boyo?' said his grandfather looking proudly at the boy.

At that moment Naomi had the feeling that someone was watching them and, as she looked over her shoulder, she could see the shapely figure of a young woman staring at her suspiciously.

Charlie left his chair and beckoned her over. The woman looked fondly at Charlie and gave him a huge kiss.

'This is Ceinwen. A little bit backward she is see, and since someone took advantage of her up on the mountain side she's nervous of strangers.' He pointed at Elwyn who was racing around the room like a tornado.

Naomi immediately went forward to shake Ceinwen's hand but the young woman drew back, staring into Naomi's eyes as if she was looking deep into her soul. She then turned and offered her a seat by a well-scrubbed kitchen table where she uncovered some bread and cheese from underneath a crisp white cloth. She made a pile of sandwiches then went over to the range and poured water out of the spitting kettle into the teapot as everyone sat down to eat.

'Not much misses our Ceinwen, you know,' said the old man. She's a good housekeeper too.'

Several minutes later Charlie stood up from the table. 'Shall we leave them to it, Da, and have a pint?'

'Duw! There's an offer I can't refuse now,' said the old man, hurrying to collect his jacket and cap from the back of the door.

'Won't be long, cariad,' said Charlie. 'I'm only going down the workmen's club for a chat with the old man and his butties.'

Naomi smiled after him, thinking it was a grand thing to do. She felt as if she'd stepped back into another era and intuitively knew that the old cottage held a mysterious past all of its own.

As Philip played games with Elwyn, Ceinwen picked up an envelope from the mantelpiece.

'I knew our Charlie would call. His divorce papers arrived in the week, you know.'

'Is that so?' said Naomi, looking surprised.

'Are you going to marry him then?' Ceinwen asked, smiling at her.

'No, I don't think so. I haven't known your brother for long.'

Ceinwen's eyes misted over. Her face took on a frown and, after replacing the envelope, she disappeared up the stairs as if in a huff.

Naomi felt dreadful for upsetting her but thought it best to leave her alone.

Some time later Charlie and his father returned with fish and chips, wrapped in newspaper, for their tea. Within a few seconds of them laying out the food on the table Ceinwen appeared through the door and sat down beside her son. Naomi hoped she wasn't still in a bad mood but as soon as she gave her a huge smile she knew differently.

When they had finished eating and put their coats on to leave, Charlie's father took down the envelope from the mantelpiece and handed it to Charlie. 'I hope you make a better job of marriage next time, my son,' he said, winking at him. 'You should have chosen a good Welsh girl, see.'

That counts me out, thought Naomi, having been born in London. But despite this she still felt Welsh through and through because she had been brought up in their ways.

Charlie pushed the envelope into his back pocket,

and Naomi and Philip followed him out. As they left the cottage Charlie and his father hugged, tears running down their faces.

'You look after yourself, Da. I'll be thinking of you.'

The old man stared after him too choked to speak.

A heavy mist hung over the row of cottages as they made their way back to the car. At the end of the road they turned and waved to the old man who was standing alone on the front door step. His image had made an imprint on Naomi's heart and she began to wonder if her birth mother was as poor as a church mouse too. In no way would this have made any difference. Just a welcoming smile and to link hands with the woman who bore her was all she really yearned for.

CHAPTER 27

After a gruelling day at work Naomi was glad to arrive home. Charlie had been on her mind and she was bitterly disappointed that he hadn't made any further arrangements to see her. She wondered whether she'd ever receive a postcard from him when he moved up north to work and she spent the rest of the evening in the doldrums.

After supper Philip went to bed clutching a ripped comic that Elwyn had swapped with him. Naomi smiled to herself. She could see that the little chap had made quite an impression on her son.

Before going to bed herself she moved the clothes horse full of damp washing away from the fireside and into the hallway at the bottom of the stairs, where it would be safe from sparks. Then she climbed wearily up the stairs, feeling a little off colour and glad to see her bed.

During the night she tossed and turned but sleep escaped her. Her whole body was itching and felt extremely hot and, as she sat up in bed to cool off, she suddenly began to feel dreadfully sick. Without further ado she dashed out of the bedroom to fetch a bowl from downstairs but as she reached the turn in the stairs she blacked out and fell headlong down into the darkness of the night.

The clothes horse at the bottom of the stairs broke her fall. The dowelled wood ripped into her neck as she fell and struck her head on the cold stone floor.

She lay unconscious in the hallway all night with the blood from her neck wound trickling down her nightdress.

As dawn was breaking Naomi began to stir. The cold night air from the gap under the front door enveloped her, making her shiver. Her hand went up to the front of her nightdress. It was wringing wet with blood and vomit, and her head ached as if she'd been struck by a sledge hammer. She felt dreadful. Semi-conscious, she managed to pull herself along the ground out of the draught and, after what seemed like an eternity, she raised herself onto the settee where she promptly slumped down and blacked out once more.

It was a couple of hours later when Philip came downstairs expecting to find his breakfast waiting. He gasped at the sight of his mother lying unconscious and in such a state, and ran over the road to Diane's house for help.

Within minutes Diane rushed into the room with Philip holding her hand.

'You stay with Mammy, Philip. I'll phone for the doctor. Be good now.'

Diane dashed through the door leaving a bewildered looking Philip sitting beside his mother.

When she returned she found Naomi stirring.

'Tell the truth now! Has that bastard Ted been here again? Because I shall set the Bobby on him if he did this to you.'

'No, it was nothing to do with him,' moaned Naomi, her head wracked with pain. 'I had a funny turn in the night and blacked out on the stairs.'

Several minutes later the doctor appeared and after seeing the state she was in he rang for an ambulance. After he'd left, Mrs Evans, Naomi's other next door neighbour, appeared in the doorway.

'I saw the doctor's car and came straight away. Duw! You look dreadful, my girl. I think it will be best if Philip stays with me for the time being otherwise they might take him into care. I know you've no relatives to speak of.'

Mrs Evans had been good to her mother when she was dying and Naomi was relieved to know that her son would be in safe hands.

'Diane, would you mind fetching me a clean nightdress and towel from the chest of drawers in the back bedroom. I can't be going into hospital in this state,' Naomi cried, trying to sit upright on the couch.

Diane left the room and several minutes later returned clutching her chest. 'I wouldn't live here if you paid me out in sovereigns. As soon as I was half-way up the stairs it felt as if someone was pushing past me and I could have sworn I saw a fleeting glance of some-one appear on the landing.'

'It's only a spirit, I expect,' whispered Naomi, managing a weak smile.

'*Only* a spirit,' screeched Diane, looking alarmed. 'The only spirit I'm interested in is vodka!' She shuddered. 'Come on let's be having you. I'll give you a quick wash and change your nightdress before the ambulance turns up.'

Within minutes of arriving at the hospital a concerned looking doctor examined Naomi and enquired how she'd sustained her injuries.

'I fell down the stairs, and the clothes-horse broke my fall otherwise I wouldn't be here to tell the tale.'

'Is that so?' said the doctor, looking at her dubiously. 'That's a nasty swelling on your forehead and the gash in your throat needs cleaning up too.'

Naomi could feel herself going giddy and was relieved to be in his capable hands. After x-rays were taken Naomi was wheeled into a side ward where the doctor called in to see her.

'You're lucky to be alive, my lady. The x-rays showed that you have a fracture of the skull. You will need plenty of bed rest.'

Naomi dreaded to think what might have become of Philip if she had died and thanked God she was still in the land of the living.

That evening Naomi couldn't believe her eyes when she saw Charlie appear at her bedside with a huge bunch of flowers.

'How did you know I was here?' she asked with a delighted smile. 'I thought you'd be half way up the map by now.'

'Well, as I was leaving the digs I bumped into an old mate of mine who's a foreman at the new steel works down in Newport. He offered me a job on shifts, paying good money too, so I've decided to stay. My first thoughts were to call around to tell you the good news. When I couldn't get an answer at your door Mrs Evans saw me through her net curtains and ran out to explain what had happened. Duw! You do look as if you've been through the mill, cariad.'

Naomi gave a huge sigh of relief. She was beginning to feel better already.

'Firstly I've a favour to ask of you,' said Charlie, taking her hand in his.

'Fire away,' said Naomi, hesitantly, wondering what was coming next.

'I don't suppose you fancy a paying guest? Only I'm finding it very cramped in my lodgings what with all the other new contractors staying.'

'You can move in any time,' she said, without hesitation. 'I'll be only too glad of your company.'

'I'd be prepared to help out with the housework and cooking till you're back on your feet, because I don't start my new job yet. Duw! There's an offer you can't refuse, my lovely.'

Naomi nodded her eyes glistening.

'That settles it then,' said Charlie looking as pleased as punch. 'Don't you worry about anything because I'll buy us some groceries and have the place spick and span for when you arrive home. That's if you'll trust me with the key.'

Naomi opened her handbag where she kept the spare key and handed it to him.

Opening his wallet, Charlie pulled out a crisp five pound note, waving it in the air. 'Is that OK to be getting on with? Only I don't want you going back on your word.'

Naomi couldn't believe it. Perhaps her luck had turned at last.

During the next few months Naomi's health improved greatly and a warm friendship blossomed between her and Charlie. Charlie also became good friends with Philip. Every day on his way home he would call at the newsagents to buy him a bag of sweets or a comic and often went out of his way to cook him his favourite meal of Welsh Rarebit.

One evening, after Philip had gone to bed, Naomi snuggled down beside Charlie and showed him her adoption papers.

'There's a draft number after you're father's name which might give us some information as to his whereabouts,' said Charlie pointing it out.

'When my aunt was dying she told me that he wasn't my real father but perhaps that was because she didn't want me to find him. I don't know,' she said, pulling a face.

'Well, there's an Air Force Record Office down Innsworth, in Gloucester that has lots of information on such things and if anyone can help they should be able to.'

Naomi's eyes shone at the thought of it. 'Tell you what I'll fix it with Rosie to have a day off and, now that Philip's in the big school and stays for school dinners, we'll have the whole day to ourselves.'

She was over the moon with his kind offer and couldn't wait for the day to come.

It was a warm sunny morning when Naomi and

Charlie travelled to Gloucester. Naomi felt as if she was wound up like a coiled spring and babbled on incessantly until they finally reached their destination.

After being asked the purpose of their visit Charlie was permitted to drive through the Air force camp to the office block where the records were kept. An airman, boasting a fine handle-bar moustache, approached them at the desk where Naomi did her best to explain why she wanted the information.

He quickly copied down the draft number she'd given him on his pad and they were invited to take a seat while he began his search. Every minute seemed an hour to Naomi until he reappeared with some papers in his hand.

'I've jotted down a few details but I'm afraid the only information I am able to give is the date your father joined up and the date he was released from the Air Force after the war years. For some reason his record stated that he was screened because of his wife. There had to be a good reason for that. Either she was mixing with undesirables or aliens during the war years.'

Naomi felt her heart sink.

'She sounds quite a rum character,' said Charlie, grimacing. 'Are you sure you want to continue this search?'

'Yes,' said Naomi quietly. 'I need to put the jigsaw together for my own peace of mind.'

Turning to the airman, she asked, 'Did he by any chance leave a forwarding address?'

'Sorry, but we're not at liberty to divulge one.'

Naomi met his eyes and felt like crying.

'There's not much else I can tell you except that your brother's birth date is listed alongside yours.'

Naomi caught her breath. '*I have a brother*,' she exclaimed, clutching at Charlie's arm.

'Weren't you aware of this?' said the airman, smiling at her.

Naomi shook her head.

'Well, his name is Richard Frank, and he was born in October, 1938.'

Naomi looked at him astounded. It was like all her birthdays rolled into one. 'Yet another person to look for with no known address,' she said, raising her eyebrows at him. 'Can't you divulge just a small clue as to where my father might have been living.'

'When he was finally demobbed he gave an address in Southend, if that's any help. But that could have been a temporary location in those days.'

'Southend,' said Naomi, putting her hand up to her mouth. She wasn't even sure where it was.

Clasping the details he had written down, a triumphant Naomi linked arms with Charlie, and thanked the airman profusely before leaving the building.

Nothing was going to distract her from her mission now that she had heard about her brother. She was determined she would leave no stone unturned until she had found him.

On returning home she applied for a copy of her brother's birth certificate, giving all the necessary details she could. And a week later it arrived in the post. Her eyes scanned the certificate and she was shocked to read the word adopted handwritten on the document just like hers. It gave her little information that she did not already know and she was deeply disappointed at her lack of progress.

After mulling things over in her mind Naomi decided to write to the address printed on Richard's birth certificate, crossing her fingers that she would receive a reply.

It was several weeks later that the letter was

returned by the Post Office stating the house mentioned had received a direct hit by a German bomber during the early part of 1944. Despite hearing this news she still had a strong feeling that her birth mother was still alive but the whole situation had left her feeling completely baffled. Why hadn't her aunt mentioned on her death bed that she had a brother, or hadn't she been aware of it?

Fortunately for Naomi Charlie could turn his hand to most things about the house but when he began to make decisions as if he were head of the household, Naomi began to resent his behaviour.

Early one Saturday morning Rosie called at the door asking Naomi if she could turn into work because she'd received a last minute invitation to a wedding. Naomi was used to having her weekends free but she remembered that Rosie had given her a day off at short notice when she travelled down to Innsworth Record Office and felt indebted to her.

It was almost tea-time when an extremely tired Naomi left work to return home. Saturday was their busiest day and she was looking forward to a quiet night in with her feet up.

As she drew closer to the house she was horrified to see that Charlie was painting the brickwork on the front of the house in a bright blue colour.

'Turning Conservative now, are we?' chuckled one of the neighbours in passing.

Naomi flashed her eyes at her. No-one had ever dared to paint the front of their house blue in such a staunch Labour constituency. Painting your house in the opposition's colour just wasn't done.

'What on earth are you doing?' she shouted angrily at Charlie.

'My butty in work gave me some paint so I thought I'd put it to good use. It's a pity to waste it, cariad.

Anyway, I thought you'd be pleased.'

'Why didn't you ask first?' she shouted. 'Don't you realise it's a Conservative colour, you silly fool? No-one leans that way in this neighbourhood.'

'So what?' said Charlie. 'I try to do you a favour and this is my thanks.'

He threw the brush in the air splattering the paint everywhere. Naomi's mouth fell open. She was so full of rage she was speechless and stomped, like a March hare, into the house. She went into the scullery and was bitterly disappointed to see a stack of dirty dishes piled high in the sink, and clutter everywhere. Naomi had always treated her son like royalty where the household chores were concerned. She waited on him hand and foot. Now she was beginning to reap the results of her foolishness.

As she wearily cooked tea Charlie appeared in the doorway. She could tell by the huge grin on his face that he thought what he'd done was a huge joke. He could not for one minute understand Naomi's reasoning and, that evening they had a fiery row which made things far worse.

This row was one of many in the ensuing months. One day on returning from work she was flabbergasted to find Charlie in the process of trying to cement the walls at the back of the house with a small trowel and his bare hands.

Her anger began to rise, as it often had of late. 'What a dreadful mess you're making of the property. You're poking your nose where it's not wanted again,' she shouted. 'This is the final straw.'

'You're never thankful for any jobs I do. You ungrateful bitch,' Charlie snapped.

'If I need something doing I shall find a tradesman who knows what he's about,' Naomi screeched, wincing at the harshness of his words.

In temper she stomped upstairs into the bedroom. She took his suitcase down from the top of the wardrobe and began flinging his clothes inside, like someone demented. She'd had enough.

Charlie came running in after her.

'Find yourself other lodgings, boyo, because I'm sick to death of you trying to take over the household. Anyone would think it was your place.'

Charlie's eyes narrowed. 'You were glad enough to have me around when you were ill, weren't you?'

Naomi's mind raced frantically. She knew he was right and felt guilty at throwing him out. 'I know that, but you continually drive my nerves to breaking point, and I can't deal with it any more. We're at each other's throats all the time, and it's not fair on Philip either.'

'Well, I'm certainly not staying where I'm not wanted,' said Charlie, snatching hold of his case. 'I'm off.'

After slinging his coat over his shoulder he walked through the door without a backward look and, getting in his car, disappeared up the street like a bat out of hell.

For a brief second Naomi was tempted to run after him but pride stopped her.

CHAPTER 28

Philip had grown into a handsome lad with his blonde hair and muscular body. He was now attending the local Comprehensive school and Naomi was proud of him.

One day Rosie took Naomi aside at work to explain that she was forced to cut her hours by half in the shop because a new supermarket had opened nearby. They were offering goods at bargain prices and there was no way she could compete with them. Naomi was downcast but knew she had no option but to move on and seek employment elsewhere.

After giving it much thought Naomi decided to call at Green's Wholesalers on the way home just to see if there were any positions available. She'd enjoyed working there and had been given a good reference when she left to have Philip.

She caught Tony Brain, the manager just as he was leaving his office and his face lit up when he saw her.

'You don't alter one bit, my lovely. I don't suppose you've come looking for a job, have you? Only one of the girls in the typing pool is on long term sick and I wondered whether or not you'd be interested in filling in.'

Naomi had always felt that he held a soft spot for her and was not at all surprised at his offer.

'You must have read my mind, that's all I can say,' she said smiling.

'It's a full time position which means nine till five thirty. Can you manage these hours with your son at school?'

'I've no option because I have to keep a roof over our heads somehow. Anyway my Philip is in the local Comprehensive school and more often than not stays at his friend's house if I'm not at home. I've also a neighbour who will keep a look out for him in the school holidays, so there shouldn't be any trouble,' she told him, feeling relieved that her son was becoming more independent.

Things were settled within minutes and Naomi couldn't thank Tony enough. She promised to begin work the following week and was over the moon with the news.

After leaving Green's she decided to call and tell Rosie about her new job as she was passing. On reaching the shop she was startled to see a For Sale sign had been erected outside and was relieved that she had already found alternative employment.

She was surprised to hear that Rosie was shutting the shop down within a few days. Mrs Jenkins was up in arms about the matter and was beside herself with worry. Unfortunately, age was not on her side and with her Idris so ill and little pension to survive on things looked bleak. Naomi realized that she was the lucky one and knew she would miss the old lady's banter each day. She was a good sort and not the type to gossip like most of the women in the area.

As soon as the alarm clock bell rang the following Monday morning Naomi hurried Philip out of bed and then got dressed for work. She was lucky as the premises weren't far from where she lived. She would have dreaded the thought of having to stand around on cold dark mornings waiting for a bus as she'd done when she worked at the foundry.

Naomi acknowledged a few old faces as she walked into Green's. She was sad not to see Sue and Maria sitting in her old office, and presumed they had moved on.

The months went by and it was Easter. Naomi loved this time of year. She had been feeling off-colour of late and was looking forward to a few days off.

Meanwhile Philip had planned to take trip up to Brecon with his Sunday school friends. The chapel had hired a youth hostel for the weekend with bed and board at a reasonable price.

It was Good Friday when Naomi waved Philip off on the coach. She was not looking forward to the prospect of being home alone, recognising that she had a tendency to brood on the past. Just when she turned to cross the road she bumped straight into Diane who was swaggering down the road in a white mini dress with matching accessories.

'Whoops! What's the big hurry, then? Going somewhere nice?' she asked, looking her up and down.

'I'm on my way to meet the girls for a drink in the local. Fancy coming along?'

'Well, I suppose I could,' she said nonchalantly. I'll only be sitting home alone now Philip has gone away for the weekend.'

'I'm just out for a good time,' Diane confided. 'If my husband can fool around with someone else so can I.'

Naomi was aware that Diane's husband had abandoned her for another woman who was now pregnant by him and she felt sorry for her.

'You never know, you might even find your Prince Charming, tonight,' said Diane.

'Huh!' Naomi scoffed. 'More like *you* will in that lovely dress.' Naomi looked down at the plain navy suit she'd worn to work and felt drab compared to her.

Both girls linked arms. 'I think a good night out is just what you need. You've been looking awful peaky of late. Still, you never did enjoy good health and that nasty fall didn't do you any favours, did it?'

Naomi had to agree with her.

As soon as they stepped into the lounge of their local pub they grabbed some empty bar stools knowing that they would be snatched up before long.

'I'll pay for my own lemonade because I can't run to buying shorts, not after paying for Philip's trip,' said Naomi, looking dolefully into her purse.

'Why on earth are you worrying about money?' teased Diane. 'We'll soon have some blokes buying us our drinks. Just you wait and see.'

The old pub doors rattled as several young men pushed their way in.

'Fancy any?' said Diane, drawing deeply on her cigarette.

'I'm off men for now,' laughed Naomi, giving her hair a quick flick of the comb.

'Oh no, you're not. Look my old flame, Roger Edwards, has just walked in through the door with his mate. I'm not going to let him pass by in a hurry.'

Roger saw Diane out of the corner of his eye and came rushing over offering to buy a drink each for the girls. Before Naomi could say a word Roger asked the bar maid for two glasses of vodka.

'Well, fancy seeing you in here Diane. Duw! There's a turn up for the books, and who's your friend?'

'This is Naomi, Diane replied, quickly grabbing her drink.

Roger took hold of her hand and kissed it. His hair was bright red and fell over his face in an unruly mop and he was dressed in an old faded shirt and slacks.

Naomi thanked him for the drink then gave Diane a glare. 'I don't generally drink alcohol,' she whispered, looking down in her glass. She hadn't touched a short since the time she went out with Rosie and didn't intend showing herself up again.

'Just get it down your neck, and no arguing,' urged Diane. 'What you can't sup, I'll polish off.'

Seconds later Diane spotted a free table and grabbed

it before anyone else could. Roger and his friend followed behind them, looking very smug.

'I'm Bryn Lewis. How do you do?' said Roger's friend, giving Naomi an admiring look.

'Pleased to meet you,' said Naomi, studying his face. She guessed he was a few years older than her by the lines on his forehead and receding grey hair. But she was quite content to sit with him because he seemed a pleasant enough man.

'You'd better be careful of my friend because she's clairvoyant, you know. So if you've any secrets look out.' laughed Diane.

'Tell the world, why don't you?' said Naomi, pulling a face. 'I haven't read a cup in ages.'

'They used to burn witches at the stake for less,' grinned Bryn.

'I know all about that,' said Naomi, indignantly. She could tell by the look in his dark brown eyes that he fancied his chances so, for want of anything better to do she decided to string him along for a laugh.

They spent the rest of the evening laughing and joking amongst themselves and, every time the men left to visit the toilets, Naomi was quick to pour her vodka into Diane's glass, hoping nobody would notice.

'I feel well oiled already. You'll have to promise to see me home,' said Diane, giggling like a fool. 'I don't know what's happened to my friends, they've probably gone else where.'

'I'll take you safely home, don't you worry,' Naomi assured her, raising her glass.

After last orders were called Diane stood up and began to sway.

'No more for you, my lady. We're going home,' said Naomi grabbing their coats.

'Is that so?' retorted Diane, looking over at the men.

'I thought you could take your liquor. You used to

in the old days,' said Roger, raising his eyebrows.

'I usually c.can,' stuttered Diane, hiccupping, 'but I've had more than my usual measure tonight.'

'How about we meet up in here again tomorrow?' Bryn suggested, looking at Naomi.

'We'll think about it,' she answered. 'At the moment I'm more concerned with the plight of Diane. But you can keep us a seat, just in case.'

Both men looked pleased and waved the girls off before catching the last bus to the depot.

The following day Diane came over to tell Naomi that she was suffering from a hangover and had no intentions of meeting up with Roger that night. Naomi was disappointed. She wasn't sure whether or not to turn up for Bryn on her own, and brooded about it all day.

There was little on the television that interested her that evening so, after mulling things over in her mind, she decided to doll herself up in her pretty green-flowered mini-dress that she'd recently bought in the C & A sale. She thought it went well with her auburn hair, which made her feel good.

After a final look in the mirror she draped her jacket over her shoulders and left the house, with a swing in her step, living in the hope that Bryn would turn up.

Saturday night was always busy and the jukebox was blaring as she made her way into the lounge. The constant ping of the cash register reminded her of the time when she had worked behind the bar in Cardiff. Those were the days, she thought to herself, remembering them fondly.

Naomi's eyes scanned the lounge for Roger or Bryn, but they were nowhere to be seen. She didn't fancy propping the bar up on her own, so decided to return home. Just as she turned on her heel to leave she heard Bryn call out to her above the level of the music.

'We're over here in the corner,' he shouted, beckoning.

With her heart beating with excitement she pushed her way through the crowds of people towards him.

'Sorry boys. I couldn't see you there with the pillar in the way. And before you ask me Diane couldn't make it.'

She noticed Rogers's mouth tighten with annoyance. 'I suppose that husband of hers is back on the scene, is he?'

'It's nothing of the sort. She's just got a bad head,' said Naomi, settling herself down beside them.

'What you having to drink, then?' asked Bryn, reaching for his inside pocket.

'Make it a pineapple juice, if you don't mind. I'm not really a lover of shorts.'

'Cheap round,' said Roger, slamming his empty glass down on the table. 'I'm off, butty. Two's company, three's a crowd you know.'

Naomi felt a bit nervous at being left with Bryn on his own but when he arrived at the table with the drinks he gave her a huge smile which made her feel more at ease.

'What do you do for a living then?' she asked, trying to break the ice.

'I'm self employed as a handy man. Jack of all trades, master of none. But since the wife and I parted I've moved around in so many grotty bed sits I'm sick of them. That's mainly the reason I spend most evenings in the pub.'

Naomi began to feel sorry for him. She could see by the creases in his shirt that it needed ironing, and on glancing down noticed his shoes were worn and needed a polish.

'Well, you're always welcome to call around my house for a chat and a cup of tea when you're at a loose end,' she said, laying her hand on his arm. 'I'm sure my boy, Philip, won't mind. He's always off playing rugby with his mates on the green. And I get lonely sometimes in the evenings.'

Naomi couldn't believe what she'd just blurted out and thought it might have made her sound cheap.

Bryn's eyes widened. 'So you've got a kid and all then. Duw! you don't look old enough.'

'Flattery will get you everywhere,' she said, laughing. He had boosted her morale, which in turn lifted her spirits. She'd had a hard time trying to juggle the spiralling household bills of late. Bed to work was all her world consisted of and Bryn seemed like a breath of fresh air for her.

When the evening was over Naomi left Bryn waiting for his last bus at the stop outside the public house. She gave him her address on a scrap of paper and felt chuffed to bits at finding a new friend.

During the following weeks Bryn became a regular visitor at Naomi's home and a good friendship began to blossom between them. As time went on she detected a snippet of jealousy between Philip and Bryn. Philip began throwing tantrums over the least little thing. His attitude made life difficult for her. She felt like piggy-in-the-middle all the time and, over the next few months, Philip's constant bickering with her began to wear her down.

One evening Bryn turned up at the house looking somewhat nervous.

'Is there anything the matter? Only you look on the pale side,' said Naomi, inviting him inside.

His expression turned serious. 'Where's Philip? I need a word with you on your own,' he said, grabbing himself a seat near the fire.

'He's in the other room watching television and there's no fear of being interrupted when the sports programme is on. What was it you wanted to say.

You're not in any kind of trouble are you?' she said, fearing the worst.

Bryn suddenly fell to his knees in front of her. 'I'm not very good with words but I would very much like us to get married, if it's OK with you.'

Naomi felt her heart rate quicken. She couldn't believe her ears. 'But I.I.. hardly know you,' she stammered.

'Please say you will. Just think there'll be no need for you to work anymore, because I earn a fair wage.'

His offer sorely tempted her. Life had been hard on her own and Naomi was heartily sick of trying to exist on a meagre income, always penny pinching. Her constant worry was that her health would fail, and where would they be then? She stood back and looked at Bryn. He had certainly taken her breath away and she wasn't getting any younger.

'Let's see what Philip has to say about the matter, shall we?' she said, with a feeling of dread running through her veins. 'After all it does concern him as well.'

Bryn nodded, and made himself comfortable on one of the kitchen chairs. 'Since I've been visiting I've noticed that your son runs circles around you. He won't think of you when he's older either. He's the type to go his own way, whether you like it or not.'

Naomi was angered by his remark. She could say what she liked about her lad, but no-one else could. After taking a deep breath Naomi walked into the living room where Philip was deeply engrossed in watching a sports programme on the television.

'I've something to ask you, Philip,' she said with trepidation.

Philip fixed his eyes on her. 'What is it then? Only you can see I'm looking at the match.'

'Bryn's asked me to marry him,' she announced,

'and I wondered what your thoughts would be on the matter?'

Silence reigned as her words went home, then his gaze returned to the television. 'Do what you want, it's *your* life.'

His few short sharp words shocked Naomi to the core. 'Is that all you've got to say, son?'

Philip shrugged his shoulders then, before Naomi could say any more, Bryn stepped inside the room, which made it obvious to her that he'd been listening to the conversation.

'Well, what do you think of me being your new step-father, then?' said Bryn, puffing his chest out.

'Just leave me to watch my programme in peace will you,' Philip retorted, staring resolutely in front of him.

'Come on Bryn, he's not really worried by the seem of it,' said Naomi, quickly ushering him out of the room.

'What's it to be then, *cariad?*'

'Yes. The answer's yes,' she blurted out, despite knowing deep down that she wasn't at all sure.

'That's my girl! I don't believe in hanging around with engagements. Let's tie the knot as soon as possible. I've no relatives to speak of so it will be just us and a few friends. Perhaps we could have a small do in the local if you like. Shall I visit the registrar's office tomorrow, then?'

Naomi was lost for words. 'My, you are a fast worker,' she said, feeling as if the rug had been taken from under her feet.

The wedding was booked for the first Saturday in September at eleven o'clock. It was to be held in the registry office at the bottom of Stow Hill in Newport, where her previous wedding had taken place. This left

Naomi little time to buy a new outfit, let alone tell all her friends.

She decided to give Diane her invitation by hand and called over at the house feeling on a high.

As she poked her head around the front door she began singing 'I'm getting married in the morning,' which brought Diane rushing out of the front room.

'I hope you're teasing me, girl,' she cried, looking at her wide eyed.

'Well, I would have loved a church do but we haven't the money so that's that,' Naomi said, handing her the invitation.

Diane opened the invite and her face fell. 'I thought you'd had your fill of men. Why don't you love them and leave them? All I can say is that you're a glutton for punishment.'

'I thought you'd be pleased for me. I'm jolly lucky to be asked a second time around.'

'If you must know I took it to be only friendship with Bryn. Otherwise I would have told you that he has a reputation for being a drunk and flirting with hookers.'

Naomi looked at Diane crossly. 'The trouble with you is that you listen to too much gossip. Anyway, I didn't think Roger such a good catch either.'

'Duw! I've no intention of marrying Roger. We're just having a laugh till my old man gets sick of his whore,' retorted Diane.

'And you'd take him back despite everything and a baby to consider?'

'Of course I would because I love him.'

'Well, I'm marrying Bryn whatever you say about him, and there's no chance he'll be spending his money on drink and women while he's living under my roof,' she said defiantly, before walking back out of the house.

They could all think what they wanted for all she cared. No one was going to spoil things for her and that was that.

Philip seemed unconcerned about his mother's impending marriage and had arranged to stay at his friend's house while they were on honeymoon. This suited Naomi as she'd always thought that both boys had a lot in common.

In the meantime, Bryn insisted that Naomi should give up her job at Green's Warehouse which was a great relief to her. She needed a rest and a husband who would help shoulder the responsibilities of running a home. And she hoped that in time her health would improve.

On Naomi's wedding eve Diane paid her a visit to make sure everything was in order, only to find Philip in a surly mood in the living room.

'Mam's moaning at me all the time, Diane, because I don't keep the place tidy. So I intend throwing a drink over her tomorrow at the wedding reception. Just you wait and see.'

'What's the matter with you, Philip? Frightened the limelight will go off you now, is it? Your mother deserves some happiness, and she could do without this behaviour,' Diane yelled, wagging her forefinger at him.

'I want everything to be just so when Bryn and I come back here, that's all. You keep messing things up as if on purpose,' Naomi said in a choked voice.

Philip smirked.

Diane's eyes narrowed. 'We'll have none of this behaviour, or threats about throwing drinks or you'll have me to deal with, not your mother. You get away with murder as it is because your Mam always sees you through rose-tinted glasses.'

Philip stood looking at her as if he was digesting her

words, then he suddenly turned on his heel and stomped loudly up every tread of the stairs to his bedroom.

'He'll get over it,' said Diane, giving Naomi a reassuring look.

'I'd appreciate it if you'd keep an eye on him tomorrow, just in case he plays up,' said Naomi, nervously wringing her hands.

'The trouble with you is you're far too soft with that boy. Always waiting on him hand, foot and finger. Anyway, I can't hang about yapping, so make sure you're ready by ten-thirty when the taxi arrives, unless you've had second thoughts of course.'

Naomi closed the door behind Diane, feeling hurt by her comments. She was fully aware of Philip's failings but, because she felt sorry that he had no-one to turn to except her, she had let him get away with more than she should have and knew only too well she'd made a rod for her own back.

After slumping down on the settee with a mug of hot chocolate in her hand she began to unwind. She found it hard to believe that within twenty-four hours her name would be changed to Mrs Bryn Lewis. She began to wonder about the wisdom of her behaviour. Then a mixture of panic and excitement flowed through her veins.

Her gaze rested on the wall directly over the fire-breast and the patterned wall paper seemed to dissolve into what looked like a mist in front of her. She stared harder, thinking her eyes were playing tricks. As the mist cleared she saw long grasses appear as if out of nowhere.

Suddenly a huge cobra reared his ugly head, twisting its body in and out of the grassland. She nearly jumped out of her skin. *He's a snake in the grass,* came into her mind as clearly as if someone was saying it to her.

Naomi shot bolt upright, staring around her. She began to wonder whether or not her imagination had got the better of her. Suddenly, the images slowly disappeared, leaving her shocked to the core. She felt the difference in temperature in the room and a cold shudder crept down her spine.

CHAPTER 29

Naomi heaved a huge sigh when she got out of bed and drew back the bedroom curtains. She had hoped to see the sun shining on her wedding day and was bitterly disappointed when she saw the rain lashing against the window pane.

Pulling her dressing gown around her she hurried downstairs to prepare breakfast for her son. Her mind flashed back to the strange apparition she'd seen on the living room wall the previous evening but, on glancing into the room in passing, she found everything in order.

Despite trying her hardest to dismiss it from her mind, it wasn't easy. In the end she tried to put the whole scenario down to her imagination running wild.

Shortly after the kettle boiled, Philip appeared in the doorway, looking for his breakfast.

'Morning,' said Naomi, trying her best to sound chirpy.

'We're going to get drenched today by the look of the weather,' he moaned, slumping down on the kitchen chair.

'It might brighten up later on so don't worry, said Naomi, gulping down her tea. She was trying to keep him sweet to avert a fit of the sulks. 'I think it's best if you hurry up and get changed into your best trousers and blazer. Diane will be arriving pretty soon, and we don't want a last minute rush do we?'

At that moment she heard Diane calling through the letter box. She hurriedly let her in.

'I've brought the flowers for your buttonholes and thought it best that I styled and set your hair before you change into your wedding outfit. Or have you had second thoughts?' Diane announced, as she waltzed into the house.

'You've got to be joking,' she said with a smile.

'I'm looking forward to being a lady of leisure at long last.'

At that moment she wished she could confide in her friend how she was marrying for all the wrong reasons. If only her financial situation was more secure, and her health stronger, she'd have thought twice about it all but as things were she didn't have much option but to give it a good try the second time around. She looked up at the sage green suit, on its hanger, that she'd bought for the occasion and hoped she'd get her wear out of it. It was a bit fancy for her liking, but she had decided to buy it because it was a reasonable price.

Just as the clock struck eleven, Naomi and Bryn stood together in front of the Registrar. Diane, Rosie and Sarah sat dressed in their Sunday best behind them, alongside Philip and the best man, Roger.

In no time at all the couple exchanged their vows, looking seemingly happy. And after the ceremony was over Naomi heard Bryn give a huge sigh. Never in her wildest dreams had she imagined marrying again and as she looked across at her new husband he grinned back at her like a cat that had licked a bowl of cream.

After signing the register Naomi linked arms with Bryn and Philip while Diane took some quick photographs on the Registry Office steps. Once that was done they all hurried out of the rain to the taxi rank.

Back at their local pub everyone sat down in the back room while the barmaid unveiled a small spread of sandwiches, sausage rolls and crisps. The single-tiered wedding cake that Naomi had purchased from the local baker took pride of place on a stand in the middle of the table along with a cheap bottle of sherry and glasses. Naomi glanced down at the inexpensive looking ring Bryn had placed on her finger and realised there was no going back. She'd hoped for far better than this for her wedding and was quite downcast by it all.

After Bryn and Roger had downed several pints of beer with their food Bryn prompted Roger to give a speech. Owing to the fact that he slurred his words every few moments Naomi guessed he'd had more than his share of alcohol and was relieved when he sat down, without causing anyone any embarrassment. At that moment her thoughts turned to her birth mother and she was glad she wasn't there to witness such a tawdry scene.

Suddenly Diane stood up. 'I'd like to take some photographs of the happy couple before they depart for their honeymoon.'

'What honeymoon?' shouted Roger in a drunken slur. 'He hasn't got two farthings to rub together, and he even owes me the money for the spread.'

A deathly silence ensued.

Naomi turned to look at a somewhat flummoxed Bryn whose cheeks had turned the colour of beetroot. 'I..I meant to tell you that I'm not in the position to take us away anywhere for the night but I'll make things up to you another time,' he said, looking ashamed. 'Why don't you help yourself to another sherry before the bottle empties, my darling?'

Cheap sherry had always given Naomi a bad stomach on the odd occasion of weddings or funerals when she'd had any, so she declined the offer. She tried hard to contain herself despite knowing what a wash out her wedding had turned into. She'd had high hopes that Bryn had secretly booked a hotel for their wedding night at least and, as she took a bite of her cream cheese sandwich, she glanced at Philip who was busily filling his plate with what was left of the sandwiches and sausage rolls.

'Don't take all the food Philip. Leave some for

everyone else,' she snapped, looking daggers at him.

His eyes flashed angrily.

'Let's take some photos of you both standing by the cake then,' Diane suggested, positioning the cake in front of them.

Naomi could tell by the look on Diane's face that she sensed the tenseness of the situation. She huddled up to Bryn for the photo shoot. All eyes were on them as Diane clicked away, which gave Philip the chance to pour out what was left of the sherry into a glass behind their backs.

Suddenly Bryn caught sight of him out of the corner of his eye. 'Put that down this minute,' he bellowed.

Naomi leapt from her seat, snatching the glass from Philip's hand. As she did so she spilled the sherry all over her new two-piece suit.

Philip smirked then marched out of the room, with Naomi running after him. 'Whatever did you do that for? Look at the state of me. I think you should go back inside and apologise for causing a scene.'

'You did it. Not me,' he grunted. 'Anyway, I'm off to stay at my friends, because your wedding is nothing but a farce.'

Naomi watched as, in a huff, her son stomped out of the building and down the road.

She feared trouble was brewing already between him and Bryn. And dreaded the thought of what might happen.

Shortly afterwards Diane, Roger, Rosie and Sarah, left the wedding party to go their separate ways, leaving Bryn and Naomi to walk home alone.

As they walked down the street they saw several of the neighbours out on their fronts, chatting. They turned silent on seeing the bridal pair.

'We heard you were getting wed today. That was quick. You haven't known him no time,' sneered Mrs

Pugh, the baker's wife, as she leant over her sweeping brush. 'Not in the family way are we?' she sniggered, looking Naomi up and down.

Naomi heard suppressed giggling from the other women and walked on, ignoring them, fully aware their mouths were always busy whenever she appeared.

'Marry in haste, repent at leisure,' Mrs Pugh shouted after her, waving her brush in the air.

Naomi put the key in the lock, seething. She'd regarded Mrs Pugh as being puffed up with self importance because her husband owned the bakery business down the road. She had never taken to the woman because of her sour tongue. Bryn traipsed in behind her, slumped down on the nearest chair and promptly fell asleep. Naomi heaved a huge sigh and was glad the charade was all over.

Within the first month of their marriage Bryn lost his job in the factory and owned up to being penniless, which went down like a lead weight with Naomi It was only now that she came to realise why Bryn had insisted on a hasty marriage, and she felt like kicking herself for her stupidity. Even the brown paper carrier bag containing a few clothes and torn sheets he'd brought with him spoke volumes. Just the thought of having to live life with a penniless, comparative stranger unnerved her but she knew she'd made her bed and had no other option but to lie on it.

After the second month of their marriage Naomi lost count of the people who came knocking at the door asking for money that Bryn owed. When his landlord came to collect the arrears on his bed-sit it took every last penny Naomi had kept by for emergencies. By now the picture was becoming all too clear. She'd become the scapegoat.

Shortly after Philip left for school one morning her heart plummeted when she was faced with an official from the tax office demanding to see her husband.

'Bryn, there's a gentleman down here for you, so you'd better shift yourself,' she shouted up the stairs as she invited the stranger inside the house, out of the neighbours' view.

Within minutes Bryn was up and dressed and ran down the stairs, looking flummoxed. Naomi made herself scarce in the other room, hoping that the official's visit might bring them a tax rebate now that Bryn was out of work.

Some time afterwards she heard the slamming of the front door and ran into the front room. 'What did he want then?' she blurted out.

'Well, if you must know, I neglected to pay any tax or insurance because I was only a self employed dogsbody at the factory. So I've been ordered to pay ten pounds a week off the arrears or I'll be summoned to court.'

'I don't believe this,' said Naomi, holding her face in her hands. 'You've promised to pay this amount and you're not even in employment. So, where's the money coming from?' she ranted at him.

Bryn coloured up, looking guilty.

'You'd better get out there and find some work, boyo, because I'm sick of keeping us all on a pittance from the dole.'

'I can do without you keeping on, woman,' said Bryn, snatching his jacket from the back of the door.

Naomi ran after him up the hallway and followed him out of the house. 'Don't you dare come back until you've found yourself some employment. Do you hear?'

Bryn carried on walking as if he was oblivious to her ranting.

At that moment Mrs Pugh came along. 'Trouble in Paradise, is it, dear?' she smirked.

'Shut your mouth, you nosy old bag,' Naomi snarled, giving her a look fit to kill.

'Don't you take your marriage problems out on me,' retorted Mrs Jones, with her head held in the air. 'You never were a good judge of character when it came to men were you?'

Naomi darted inside, fuming. What with Philip and his moods, spending most of his spare time out with friends, and her husband taking her for a fool she felt fit to scream.

Several hours later Bryn staggered home, reeking of drink.

'So you've been over the pub getting drunk, and with what?' Naomi shouted, as soon as he appeared through the door.

'It went on the slate, woman, so don't worry,' he slurred, falling down onto the nearest chair.

Naomi shook her head in desperation then stamped out of the room, afraid of what she might do next.

Later that evening she became increasingly worried when her son hadn't returned from the Youth Club, at his usual time of ten thirty. Just as she was about to put on her coat he appeared in the doorway looking somewhat dishevelled.

By now Bryn had slept the drink off and, as soon as he heard Philip's voice, he looked at his watch and dived into the hallway. 'What time do you call this?' he growled. 'You've been up to no good, I expect.'

Naomi ran to her son's side.

'He's not my father so I don't have to answer to him,' Philip grunted, staring hard and long at Bryn.

Naomi recoiled, looking shocked. 'What's your real father ever done for you, my boy? Not even a birthday or Christmas card. And he only ever paid a few bob maintenance because the courts demanded it.'

With a defiant look Philip ran up the stairs,

slamming his bedroom door behind him.

'You're too soft with that boy, that's your trouble. He doesn't even wash up a cup for you,' sneered Bryn, looking full of himself.

'Hark who's talking,' snapped Naomi, fuming.

'Shifting things onto me now are we?'

Naomi looked at him, exasperated. 'Before you start whingeing about my son I think it's high time you found yourself work. It's either that or I'm throwing you out.'

Bryn went quiet. Naomi knew by the solemn look on his face that her words had taken effect. She was riddled with worry. The household bills were long overdue so she knew she had no alternative but to return to work herself otherwise things would really get out of hand.

On her arrival at Green's Warehouse the next morning Naomi called into Tony Brain's office, dressed in her best suit hoping to create a good impression.

'Morning, Mr Brain. I don't suppose there's any chance of some work going, only I need a few hours to help keep the wolves away from the door, so to speak.'

Tony Brain's eyes held hers for a few seconds in an intense, almost intimate stare. 'Good morning. It's a lovely surprise to see you, and we are a typist short as it happens now Rhiannon is on sick leave. There's no-one I'd like better than you to fill the space.'

Naomi's eyes lit up. 'When can I start then?' she asked with desperation in her voice.

'Tomorrow morning suit you? Only there's a huge pile of paper work to catch up on and I know you're quite capable of handling such things. By the way I was under the impression you'd retired from work in order to marry.'

'Well, that's another story, shall we say,' said

Naomi, not wanting to go into details.

'You know I'm always around for a shoulder to cry on, don't you?'

'I'll bear that in mind, thank you,' said Naomi, enthusiastically. She had an idea there was much more to Tony Brain than met the eye, and had always felt her heart pounding in her chest whenever he was near.

On her arrival home she was flabbergasted to find a note left on the table from Bryn, saying he'd found himself employment in the new supermarket up the road. She sighed with relief. At least her marriage might stand a chance now.

Naomi settled back into working at Green's Warehouse as if she'd never been away from the place and she was pleased to see Bryn was a reformed character now he was back working. Occasional rows still flared between him and Philip but, more often that not, Naomi turned a blind eye because she lived in the hope that they might eventually bury the hatchet.

Shortly after her arrival home from work one tea time Naomi was peeling some potatoes to cook with liver and onions for their evening meal. Just as she was lighting the gas under the pans she heard a knock at the door. On opening it she was confronted by a well dressed, middle-aged man, with a trilby hat on his head.

'Am I addressing Mrs Lewis?' he asked in an official voice.

'You are,' said Naomi, looking at him curiously.

'I'm Mr Price, the Bailiff, calling about Mr Bryn Lewis's debts,' he announced loudly, thrusting a document into her hand.

Naomi nearly choked. 'You'd better come inside,' she whispered, fearing the neighbours might hear.

The man followed her down the hallway and into the kitchen where he took a grubby looking notebook out of his pocket and began writing in it.

'What on earth are you doing?' she asked angrily, watching his every move.

'Just taking an inventory of what furniture you have, my dear.'

Naomi stared at him in disbelief. She stood holding onto the table to steady herself. 'Stop that! You can't take anything from here because *I* own all the furniture *not* Mr Lewis.'

'I'd like a quid for all the times I've heard that old tale. You're man and wife, aren't you?' smirked the man, as he carried on looking over the place.

'Just how much does my husband owe then, and what for? Only we haven't been married for long and I've not seen anything new being brought into this house.'

The man's face hardened. 'I have it on good authority that Mr Lewis bought some electrical goods on hire purchase over two years ago, which come to just over the two hundred pound mark.'

Naomi looked at him stupefied. Apart from not liking his manner she felt extremely humiliated by it all and she could feel her insides knotting up to such an extent that it hurt.

'Don't tell me you didn't know about all this because we've written to your address on several occasions, and he's had ample time to reply.'

'I haven't seen any letters,' moaned Naomi, suspecting that Bryn had probably hidden them from her.

'Surely we can pay this off weekly,' she begged, feeling acutely embarrassed.

'It's too late for that, I'm afraid,' said the bailiff, frowning.

'W..what if I told you that I could find the money by tomorrow?' she stuttered in desperation, hoping to stall him.

The bailiff stopped in his tracks rubbing his chin. 'I've heard that one before too, so don't waste my time,' he grunted.

'No. I promise I'll find you the money by tomorrow,' she cried, wringing her hands.

'Well, I'll give you the benefit of the doubt, but you've only got twenty-four hours or goods will be taken equivalent to the sum owed.'

Naomi's face turned white.

After closing his notebook the man walked out of the house leaving Naomi in a state of despair. The shame of it all creased her. For years she had scrimped and scraped to keep a roof above her head. She had thought that by finding a husband it would be the answer to her prayers. She broke down in tears, wondering where it would all end.

Naomi fought to control her anger when Bryn returned from work that evening.

'What on earth's the matter with you?' he asked. 'You've a face like a bloody smacked arse.'

Naomi hated his crude remarks. They only fired her up even more. 'I've had the bailiff calling, dear husband, asking for over two hundred pounds for outstanding debts you owe. And, if it's not paid by tomorrow, they intend taking my furniture away,' she cried, thrusting the bailiff's document into his hands. I've never felt so humiliated in all my life. What I saw in you in the first place I'll never know.'

Bryn glanced down at the document and shrugged his shoulders. 'Well, we'll just have to sit on the floor, won't we? There's no chance of me finding that kind of money.'

Naomi was outraged by his flippant attitude. She felt like punching him.

'What do you intend doing about it then?' she screamed, getting angrier by the minute. 'You can't

289

hide in a corner pretending it's not happening.'

Bryn banged his fist down on the table. 'I'm off to the pub. You work it out.'

'Drowning your sorrows in drink's not the answer.'

'Nor is it listening to a whinging woman.'

Turning on his heel Bryn left the house just as Philip strolled in looking for his tea.

Naomi forced back the tears and quickly dished up his food.

'Don't tell me its liver and onions again?'

'What's wrong with liver and onions when some people are starving?'she snapped, trying to control her temper.

'Well, I don't want it,' he cried, pushing the plate from him. 'I'll take some biscuits from the tin. I'm off with Johnny Hodges tonight.'

Naomi wasn't keen on him keeping company with Johnny. He had a bad reputation in the neighbourhood for hanging round street corners looking for trouble but she knew there would be a huge row if she tried to intervene and anyway she was in no mood for any more hassle.

Shortly afterwards she heard her son leave the house. She felt so alone in her troubles and was loath to tell him what had happened, knowing he would fly off the handle with Bryn causing more problems.

Her stomach churned as she stared down at her wedding ring. It was a sure fact that marriage hadn't brought her bliss and she wished, with all her heart, she hadn't got herself in such a mess.

Before starting work the next day Naomi walked into Tony Brain's office, with tears in her eyes.

'What on earth's the matter?' he cried, coming to her side. 'I can't have my work force looking unhappy.'

She felt his large hands grasp her shoulders and caught her breath. 'The bailiff called yesterday asking for money for my husband's debts. I desperately need to borrow two hundred pounds from somewhere because he's returning today to take my furniture, and it's not even Bryn's stuff at that,' she poured out.

'I can't believe that a lovely girl like you has got herself entangled with yet another waster. With your looks you could have had your pick of men. I thought you might have learned after being married to Duncan.'

'Believe you me, he's a saint compared to Duncan Campbell, but he'll never have a penny to his name as long as he drinks like a fish.'

'If I had someone like you at home I certainly wouldn't be spending my time in a public house,' Tony said, pulling her close to him. 'I've always had a yearning for you,' he added, gazing into her eyes. 'And I'm prepared to lend you the money on one condition. That you pay me back in kind.'

Naomi looked at him, flabbergasted.

'Think it over, and as long as you promise to keep things to yourself, we could perhaps go for a run in my car at lunch time.'

'You don't waste any time about things, do you?' said Naomi, her stomach churning over.

He shook his head then walked over to the safe.

She'd always fancied him but never in her wildest dreams did she think he would make such a proposal. She was completely unaware of his marital status and she had no intentions of making their private business common knowledge, being up to her neck in debt as she was.

Tony Brain walked back from the safe with a wad of money in his hand.

'What do you propose then?' asked Naomi, willingly offering herself on a plate.

His eyes glistened.

Desperate for him to hand the money over, she

sidled closer to him.

'See you at one o'clock then,' he said, pressing his body up against hers.

'I won't tell a soul,' she promised. 'It will be our little secret.' As far as she was concerned it would just be a physical thing but, deep down, this still made her feel little better than a prostitute.

Before she had time to think of anything he lowered his lips to hers and rendered her senseless, something which Bryn wasn't capable of.

'Where on earth have you been?' asked Bryn, as soon as Naomi came through the door that evening.

'Paying off your debts, if you must know,' she answered, feeling her colour rise. 'I took time off in order to visit the County Court Offices with the money. So you want to thank your lucky stars I managed to get a loan.'

'Good for you. Now what's for dinner? I'm starving.'

Naomi sighed with the relief that her husband seemed content with her explanation.

She looked in the pantry to find something for their meal and gave a wry smile as she thought back to her afternoon of passion.

CHAPTER 30

One day, on her arrival home from work, Naomi found Philip sitting in the kitchen with his friend Evan, drinking tea.

'You'll never guess what, Mam. I've got myself a job,' announced her son, beaming all over his face.

'I thought you were staying on in school,' said Naomi, gaping at him in amazement. Time was slipping away too quickly for her. She couldn't believe that her son was growing into a man, and she into a middle-aged woman.

'You've no chance of that,' he retorted. 'Evan and I have found ourselves shift work at the Engineering firm off the High Street, and we start just as soon as we break up for the summer holidays. There's also talk that the firm is moving to London. That will be fun if it does.'

Naomi looked at them both with gaping mouth. It was as if a bolt out of the blue had hit her. 'Well, I hope you land on your feet, son, and wish you all the luck in the world but I'd think it all over carefully if I was you.'

She had hoped her son would have done better for himself and wondered whether or not he had been talked into finding work by Evan but, she told herself, perhaps it was time to cut the apron strings.

The following day Naomi was surprised to see Rhiannon who used to work beside her in the foundry sat at her desk

'Good gracious me, fancy seeing you here,' said Rhiannon, gawping at her.

'So it was *your* job I took over,' said Naomi, looking shocked. 'I'd best go and ask Mr Brain if he needs me anymore, because he did say that the position might be only temporary.

As soon as she walked into Tony Brain's office he looked up at her with a smile on his face. She was wearing her green spotted, see-through blouse, the one she so eagerly threw off during their afternoon of pleasure. Tony's sexual performance had already ruined her with regards to making love with her husband. He had worked her body knowing her every weakness, giving her pleasures she'd never known. What had started out as meaningless sex had gone far beyond that.

Up until then Tony had not made any further advances towards her but was polite when their paths crossed in the corridors between their offices.

She stood before him quaking in her shoes at the thought of losing her job. Bryn only gave her a pittance in money for housekeeping and she knew that without her wage they'd find it hard to live.

'I was hoping you could find me another position now Rhiannon's back in the work force?' she said with trepidation.

'Well, well, it's a long time since we've had a chat together. So how do you fancy another outing one lunchtime?' he asked with a wicked smile on his face. I'll have to share you with my other girlfriend and wife mind. But I can assure you that I'll always find the time to accommodate you.'

I've no intentions of being a convenient m.m.mistress.' stuttered Naomi.

He had taken her unawares. She wondered whether or not he was joking. He was flirting outrageously with her and she was enjoying every minute of it. He'd never ever mentioned the two hundred pounds he so willingly gave her. But in her eyes she thought she'd earned it, and the subject had never arisen.

'Does my answer determine whether or not you'll find me a position in the firm then?' she asked him, smiling sweetly. He put his arm around her. For a brief moment their eyes met but she was first to look away.

'I can't stop thinking about you,' he whispered in her ear, running his hand down the front of her blouse. 'For the time being I can certainly fix you up with some relief work on the switchboard until things are more amenable between us.'

'Naomi nodded and pushed his hand away. No way was she going to play such a dangerous game. She could feel her body shaking and knew the inevitable would happen if she allowed her feelings to get the better of her. 'I'll run down to the switchboard and see what shifts are on offer,' she cried, knowing full well she was losing control of the situation. Suddenly, without a backward look she ran out of the office like a bat out of hell.

From that day on Naomi began to look for other employment. She was fully aware that she could easily succumb to Tony's advances and thought it best if she broke all ties from him.

One afternoon, when sharing a tea break with Rhiannon, the subject of clairvoyance came into the conversation.

'I've heard there's a very good card reader down in Newport, near the docks, named Kate. I've written her number down in my diary somewhere,' said Rhiannon, pulling a small note book out of her bag. 'How do you fancy coming along? Only, I don't relish walking down the dock area of Newport on my own with all those seafaring men about.'

Naomi looked at her eagerly. 'I could do with a glimpse into the future myself but would rather make it on the weekend because I'll have to juggle the housekeeping around for the clairvoyant's fee.'

'That's alright. I've man trouble to contend with, and that's not the half of it.'

I know the feeling only too well,' Naomi answered, looking at her in amusement.

When the bus pulled into Newport town centre Naomi was delighted to see Rhiannon waiting for her at the bus stop. It was a hot sunny day and Rhiannon's long black hair was tied up in a pony tail which showed off her prominent features.

They linked arms then eagerly made their way in the direction of Pillgwenlly, affectionately known to the locals as Pill. After enquiring the way from a police constable on his beat they turned in the direction of the Transporter Bridge, which towered across the murky waters of the River Usk. Not far from the bridge was the entrance to the Newport docks, a thriving port and hub of industry.

Rhiannon clutched a piece of paper with Kate's address on and, after passing several streets of terraced houses with people of all nationalities going about their business, they finally found their destination.

Looking up at the red brick house Naomi gingerly knocked on the newly varnished door, noticing how well kept the place looked with its clean windows and well scrubbed step.

Within seconds the door was opened and they were welcomed inside by a plump, jolly looking woman, whose greying hair was wrapped up in a bun.

'Through here, my lovelies,' she said, in a strong Welsh accent, taking them into the kitchen. 'Now who's first?'

Rhiannon pushed herself forward while Naomi made herself at home on an easy chair near the window looking out on the yard where there were several beautiful rose bushes. She was glad of the time to sit and stare into space. Relaxing in the warmth of the sun's rays she soon dozed off to sleep.

Twenty minutes or so later Rhiannon returned looking far from happy.

'Is everything OK?' Naomi asked, struck by the paleness of her face.

'Yes fine,' mumbled Rhiannon, with a resigned smile.

Before Naomi could comment she heard Kate calling her into the parlour, and made her way down the long hallway. As she stepped into the room a beautiful oak dresser full of china ornaments, and photographs took her attention when she pulled out a chair and sat down.

Kate immediately thrust a large crystal ball into her hands then placed some playing cards in front of her. Naomi held onto the crystal carefully, and stared into the woman's eyes.

'Make a wish on the crystal then shuffle the cards, putting them into three piles,' urged Kate.

Naomi immediately thought about her birth mother and made a wish regarding her. She passed the crystal ball back into the old lady's hands and couldn't wait to hear what the clairvoyant would pick up on. Then she shuffled the cards and placed them down in three piles, hoping for good news.

Kate began staring into the crystal ball, turning it one way and then another.

'You have part of your life missing and will be granted your wish, dear, but no good can come of it, mark my words,' said Kate, shaking her head.

Naomi sat riveted to her seat, gulping hard.

'I'm seeing the Houses of Parliament, which means a person connected with you must be living somewhere in London.'

'What else can you see?' asked Naomi, excitedly.

'There's a woman with dark curly hair coming into view. Once she was a good time girl, but now she's portraying herself as Miss Goody Two Shoes,' said Kate, frowning. 'This person gave several children away and doesn't want anyone to haunt her from the past. But mark my words, justice will be done. She's fooled many people, and didn't play fair with an elderly lady either. Was this your grandmother?'

'I wouldn't know,' said Naomi, shaking her head.

'I can see that the dark curly headed woman moved house several times and lived in fear of her past catching up with her. I can also see several men around her.'

Silence reigned for several seconds as Kate stared back into the crystal. 'I'm sorry but the crystal is misting up. Let's see what the cards have in store, shall we?'

Naomi took a deep breath as Kate placed the crystal back in its box, and began handling the cards. She was deeply moved by what the old lady had told her, and was amazed at her accuracy.

'There was a very tall man who turned his back on the dark-headed woman I was talking about. When he eventually settled down he chose someone who would look after him. The dark-headed woman only wanted fun.'

'Is that so?' said Naomi, taking in every word she was saying.

Then a grim look suddenly appeared on Kate's face, as she turned over more cards. 'I can see a broken wedding ring as plain as day. There is a woman dressed in a fur coat who will cause trouble. She's not Welsh either. So be warned!'

Naomi's heart began thumping twenty to the dozen. All sorts of fears began to flood through her brain. What if Bryn *was* having an affair? Would she be able to turn a blind eye after breaking her marriage vows herself?

Kate gave her a wry smile, as if she was reading her mind. 'You have lots of spirit people around you, and are psychic yourself.'

'I know,' said Naomi. 'I used to read the tea-leaves and visit the Spiritualist church but since marrying again my husband doesn't approves of such things.'

'Always remember that the gifts you don't use you will lose, my dear. But be sure to take care of yourself, my lovely, because you've a hard road to tread.'

Kate stacked the cards to one side while Naomi reached inside her bag for her purse. Despite being told some more home truths about her birth mother she was still determined never to rest until she'd found her.

'Well, what did you think of Kate the Clairvoyant then?' said Naomi to Rhiannon when they were out of earshot of the house.

'I'm still trying to come to terms with her predictions because she told me something I didn't want to hear. Look, there's a café further on down the main road,' she said, pointing to it. 'Just over the road from the dock gates. Let's stop there for a bite to eat. I'm starving.'

Naomi followed behind her into the café which was mainly full of sea-faring men having arrived off the boats at the docks. They eyed the girls as they walked inside. Naomi quickly ushered Rhiannon to a table laid with a red and white checked cloth by the window then went up to the counter to place her order.

'Two pasties and a pot of tea for two, please,' she said, counting out the last of her change from her purse.

After eating their pasties Naomi sat back in her chair and mentioned a couple of the things that Kate had forecast.

'So you were pleased with her,' said Rhiannon, pulling a face. 'Well let me tell you I was devastated when she told me I was *pregnant*.'

Naomi nearly choked on her tea. 'I didn't know you were even courting.'

'Well, sort of. But it's complicated if you get my meaning. Anyway I've had suspicions I was in the pudding club for quite some time now. And to think the doctor put me on the sick with a virus. Virus, my arse! Just wait until I drop the bombshell in my man friend's lap. He'll have a fit because he's already spoken for. But I'll stir things up just you wait and see.'

'I'm sorry to hear about your trouble,' said Naomi, pulling a face. She wondered who the man friend was but thought it none of her business.

After they'd finished eating Rhiannon stood up to leave. 'I think it's time we made our way to the bus station, only I've some shopping to do before the indoor market closes,' she said, slinging her shoulder bag over her arm.

Naomi followed behind her. She was so glad to have taken the birth pill during her marriage with Bryn and wouldn't have changed places with her friend for the world.

Shortly after Naomi arrived home she made a cup of tea for herself and, just as she was taking some biscuits out of the tin, Bryn entered the room.

'Well, what did the fortune teller have to say then?' he asked, looking at her eagerly. 'Are we going to win the pools?'

'Seeing we don't do them I very much doubt it,' retorted Naomi, surprised that he took such an interest in it all. She settled herself down on the kitchen chair before kicking off her shoes. 'There was no mention of money but I thought she was quite good actually, although she didn't tell me a lot.'

'Did she mention me?' said Bryn, staring hard at her.

'No not really, nor did she speak of Philip. Anyway

why are you so concerned? Got something to hide?'

'Don't talk daft,' said Bryn, colouring up. 'Where did you say she lived? Only I thought I might just pay her a visit, just to see what the old girl has to say.'

Naomi gave him an odd look. She didn't trust him an inch.

CHAPTER 31

That evening Naomi slumped in the armchair wanting nothing more than the touch of Tony's hand on her breast, but she knew deep down it would have been a recipe for disaster. She wanted her marriage to work but lately drink seemed to take Bryn's preference and by the time he returned home after an evening at the pub he was so full of booze he could hardly stand, let alone interest her with a night of passion.

One Saturday evening, as Naomi was working her way through a huge pile of ironing, Bryn appeared in the doorway looking very pleased with himself.

'I've just returned from visiting Kate the clairvoyant. She told me there'd be another women in my life and I'll be moving house before long,' he boasted.

'You're a dark horse. I didn't even know you'd made an appointment with her,' said Naomi, looking surprised. 'Well, I've always wanted to live in the country and have chickens,' she mused. 'And as for another woman in your life, perhaps it will happen when I'm dead and gone.'

Before Bryn could answer there was a loud knock on the front door and when Naomi opened it she found herself confronted by two strangers.

'Can I help you?' she asked hesitantly, hoping they hadn't called for money. Up until now Naomi had managed to keep Bryn's debts under control and she certainly didn't intend forking out for any more.

'We wondered if Bryn was coming over for a drink. When he didn't turn up as promised we were worried,' said the woman.

Naomi eyed her up and down and thought she looked mutton dressed up as lamb. Crossing her arms over her chest she called out to Bryn. 'It's someone for you.'

Bryn ambled to the door and looked shocked on seeing who was there.

'Come on in and take the weight off your feet. This is the wife.'

'I'm Fiona, an old friend of Bryn's, and this is my husband, John,' said the woman in a broad Scottish accent. Her eyes flitted around the room taking everything in, which riled Naomi. She'd met her type before – nosey and all show.

'Feel free to join us if you want to,' said Bryn, looking over at Naomi as he dipped into the wooden biscuit barrel where the housekeeping money was kept.

'I suppose a quick drink won't hurt. It's not often I get invited out, is it?' said Naomi, pursing her lips. 'I'll just give my hair a quick comb.'

Despite feeling tired she thought she'd tag along because she found it odd that Bryn hadn't mentioned the couple to her before.

After settling themselves down in the local pub Naomi noticed that Fiona was too chummy with Bryn for her liking. But she decided to ignore it and took a seat beside John, who she thought looked much older than Fiona.

During the course of the evening Naomi got the impression that John was under Fiona's thumb, He rarely made any comment unless prompted to do so by her. Although her Scottish accent made it difficult for Naomi to understand what she was saying, she soon realized that Bryn had known her for quite some time. She could sense a familiarity between them, as if they had once been lovers, so she sat watching points all evening, thinking back to what Kate the clairvoyant had predicted.

Just as last orders were being called Bryn stood up to leave. Naomi was ready to go as well. She guessed the housekeeping money was now spent and was glad to be going home to her bed.

'It's John's fiftieth birthday next Friday. You must come around to the party,' said Fiona, with a big smile on her face.

'Never let it be said that I'd stay away from a good shindig with such a pretty hostess,' answered Bryn, grinning.

Naomi followed him out of the pub, seething. 'How well do you actually know Fiona?' she asked, stopping in her tracks, and looking at him.

'Well enough,' he smirked, sauntering on down the road in front of her.

Naomi didn't respond. She was determined she would find out in her own good time. All she had to do now was to stand back and give Bryn enough rope in the hopes that he would hang himself.

On the following Friday Bryn finished work early and happened to walk into the bedroom just as Naomi was going through her worn out clothes in the wardrobe.

'What do you think of the shirt I've bought then? I thought it would look great for tonight.'

'I could have done with something new as well,' Naomi moaned, surveying a black and white spotted dress that she'd kept, for best occasions, over the years

'There's nothing wrong with that,' said Bryn, turning his head.

'Make do and mend, that's all I ever do,' Naomi snapped. 'I thought things would be *so* different when I married you.'

'Don't keep on, woman, for God's sake,' said Bryn, looking at himself in the dressing table mirror. 'No-one's going to notice you anyway.'

She felt like boxing his ears but decided to keep the peace because she had no wish to forego a party.

When they eventually arrived at the house Fiona opened the door herself and cheerfully welcomed them inside. Naomi thought how smart she looked in her flame red mini-dress, and any self esteem that she had left about herself plummeted.

'Help yourself to a drink while I steal your Bryn away for a while,' said Fiona, as she ushered Bryn towards the kitchen.

Naomi took a deep breath then made herself comfortable on the settee, next to a young girl who was tapping her foot to the music.

'I'm Joy. Known Fiona long?'

Naomi shook her head and smiled sweetly.

'Well, when you get to know her you'll find out she's one hell of a flirt. I'd watch your husband with her if I was you,' she sniggered.

'Is that so?' said Naomi, wondering what was taking her husband so long in the kitchen. She sat back in her seat and glanced around the room at the large sculptured figures and flowing silk curtains. They were far too ostentatious for her. It was certainly not a place she could feel at home in.

Suddenly she looked up and saw Bryn enter the room with his hair looking ruffled and tie askew.

'What on earth have you been doing with yourself?'

'Just fixing Fiona's plumbing, you could say,' he said grinning.

Naomi couldn't be bothered with playing games and was determined not to let her husband spoil her evening. The room began filling with people just as John brought in several plates of sandwiches and fairy cakes.

At that point Naomi stood up and began to mingle with the other guests. She soon learned that John spent most of his time working as a contractor in Scotland, which was where he and Fiona first met. Alarm bells began to ring in Naomi's head. She wondered if Fiona was playing away with her husband. Was that the reason he spent so much time in the pub? If indeed he was in the pub. All sorts of things raced through her brain and she decided to keep a close watch on him as the evening wore on.

Much to her surprise nothing untoward happened for the next couple of hours but, by the time the clock struck ten, she could see that Bryn was the worse for drink. He was swaying and talking absolute rubbish.

'I'm taking you home before you embarrass me any further, Bryn,' she shouted, gathering up their coats from the hallstand.

Fiona and John heard her raised voice and quickly appeared on the scene. 'You can't leave now,' said Fiona. 'Things are only just starting to warm up.'

'Sorry about this,' said Naomi, pushing Bryn out of the front door. 'Look at the state of him.'

'I do see your point,' said John, looking embarrassed. 'By the way I've tickets for the Rugby Club next weekend. What say we meet up there? I'll keep you some seats, shall I?'

'That's a d.d.date,' stammered Bryn, ogling at Fiona who was grinning all over her face.

As Naomi pulled him out into the street she mumbled a quick goodnight to her hosts and began to steer Bryn down the road towards home. It took her ages to drag him through the back streets but she felt too ashamed to be seen walking with him along the main road for fear of people recognising her. How she bitterly regretted marrying him and, as the anger whelmed up inside her he began to stumble, nearly dragging her down onto the pavement as he made his way to the gutter to vomit. Just the thought of having to share the same bed with him made her cringe.

When they eventually arrived outside the house

Naomi quickly opened the door and pushed him inside, where he fell headlong in a crumpled heap on the hallway floor. Too wound up to speak she decided to leave him to his own devices. The subject of divorce loomed into her mind. She had no intentions of carrying on like this anymore.

As she was making herself a nightcap Bryn stumbled into the kitchen putting a firm hand on her shoulder. She shuddered as she smelt the stale smell of drink and vomit on his breath.

'Let go of me,' she shouted, pushing him from her.

Bryn fell against the wall. 'You'll be sorry for this, my lady. I've been offered cock down the road, so don't you forget it.'

Naomi looked at him shocked. 'She's welcome to you, boyo. Who on earth in their right mind would want a lout like you? Anyway I've had enough.'

Gathering up her handbag and nightcap Naomi climbed the stairs with a heavy heart. She'd hoped Philip's hadn't heard the kafuffle downstairs so she quickly peeked into his bedroom. She sighed with relief at the sight of him soundly asleep, and quietly closed the door before going to her bed.

Later that night she heard Bryn rummaging around in the spare room. She was hoping he was making himself at home on the put-u-up bed. At least she would be spared having to contend with his snoring and fumbling hands.

During the following week Bryn acted like a stranger towards her. When Philip asked his mother what was wrong she fobbed him off with a white lie not wanting to go into details. She had always prayed that he would have an easier life than hers and was pleased that he was doing well in his new job at the engineering works.

Shortly before leaving for work one morning Naomi

decided to soak her husband's dirty jeans in the galvanised tub. As she emptied his pockets she found a wage slip screwed up with two dirty handkerchiefs. She caught her breath on seeing the total amount of money he received each week. It was treble the measly sum he gave her. Her emotions began to run high as she crammed the slip into her pinafore pocket, furious to think of the steps she had taken in order to clear his debts.

That evening, as soon as Bryn came through the door, she pounced on him, waving the wage slip like evidence in his face. 'What have you got to say about this then, Bryn Lewis?'

Bryn's eyes flashed in anger. 'Been snooping, have we?'

'So what if I was? I always turn out the pockets of your jeans before soaking them. Anyway don't change the subject. I've had all your debts to contend with and this is how you pay me back by keeping me short of money. I can understand where the money came from to go drinking now.'

'So what?' snorted Bryn, grimacing. 'You'd drive anyone to drink.'

'Our marriage is in tatters and you couldn't care less. Why don't you turn over a new leaf then perhaps we could visit a marriage counsellor before it's too late?'

'I'd have to be desperate to be seen entering one of those places. Anyway, I've better fish to fry so don't wait up.'

'What about your tea?' she demanded. 'There's a casserole cooking in the oven.'

'You eat it then, and I hope it chokes you.'

With this threat Bryn left the house, banging the door angrily as he left.

They passed like ships in the night until Saturday evening came around.

'Don't forget to have your glad rags on before seven because we've a date with Fiona and John. Or had you forgotten?' muttered Bryn, on his arrival home from work.

'Oh! You surprise me. I didn't think we were going,' Naomi answered mournfully. She felt so cold and empty inside.

She reached out to him but he pulled away.

'Well aren't you going to put your glad rags on then?' said Bryn, looking quite indifferent.

What glad rags? Naomi thought to herself as she stood before the mirror in her well worn black and white spotted frock.

The nights were drawing in and there was a chill wind blowing, so she decided to wear her black woollen jacket over her dress. Much to her surprise Bryn took her arm as they were leaving the house. As far as she was concerned it was Bryn's last chance at saving their marriage, which she knew was well on the rocks.

As they jostled amongst the crowd in the Rugby Club it wasn't long before they came across Fiona and John who beckoned them over to their table. Naomi seated herself in the well furnished lounge bar and noticed that Fiona had a fur coat draped over the back of her seat.

'Posh gaff,' said Bryn loudly. 'I'll get the round then, is it?'

'Mine's a pineapple juice please,' said Naomi, sitting down.

'I'll help you with the drinks,' chimed in John, rising out of his chair. 'We're glad you could make it on time, only it does get rather packed.'

Fiona stared across the table at Naomi. 'You're

looking peaky tonight.'

'Well, things between Bryn and me have been strained of late. Or didn't you know?'

'Yes, he did tell me the other evening when we bumped into each other in the pub. Still, men are strange creatures aren't they? But once you know how to handle them they melt like putty in your hands.'

Naomi's eyes flashed. She was annoyed to think that Bryn had discussed their private life with this woman and looked coldly at her. Her low-cut black dress revealed most of her ample bosom. Bryn would have had a fit if he had found her wearing the same, but she noticed it didn't stop him ogling Fiona when he returned with the drinks.

Bryn smirked at Naomi before he began to swallow his drink down in gulps.

At that moment the band struck up. 'Are we dancing then?' she asked him.

'No, I need to get myself drunk before I get up on the floor with you.'

Naomi was hurt and infuriated by his cruel words and stormed off to the toilet to calm herself down. On her return she was flabbergasted to see Bryn cavorting on the floor, like a penguin, with Fiona. She stood staring at them in disbelief.

'What have you got to say about my husband making a display of himself with your wife?' she said to John, who was busily trying to light up a cigar.

'It's a free country and, to be perfectly honest, Bryn's doing me a favour because I can't dance for toffee.'

Naomi clenched her teeth. She slumped down in her chair, angry at his reply, and felt like a wilting wallflower.

Her eyes were glued on Bryn and Fiona who were all over each other. All she wanted was a bit of happiness in her life but it always seemed to elude her.

When the music eventually stopped a young woman in a black sequined dress took to the stage and began to sing some old time favourites.

By now Bryn and Fiona had returned to their seats and were deep in conversation together. John took no notice of them and sat quietly in his chair listening to the woman singing, whilst Naomi sat beside him, fuming.

As the night progressed Bryn and Fiona looked the worse for drink but they continued to hog the limelight on the dance floor. Naomi was amazed that Bryn was still on his feet and astonished that John seemed quite oblivious to the fact that his wife was flirting outrageously with him, for all to see.

Her mind began to race as utter desolation and hopelessness whelmed up inside her. Bryn had hurt her to the quick and this was the final straw.

After the last dance Bryn returned to the table and bent down to whisper in her ear, 'She's mine for the asking and, as I get nothing from you, I'm taking.'

Naomi was enraged. She stood up and slapped him hard across the face as her blood boiled over. 'You've just overstepped the mark for the last time Bryn Lewis. I'm off.'

Bryn reeled from her blow but carried on grinning, just as if the slap and words hadn't penetrated his brain. Staggering from his chair, he pulled on his coat then made his way towards the exit after her. Then Fiona jumped up, pulling John with her, and they quickly followed each other out of the club.

Bryn lurched up the road shouting obscenities at Naomi. This made her even more furious.

She could hear Fiona in the background chuckling at his behaviour and couldn't for the life of her see what was funny about the situation. She turned around and gave her a look fit to kill.

'You want to lighten up, girl,' Fiona sneered sarcastically.

'You think so, do you?' Naomi snapped. She was having great difficulty in keeping her hands to herself.

At that moment the heavens opened and heavy rain began to fall.

'Shall we shelter in this shop doorway?' John suggested, ducking out of the downpour. 'It might be only a passing shower.'

Without any warning Bryn took off his jacket and threw it into a large pool of water on the road. Naomi tried to grab it but the jacket was quickly knocked down by an articulated lorry that drove over it rendering the garment unfit to wear.

'Think your-self funny?' she shouted, extremely annoyed at Bryn's reckless behaviour. It was only the other week that she'd spent her hard earned cash on the jacket for his birthday.

Bryn stood, leering at her. 'I don't want you or your jacket in my life any more. Do you understand?' he growled, kicking the sodden coat into the gutter.

Naomi's rage intensified. 'That's it! You can rot in hell for all I care.' With a quick twist of the wedding ring she tore it from her finger and flung it at him. 'You can have your ring too,' she shouted, her voice hoarse with emotion. 'It was never much cop.'

Bryn, Fiona and John, stood looking on in silence as she turned on her heel and stomped up the road in the pouring rain.

That night sleep eluded her so, after putting on her dressing gown, she made her way down stairs in order to get her thoughts straight. She had bolted all the doors to keep Bryn out, presuming he was more than likely staying away until her temper had died down. She felt a great need to talk with someone who would share her grief and, as her son was staying at his mate's house for the night, she decided to dial the Samaritans' number, hoping she would be able to speak with someone who would be unbiased about her situation.

Her heart began to pound as she waited for someone to answer the phone and, as a man's voice spoke on the other end she began to pour her heart out to him, only stopping to sob every now and then.

'I'm listening. Do carry on,' the voice encouraged, with all the warmth of a sympathetic friend.

'I hope I've done the right thing by locking him out,' Naomi cried, wiping away her tears.

'I'm sure you have,' replied the voice from the other end. 'You couldn't be expected to continue living under these conditions and, unless your husband is willing to change his ways, there doesn't seem to be much hope.'

After thanking him for his kindness she replaced the receiver. It soothed her to think that a complete stranger could understand her situation and could be so sympathetic. There was no turning back. Her marriage was definitely over.

After a fitful night's sleep she woke up the next morning with the intention of packing Bryn's belongings in carrier bags. She wanted no part of him left in the house and made sure that everything was ready before deciding to telephone Fiona.

Before Fiona could speak Naomi blurted out, 'I'm sending Bryn's belongings round to your house in the next few minutes by taxi. Last night was the final straw.'

'There's no need for that. We were only having a laugh,' Fiona cried, quickly springing to Bryn's defence.

'Well you two will have all the time in the world to laugh now, won't you?' Naomi shouted before slamming down the receiver.

She telephoned a taxi firm, asking them to call at the house as soon as possible and within minutes a car pulled up outside. Naomi bundled her husband's belongings into the boot and, with the last few pounds in her purse, paid the driver.

She stood and watched as the taxi disappeared from sight. At that moment a huge feeling of relief flowed through her veins and her thoughts went back to the time when she'd seen the apparition of a snake in the grass on the living room wall. She sorely wished that she'd cancelled the wedding plans then.

Nine months later Naomi was granted a divorce on the grounds of her husband's unreasonable behaviour. She was relieved it was all over at last and remained determined that no-one would ever entrap her into marriage again. She had learnt her lesson the hard way.

CHAPTER 32

When Philip heard that the engineering firm he was working for was moving to new premises on the outskirts of London he jumped at the chance of accepting a position there. It meant better pay with the bonus of a lodging allowance.

If the truth was known, Naomi was relieved that her son was leaving the small valley town to better himself. He'd become quite a rebellious teenager who was easily led, and needed a much firmer hand than she was able to give.

On one occasion she'd mentioned to him that his father was living on a council estate nearby, with his wife and two children, but as soon as the words council estate were mentioned he turned his nose up. Although taken aback by his contemptuous manner Naomi was greatly relieved that he hadn't shown any interest. She knew only too well that his father was capable of putting on a false front and could charm the birds off the trees with his glib talk.

Several days after Philip had left home for London a programme about adoption appeared one evening on the television, mentioning a social worker named Jack Stevens. It went on to say that he specialised in re-uniting twins who'd been adopted at birth and, up to date, he had helped over one hundred and fifty people discover their roots. Before the programme finished the commentator explained that there would be an address for people to write into at the end of the television broadcast. He also went on to say that the law had now changed with regards to adopted adults tracing their birth parents.

Naomi was ecstatic and quickly jotted down the address that came onto the screen. Within minutes she began to write a letter to Jack Stevens and she hoped and prayed that he would be of some help.

A week to the day of sending off the letter Naomi received a reply from Jack asking her to fill in all the relevant details on the form provided so that he could deal with her case. She was thrilled to think that at last she was getting somewhere and she quickly put pen to paper with what little information she could see on her adoption documents.

That evening as she made her way home from work Naomi bumped into Jenny, who was one of her neighbours.

'Just the person I'm looking for,' said Jenny. 'How do you fancy working alongside me in the local pub? Only the girl I work with is moving away. I happened to hear that you once worked in the trade, and they would prefer experienced workers.'

Naomi quite liked the idea of returning to work behind the bar. Her full time position at Green's was wearing her down, because Rhiannon had left and she was missing her company. Also Tony Brain was forever on the prowl in the office giving her the glad eye. She'd had her fill of men and although she was fully aware that she would have to take a drop in wages she decided it was time for a change.

'I'm tempted to give it a go,' she answered. 'Because I was thinking of leaving my present job anyway, but that's another story.'

'Well, you'd better get your skates on because Mr Morgan, the gaffer, is holding interviews Saturday morning. That's tomorrow so I will put a good word in for you.'

'Thank you Jenny. I think it might well be the pick-me-up I need. Being bogged down in an office job every day can be pretty boring you know.'

Jenny gave her a broad grin and proceeded to walk in the direction of the shops.

The following morning Naomi was up early as usual and took her time with her make up and hair before presenting herself to Mr Morgan. She thought her best suit would be most appropriate for the interview and as she walked out of the house she felt like the cat's whiskers.

After explaining that she'd previously served in a public house and understood the running of the bar she was over the moon at being told that the job was hers. She couldn't wait to give in her notice to Tony Brain and hoped that he wouldn't be awkward in any way.

Before hanging up her coat, on Monday morning Naomi boldly walked into Tony Brain's office and was shocked to see Mr James, his understudy, sitting at the desk.

'Morning, Mr James. I've come to give in my notice to Mr Brain. Only I've found alternative employment,' said Naomi, hesitantly.

'Well, I'll have to accept your notice because Tony Brain is no longer with us.'

Naomi looked at him amazed. 'Do you mean he's died?' she gasped.

'Died be buggered. He's only cleared off with Rhiannon out of the typing pool.'

Naomi felt her legs going from under her and she quickly sat down on the nearest chair. 'How do you know about this?' she asked, looking at him astounded.

'Well, on all accounts Rhiannon paid a visit to Tony's wife with Tony's baby in her arms, which led to him being thrown out. And I haven't a clue as to where they are or if he'll ever return to the company. He's left us in a right pickle, I can tell you, because he's cleared the safe of the firm's money on top of everything else.'

Naomi's jaw dropped. She hadn't thought of him as a thief and was utterly flabbergasted. No wonder her friend Rhiannon hadn't disclosed who she was pregnant by. It was too close to home.

It wasn't long before Naomi was back into the swing of things, working in the pub. Despite feeling tired out by the end of each shift, she enjoyed every minute of it and mixed in with the other bar staff really well.

After corresponding with Jack Stevens for several weeks Naomi was thrilled to bits when, one morning, she received a letter with a copy of her birth mother's second marriage certificate pinned onto it. She was shocked to read that during 1943 when she was twenty-eight years old, she had married a much younger man than herself in a London registry office. Naomi was aghast because she thought it spoke volumes as to why she was probably given away and perhaps her first husband had died

Jack Stevens ended the letter by offering his services as an intermediary between them both as soon as he could find out where Naomi's mother was now living.

Within minutes of reading the letter Naomi telephoned her son with the good news, and blurted everything out to him before he could speak.

Philip was in the process of leaving for work and hurriedly told her that he would check the relevant telephone directories in the area to see how many people of her mother's name there were.

Naomi sat down with a cup of tea, mulling over in her mind as to what could happen next. She began to wonder how her birth mother would react to the news, once Jack Stevens had traced her. A huge smile came over her face as she looked forward to the prospect of a wonderful reunion between them.

On arriving home from work later that afternoon she did some household chores before making herself some scrambled egg on toast.

Just as she was putting on her coat in order to return to work the telephone rang and she quickly picked up the receiver.

'Is that Philip's mother?' said a man with a gruff voice on the other end of the line.

Naomi's heart lurched, wondering who it could possibly be. 'Speaking,' she said.

'I'm Kenneth, Philip's friend. He wasn't able to ring so he asked me to contact you with the latest news regarding your mother. We found her address and phone number through the telephone directory so, as your son was working late, he told me to telephone her instead. Anyway, to cut the story short, I explained that you had been searching for her and would be in touch.'

The blood drained from Naomi's face. How dare a complete stranger take it upon himself to meddle in something as sensitive as this!

'What did she say?'

'Well, she was perfectly pleasant to me, possibly because I took her unawares, and said she would be willing to help in any way.'

Naomi felt helpless.

'I have her telephone number to hand if you'd like to write it down.'

'Yes, please,' said Naomi, tears pricking her eyes. Inwardly she was fuming that this outsider was intervening in her affairs, fully aware that Jack Stevens would be extremely annoyed as well. She certainly didn't want a complete stranger breezing in for the fun of it.

After jotting down the number she replaced the receiver feeling agitated. She was late for work as it was so she put the number into her coat pocket and left the house.

As soon as she walked into the pub the landlady

called her over. Mrs Morgan was a jolly middle-aged woman. Naomi enjoyed working with her because she was a good landlady and kind to her staff.

'You don't look your usual cheerful self. What's the matter?' Mrs Morgan asked, looking most concerned.

'I've waited for what seems like a lifetime to make contact with my natural mother and out of the blue it's all been taken out of my hands by my son. Trust him to barge in. I'm the adopted one, not him. I had a chance of it all being handled in the correct manner by a social worker but my son has wrecked things for me by taking over. He shouldn't have asked his so called friend to speak with her and he ought to have had more sense.' she cried, looking mournful.

'I'm sorry to hear about your troubles. Is there anything I can do to help?' said Mrs Morgan, putting her arm round her.

'Well, I do have her phone number to hand,' Naomi said, taking it out of her pocket, but she's probably still reeling from the shock of it all.'

'Take a chance and ring her on the telephone in the bar while we're quiet.'

Naomi shook her head. She didn't want any background noises like the fruit machine to give away the fact that she worked in a public house. She knew some people looked down on bar staff, and wanted to give her birth mother a good impression.

'To be honest, I'd rather ring her in the morning when I've collected my thoughts together,' said Naomi, with a glint of tears in her eyes.

At that moment a steady flow of customers began flooding into the pub and having to serve them took Naomi's mind off things.

After a fretful night's sleep Naomi rose from her bed and drew back the curtains on a dull dreary day. She'd made up her mind to telephone her birth mother after breakfast. She longed to see her face to face and couldn't believe that her dream was at last coming true.

At the sound of the clock on the wall striking nine, she wondered if it was wise to telephone so early. After all her mother would be in her sixties by now and may not be an early riser. On no account did she intend getting off on the wrong foot with her so she waited a little longer feeling more wound up by the minute.

After several more minutes had gone by she couldn't wait any more. A mixture of excitement and anxiety ran through her veins as she slowly dialled the number, holding her breath after each digit.

Her pulse quickened when she heard the receiver being picked up.

'This is your daughter Naomi, speaking,' she said, trembling.

The line went silent for several moments.

'I don't want you ringing my home,' said a cultured, dignified sounding voice.

Naomi was shocked. This unexpected reply threw her completely. 'But I've been longing to meet you for years,' she cried.

'Don't you realise that you're nothing to do with me now you've been adopted? I gave away all rights to you years ago.'

'B..but my adoptive parents have died now and there's so much I need to know, like are there are any hereditary illnesses in the family?' Naomi pleaded, trying to keep the conversation going.

'There are no illnesses in *my* family. We're all perfectly healthy,' the voice on the line snapped. 'But I do have a son in a Holy Order who mustn't, under any circumstances, find out about you.' Her voice grew cold, almost harsh.

'*Please,* I just want to talk with you,' Naomi implored, completely at a loss as to why this woman had no compassion in her heart for her.

'I was intending to go on holiday shortly but this has really spoiled the whole thing for me.' Her voice ranted down the phone.

Naomi was speechless. Nothing had prepared her for this. To think that she was worrying over a measly holiday when her own flesh she'd discarded so long ago needed to speak with her.

'I..I..I only want an hour in your company, *please,*' begged Naomi, thinking she owed her that much at least.

'I cannot see any point in that. So don't you ever ring this number again. Do I make myself clear?' the voice thundered down the phone and, before Naomi could answer, she heard the sound of the receiver being slammed down.

She held her head in her hands and sobbed her heart out. The moment she'd waited almost a lifetime for was over. She would have given the world to have heard her mother speak kindly. Her motives were only pure and simple, but she hadn't been given the chance to say she had no intentions of upsetting her mother's family. Just a few minutes of her time would have meant the world to her.

Naomi tried her best to pull herself together but as soon as she arrived at work she broke down into tears as she told Mrs Morgan the latest news.

'It sounds to me as if you're a lot better off without someone like her,' said Mrs Morgan. 'She certainly doesn't deserve a daughter like you. Now, dry your eyes because she's definitely not worth crying over.'

The landlady's kind words could not soften the blow. Naomi felt that the very core of her existence had been ripped from within her. The image of a reunion with her birth mother had been swept away by a huge tidal wave of tears, and by the end of the lunchtime shift Naomi felt exhausted and was glad to go home so she could grieve alone.

After tea she decided to telephone her son to explain what had happened and prevent any more interference. She couldn't help wondering how different things might have been if Jack Stephens had taken over the matter, and she continued to wring her hands in despair.

When Philip eventually answered the phone he sounded most irate about things. 'Talk about skeletons in the cupboard. She's got a nerve to speak to you like that.'

'Well, to be honest, I'm hoping to try and salvage things by contacting Jack Stevens. It might be worth a try,' said Naomi, holding onto her tears.

'Alright then, but I must go as I'm on my way out,' cried Philip. I'm off to meet up with some friends.'

'I'll write and let you know what Jack has to say when I hear from him,' Naomi added hurriedly.

After putting down the receiver she flopped down into the nearest armchair and sobbed. It was an experience she would never forget.

CHAPTER 33

It was Sunday and Naomi was in the middle of cooking herself lunch when the telephone rang. After turning off the stove she hurried into the hallway to answer it, and was surprised to hear her son speak on the other end. 'Guess where I've been to, Mam?' he said in a voice louder than usual.

'I haven't a clue' answered Naomi, hoping against hope that he hadn't been meddling in her affairs again.

'I've been to visit your mother but no sooner had I introduced myself than the door was promptly closed in my face.'

Naomi's blood ran cold. She swallowed hard. 'I wish you'd leave things be. She's made it quite plain that she wants nothing to do with us. Anyway, I look upon *my mother* as the woman who nursed me when I was ill and went without to make sure I was clothed and fed.'

'That's as may be. But I had a shock when I saw her because she didn't look remotely like you at all.'

'Is that so?' said Naomi, sighing. She knew only too well that her birth mother must have been frightened out of her wits by Philip's visit. So there was little chance of her ever consenting to a meeting with Jack Stephens. She could have wept.

'Well, it's such a shame you've knocked on her door. You've probably done more harm than good now. Anyway, I fully intend contacting Jack Stevens my Social Worker next week, in the hope that he can unravel this mess.'

Naomi heard the phone cut off as the money ran out. She was literally tamping. What chance did she have of finding out the real truth of her adoption now that everything had been taken out of her hands again.

That afternoon Naomi decided to visit the local

Catholic Church where she hoped she would be able to unburden herself to the Priest about the whole issue. Although she was not of the Catholic faith she knew Father O'Kelly to be a good man and trusted in him.

After being invited into the Presbytery Naomi explained to the Priest the predicament in which she found herself and asked his advice on the matter. He sat back in his chair as if in deep thought then surprised her by suggesting that she wrote to her birth mother, making it clear how she felt.

Naomi accepted this idea eagerly and, after thanking him for his kindness, she left the church feeling as if a burden had been lifted from her shoulders. In her eyes there was hope yet.

Immediately upon returning home she gathered her thoughts together and put pen to paper. She explained how upset she'd felt over her mother's rejection of her then carried on to apologise for her son's unannounced visit, adding that the thought of her shutting the door on him was deeply hurtful. She finished the letter by stating that if she still wished to remain anonymous, she Naomi, would appreciate it if she would inform her Social Worker, Jack Stevens, as to the whereabouts of her brother.

After writing Jack's telephone number and address on the bottom of the page she signed the letter with the words. 'Your forgotten daughter.'

At the same time she dropped a line to Jack Stevens asking for help in the matter now that things had gone haywire.

Several days later she received news from Jack stating how shocked he had been about everything, seeing that he had warned her that a cautious approach was necessary and should have preferably been instigated by him. He then went on to write that after much thought he'd written to Naomi's birth mother explaining that he understood the state of shock *she* must be in. He'd given her his telephone number asking her to make contact with him at her earliest convenience, and stipulated that Naomi's prime concern now was to make contact with her brother and any help she could give him regarding his whereabouts would be much appreciated.

This letter was never acknowledged. But several weeks later Naomi was horrified when she received a solicitor's letter from London, stating they were writing on behalf of her birth mother. It carried on to say that she had found the telephone calls and visit very difficult to cope with. Further down the page the solicitor explained that her birth mother had no information with regards to where Richard was living as she had left him in the care of his father on an RAF station sometime during the war years. The letter concluded by stating that Naomi's interference had caused her a great deal of distress and further steps would be taken if she ever tried to make contact again.

Naomi was flabbergasted. She kept reading the letter over and over again until she knew it off by heart. She doubted very much that her brother could have been left on an Airbase, especially when it would have happened during wartime. The questions and possible answers filling her mind gave her no rest. The deep scar she bore from her adoption she felt was now a gaping wound.

It was around this time that Naomi met Don whilst she was working at the pub. He was known locally as the odd-job man because he could put his hands to most things that needed repairing.

Naomi was quite attracted to the middle-aged man who had strong features and thick black hair. He reminded her of a gypsy who used to sharpen scissors and such like on his occasional visits to the neighbourhood.

One lunch time when the public house was quite busy Don ambled up to the bar with a worried look on his face.

'Are you alright, Don, only you don't look too good,' said Naomi, as she pulled his pint of beer.

'My place has been broken into for the umpteenth time, mainly for the tools I keep, so I'm looking for other lodgings. You wouldn't happen to know of any would you?'

'Sorry to hear of your troubles,' said Naomi, sympathetically. She felt sorry for the man and wondered whether or not to let him have the spare bedroom. She could do with the extra money, and company, if truth was known and he didn't look the type that would cause any trouble.

'I've a spare room at home if you're interested,' she blurted out, wondering as to whether or not she'd made the right decision. 'And, if you've the time I can show you around when I've finished my shift.'

Don's big brown eyes widened. 'That's very kind of you. I'll take you up on that if I may.'

Naomi watched Don as he ambled back to his seat with his pint of beer. She'd known him at the pub for some time and thought him to be a quiet, placid man.

Within seconds of viewing the room Don took Naomi up on her offer, but just as he was leaving his eyes caught sight of a damp patch on the ceiling.

'How long has that been there then?' he asked, pointing to it.

'Not long,' said Naomi, hoping it hadn't turned him off renting the room. She didn't have the money to have it repaired and was living in the hope that it would dry up on its own.

'To be honest, I think one or two slates were loosened through the dreadful storm we had a few weeks back.'

'Consider the job done and dusted before I move in then,' said Don, smiling. 'I'd rather mend it just in case the ceiling falls down on top of me,' he joked, with a grin on his face.

Naomi couldn't believe her ears. 'I'll gladly pay for the materials,' she said, smiling.

The house was old and it needed lots of jobs doing. She could never have afforded a tradesman to call.

The following day Naomi bought a rent book from the local newsagents, and marked it up accordingly. At this rate she'd look no further for a better paid job, being quite content and happy with the way things were.

That evening she wrote to her son telling him about her new lodger, along with other snippets of information. He seldom visited, now that he'd obtained a flat of his own, but Naomi was comforted to think he'd settled down so nicely.

Several days later she was surprised to receive a letter from Jack Stevens explaining that he'd found out that the man assumed to be her father on her adoption papers had died suddenly during 1956. Naomi was extremely interested and hurriedly sat down to look at the marriage certificate that was enclosed. It stated that he had been married to a Miss Lena Johnson, and their marriage had taken place in a Methodist church in Newcastle. Also attached to the certificate was a piece of paper with his widow's telephone number on. Naomi was thrilled to bits and decided to ring the lady in the hope that she might throw some light on the matter of her adopted brother. She had no intention of giving in to unfair fate and needed to unearth any snippets of information that would help.

Her head was bursting with questions as she dialled the number and within seconds a woman with a strong

Northern accent answered, stating who she was.

After explaining the purpose of her call Naomi was surprised to find that the woman was more than willing to share what she could remember from the past.

'When I first met my late husband we were working alongside one another on an Air Force camp during the war. Apparently he was separated from your mother then, and she was quite a rum character by all accounts. I can even remember him being screened by the Royal Air Force for three months, before demobilization, because of his wife.'

'Why was that, then?' Naomi asked, holding her breath. She could recall being told a similar thing when she visited RAF Innsworth. Since then she'd had visions of her mother being someone like Mata Hari, the exotic dancer and spy.

'I don't know for sure but if my memory serves me right she also spent time in a London prison during the war, for bigamy. Apparently, she wrote a book whilst she was locked up about the monstrosities that went on behind closed doors when she was serving her sentence. She fully intended sending this book to the News of The World Sunday Newspaper but the governor got wind of things and it was confiscated.

'Never,' said Naomi, clutching hold of her mouth.

She was also very friendly with someone who was connected with the sea and apparently had numerous love affairs,' she continued. 'God knows what she got up to really. My husband must have found me quiet in comparison to her.'

Naomi was speechless.

The line went quiet for several seconds. 'Are you still there?' said the voice on the other end. 'If you hang on a minute I'll look through some of the old documents I still have of my late husbands.'

'Thank you very much,' said Naomi, who was

finding it difficult to comprehend everything she had been told already.

Several minutes later Lena returned to the phone. 'According to the RAF documents from the forties my Frank was having money sent to an address at 7, Mill Parade in Newport.'

'Well I Never! That's not far from where I live,' cried Naomi, her mind boggling. 'But that's the dock area of Newport, which would have been a target for bombing during the last war.'

To be honest I think one of Frank's relatives by the name of Cooke might have had something to do with it but it's all so long ago and everyone concerned will have forgotten by now.'

Naomi heaved a huge sigh. 'Is there anything else you can remember?'

'There were other stories, too vague to remember properly, but I did hear a rumour that she was pregnant towards the end of the war but I wouldn't swear to it. My late husband divorced her during 1946 and never really spoke about her much after that, except to say that she had taken on a different name and had moved to a new area in London when the war ended. He thought perhaps to cover her tracks. But who knows?

Everything had become clear to Naomi now. No wonder her Aunt Maud didn't want her to go raking things up all those years ago.

'I don't suppose you can remember anything about my brother, Richard, who was also given up for adoption?' she asked, crossing her fingers.

'Come to think of it I do recollect that he had a son who was living in Bristol some time in the war years. My late husband's friend took him on. But I believe he finally landed up in the Suffolk area.'

'They shouldn't have been allowed to split brother and sister up,' said Naomi, feeling angry about it all.

'I've also got my doubts as to who my birth father really was.'

'I didn't like to comment but to be perfectly honest there was a lot of speculation in the family about that. My late mother used to say that morals and knickers fell along with the bombs during the war, and anyone who might have known the truth about the matter would probably be dead and buried by now.'

Throughout the call Naomi listened intently, trying to piece the jigsaw together. It was all making sense to her now. If her birth mother was a good-time girl her father could have been anyone, so there was little likelihood of her finding out the truth. Not that he would ever replace her late beloved Da.

'Well, I'm sorry but I must go now because I'm in the process of packing. I'm moving to the sea side to live with my sister. And if I were you I'd put all these things I've spoken about behind you. .

'That's easier said than done,' cried Naomi.

'Well, I suppose so but I'm sorry I can't help you any further. It was nice talking with you.'

Naomi thanked her for all her help and hung up the phone. For the rest of the evening she sat down on the nearest chair trying her hardest to come to terms with what Lena had told her. She thought back to what she'd heard behind closed doors at her adopted father's funeral. And knew there was little chance of her ever finding out who her birth father was now that her Aunt Maud was dead. She wished her adopted parents had told her the truth about her background instead of sweeping things under the carpet.

The longing to see her birth mother had haunted her all her life and to be rejected yet again was beyond belief. She felt deep down there was a reservoir of unhappiness waiting to surface through her being abandoned which would always be there. But she was determined not to be beaten and would carry on searching for her brother come what may.

Naomi decided that her next line of approach would be to contact as many newspapers as she could in the Suffolk area asking for an advertisement to be placed in the Personal Column with regards to the whereabouts of her brother. She realised that through being adopted his surname would have changed but she lived in the hope that someone might possibly know of him.

In the meantime Naomi made some enquiries regarding the address Lena gave her in Newport. Through a friend she contacted the Landlady of a Public House in the Baneswell area of the town who was said to have had family that had lived at the address during the war. But on speaking with her she denied having any knowledge of her mother.

Several weeks elapsed without receiving any news and just as she was about to give up hope the postman delivered a handwritten envelope through the letter box. She knew instinctively who it was from and tore it open.

'I'm almost sure it's a letter concerning my brother,' she said to Don, who was sitting at the table eating his breakfast.

'Oh yes,' he muttered, looking disinterested.

Naomi's face flushed red with delight as a photograph fell out onto the table. Holding it up to the light she saw it was of a middle-aged man who was tall and good looking.

'I've found my long lost brother at last!' she shrieked, dancing up and down on the spot.

'Calm down. You'll be having a heart attack if you're not careful,' grinned Don, who was in the act of putting on his jacket for work.

Naomi knew he didn't have a clue as to how she felt and, as her eyes scanned the contents of the letter, she was thrilled to read that Richard wanted to meet her as soon as possible. He suggested that Trafalgar Square might be a suitable venue and signed the letter with love and kisses.

Naomi clutched at her chest and began to panic. She knew it would be impossible to afford the fare at the moment because she was only just getting her finances straight as it was.

'What's the sudden glum look on your face for?' asked Don, as he was just about to disappear through the door.

'My brother wants me to meet him in London but, what with the fare and the expense of everything a day out in London would entail, I don't think I can stretch to it. And I've not got any savings to fall back on,' she said, looking downcast.

'I could afford to give you a month's rent in advance, if you like. I had a nice little pick up on a horse yesterday, and knowing me I'll only squander it.'

'Squander money? I wouldn't know how that felt,' Naomi said, pulling a face. 'But I'll certainly take you up on your offer.' Naomi couldn't believe her luck and practically snatched the money from him as he counted it out from his inside pocket.

'You don't know what this means to me,' she said, planting a kiss on his cheek. 'Thanks ever so much.'

Don raised his eyebrows and gave her a grin. 'I've got to be going now. See you tonight.'

Naomi waved him off and, as soon as the front door was closed, sat down to reply to the letter, shaking from head to foot. Her nerves had got the better of her. She spent the next hour staring at her brother's photograph looking for similar features to her own.

Naomi was eagerly counting the days to their meeting. She'd deliberately neglected to tell her son about what had happened because she felt the need to speak with Richard alone, so she could absorb everything he said without any-one else taking over.

She left Wales on the early morning train to Paddington and sat in the railway compartment staring out at the passing scenery, her mind in a whirl. She could hardly believe this was happening to her and hoped all would go well.

The train eventually ground to a halt at its destination. Naomi gathered up her things then apprehensively stepped out onto the platform, clutching tightly at her handbag which contained her adoption papers together with photographs of herself and Philip. The station was crowded with people, more than she had ever seen in one place. She stood still looking around her for a minute or two then decided to follow the mass of people out of the station and into the street.

Outside the station she was relieved to see a taxi rank. She was terrified of getting lost on the tube. Not being well travelled she thought it best to treat herself. She soon found a vacant cab and as she stepped inside she felt like a queen. She was determined to savour every moment as she looked out at the passing scenery of the City she had been born in. But she knew in her heart of hearts that London could never replace the huge mountains and valleys of the Wales that she loved.

Once she had reached her destination she glanced down at her watch and saw it was nearly time for their arranged meeting. She stared in awe at Nelson's column and the hundreds of pigeons that had made their home there. As she stepped out of the cab she began to shiver in the keen November wind and, just as she began to draw the collar of her coat up round her neck, she noticed a tall dark-haired stranger striding towards her. With no doubt at all she knew this man was her brother. 'It's Richard, isn't it?' she said, looking at him in wonder.

'Yes, sis, it's really me. Your big brother,' he answered, putting his arms around her. After hugging each other for several minutes they stared into each others eyes in wonderment. Naomi found it hard to believe how much of her life had passed without ever knowing of his existence and gave a huge sigh, wishing things had been different. She thought how smartly turned out he looked in his navy blue blazer and grey slacks, but although slender in build like herself she could see no other resemblance at all.

Before moving on Richard drew out a small camera and asked a passer-by if he would take a photograph of them both. Naomi was enthralled and as the two of them stood together she couldn't believe what was happening.

'I noticed a lovely little pub that sells food just up the road,' Richard said, taking her arm. 'Perhaps we could have a bite to eat in there?'

Naomi enthusiastically agreed to his suggestion, hanging onto his every word.

Once inside the lounge they quickly found a suitable table for two. After ordering their meals it was Naomi's turn to listen as Richard told her all about his childhood. She was surprised to learn that his birth father had kept in touch until he died. Although he had often mentioned to Richard that he had a sister somewhere he was always more interested in looking at the present his father gave him.

'But the name of Naomi was always lodged in the back of my mind,' he told her smiling.

'And here we are actually having lunch together. My treat as well,' he insisted.

Naomi hesitated to tell him that she thought she was not his full-blooded sister, not wanting to spoil the moment. She so needed him to be her full brother, and although any chance of them forming a close bond so late in life was slim, she knew in her heart they would always be good friends.

After their meal they went into the bar to make room for the droves of people laden with shopping bags who were queuing up for tables. Naomi insisted that she bought the drinks, wanting to contribute something to the day, and sat down beside him nursing a fruit juice. While they talked about the lost years between them she began to feel as if she had known him all her life. And on mentioning what had happened when she'd made contact with their mother Richard looked shocked to the core.

'Perhaps she'd be different with her first-born,' he joked, drinking up his beer.

'I don't know about that,' said Naomi, wondering what he was leading up to.

'I don't suppose you have mother's telephone number to hand. She might be willing to join us, if only for an hour. I'd pay her taxi fare if needs be.'

Naomi was totally flabbergasted and amazed at the ease with which he used the word mother, which was something she'd never felt able to do.

'It might be worth a try,' said Naomi, living in the hope that she might have a change of heart. She opened her diary and gave him the number and, after checking the change in his pocket, Richard went into the telephone booth in the corner of the bar.

Naomi sat biting her lip. Her heart went out to him, fearing what could happen, and she waited on tenterhooks until he returned.

'Well?' she almost whispered as he sat back down beside her. 'What happened, then? Is she coming?'

'No she's not. After explaining who I was, she promptly slammed the receiver down on me.' His face was ashen. 'I can understand that she's made a new life for herself but she didn't even give me the chance to speak. We could have met up in secret in here and nobody would have been any the wiser.'

Naomi caught her breath. She could have wept for him. At that moment she felt a genuine need to throw her arms around his shoulders, feeling his pain as if it were her own.

Richard clung on to her tightly, with tears in his eyes.

'Just remember that we have each other now, Richard, and no-one will ever spoil that.'

All too soon the time came for them both to go their separate ways. They vowed to always keep in touch. Richard accompanied Naomi to the station and waited as she boarded the train back to the valleys. Blinking back the tears she waved to her brother until the train gathered speed and she lost sight of him. Sitting down in her seat she began to mull over the day's events and her thoughts went back to the Bible she had been given as a child by her Sunday school teacher. Inside the first page was written, 'In all thy ways acknowledge Him, and He shall direct thy paths.'

Naomi had always felt that she'd been touched by a power beyond this world, a power that was always within her. She looked up towards the sky, through the carriage window, and thanked God for the most wonderful day of her life.

IF YOU ARE AN ADOPTED ADULT, BIRTH PARENT OR OTHER RELATIVE AFFECTED BY ADOPTION PLEASE CONTACT THE ADDRESS BELOW IF YOU NEED HELP WITH SEARCHING FOR FAMILY CONNECTIONS.

NORCAP
112 CHURCH ROAD
WHEATLEY
OXFORD
OX33 1LU
Telephone 01865875000
Website: http://www.nocap.org.uk